ALL FOR PEACE
A SAFE HAVEN SELF-DISCOVERY NOVEL

LYNN BOIRE

With much love,
Linda

Copyright © 2021 Linda Glazier

All for Peace is a work of fiction. All characters and events in this publication, other than those clearly in the public domain, are fictitious and any resemblance to real persons, living or dead, is purely coincidental.

All rights reserved. No part of this publication may be reproduced in any form or by any electronic or mechanical means, including information storage and retrieval systems, without written permission from the author, except for the use of brief quotations in a book review.

Cover design by Steven Novak

ISBN eBook: 978-1-7771458-4-2
ISBN Print: 978-1-7771458-5-9

PRAISE FOR LYNN BOIRE

All for Love

"It's what many of us have feared....the time climate change becomes a reality. *All for Love* is about a family enduring all the trials, tribulations, and uncertainty they face, trying to find a new normal in the midst of chaos. Riveting!" ~ *Dave*

"*All for Love* opens a readers' eyes to how easily the idea of security can shift. Prepare yourself for a thought provoking tale." ~ *Suki Lang*

All for Family

"Enjoyed this one tremendously!" ~ *Darlene Y.*

"I really enjoyed the snappy dialogue. Perceptive glimpses into an Intention Living lifestyle opened my thoughts on this way of life." ~ *Karen G.*

All for Peace

"A refreshing novel that shows no one is perfect, but with love and honesty, relationships can work. Loved it." ~ *B Johnson*

"It was hard to put the novel down, the intriguing plot of romance, illusions, and murder kept me engaged until the end." ~ *A. Evans*

CHAPTER 1

"No, I'm not going there!" Ellen refused to raise her eyes as she repeated herself. "I'm not seeing anyone. Tell him to—" She clenched her hands and lowered her voice to a growl. "Go. Away. Now."

"Alright, Mrs. Peterson, I'll ask your husband to leave. He's going to be very sad and hurt by your decision. You promised Dr. Hallden you'd see him today. He looked so excited to see you. Won't you at least give it a try?" Nurse Reid stooped to get to eye level with Ellen. When Ellen didn't respond, she sighed and shook her head, then retreated from the parlor. "I'm sure Dr. Hallden is going to be disappointed too."

Glad that the nurse hadn't forced the issue, Ellen barely noticed her leaving the room. She sat in her favorite chair in St. Joseph's Hospital's lounge area. She wasn't fully aware that she had won the battle, only that everything around her had closed in again, keeping her safe.

The walls were growing around her, and she wasn't going to let anyone in. Ellen hummed a tune and let her mind float. She was getting to be an expert at shutting things out and was proud of it.

Ellen gazed out the big picture window at the mesmerizing view in front of her. The waves on the sea were hypnotic. Today, a north-easterly wind blew, and whitecaps danced across the bay. The early sunset turned the horizon a soft coral color. Wispy clouds tinted in shades of mauve against the baby-blue sky created a breathtaking effect.

That's what made her calm. Peace, beauty, things as they should be. She was content. Nothing existed except being here. No past, no future, no pain. She closed her eyes and let herself drift.

An hour later, Ellen sensed a presence and stirred. Laura had joined her. Like herself, she never caused a fuss and seldom spoke, a perfect dinner partner. Laura smiled at her, and Ellen smiled back. They understood each other. As long as they were at St. Joseph's Hospital, no one could hurt them. That gut-wrenching, screaming pain would never tear at them again. Instead, every evening they teamed together to witness the lights flickering on in houses surrounding the bay and silently rejoice they were not part of it.

After a dinner that she had seldom had an appetite for, Ellen constantly watched the clock as the evening programs completed, and she was allowed to go to bed. Ellen took her anti-depressants, patted Laura's hand, and made her way back to her room. She loved her bed and could sleep deeply, totally cut off from everything.

ELLEN SAT on a maple rocking chair, staring out the window. The gnarled branches of the fruit trees intrigued her as a distant memory tickled her mind.

"Ellen, if you're not talking to me, you might as well leave." Dr. Hallden put his notebook down on the table between them. He noted Ellen's hair was well brushed today. The sunlight streaming through the window caught a hint of auburn in her chestnut hair. He hoped one day he'd be able to break through her sad and lonely demeanor so that he could get to the root of her problem.

"Are you pleased with yourself? You've built that fence up nice and high again. I thought you said you would try to see your husband." Dr. Hallden leaned forward, slapping his hands on his thighs, capturing Ellen's gaze and holding it. "What's changed? You didn't even try."

Ellen looked at him, then lowered her gaze. Her cheeks warmed, and her palms began to sweat. She had grown to trust Dr. Hallden, nevertheless, it was still hard for her to speak about her feelings for her family. "I just got this queasy feeling in my stomach, as if I'd been on a roller coaster for the last hour." Her hands twisted in her lap and shredded a tissue. "I tried to ignore it. I went for a cup of tea to calm me, but I threw it up." Ellen paused. "I was so scared of seeing him that I simply couldn't do it," she whispered.

"And yet, you told me that although he usually put his business first, he was a loving husband. Always treated you well. So, what scared you?"

"I don't know. You're right, and he was a good husband. He was very ambitious in the early days. His life was all about his work. I know financial success was important to him. But there were times that I wished he could be happy with less and spend more time with us."

"If he was always busy, you must have been the one holding the family together on a day-to-day basis. Am I right?"

"Yes. Once Dan hit pre-school, I worked part-time in

finance at a bank, then I left when Sara was born. There was a time Barry let me help with the business doing the books, but as soon as the financial crisis was over, he didn't need me anymore."

Ellen glanced outdoors again, avoiding Dr. Hallden's eyes. She gnawed on her bottom lip as the blood pounded in her ears, warning her. Time to stop talking.

Dr. Hallden paused, letting his patient calm herself. He noted her fingers were tapping on the rocking chair and her nervous habit of nibbling on her lower lip. He stood up and retrieved a bottle of water each, then opened them. Taking a sip, he settled comfortably. As she took a swallow, he began again.

"How did you feel when your husband's business became more successful, and your kids grew more involved in their own social life? Were you lonely?'

"I was. I used to envy Barry his freedom and ambition, along with all his friends in the business community. He had a full life." Glancing at her doctor, she noticed his concerned gaze and flitted her eyes outside again. She took several sips of water to quieten her breathing while she rocked her chair more quickly. It was a time she didn't want to remember.

"Take deep breaths, Ellen. Long, slow, deep breaths. In and out. That's it." Dr. Hallden let her calm down and waited 'til the rocking had almost ceased. "Do you feel angry about being left out?"

"No." Ellen cocked her head to the side, reconsidering. "Maybe. More envious, I think, but not angry. I loved Sara and Danny a lot. I was so fortunate to have a child like her. She was dyslexic, you know, yet she worked hard and learned how to handle it. She had such a positive attitude." She smiled as she remembered her daughter.

"How was Danny different?"

Her hands began fidgeting as she played with the clasp on her watch, opening and closing it. "Danny was always on the go, but a loner too, if that makes any sense." Ellen stared out the window at the wintry garden. Fall leaves rotting on the ground. A rake leaned against the trunk of a massive maple tree.

Dr. Hallden remained silent, waiting for Ellen to gather her memories.

"Nothing kept his attention for very long. He was bright when he wanted to be, even perceptive at times. Or he could be withdrawn and suspicious, imagining situations that weren't there." Ellen paused, confusion briefly tightening her face. "He could get furious, too. I think he cared a lot about me, even if he didn't let it show."

"Families show their love in different ways, Ellen. Think about that for our next session."

Ellen paused as she considered his request on the heels of her newest revelation. Ellen's eyebrows knit together in a frown as she thought about her response. It usually made her feel guilty if she criticized her children or showed their imperfections. She should've been a better mother.

Glancing at Dr. Hallden, a sigh of relief escaped her lips. He was making notations on his tablet, a sign he was ending the session. He pushed his chair away from the table and placed his notes in his briefcase. Thank God.

"You've done well today, Ellen. I'll have you return to see me soon. I want you to think about your early years with Barry, what you remember about your marriage." Dr. Hallden observed Ellen. "Let your mind relax and wander. You'll probably start remembering little things at first. Write them down before you push them away again." He stood up and walked over to her chair, gently laying his hand on her shoulder.

"The past can't hurt you anymore, Ellen, so don't be frightened. When you feel the darkness pulling you down, imagine sunlight coming in the window and push a little harder—reach for it."

"I'll try, Doctor. Not now, though. I'm too tired."

"Take your time. Go slowly. Force yourself slightly further every day. Just remember, rest is not peace." He tapped her arm twice and said goodbye.

Acknowledging his advice, Ellen nodded. Weird, how all her energy seemed to drain after she saw him. She stood up and left his office, passing him in the reception room before returning to the main living area.

Ellen tiptoed quickly back to her private room and shut the door, breathing a sigh of relief. This sparsely furnished room had been her safe haven for a long time. Now, as she looked around her, she wondered if this was enough. Even though her heart was pounding and her palms were damp, she was proud of herself.

Amazed that she had talked about Sara and Danny, she began to hope that she'd continue this progress. Her children were always in her mind's eye, creating a warm, comforting aura around her when she thought of her babies. Sometimes a marbling of fear penetrated it, making her retreat from them. But why??

Drained, she flopped on her bed and curled up, surrendering to the exhaustion sweeping across her body. Sleep. The best way to get the peace she craved.

Dr. Hallden's voice drifted through her mind. *I want you to think about the beginning of your time with your husband.*

Her heavy eyelids closed, and suddenly she had a flash of recognition.

She was in the old house she grew up in. She smiled and drifted...

FOR THE THIRD night in a row, Barry poured himself a scotch and downed it. He knew he should cut back on the drinking but the hurt and anger from his last attempt to see his wife hadn't left him. His hands still shook. He'd been so sure from Dr. Hallden's comments that he'd finally spend some time with his wife and be able to touch her, maybe even hold her. Or at least talk with her.

He stared at the family picture taken last summer at their Comox Lake cottage, and his eyes blurred with tears. Barry poured himself another scotch and plunked down in his leather recliner. Would it ever change? He was no closer to the answer than he was four months ago when they'd placed Ellen in the psychiatric ward.

The house was empty now. Sara was in her first year of University in Victoria, sharing an apartment with her best friend and cousin and loving it. Their son, Dan, had never been here, and he probably never would be. Semi-retirement should've been the best time of their lives. Instead, Ellen was lost, and he was alone and confused. Barry sipped his drink, then closed his eyes and savored the smooth bite of single malt, waiting for it to ease his tension.

Would she ever return to share their love? When they moved here, they had such optimism, a new beginning to enjoy and explore, a fresh start to their future with no regrets. His tension eased as the scotch sent a warm wave over him. He gazed outside, letting his mind wander as he stared at people strolling the beach at Goose Spit.

He could retire early after selling his restaurants in

Victoria and Nanaimo, leaving them financially well off. Hoping to rekindle his early ambitions to enter politics, he and Ellen completely changed their lifestyle. They moved to the Courtenay-Comox area and became involved with the local liberal party. Barry loved challenges.

At forty-six years old, he was in great shape, both mentally and physically. He jogged three miles every day, played golf two to three times a week, and kept abreast of local and provincial issues.

Since the start of their marriage, Ellen had been the cornerstone of his success. She believed in him, giving him the freedom and the confidence to accomplish what he had. It couldn't have been easy having a workaholic husband. She must have felt like a single parent at times. And for that, he'd spend the rest of his days making sure she was happy.

Handling a difficult son almost broke Ellen, but to her credit, she kept trying. For Ellen, everything was about family, and she'd figured out how to balance everyone. Lord only knows how she managed to stop him and their son from killing each other.

Since moving here, she'd stood beside him proudly, helping his campaign when he'd entered the provincial elections for a seat in the legislature. She'd offered her advice when she noticed something he missed. She was his personal campaign chairperson. With her at his side, Barry finally realized his dream of working in the political arena.

Ellen had regained her confidence since moving here. She joined the Crown Isle Ladies Golf Club, telling him she'd surprised herself at her love and aptitude for the game. Ellen joined the St. Joseph's Hospital Ladies Auxiliary in Comox, fundraising for a state-of-the-art cancer diagnosis and treatment wing. She'd looked better and seemed happier than she had been for years. They made a striking couple. His solid physique, blond hair, and brown eyes were a perfect foil for Ellen's delicate frame, chestnut brown hair, and hazel eyes.

Then Ellen's mind fell apart.

His cell rang, interrupting his reverie. When he glanced at the caller ID, his heart lifted in anticipation.

"Hi, Dad, how was Mom today?" his daughter Sara asked. "Did you give her my love and tell her I'm all settled for my third term?"

"So good to hear from you, sweetie. I'm afraid it's the same thing, she broke her promise and refused to see me. I haven't been able to tell her anything. I don't get it, Sara. If only she'd talk, and we could find out what caused all this. She's been in there four months, yet she still won't see anyone." His voice turned thick and full of anguish. He took a sip of scotch to clear his throat.

"Maybe I should come home this weekend, Dad. We could go fishing or something. Just like we used to." When he didn't answer, she continued. "You know she loves you. You're all she's ever thought about. Everything we did as kids revolved around your schedule and what you enjoyed. C'mon, Dad, cheer up! Dr. Hallden says it'll all come out one day, and she'll get better. Trust him."

"I guess I have to, Sara. I don't know what else to do. I miss her so much. I've taken her for granted. We all have. She's always been beside us whenever we needed her. Remember how she helped you when you were in grade school? The teachers were too busy to spend extra time with you."

"Y'know, I still taste grape once in a while, when I write certain numbers like 5 and 3. And lemonade or orange for my b's and d's. Those teachers used to make me practice line after line. As soon as I'd get back to other work, I'd fall right back into reversals. Mom cured me."

"She was a pretty smart cookie." A yearning note crept into his voice. "She never let anything beat her. Not even Dan."

He heard Sara groan. He knew she disliked talking about her older brother.

"No kidding. I wonder what my brother's up to now? He sure left fast after the accident, and he hasn't even come home to see Mom."

"I hate to admit it, honey, but he's always looked after number one first. I don't know how your mom never gave up on him."

He rose from his chair and began pacing in the kitchen as he reflected on their relationship with Dan. "The little jerk hasn't even come by since I called him about your mom's breakdown. He doesn't even respond to my texts anymore." His stomach churned as he thought about his only son, who should've been his pride and joy but had always proved to be his nemesis.

"Until I see a big change from what I experienced this summer, Dad, no news is good news as far as I'm concerned. Let him stay in Surrey. Anyway, if I get my English term paper outlined this week, I'll drive down and make your favorite lasagna, ok?"

"Sure, sweetheart, I'd love that. But don't let yourself get behind," he warned.

"I won't. Love you."

"Love you too, sweetheart." He shut his cell off and breathed a sigh of relief. He felt a hundred percent better.

He looked at his favorite picture on the oak coffee table and noticed how similar his wife and daughter were. Sara was a brunette with hazel eyes like her mother's. She also shared Ellen's fair complexion but had a rounder face and had inherited Barry's dimples.

He had always been so proud of the two of them—both so independent, responsible and loving women. Ellen had done an excellent job raising Sara. She had almost been a single mother for the first half of Sara's childhood.

His priority had been getting his first restaurant established then multiplying it when opportunities arose. He only leveled off after a fainting spell coupled with a nose bleed signaled problems with high blood pressure. Barry had reduced his workload then, eventually retiring almost three years ago to Comox.

He wasn't able to stay idle, however, and had involved himself in politics again. He'd renewed old acquaintances and made new contacts at local town hall meetings and service clubs, always keeping in touch with the regional issues. He knew his easy smile and ability to engage people made him popular. His prompt attention to their requests for information or action soon built a loyal and trustworthy reputation, garnering him the liberal representative in Comox-Courtenay.

Last year had been the most exciting time of his life when he ran for public office and was elected to parliament. He promised to make his constituents his priority and worked hard, long hours to earn their respect. Ellen and Sara had stood by his side on election night as the results poured in. He remembered their excitement and happiness in his success. The three of them were one proud family.

Then Dan came home.

The same question always came to mind. Did Ellen's breakdown have anything to do with Dan's visit?

They had spent a lovely summer at their secluded cabin on Comox Lake. She had been so excited to see Dan arrive with a few friends in August. Then, after that horrible accident, she couldn't seem to sit still or concentrate on anything. Dr. Hallden had suspicions that there was more to it, but if there was, Barry didn't know what it could be.

As far as he remembered, the visit had gone much better than they had hoped for until the tragedy occurred.

CHAPTER 2

Her ringtone buzzed again. Ellen had barely turned her pager back on, hoping that the sexy guy who'd caught her attention three weekends ago would stop his constant calling. Now the home phone was ringing, and angrily she picked it up.

"Give it up, Barry! I'm too busy for this," Ellen barked. She hated to be rude, but sexy or not, she didn't want to encourage his attention.

A playful voice answered. "Be fair, give me a few minutes, *please*. My pride can't take many more hang-ups. It's had a tough couple of weeks."

Ellen laughed nervously. She imagined that it probably had driven him crazy. He must be used to girls begging for his attention. She gripped the phone tighter but didn't disconnect.

"That's better. I love your laugh, but we still need to talk and get a few things straightened out. I need to see you—and soon."

Ellen wasn't sure that was such a great idea. Whenever

she was near him, saw his text, or heard his voice, her stomach flip-flopped with anxiety. "Look, Barry, I think you've got the wrong idea about me. Tom and I have been going together for over a year and-"

"And you've been coasting all the way through it. What do you see in him? He's going nowhere. Tom is content with working in a mill and spending his life here. I'll bet he never even talks about traveling or exploring new horizons anywhere else. You're way too good for him."

"And I suppose you're better?"

"Baby, you know I am," he whispered huskily.

"No way. Uh-uh." Ellen clutched the phone tighter and lowered her voice. "I don't know what got into me, but *that* won't be happening again."

"Look, I know I act like a big shot sometimes and come across like a smartass, but I'm not that bad. Honest."

"Really? I know your type. You're here to make a few bucks, break a few hearts, then go back to Victoria."

"You're right on half of that. I plan on making my tuition and living expenses for next year, but I hadn't counted on meeting you."

Ellen shivered at his hidden message as he whispered suggestively. "Stop that. I bet you've used that line several times, and I don't want to be another conquest in a summer romance." She could have sworn she'd just run a sprint, as her breath quickened while her heart thudded in her chest. "I have to go." She didn't want to fall for his smooth lines and make another mistake.

"Come out with me tonight."

"No. I'm not seeing Tom or you."

"Please? I promise I won't even kiss you. I need to talk to you, to see you again."

"No. I'm setting a record. Two Saturday nights at home in a row. I'm going to help my mom with my grad dress then study for finals on Monday."

"Tomorrow then," Barry pleaded.

"Not likely. I have to attend church, then have lunch at my grandma's. You better face it. You're out of luck."

"Sorry, Ellen, but that's not going to happen. I've fallen for you. And I think you're falling for me. I can't get you out of my mind."

She shook her head in disbelief, then hung up the phone. Going over the conversation, she wondered if he was right. She'd never believed in true love at first sight. This thing between them was only physical, she was sure of it. If she could resist him for a while longer—and if her period came, then she could pick up the pieces and go back to Tom. Safe, dependable, adorable Tom.

She turned and saw her mother watching her as she stirred a pot of homemade chili.

"Who was that, dear?" she asked.

"One of the guys we hang around with," Ellen lied, her face flushing.

"Same fella who's been driving by every day?"

"I don't know, Mom."

"What are you doing tonight?"

"Nothing."

"I haven't seen Tom around here lately."

"Tom's busy. Don't you need help to sew some pearl beading on my grad dress?" Ellen slipped by her mom and sprinted down the hall to the dining room to set the table.

Her mom's footsteps followed her closely. "There's no hurry. We still have time for that. What's going on? This is two weekends in a row that you've stayed home. You have two boys phoning you, and you're avoiding them both." She eyed Ellen carefully. "Better watch yourself, young lady, you don't want to be getting a reputation."

"Mom, this isn't the dark ages. Seriously. A bunch of girls hangs out with a bunch of guys as good friends. It's nothing to worry about, honestly. We all get calls from each other in our group. It doesn't mean anything."

"It better not. Remember, you're a Dalmy. That's a well-respected name in this town. I hope it stays that way."

"Yes, Mom, it will." Ellen finished adding the buns and butter to the table. "You think you'd be pleased to see me at home, studying for finals and helping you."

"I am, dear. We'll work on the dress after dinner."

"OK. Call me when dinner's ready." She scooted up the stairs to her room, inserted her favorite Bryan Adams CD, and turned it up. Hot tears rolled down her cheeks as she flopped onto her bed. She pulled her pillow over her head to help muffle the sobs.

Her emotions were all over the map. That's all she needed was to have her mom give her a lecture.

What was she going to do if she was pregnant? She probably wasn't. After all, her friends said you couldn't get pregnant the first time. Wouldn't Tom have a fit, after all the rejections and alternative loving she'd given him?

Maybe she should take a hot bath. She heard that it was guaranteed to bring on late periods. Ellen pulled her thick, shoulder-length hair into a French knot, then stripped and looked at herself in the mirror.

She ran her hands over her belly. She was an athletic girl with a healthy appetite, involved in running and basketball, so the slightly rounded curve couldn't be proof that she was pregnant. Her hands went to her breasts. They didn't feel or look any larger, although they were slightly tender.

As she watched herself, she remembered Barry's fingers touching her, his lips nibbling and tasting her. Her nipples hardened as she stood there, remembering. *Stupid, stupid girl.* She shook her head to rid herself of the memories and slipped on a housecoat to go downstairs for her bath.

Her face flushed as a niggling feeling of shame washed over her. Minutes later, she lowered herself gingerly into the hot, steaming tub. Her ivory skin reddened in the heat. A dizzying sensation threatened to overtake her as perspiration beaded on her upper lip.

Stoically, she added more hot water, determined to start her menstrual cycle. If this didn't bring it on, she'd have to borrow her dad's car and slip over to Parksville, where she wouldn't be known, to pick up a pregnancy test.

Gravel crunching in the driveway alerted her to her dad returning from work. The back door opened, and Ellen could hear his boots tossed into the closet.

Last year, her father took the leap and started his own business as an electrical contractor in Port Alberni. He was also recently elected as an alderman on the town council. A well-respected man about town, his word meant something. *A teenage daughter, unwed and pregnant, would kill him.*

A mumbled conversation between her parents made her decide she'd better get out before he wanted to clean up for dinner. She blotted her reddened skin carefully, then hurried out to her bedroom, hoping the bath would do the trick.

Opening the window in her bedroom, she let the light breeze cool her. She loved her room. She had re-decorated it last year with Miami Vice colors and pictures of tropical beaches she hoped to one day visit. She dreamed of being a travel agent, which would let her explore all those exotic locations and more.

Pictures of Mariah Carey, Jennifer Lopez, Bryan Adams, as well as Brooks and Dunn showed her eclectic taste in music. Her earphones sat on the night table so she could listen to it at night, even if her parents were in bed. The short wall near her closet contained a shelving unit filled with her favorite stuffed animals, school pictures, and books. A turquoise rug with a musical note hooked into the center lay beside her bed. Hardwood floors were cold in the morning, and she had hooked this rug herself.

It would be hard to leave this room.

Leave? The idea popped into her mind. *Well, I guess I might not have much choice.* If her period didn't come, should she tell Barry or her parents? Or simply take off and never come back? But where to?

"Ellen, dinner's almost ready." her mother called.

"I'll be there in a minute," she replied. Before joining her parents, she hopped into a pair of neon pink capris with a short crop top.

Dinner was predictable. Salad, buns, and chili every Saturday night. Each day of the week had a special menu. Boring, boring, boring.

Her dad was quiet as usual, always tired by the end of his work week.

Ellen picked at her food, then excused herself, pretending not to see her mother's stern reproach. She scraped her plate into the organic bin, rinsed it, and placed her utensils in the dishwasher. Her mom always looked after the rest. No one else cleaned up to her satisfaction.

Ellen leaned over and gave her dad a peck on the cheek, which produced the smile she always strove to find. "I have homework to finish, and then I'm going to work on my dress with Mom. See you later."

With a mouthful of salad, he nodded and waved his fork to her, and Ellen escaped.

She went to the spare bedroom upstairs that doubled as a sewing room and picked up the tiny faux pearls. Ellen loved how they glowed against the pale-yellow satin material she and her mom had selected for her grad dress. The color would set off her deep brown hair perfectly. The sweetheart neckline angled to show off bare shoulders a la *Pretty Woman* rage. The bodice hugged her, then fell in a straight line to the tops of her feet. A slit on her left side that led above the knee gave her movement without trepidation.

It was glamorous, and a bit outrageous, but Ellen had stuck to her guns for a change.

She already had white patent flats and a purse, so no money need be invested there. And two rows of tiny pearls were being sewn near the dress's neckline to add some class.

Only two more weeks to go, and she'd be graduating with the rest of the class of '93. Tom was supposed to be taking her, but now she wasn't so sure.

The night dragged by.

Her mind drifted to the first time she had met Barry. She and Tom had double-dated with her best friend, Paula, and the new guy she had recently met. It had been a lot of fun, but Barry had never called Paula for another date. Yet somehow, he was always around their group when he wasn't working at the mill, and Tom had become jealous.

A month ago, at the pre-grad beach party, a fight flared up between Barry and Tom. Everyone had been drinking and singing along with the kids who'd brought their guitars. A cooler full of wieners and buns to cook over the campfire went along with the beer. Everyone was having a good time until Tom thought he saw Barry make a pass at her.

After the brawl, Ellen was so mixed up and upset, she'd run off alone along the beach.

Barry had found her and apologized. They'd sat on the sand, knees to chest, sharing their dreams. His attentive manner eased her distress as they listened to the waves lapping on the shore. Falling back onto the sand, they stared at the night sky above them, identifying constellations in the sky.

A current of electricity hummed then zipped between them, so when he finally kissed her, a lightning response shot through her. It seemed so right. She still couldn't believe the fiery passion that flowed between them. Was she going to pay the price for that fire now?

Ellen's daydream was broken by the annoyance in her mom's voice yelling, "Ellen? Wake up. This is the second time I've asked you to put your dress on. I want to mark it for the hem. You'll need to put your shoes on too."

Ellen took the dress to go and change in her room.

"Really? Do it here, Ellen. I certainly know what you look like by now."

"Mom-"

"C'mon, put it on," her mother commanded. She helped Ellen pull it over her head and adjusted it over her shoulders. "Suck it in," she advised, as she began to zip the dress up. "You better watch those French fries, girl, or you'll be wearing control tops underneath."

"Holy crow. I had a milkshake today too. That does it, the diet starts tomorrow."

Her mother looked at her and laughed. Ellen was always starting a diet but never completing one, which was alright by her mother.

Mom didn't believe toothpicks made beautiful and healthy girls.

"Just quit fidgeting and let me finish pinning this, then you can go. Why don't you call Paula and head out to the movies or something?"

Ellen carefully removed her dress and changed. "I'm beat, Mom. I've been doing a lot of studying, so I think I'll just listen to my new CDs and hit the hay."

Her mother looked at her worriedly. "Everything ok, dear?"

The doorbell rang, and Ellen, eager to escape, ran downstairs to answer it.

Tom stood outside, a glint of anger and confusion in his eyes. "We need to talk."

Ellen tried to postpone the inevitable. "I'm helping my mom with my grad dress."

"Look, we can't keep going on this way. I've had enough. Either we iron it out now, or you can forget about us forever. I'm sure your mom can spare you for a while, so what's it gonna be?"

Ellen didn't like the rising growl in his voice. Before a scene broke out, she'd better get him out of there.

"Alright." She reached for her purse, then called her dad that she was going out for a bit with Tom. Outside, she shrugged off his hand.

He glared at her, and when he grabbed her arm again and steered her toward his '86 Camaro, she gave up. Inside the car, she stayed close to the door, not cuddling him like she used to.

Her gaze drifted to the skeleton-head gear shifter she had bought him as a joke for his birthday, and she groaned inside. They had spent a lot of time in this car and made a lot of plans together. A queasy feeling rocked the pit of her stomach. She glanced at Tom. His biceps rippled under his black spandex and mesh T-shirt as he put the car in gear and peeled out.

He was quite a catch by most girls' standards, yet here she was, ready to throw that all away. *I must be nuts. What more could a girl ask for?*

"Thanks for sticking around after the fight," Tom hissed. "Of course, I guess that's a good way not to have to choose who you want. I get my head kicked in because that asshole makes a pass at you, and you don't even come and see how I'm doing." His voice grew louder, his frustration evident. "Maybe you wanted him to feel your ass, is that it? Did I break something up for you two?"

"Are you still hung up on that? Every time I see you, that's all you ever want to talk about. Can't you lay off? You're letting your imagination run away on you."

"Everybody knows he's got the hots for you. He's down here working at the mill only to earn money to go back to college. Barry figures he's a big man around a hick town, so he can screw anyone he wants."

"I haven't seen him with any other girls," Ellen declared defensively.

"You've been noticing that hey? Admit it, he was coming on to you ever since you and I double dated with him and Paula." Tom swerved off the road and parked by Paper Mill Dam, a favorite spot for swimmers who liked to test themselves against the rapids and currents. It was also a favorite hangout for a lot of teenagers in love.

"Give me a break. I can't help it if Barry likes me." She sniffled as tears welled up in her eyes. She hunted for a tissue in her purse. She was *not* going to cry. It seemed that's all she'd been doing lately. She was so confused.

Tom moved over and gathered her in his arms, smelling

the scent of Tommy Girl, that lemony, floral blend that he bought for her birthday. "The day after the fight, you said you needed time on your own for a while. I can understand that, with exams, graduation, and everything else, but these past few weeks have almost driven me around the bend. You weren't even answering my calls lately." He lifted her chin and kissed her lips, then her salty, damp cheeks. "All you gotta do is tell me you're still my girl, that you still love me," he whispered, his voice hoarse with emotion.

The security and safety she'd always felt in Tom's arms were still there. It seemed like her second home in the past year. When he began kissing her, she drooped inside. There was no fire, no magic there anymore. Barry had awakened a passion in her that she never dreamed existed.

"Honestly, he's not good enough for you," Tom whispered. "Not good enough for anyone around here. He's only here to make big bucks at the lumber mills, turn his nose up, then return to the city life. You watch him charm Paula or another girl and then break her heart when he leaves for Victoria. He's just a puffed-up asshole. But I'm here for you, babe. I always have been, always will be. I don't have my head in the clouds like he does. Like I told you, it won't be long that I'll have enough saved for a down-payment for our home, then we'll start our life together. Life's good here, Ellen. Don't screw it up."

Confused by her lack of desire for him, Ellen pushed away. Trying to avoid an answer, she focused on fixing her hair in the rear-view mirror. Her cheating eyes stared back, and she lowered them as she tried to sort her jumbled emotions.

"You know how much I care for you. But with graduation and everything happening so fast, I'm mixed up. I don't want to hurt your feelings, but I need a break. That's why I haven't been talking to you lately, or to Barry either, for that matter. I need some time to myself to make sure how I feel about things. You know where you're going, but I'm confused about my future."

Trying to avoid Tom's eyes, she reached for another Kleenex in her purse. Her nose was probably chafed and red from blowing it. Her parents would notice it for sure. Another situation to try and explain. "I don't know what I'm going to do next. I don't want things more complicated than they are now."

"I don't get it. How much more time do you need? It seems pretty damn straight forward to me, you either love me or you don't. Our future was always going to have *us* in it, in this town. What's changed?" Tom's stormy eyes glared at her.

A thread of anxiety snaked through her. "I don't know, give me a few weeks, maybe?" Ellen took a deep breath, then blew it out, trying to regain some composure. She wiped her tender nose again. "I have so much to do. Mom and I are finishing the alterations to my grad dress. I have to finish cramming for my finals." Ellen threw her hands up in frustration. "I can't add the pressure from anyone else right now."

"Are we still on for your grad? Everybody thinks I oughta dump you. You're making me look like a fool."

"Who cares what they think?"

"Obviously not you, which brings me back to the fight. You disappear. I get flattened, and the sonofabitch who does it takes off. Nobody sees him-or you."

"What are you trying to say that we got together?" Her voice went shrill in self-defense. "I can't stand to see you two jackasses fight, and then I'm accused of going off with the winner? Great." she ended sarcastically. Her heart was beating a mile a minute.

Tom's frown deepened as his eyes narrowed, assessing her unusual explosion. She wasn't a good liar, so she decided to go on the defensive.

"Take me home right now. If this is what you think of me, then to hell with you," she growled as she jumped over to her side door. "Either that or I'm gone."

"Getting touchy, aren't we?" Tom probed. "You got something to hide?"

"I told Paula. Now I'm telling you-I went for a walk down the beach to cool off. I didn't want to spend another minute at that stupid party. So, I decided to head home and hiked up to the Esso on the highway. I called my dad to come and get me." At least part of that was true. "Now, will you drop it?"

Tom glared at her for a full minute, deciding whether to believe her or not. He started the car and revved the motor several times, his way of trying to make up his mind. Exasperated, he threw it into reverse, spitting gravel behind them before putting his Camaro in first and driving her home.

Neither Tom nor she spoke a word. She opened her door then he touched her shoulder.

"One more week. That's it. I'll call you next Saturday morning. You better have the answer I want to hear."

She looked over her shoulder at the guy she had fallen in love with over a year ago. He wasn't happy with her right now, but he would wait for her answer. Not many fellas would do this, she knew.

"Thanks, Tom." Tears threatened again, and she quickly brushed them aside before she slammed the door shut behind her. She blew him a kiss and waved goodbye. She was giving mixed signals but damned if she knew how to straighten them.

When Ellen entered the house, she went straight to her room, then to bed. There she lost control, shedding the pent-up tears of confusion and fear. Ellen tossed and turned most of the night, wondering what her options were. She eventually gave up and got up at 6:30, going downstairs for some yogurt and a banana to settle her stomach. She hadn't gotten her period after all. She caught her mom whispering to her dad that the young couple was fighting. Right now, anything but the truth that would explain her mood was ok by her.

Ellen joined her parents for the mid-morning church service. Father Kevin was again preaching on the evils of drinking, drugs, and the poor decisions they encouraged. Her conscience twinged a few times as she remembered her actions, then she pushed those thoughts aside. The service dragged by, and she couldn't keep her hands still.

It was stuffy in the church on this warm June day, and Ellen began to feel claustrophobic as well as lightheaded. Mercifully she sang the last chorus, then quickly left to inhale the fresh air outside. A warm hand settled on her shoulder, and she promptly turned around to see Barry.

"What are you doing here?" she squealed.

"Better smile. Your parents are staring at you and coming this way. Can't a fella go to church? I told you I don't give up easily. Now be a good girl and introduce me to your parents." He turned to greet them, extending his hand to her father. "Good morning. Beautiful day, isn't it?"

"Dad, Mom, this is Barry Peterson. He's a student from the Lansdowne campus in Victoria, working at the mill for the summer. Barry, these are my parents, Mr. and Mrs. Dalmy."

The Dalmys eyed him over, taking in his sharply pressed khakis, his navy-blue polo shirt, and casual boat shoes. They smiled and shook hands with him.

"And how do you like it here in our Valley?" her father asked.

"Just fine, sir. I'm working at the Somass Division, pulling off the chain." Barry smiled. "It's great money, but it reminds me of why I'm going to school. I can't see myself doing millwork for the rest of my life."

Ellen could tell that her parents were a bit uncomfortable. Barry was much too familiar and charming for their taste. Her father looked Barry over and then Ellen as he tried to figure out the story.

"Is it okay if I take Ellen out for lunch?" Barry asked.

"You'd better ask Ellen that question. She usually accompanies us to her grandma's most Sundays for brunch, but it's up to her."

Ellen hoped her nervousness wasn't showing. She knew her dad would be impressed with Barry arriving at the church, dressed impeccably. Maybe the charm was somewhat overdone, yet her parents were warming up to him, just like she had.

Ellen was too stunned to make any comment. She was still angry that Barry had shown up here. *He had a lot of nerve.* Her face was flushed, but whether it was just embarrassment, she wasn't sure. She couldn't deny how her pulse raced when he held her elbow.

"C'mon Ellen, please," Barry begged impishly.

Ellen shrugged, then glanced at her parents. From the smile on their faces, they seemed to approve of him, so she nodded. They waved goodbye to her parents as he guided her to his black Ford Escort.

"After you."

She slid in, then Barry reached inside and handed her the seatbelt before closing her door. She glared at him while he smiled and started his vehicle. "What did you think you were doing coming to my church? I told you I didn't want to see you."

"Why didn't you tell me to get lost or tell your parents you weren't interested in going anywhere with me?" Barry shook his forefinger at her as he chuckled. "You don't know what you want right now."

"That's true. A lot is going on in my life, and you're not making things any easier. You've been pushing me ever since I met you." Ellen crossed her arms, wanting him to see how upset she was. "Can't you tone it down and give a girl a chance to think?"

Ellen watched his cockiness disappear as he finally recognized her unease. *That's better.* He was too smooth for his good and hers. Barry needed to be taken down a peg or two. He pulled away from the parking lot and turned left on Johnson Street, heading out of town.

"Where are we going?" Ellen asked.

"Let's get out of the Valley for a while, go over to Parksville or Qualicum. Sit on the beach and enjoy the sun." His tone of voice was serious now, warm and gentle.

Ellen bit her upper lip, a habit she had when she was confused. His voice was like honey, and it scared her. It scared her because it felt so good that it sent chills down her arms.

They drove around Mount Arrowsmith through Cathedral Grove. Douglas fir towered around them, blocking direct sunlight. As a child, Ellen had often begged to stop and walk there. Thick with moss and shedding needles, the paths were full of surprises if you were observant. The family competed to find mushrooms of various shapes, sizes, and colors. Burls were spotted, and feathers from hawks and eagles were collected and treasured. It was always a contest between her and her dad to collect the most unusual items.

As the road curved onwards, the cool green water of Cameron Lake hugged the highway. The Beaufort range was mirrored in its calm reflection.

"I hear this is a cold lake to swim in. Do you ever come here?" Barry asked.

"Not often. I love it, but most people can't handle it once they're used to Sproat Lake. You'll probably be back home before you see this in the fall. It's gorgeous then, the mountains dotted with red and gold deciduous trees mixed between the evergreens. I love living here."

A smug smile crossed Barry's face. "We're lucky. I plan on traveling in the future, but I never want to move from Vancouver Island. How can you beat this place?"

"I know. We're never more than an hour away from a lake or the ocean. There's always a corner somewhere that you can find privacy and enjoy nature. Do you do any climbing or hiking?" Ellen asked.

"Not often enough. School and work keep me pretty busy."

Ellen flicked through the stack of CDs and chose a Brooks and Dunn greatest hits. "I didn't know you liked Pop Country."

"Some call it the new rock-and-roll. There are lots of clubs in Victoria that play it, and line dancing is popular. Have you ever line-danced?"

"Not really. Not my thing, but it's fun to watch."

They sang along with Boot Scoot Boogie and laughed with each other, dissolving the tension between them. The diverse scenery around every corner kept Ellen busy explaining what was where.

When it ended, they didn't replace the CD, choosing to absorb the serenity and natural beauty to sort their feelings and thoughts. When they reached Parksville, Barry pulled off onto a beach access, and her gaze scanned the long stretch of sandy beach.

"I'm sorry I've rushed you, Ellen." Barry's hand covered hers, and that thrilling electricity flowed through her again. "I know it's only been a few months since we first met, but you're special. I sensed that as soon as I saw you."

"Thank you, I'm flattered. Honestly, I don't know what to think. I don't know whether to trust you or not." She withdrew her hand and fiddled with her watch again. "I don't want to be just a summer romance and forgotten when you go back to college in the fall. I'm not interested in getting involved with a player." She couldn't look at him. She was too nervous. She took a deep breath to explain herself.

"The other night was a mistake. I don't usually have more than a beer or two in an evening. I'm not sure why I became so reckless. I must have drunk three or four cans before the fight broke out. So when I took off, I wasn't feeling any pain." She turned her face away from him, too embarrassed to go on.

"Don't, Ellen." He pulled her back towards him. "Don't say the most wonderful night in my life was a mistake." His chocolate-brown eyes mesmerized her.

Barry bent to kiss her while she leaned towards him, parting her lips slightly and closing her eyes. His lips touched her softly, breaking away, then meeting them again. Her senses reeled, and she pressed herself against him wanting more.

He stopped and tipped her chin up until she opened her

eyes. He groaned. "Don't blame it on the beer. We may not know much about each other, but we both feel the chemistry. I want you." When she lowered her gaze and pulled away, he made her look at him again. "And you want me. And that's the way it should be. Life without passion is dull, safe, boring. If you want that, then go back to Tom."

"I can't believe this," she murmured. "It sounds crazy, I know, but I've never experienced this before. I like having fun. I enjoy some harmless flirting, but I'm not a girl who fools around. Ever. That's what's confusing me now. I don't know what to do."

"I think I know the difference between a good girl and a sleaze, Ellen." His fingers stroked her soft, silky tresses.

Ellen leaned against him, feeling the taut muscles of his chest, the wild beating of his heart. It reminded her of their night on the beach when she discovered what passion truly was. Aware of the evidence of his growing desire, Ellen pulled away. Needing to put some distance between them, she challenged him.

"I'll bet I can run faster than you can. I'll race you to the water. The last one there is a rotten egg." Ellen kicked off her shoes, jumped out of his car, then lifted her skirt to mid-thigh as she stumbled through the soft sand. Once she hit the packed, damp beach, she ran faster. She giggled when she glanced back to see Barry struggling to remove his socks.

The tide was out quite far, at least a few hundred feet. Barry's footsteps were soon slapping the sand behind her, gaining on her.

"Ha-ha," Barry panted as he came level with her. "Think you're an Olympic racer, do you? Well, you're beginning to smell rotten now."

They ran through warm, shallow tidal pools, and after a

final burst of energy, Barry beat her to the gently lapping waves. He bent down and used his hand to splash her, so she kicked water back at him. And the water fight was on.

"Stop it! I'm going to get soaked," she shrieked between her bouts of laughter. "Stop, please."

"Are you ready to give up?" he bantered, poised to send another spray of water over.

"Yes. Yes!" Ellen gasped, trying to catch her breath from the laughing and running. She shook her head and wiped her face free of the salt water and sand.

BARRY MOVED CLOSER to Ellen and rumpled her hair. Those eyes. Flecks of green in her hazel eyes had a pull that magnetized him. Merely making eye contact with her sent him into a tailspin. She looked innocent, but there was a passion hiding in her that surprised both of them.

He soon found out, though, that her keen sense of dry humor kept him off guard. He liked that. She had long, long legs that made a guy look twice. The rest of her was just as sexy as he remembered how she looked and felt beneath him. Soft, warm, giggly, and passionate all at the same time. He had to convince her how much he cared.

"Ell? Can I call you Ell? " His hand reached out, and waiting for her answer made him hold his breath

She looked at him thoughtfully for a moment. Then with an impish smile, a shrug won out. "Sure, why not? No one's given me a nickname before." She reached out and grasped his hand.

"Good. Let me be the first." Barry squeezed her hand and swung their arms in an arc as they splashed through the warm, shallow surf. "I guess you want to know more about me, right?" When she nodded, he continued.

"In a nutshell, here it is. I'm twenty-two, an only child like you, but my dad died when I was seven. My mom's worked in the kitchen at the hospital ever since. We live in an apartment on Fort Street, and I'm working through a business administration course. When I was sixteen, I washed dishes on weekends at the Chateau Victoria. It was hard work, but I kind of liked watching what went on, all the ordering and organizing that the kitchen staff did for banquets and special events. We had a great reputation for our food, décor, and service. After I graduated, I did guest services for a while, eventually bartending at dinners or whenever they needed an extra hand. It was fun."

Barry held her hand lightly, tracing from her palm to each fingertip and back with his thumb, as he viewed the incoming tide. "I moved out with a friend for a while and did the usual partying routine. We got kicked out of the apartment we had rented. When I asked to move back home, my mom read me the riot act. She said I had to decide what I wanted to do with myself first. She had no use for a loafer."

Ellen laughed. "Sounds like a smart mom. My parents would do the same thing. They expect nothing but the best from me, so I try hard to make them proud with good grades. And all the studying that it takes has kept me out of trouble. It makes it so much easier at home."

She raised her eyebrows at Barry, then continued. "It may be difficult for you to believe their attitude, but forestry operations here have given them a good life. In return, they're very involved in community events and committed to making this town great. I doubt they've even considered me leaving here to better myself. In their opinion, nothing else begins to compare."

"I guess so, but I can't imagine not being encouraged to explore options. There's a big world out there full of things to experience. I'm surprised you haven't rebelled," Barry replied.

"To be honest, so am I. But then again, very few graduates move out of the valley. Why would they? High wages and security are powerful motivators. Although, sometimes, I want to chuck the whole thing, do something no one expects me to do. Do something daring, something exciting. I'm such a boring person sometimes. The most exciting times I've had are when my cousin Matt visits, and we go camping every few years."

"Where's he from? Where do you go?"

"He lives in Olympia, Washington. He tries to vacation here every few years for a week or two. We went to Cape Scott about three years ago, then hiked the West Coast Trail with a group last year. Matt's my only cousin and an amazing outdoorsman. We have a lot of fun together. He even taught me to ride an ATV one year in Bella Coola."

"Really? I'd say that was very adventurous. What were you doing there?"

"My grandmother and his grandmother were sisters. They moved from the prairies and bought some property up there. My grandparents sold and moved here when my mom married my dad. We'd go to Bella Coola to visit the relatives now and then. Eventually, Matt inherited his grandparents' land. I prefer more access to civilization, though, so we mainly get together on the Island now."

"Looks like I have a lot to learn about you. But you're interrupting an autobiography of the next extremely important person in your life."

Ellen flipped her hand towards him, entreating him to proceed, "Excuse me. Please continue, your highness."

Barry bowed to her apology. "Where was I? Oh yeah, my mom made me look more seriously at the future. I liked the hotel industry and working with the public, so I decided to take a business administration course. It will give me a good background to explore different opportunities. After I finish my course and become more experienced, I'd like to buy my own place, eventually. Get into the big league. I plan on making her proud of me and making her life a little easier. She's not as well as she used to be. Anyway, that's about it."

Barry watched Ellen's reaction and hoped he'd conveyed the confidence he had of himself and his future. He was more ambitious than she probably realized and wondered if she'd be okay with that.

"Doesn't sound like the typical playboy that I thought you were," she conceded, "but what about girlfriends? You're not exactly ugly, and I know you're not blind." Ellen's wink took away any perceived sting.

"Thanks, I think. Sure, I've had a few here and there. But sometimes, they wanted more than I could give, like moving in together. Or sometimes, I wanted more than they could give. Anyway, there's no one I'm serious about. Except you." Barry watched the delicate pink tint her face, and his pulse quickened with hope. He tipped her chin up so she could hopefully see the intense love he had for her in his gaze.

Their eyes met, and a deep, profound emotion passed between them before Ellen glanced away. He sat on a long piece of driftwood and pulled her hand so she'd sit beside him.

"You must think I'm easy, but I'm not. I go over and over it. I'm shocked at myself. It's hard to believe we did it." Ellen dropped her head in her hands and whispered, "What happens if I get pregnant? I hardly know you, and vice versa."

He needed to tread carefully here, give her some time to think. "I know all I have to know, Ell. I wasn't expecting what happened either, and I wasn't prepared. That's on me." Barry kissed her fingertips, then continued.

"Don't you ever wonder what life would be like outside of the Valley? To leave the ups and downs of the forestry industry and the narrow thinking that job security is worth leaving your dreams behind? You're about to graduate, yet I haven't heard a word about your dreams for the future. There's so much diversity in Victoria, and with hard work, the sky's the limit. You could explore so many avenues and make your wishes come true."

"That's just it. I'm not sure what I want, other than finding a job in September. Port Alberni's a safe place for me, where my family is known and respected. Truthfully, I'm almost afraid to even think of leaving them and my friends."

"If you followed me, you wouldn't be lonely. You wouldn't need to be afraid. We could make a future together." Barry watched her cheeks turn even rosier as her eyes flitted around them. He realized she was probably overwhelmed with her predicament and what it would mean for her future.

He turned her flushed face towards him, sensing the lingering shame within her. "We've got the whole summer to get to know each other more, but if you do get pregnant, it will only mean one thing." Barry paused, waiting for her to look into his eyes.

When she lifted her eyes to his, he could see the insecurity within her. He could see her breath quicken as tears glistened. He hoped that she was as smitten with him as he was with her. No matter how quick this courtship had progressed, he was sure it was the real thing. But would she be brave enough to break free of her family and her small hometown?

"One thing?" Ellen's voice trembled.

"Yes, I'll have to ask you now instead of later. Will you marry me?"

CHAPTER 3

Ellen remembered the last time she saw Tom. It was the day after Barry picked her up from church when they'd bought a pregnancy test, which confirmed her worst fears. She had called Tom and arranged to meet him at the Golden Dragon, a popular Chinese restaurant. It might not have been the ideal place, but she didn't want to be alone with him. Do it fast, do it cleanly, with no guilt. It was fast, alright, but she couldn't escape the blame.

"That was quick," Tom commented as she sat down at the booth. "You wanted a few weeks, and you did it in a few days."

Ellen looked at him, the recently grown mustache framing his familiar lips. A new leather jacket with shoulder pads nodded to the latest fashion craze. Fast cars and high style. It was a surprise he had stayed with her as long as he had. He'd been a big part of her life, but now he was a part of her past.

"Tom, you know how much I care for you,"

"Don't draw me a picture, babe. I'm not stupid. I saw your answer written all over your face as soon as I walked in.

All I wanna know is if there's someone else." He glared at her as he lit a cigarette.

"I didn't mean for this to happen, honest. But I'm not going to lie about it. I'm seeing Barry. I don't know if I'm making a mistake or not, but I can't ignore it either. I'm sorry." Ellen couldn't bear the pain she saw in his eyes. She dropped her gaze.

"You don't know how sorry. That sonofabitch is gonna dump you, but if you're too bloody stupid to see that, don't expect me to pick up the pieces. There's a lot of chicks out there, and I'm gonna have fun finding a new one." Tom threw a few bills on the table, stubbed his cigarette out angrily, and jerked out of the booth.

Stunned and embarrassed, she left the restaurant quickly.

The following day Tom called and apologized. Ellen hung up the phone then ran up the stairs while trying to contain her tears. She hoped she'd made the right decision. A few minutes later, a soft knock at her door grabbed her attention. "Go away," she begged in a muffled voice.

Her bedroom door slowly opened, and her father stood there looking ill at ease. "Just one thing, sweetheart. No man is worth all those tears. Love has to last a lifetime, so make sure you pick the right one who loves you as much as you love him. One that makes the sun shine for you every day, ok?"

She grabbed a tissue and blew her nose, then nodded in amazement. She knew her dad didn't know what exactly was going on. He was a quiet, private man. She knew by instinct how much her father loved her. Here in a rare moment, he was showing his support. It touched her to think how hard it must have been for him to come into her room.

"Thanks, Dad. I'll be ok." Ellen tried to reassure him with a smile but didn't quite make it. She watched him nod compassionately, then back out of her room, giving her the privacy that she needed.

~

Click, Click.

"Smile," her father encouraged. He still favored the old Canon, where the flash almost blinded you.

Click, Click. Graduation! At long last. Ellen thought it would never come. The past three weeks had been so hectic and emotional. Her parents still didn't know what to make of Barry. Her mom still preferred Tom. Luckily, she'd avoided the questions and the lectures.

"My baby's all grown up," her dad continued. He came over and hugged her.

She inhaled his Old Spice shaving lotion, the scent of Sundays, weddings, and special occasions. She hugged him back, feeling his strong, slender frame against hers. She wished they would do this more often, but love was implicit in daily family life. Only occasionally was it ever put into words or gestures such as this. A loving feeling grew between them, and it felt so good.

"I'll always be your baby, Dad. No matter how old I am." Ellen reached for him again, kissing him on the cheek. *Oh, Daddy, I love you. I wish I didn't have to hurt you.*

"You look beautiful. Call your mother. I want to take pictures of the two prettiest women in town. That dress turns you into the princess you are, my dear."

She pirouetted for him, the yellow satin swishing around her hips. The glamourous neckline emphasized her creamy slender shoulders, and only a demure swell of her breasts showed.

Her graduation gift from her parents had been a gold chain with a pearl pendant, matching earrings, and a ring. Ellen had swept her hair into a French roll with loosely coiled tendrils framing her face. Applying a smidgen of eye shadow that emphasized her hazel eyes and a touch of blush to her cheeks, Ellen critically examined and approved of the sophisticated look it gave her. She wore a pale pink lipstick outlined with a slightly darker pink to emphasize her full lips, although now she was nervously chewing them.

"Mom? Dad's waiting. He wants to take more pictures of you and me."

Her mother entered the living room dressed in a pink suit.

Ellen gazed lovingly at her elusive mother. "You're beautiful in pink, Mom."

"Like mother, like daughter," her father teased. "Give us a twirl, Ellen."

Ellen reached for her father's hand and let him twirl her around as he used to when she was a child. "Thanks for everything, Mom and Dad. I feel like a glamourous movie star tonight." As Ellen thought of the heartache to come, she bit her lips. She doubted her father would consider her a princess once they found out what was in her near future.

"Don't bite your lips, dear. You're smearing your lipstick." Ellen's proud mother stood beside her for the photo, smiling brightly.

"Alright, ladies. One more." commanded her father.

Then her mother took a few more snapshots with Ellen and her father before they collected their things to leave. Ellen noticed Tom's Camaro drive by their front door. Poor

Tom. Ellen still loved him, but not in the way he wanted. And now that she had been with Barry, she knew the difference.

She could never be content without him beside her.

When Barry arrived to escort her to the grad pre-dinner party, her father welcomed him. She walked towards him, her chin high, her eyes misting slightly with her love for him.

He handed her a wrist corsage of tiny white rosebuds. "You look beautiful, Ellen. I hope these roses are ok." For a change, Barry seemed tongue-tied.

Smiling, she smelled the delicate scent. "They're perfect. I love them. Thank you."

After the pre-dinner party at Paula's house, Barry would hang out with the other dates, as the first part of the evening was for the graduates and their parents only. Afterward, Barry would pick her up, then the rest of the night belonged to the young.

After dinner at the school, she joined Paula, Carole, and Danielle, her best friends since she started grade school. Everybody seemed nervous as they shared plans about their futures. Danielle was going to B.C. Institute of Technology in Vancouver to be a legal secretary. Carole was promised a full-time job at the Rexall Pharmacy downtown. To no one's surprise, Paula was undecided. She never planned much for the future as long as things were going well today.

The girls began recounting the fun they'd enjoyed during their school years.

Soon Carole was practically doubled in half, laughing so hard that she was almost crying. "And remember when we were in that play in grade nine, and Paula dressed up as a *lady of the evening*? We used black kohl to dramatize your eyes then we made you wear a large bra with balloons stuffed in the cups to appear sexy. When you tripped in your red heels and fell against the table, a balloon burst, and everyone started laughing."

Paula nodded. "I was so embarrassed, I forgot my lines and started laughing too. Then the kohl began running down my face. So much for the provocative lady of the evening. That was the end of my acting career. On the bright side, my performance was the highlight of the play."

Ellen had always been glad that she had managed to switch roles with Paula. If that had happened to her, she would never have been able to take the teasing that Paula endured for the rest of the drama term. "The rest of the actors were trying to control themselves and get the play back on track, but they gave up and laughed along with the rest of us."

"That performance made the rest of my year. I'd *never* been so popular." Paula deadpanned.

Danielle was now laughing in her unique way that caused the rest of them to giggle uncontrollably. Ellen hiccupped as she tried to calm her breathing and reminded them of another escapade involving a 'borrowed' family car.

Paula agreed. "Yup. We've had a blast, that's for sure. Let's make sure we never forget each other. No matter what. We should make a promise. No matter where we are, we get together on our birthdays, go a little wild, and remember when."

The girls agreed with pinkie swears. Suddenly, the mood changed as they looked at each other. Ellen knew they were each wondering what their future would bring.

The chatter and laughter of over two hundred graduates grew. Mrs. Burke, the vice-principal, came over the intercom, telling them to calm down and reassuring them that the ceremonies were about to begin. Cheerful memories balanced the sadness that they were all feeling. Nothing would be the same again.

Where would her childhood friends be in ten years? What about her future now that she was sure she was pregnant? She hadn't told anyone.

Her friends had been shocked when she broke off her relationship with Tom and started seeing Barry right away. Danielle and Paula had even tried talking her out of it at first. True friends as they were, they backed off and stood behind her. Now, she would tell them part of her secret.

"Well, girls, want to hear the latest?" Ellen ventured.

"You bet, what's up?" Carole asked.

"Guess who's getting married?"

"Who?" they all chorused.

Ellen motioned them closer and wrapped her arms around them. "Me! Barry's asked me, and I've said yes. I haven't even told my parents yet."

Amidst squeals of disbelief, the girls kissed her and congratulated her. Paula threw her a look that Ellen knew very well, which said, *not now-but we'll be talking later.*

Ellen had timed her announcement well. Her friends didn't have time to ask the rest of the questions Ellen was sure to come. The doors opened, and the graduates entered single file into the auditorium. Amy Thompson's hit song, *I'll remember you*, was playing. Ellen's throat thickened with emotion as she held onto threatening tears. Her heart swelled with pride as she looked around her.

No matter what was ahead of her, she promised herself, she would handle it and handle it well.

WHEN IS she going to stop? Ellen's pulse quickened as her mother's sad face passed by her. The sniffles and the tears had been going on for two days. Every time Ellen glanced in her direction, her mother would begin to cry again, blowing her nose so often that she had chafed it.

"And I'm not going to tell him. No sir! Your dad will be home this afternoon. You can tell him what you've done. I don't know where I went wrong. Lord knows I did my best." Another series of quiet sobs would begin again.

Ellen had tried comforting her mother at first, reassuring her that she had done everything, as well as other mothers had. It hadn't helped. The gossip that would start flying would hurt her parents deeply.

Barry wanted to be there, but she had refused. She hadn't agreed when he'd said she was only punishing herself. Ellen wasn't sure if she was stupid or courageous, only that this was something that she needed to do on her own. Ellen would face her parents' disappointment alone.

Hearing her dad's diesel truck pull in the driveway, Ellen went to meet him.

"Hi, Ellen. Where's Mom?" her dad asked as he put his overnight bag down. He had left Monday on a business trip to Nanaimo to bid on a large construction project.

Ellen suddenly wondered if she had done the right thing, breaking the news to her parents separately. Too late for regrets. Besides, honestly, she could stand only one disappointed parent at a time.

"She's lying down with a headache right now. How did the negotiations go? Did you get the contract?"

"Looks good, really good." He beamed. "We'll know by the end of next week. It's a whole new concept. Retirement in style. Condo living in luxury and privacy, with options for joining dining and recreation facilities. They're calling it the Georgia Villas."

Her dad hung up his jacket and eased into his La-Z-Boy rocker. "The idea's a big hit in the States. You can opt-in for as little care as you need or full care if necessary. The theory is that seniors are more educated and fit than ever before. They're ready to let go of maintaining their homes, yet they want to continue a great quality of life. It's not for everybody, as the design and service are top tier, so it's pretty expensive. We'll see if it catches on. Who knows?"

"Are you thirsty, Dad? Want something to drink, a soda or beer?"

"Not often I feel like a beer when I get home, but sure, why not? I'm very optimistic about this trip. It could set my company on the map."

Ellen fetched him a beer and brought a soda for herself, popping the tab. "Hey Dad, have you got a minute? I need to talk with you." She sat on the couch opposite him, fiddling with her pearl ring, twirling it around and around her finger.

Ellen saw her father glance at her hands, and his expression turned serious. She remembered that was one of her tells, so she quickly tucked her hands under her thighs and glanced around the room.

"Sure, dear. What's the matter?" Her dad crossed one leg over the other towards her.

Ellen could feel his gaze burning into her. Her eyes flickered up to him, and she smiled, then looked away.

"Nothing really," She paused. "Well, that's not exactly true." Her hands appeared of their own volition, and she began twirling her ring again. "Um, Dad? Barry and I want to get married this month."

Her dad began to cough, choking on his sip of beer. His

blue-grey eyes watered as he cleared his throat. "And when did this happen?" he asked as he struggled to regain his breathing.

"He asked me before graduation, but I wanted a bit of time to think it over." Ellen's pleading eyes and lopsided smile didn't go unnoticed.

"Hmmph." He rocked in his chair, saying nothing.

She was silent. Ellen knew he was taking his time, analyzing the situation before replying. She saw his Adam's apple shift as he cleared his throat again, then swallowed a few times. "Do you *have* to?" her father asked softly.

"No-o, not really. I mean, we don't *have* to. We've talked it over, and we should. We wanted to wait a while longer, but..." Her voice trailed off, faltering. Knowing how uncomfortable her dad was talking about the facts of life, this was as close to mentioning the pregnancy that they would get.

Again, silence. The only sound was the rocking chair and the clock on the mantle, ticking.

"Do you love him?" Her father's voice seemed void of emotion, and she was glad.

She had dealt with as many tears and displeasure as possible. "Yes. More than I ever imagined. Barry loves me, and he makes me laugh. I adore him."

A long silence ensued.

"I hoped you'd have been smarter. More careful." Her dad looked straight into her eyes for the first time.

Ellen saw his distress, his lower lip quivering slightly.

"Tell Barry I want to see him. He needs to ask for your hand in marriage in the proper way. Let's make it Sunday."

She breathed a sigh of relief. It was ok. Her dad was disappointed, but he still loved her and would stand by her.

"Is that why your mother's laying down?" he asked.

She nodded, remembering how differently her mother

had reacted to the news. Although she was cordial to Barry, she hadn't warmed up to him. She'd always liked Tom, who would never have moved her daughter away. Now her mom probably felt justified.

"Has he told his parents yet? Have you decided anything about the ceremonies?"

"He only has a mom. His dad died when he was young. Barry's in Victoria telling her now. If it's ok with you, we planned on having a quiet ceremony here in mid-July, then we'll be moving in with her. He's already registered in the fall program at Camosun, but he wants to add his last two courses before the end of the year. Then he'll have his certificate in business administration by late spring, and he can start looking for a full-time job."

"Sounds like he's planned it well. And you're okay with all of this? It'll be a big step for you, moving away from us."

"Yes, it makes the most sense. Besides, I think Mom will be glad I'm gone. She can't stop crying, and she's ashamed of me. She even asked me if I'd like to go *away*, have my baby and give it up. Then I could start over." Now Ellen's voice trembled, and tears threatened to spill over. "I couldn't believe it, Dad. She doesn't seem to care how we feel, only about the gossip that's going to fly around town."

"Well, your mom always did care a bit too much about other people's opinions. You *are* her only child. Understandably, she's a tiny bit upset."

"There are lots of nice people that end up like Barry and me. It doesn't make us bad people. I'm still the same as I've always been."

"I know, sweetheart. It's the naïve girls that usually get into this kind of trouble. I think a major part of this is that you'll be moving away, and that's going to be hard for all of us. Your mom will get over it. You'll be fine. You and Barry will make this work." He excused himself, kissed her, and tapped her shoulder as he left her to console her mother.

Ellen's dad had hit the nail on the head when he said she was naïve. She had been caught up in a tide of rising passion that Ellen assumed she'd control, just like she had with Tom. Inexperience had tripped her up, but it wouldn't define her. She and Barry would have a great life together, even if they became parents at a young age.

Ellen raced to the phone and called Barry. His mother answered and told her that he was still at the college, trying to pick up some correspondence courses to do this summer. His high grades gave him some pull as he was approved for the September enrollment in two additional courses.

"Would you tell him to call me back tonight, please, Mrs. Peterson?"

"Yes, dear. By the way, Barry told me all about you. This apartment is a small place, but you're welcome to stay for as long as you need." Her voice was warm and welcoming, although slightly shaky, then she began to gasp.

"What's the matter, Mrs. Peterson?" Ellen asked worriedly. "Have you been sick?"

"Not really, dear. Don't worry. I often get this. I have trouble with allergies. I'll tell Barry you called."

"Ok, Thanks. Hope you feel better soon," Ellen added as they said their goodbyes.

Dinner that night was strained. Her mother made no effort to prepare a meal, so Ellen made a salad and threw together spaghetti and meat sauce with garlic bread. Her mother appeared looking bereft but barely ate anything.

"Claire, you'll have to make some arrangements next week. Ellen should choose her dress and accessories, then call Father Kevin and pick a date for their wedding ceremony."

Ellen glanced between her parents to gauge their reactions but saw nothing but a studious attempt at organizing the event. Her father's planning initiative seemed to spark interest in her mother. Her mom livened up as they began discussing who they should invite, yet she avoided asking Ellen for her opinion. Ellen closed her eyes briefly, then stifled a sigh.

Obviously, she didn't deserve to be consulted for her opinion. It didn't matter about the details. When all was said and done, she'd be Barry's wife.

"We'll all go on Saturday and shop for a bedroom suite and some basic household items. She'll need a few good suitcases too. They've decided on a small wedding, so see about the cost of a private reception at the Hospitality Inn or the Best Western."

Ellen listened to the conversation, feeling left out. Her parents didn't even consider her wishes. She supposed her predicament forfeited her right to the type of wedding she wanted. So be it.

Ellen sighed deeply. *If this is what they want, then this is the least I can do for them.* Maybe it was their way of saving face in the community. She knew that they had always dreamed of an extravagant affair for their only child's wedding. That wasn't going to happen now, but Barry and Ellen had agreed to compromise between their wish of immediate family only and her parents' dream.

She knew they wondered if their marriage would be a dreadful mistake. That would never happen. No way would she screw up twice. They might be ashamed of her now, but come hell or high water, she'd make a success of her marriage and make them proud of her again.

That night she waited impatiently for Barry's call. Restless and fretful, she called again at 10:00 p.m. "Barry, I paged you, then I called your mom. Didn't you get my messages?" she asked after he answered the phone.

"Dammit, sorry, sorry. I did get them, but then I started organizing my books to bring back to Port with me. I forgot all about it." Barry sighed deeply, his voice full of anxiety. "It's going to be hectic working and taking a correspondence course this summer. I'm afraid I won't be seeing a lot of you for most of it."

"I know, I'm sorry. This pressure must be rough on you, too." She paused. "I told Mom two days ago, and then I told Dad today."

"Oh, God. How did they take it?"

"Mom's been crying ever since, but Dad's been great. He was surprised and wanted to make certain that I was sure about marrying you. I think that's why he wants to talk to you. And remember I told you about our old-fashioned ways? Be prepared—you're instructed to ask him for my hand."

"What? You must be kidding!" exclaimed Barry. "I asked you, and you said yes, and that's it. I'm not marrying your parents."

"Barry, please. It's traditional in our family. It shows respect for the parents."

"Will it make it any easier on you?" he asked.

"Yes. I think my parents would feel a lot better if you did."

"Ok. I'll be finished the counseling session and registration on Friday, so I'll be back on Sunday to make it official. Then it's the nose to the grindstone. I've got an awful lot of work to do. Have you decided where we are going to get married?"

She knew he would have it in Victoria with just her parents and his mom attending a civil service if it was up to him. And truthfully, she'd always dreamed of being married in Beacon Hill Park. Although, with their situation, she'd feel better if they did things her parents' way.

"Here. Mom and Dad are having a small reception for us after we get married. I'm going to have one bridesmaid, and I hoped maybe you'd like to have one of your friends be the best man."

"This sounds like a bigger deal than what we wanted."

Ellen could hear the exasperation in his tone. "I know, but I'm also the only child my parents have. They'd feel cheated any other way. Besides, if we didn't do it their way, it would be one more thing my mom would hold against you."

"Alright, I'll leave it up to you. But nothing extravagant. In twenty-two more days, we'll be together forever. I can't wait to have you here, babe." His voice became huskier. "I've only been gone a few days, but already I miss you. Do you miss me too?"

"Of course, I do," she whispered into the phone.

"Then I'll see you Sunday. Love you."

"Me too, bye." Tomorrow was Tuesday, and if she and her mom could get a lot accomplished in the few days, maybe she'd leave Friday morning to go to Victoria. She'd surprise Barry and meet him at school, then meet his mother.

Ellen was sure she'd need a break by then. She longed to have Barry's arms around her. He made her feel so secure and loved by his side. They'd made love only twice since she tested positive. It may seem silly, but they agreed to stop making love until after they got married. She wanted to feel the anticipation of a blissfully romantic wedding night.

Ellen was highly aware of her emotional ties to her hometown as she and her mom shopped the stores for the appropriate trousseau articles. Not a speck of snow was left on Mount Arrowsmith, the landmark that identified the town. She would miss seeing it in all the seasons. In the summer, she would miss Sproat Lake, Mount Klitsa with its glacier nestled in her crevices, and the ease with which they could access the wild west coast of Ucluelet and Tofino. She knew the name of every street in Port Alberni.

Although Ellen had heard of the problems with log exports to countries with cheaper labor, it didn't seem like a big deal. But when that materialized into cutbacks in the local mills, the town experienced its first recession. Nobody wanted to believe the booming forestry economy couldn't be fixed, but the writing was on the wall.

Already, a few shops had closed, the owners moving to Nanaimo, where the labor base was more varied. Just last week, the mill was notified that the midnight shift would be canceled. Maybe this downturn would be a blessing in disguise, making it easier for her to leave. She wouldn't be the only one leaving her hometown for greener pastures.

Now she'd have to learn the nooks and crannies of the big city of Victoria. Although she'd miss this corner of her world, she looked forward to her marriage with Barry and the opportunities of life in his beloved city.

Ellen and her mother quickly chose the lingerie and bedding supplies. They finished picking out the wedding invitations and settling the details for dinner at the Hospitality Inn. The preparations were going smoothly until an argument flared on the type of wedding dress Ellen would wear.

"You may be pregnant, but I see no reason why you can't wear a traditional long white dress and veil. Heavens, you're not due until February, and with any luck, you'll be late. Then we could say you were early."

"Mom. I wouldn't feel comfortable. I'd feel like a hypocrite. Don't you think a suit would be more appropriate? Besides, times have changed. For heaven's sake, there are tons of people that don't even bother getting married. They start a family without a church blessing."

"I don't care what other people do. Would you deny your father the pleasure of walking you down the aisle in a beautiful wedding dress? I don't believe it. I never imagined you were so selfish."

Ellen withered under her mother's glare. She took a deep breath and made herself stand tall. "I'm not. I'm practical." She stopped in the middle of the sidewalk and faced her mom. "Mom, please listen to me." Ellen put her hand out towards a storefront as a dizzy spell came over her. A sheen of perspiration covered her forehead and her upper lip.

Worried, her mom grasped her arm to steady her and whispered a change in plans. They walked arm in arm to her mother's car parked half a block away, then drove home. She sent Ellen upstairs to rest in her room and brought in the purchases from the car.

Claire sat at the dining room table with a cup of tea, deliberating the next step. Ellen was right. It was time to make some compromises and lower the stress levels. Nevertheless, Claire couldn't hide the fact that she was disappointed. Yet, she didn't want to risk Ellen or her baby. It was time to slow things down. She was looking forward to being a grandparent, even if it would be a long-distance relationship.

Although Claire believed Ellen was too young to start a family and tie herself down, she only wanted the best for her. A few bridal shops and top-end ladies' stores in Nanaimo might offer them a compromise they both could live with. She'd try harder to make their wedding day a festive occasion for all of them.

As the family sat down to dinner, Ellen's mom continued to update her dad. "I'm happy with what we accomplished today, Fred. But tomorrow we'll have to go to Nanaimo. There's more choice in stores that handle bridal wear. If we don't find anything in them, we can look at formal wear shops on 5th Street."

Ellen had little to contribute, politely listening to the lists and decisions that needed a decision. At one point, she looked over and saw her father's sparkling gaze upon her. He was amused at the scene playing out before him. When Ellen rolled her eyes with frustration, he winked at her. Lighten up, he seemed to say. Her gratitude for him grew. She would persevere for him.

"I'm sorry, but I'm getting stressed out with all the decisions we have to make. It makes it hard when there's so much to choose. Could I bring Paula along? She has a good eye. She'd be a huge help."

"Why not? You won't be seeing her that often once you move. You'll need these memories. But I get the final say."

Ellen excused herself from the dining table, went to her room, and immediately called her friend. Five minutes later, she returned to the table with a happy smile. "Thanks, Mom. I have another idea too." She took a deep breath, nervously fingering her napkin as she looked to her father. "Dad, do you think I could borrow the car on Friday to go to Victoria? I've talked to Barry's mom on the phone, but I've never met her. And if Mom, Paula, and I can't find everything in Nanaimo tomorrow, I can look in Victoria."

"Will you be back the same day?" he asked.

"Probably not. It's almost three hours each way, and if I do any shopping, I'd be too tired. I can sleep at their place. They have a sofa bed in the living room."

" Ellen? I'm not sure that's proper. We'll give you money for a hotel room for the night."

Fred saw his daughter flush, and her eyes began to water. He gave his wife an icy glare. Ellen was still too naive to have been intimate very long. Just bad timing, he figured. Those girls who slept around regularly knew what precautions to take. Often, the shyer and more introverted girls paid the price of a passionate necking session that broke the limits.

"I don't think that's necessary, Claire. Ellen's told us a lot about Barry and his mom. She'll be fine staying there," her father said brusquely. "You look tired, dear. Maybe you'd better go rest. It'll be a big day tomorrow."

"You're right. I am quite tired." Claire kissed him on the cheek, glared at her daughter, and retired.

THE FOLLOWING EVENING, after Ellen and Paula treated themselves to a burger at the J&L drive-in, Ellen counted her blessings. Paula would always have her back, and today cemented their friendship for the future. She laughed along with Paula, thankful for her outspoken best friend.

"Honestly, I just about burst out laughing when your mother tried to make you model that dress. You should've seen the two of you. If looks could kill, your dad would be going to a double funeral instead of a wedding."

Ellen's face colored, remembering the surge of anger towards her mom. She was so relieved to have the day finished. With Paula by her side, she had found it easier to override her mother's master plan. She refused point-blank to try on long wedding dresses, which had sent her mother into an acute state of anxiety.

Paula had fetched water and coaxed Ellen's mother into taking deep breaths to calm down. They took a break for lunch with her mom, downing two glasses of chardonnay before they returned to the search. Finally, they agreed upon a cream colored, short satin brocade dress with a matching jacket.

Ellen chose a vintage satin cap, beaded with pearls and tiny white silk roses in a nod towards her mom's wishes. A matching studded netting could be pulled over her eyes and serve as a demure veil.

Paula and Ellen chose a pale blue satin dress for the maid of honor. It was sleeveless, and the wide shoulder straps deepened into a sweetheart neckline and fitted bodice. Paula loved it but didn't think Ellen should pay its outrageous price. As far as Ellen was concerned, her mom had saved enough money on the wedding dress that she could afford to spoil Ellen's best friend.

They would both wear white accessories, with Paula carrying a bouquet of white carnations intertwined with blue satin ribbon. Ellen would have white roses with the same ribbon. Simple, and in Ellen's eyes, perfect. As the mood lightened with each decision and purchase made, her mother began smiling more often.

Eventually, her mother had chosen a navy and white suit with navy accessories. It was amazing to think how much they'd accomplished in two days. Next week would entail calculating the response to the wedding invitations already mailed to the forty guests invited.

The guests consisted mainly of close family and friends of her parents. Ellen included Danielle and Carole and their dates, plus Paula's date. Matt and his wife Anna would also be coming from Olympia. They'd be staying with them for an extended long weekend.

Barry, his mom, and his best man, Ken, would arrive on Friday. They were staying at the Hospitality Inn to help with decorating and prenuptial preparations.

Ellen's mother would look after the rest of the details for her. The last detail was the reservation at the Coast Bastion in Nanaimo, where they would go after the reception for their first night as husband and wife.

Paula noticed how tired her friend was and was worried for her. Ellen's pale face and dark shadows underneath her eyes told the tale she hadn't been telling. Paula had made her mind up not to ask the obvious question, leaving it to Ellen to share when the time was right. She poured another glass of Coke for her and turned the music up. They laid stretched across the bed in Paula's bedroom, looking at the disorganized mess that always filled the room.

"I'm going to miss you, girlfriend."

"Now, don't get all mushy," warned Ellen. "You can always take the bus and visit me in Victoria, and I'll come back now and then. It's not like Victoria is the end of the world. You never know, you might decide to expand your horizon and move to the big city too. You haven't got anything else planned yet, have you?"

"No. It's kinda scary though, going somewhere you hardly know anyone."

"You were always the daredevil in our group. Don't tell me you're changing? Besides, no matter where we are, we'll always be best friends. Moving away is going to be tough enough as it is. Please don't make it worse," Ellen begged.

"No sweat, sweetie. I think you'd better let me drive you home. You look beat."

Ellen agreed, and within an hour, she was easing her

tired body into a warm bath. This week had flown by, so much was accomplished, but all the decisions had drained her. Planning on seeing Barry tomorrow brought back a sense of confidence their decision was the right one. She closed her eyes, smiling at the surprise he would have.

IT WAS the beginning of a typical warm summer's day when Ellen left Port Alberni, filled with anticipation and happiness. She loved her parents, yet this crisis had taken its toll on her. Ellen was anxious to escape the frenzy she'd created in their home. Ever since that tall, handsome hunk came into her life three months ago, her life had been a roller coaster—but not one she regretted. She put an old Bryan Adams CD in her dad's car stereo, thinking that her song was Summer of 69, only a different year. The summer of '93 was the one that changed her life, but in her case, it would last forever. She could hardly believe that Barry wanted to marry her.

At least she now knew he wasn't a player, making the rounds and then moving to new conquests. *Thank God he's proved me wrong.* Imagine the nightmare if he had been the jerk she was afraid he was. The reaction of her parents was bad enough, considering they were being responsible and getting married. Suddenly, she couldn't stop smiling as her heart lightened when she passed Cameron Lake, leaving the Valley behind.

Her dad's old Topaz wasn't a speed machine, although it was a reliable second vehicle. She passed through Nanaimo, stopped for gas in Duncan, then began the Malahat Drive. This section of the highway would take her over some of the highest mountains to Victoria on the island's southern tip.

Their honeymoon would take place in Victoria because of finances but also because Ellen was eager to see more of her beautiful new home. She was looking forward to going to the Butchart Gardens. The meticulous care and planning that developed the old lime pit were famous internationally —just one of the so many places to explore.

At the top of the Malahat, she stopped at the Chalet, a small motel complex and restaurant perched on the mountain's edge. Floating like a precious jewel, the Saanich peninsula below was sandwiched between Swartz Bay and the Salish Sea. Expanses of evergreen forests were broken occasionally by a patchwork quilt of rolling parcels of farmland, fitting together like a puzzle, their various hues inducing a sense of tranquility.

Surrounding her, the Arbutus trees clung to the edges of the cliffs, their red peeling trunks catching her eye. Ellen tried identifying all the trees around her. The familiar cedar, fir, and pine were easy to identify, but her favorite evergreen, the spruce, was few and far between. Here and there, she spotted the dogwood, its beautiful white blossoms swaying gently in the wind.

The patio door was open, and Ellen breathed in deeply, enjoying the slightly sharp evergreen scent. Pots of red geraniums and rainbows of hyacinths adorned the porch. Now and then, she'd catch a whiff of their perfume. She couldn't imagine a day more perfect. Sitting there, she sensed a new world opening up for her.

The smell of fresh cinnamon buns arriving at the table next to her caught her attention. She was starving and ordered the soup and sandwich special of the day along with a cup of tea. She was making a special effort to cut out junk food so she'd have a healthy pregnancy.

She caught a young guy staring at her and smiled

demurely, lowering her gaze. It was nice to be admired, even though she was engaged. She promised herself she'd get back her figure right away. Barry should always be able to look at her as he did now and be proud of her.

She glanced at her watch and figured out her schedule. She should have plenty of time to go directly to Lansdowne college and surprise him there. Hopefully, they would be able to have an hour or two alone before going to his place. She hurried through her lunch and resumed her drive.

An hour later, she was making her way down Douglas Street. No mountains blocked the sky, which she appreciated. She had never noticed before how hemmed in and restricted she felt in her hometown. Here, her eyes could sweep the horizon and not bump into anything. It made her feel lighter, freer somehow.

Ellen always appreciated the eye-catching lamp posts that adorned Victoria's main downtown streets. They consisted of three circular domes fashioned in a triangular shape, and in the summer, colorful hanging baskets hung from them. Victoria's pride in its British roots was captured in its classical buildings and restorations throughout the city, integrating the old-world class into this modern, new world. Now Ellen would be one of the proud residents too.

She'd miss her friends and family, but it wasn't as if they lived a thousand miles away. They would see each other often, revisiting their old haunts in China Town on Fisgard Street or wandering through the two hundred acres of Beacon Hill Park. She never tired of ambling along the Inner Harbor of James Bay, where the prestigious Empress Hotel sat perpendicular to the majestic, domed Parliament Buildings.

If Ellen could've chosen their wedding site, it would've been in one of those cultivated gardens behind the Inner

Harbor in Beacon Hill Park. Expansive beds of roses and rhododendrons always lured her into the Japanese gardens. With bridges over manicured streams, it offered privacy for lovers and nature lovers alike. She smiled as she imagined the romantic scene in her mind. Maybe they'd have another private ceremony there, a picnic, a blanket, and their arms wrapped around each other.

Just thinking of the romantic times she would be spending there with Barry made Ellen cheerful. Hopefully, they'd make an effort to walk there before they returned to Port Alberni. She was going to love exploring every hidden corner with her husband in their new home.

Turning left onto Hillside Avenue, Ellen followed it a few miles until she reached Camosun College. She found a parking spot and glanced at her watch. Perfect. 4:45 p.m.

Freshening up in the rear-view mirror, Elen applied a swipe of lip gloss. Too hot to stay in the car for long, she decided to walk around. She'd wander close to the parking lot so she could see Barry approach his vehicle, parked only a few hundred feet from hers. She strolled across the well-kept lawns, noting the huge Garry Oaks, native to the Island.

Small clusters of students sat beneath them, some studying, some laughing and talking. She sat on one of the wooden benches placed haphazardly around the college and waited for him. Optimism for the way things had turned out filled her.

The warm summer breeze caressed her skin ever so gently, carrying the scent of freshly cut grass. She breathed a sigh of contentment. Careful not to wrinkle her patterned blue and purple sundress, she leaned back and relaxed, letting the tension of the long drive ease slowly away with the wind. She noticed the hair styles and fashions the kids wore here, slightly more adventurous than she was used to, scrutinizing ones she would like to try herself.

Her heart stopped.

It can't be. Ellen put her hand over her eyes to cut the glare. Lots of fellas had blond hair and styled like Barry's. When she had first noticed a familiar guy strolling down the sidewalk, with his books under one arm, she wondered if that might be him. Then a dark-haired girl ran to catch up to him, and as she hugged him, Ellen had turned away, switching her attention to other students that could be Barry. But now, as they came nearer, she could see clearly.

Barry was teasing the girl and reaching to take her books from her.

Oh my God, what am I going to do? How could I have been so stupid? Her heartbeat accelerated, and her eyes filled with tears. She picked up her purse and quickly jumped to her feet, almost running across the lawn to her car.

She backed up and slammed the Topaz in gear. Ellen thought she heard her name called, but by now, she was sobbing uncontrollably. She cursed herself for being a romantic fool. She wished she had never been so impetuous as to come here and surprise him.

"Damn traffic," she swore as she eased her way down Cook Street towards Beacon Hill Park, her beautiful and peaceful haven. She needed time to think, to be by herself. She wasn't expected home until tomorrow. Now, she wasn't sure what to do.

Damned, whichever way she went. Concentrating on the traffic, Ellen tried to keep her mind blank. Usually, she entered Beacon Hill Park and parked near the animal petting zoo where she began her visits. This time she needed more privacy and circumvented the park. Ellen drove along the scenic Dallas Road, which followed the coastline. She entered Clover Point, parked, then collapsed her head onto the steering wheel, releasing hot tears of anguish.

Slowly her sobs diminished. Reaching for tissues, a sunhat, and her purse, she left the car. Ellen needed to burn off her anxiety so she could think and make some decisions.

Clearing her throat, she dabbed at her eyes, trying not to make a scene. Ellen slapped on her sun hat, pulling it low as she started walking briskly, away from the congested parking area. She didn't want to think of what she witnessed would mean to her.

She continued walking east towards Ogden Point and the sea wall, drinking in the fresh, salty scent of the ocean, concentrating on the beauty around her. She remembered the waves that came crashing in there during winter storms, sending sprays of seawater high onto the road at times. She used to dream that she lived in one of the old restored homes across the street from the sea wall, able to watch the majesty and devilry of the ocean in all its moods.

This was no time to dwell in the past or waste her time on dreams, as she reminded herself as she stopped for a rest. She sat on the grass, her sundress no longer important, and tried to analyze what she had witnessed.

Barry had another girlfriend. There was no mistaking the love between them. *He obviously hasn't told her about me. Maybe he was going to keep her a secret and see her behind my back.*

To hell with him. I don't need his pity or his act of chivalry. He doesn't have to marry me. Humiliation stole over her, and once again, a week's worth of frustration and pain broke through her defenses. She pulled her knees up and her straw sun hat further down and cried furiously, releasing a torrent of hurt feelings.

Ellen didn't care if anyone saw her. No one knew her here. No one would care.

Exhausted, she slowly came to her senses, unaware of the time she had been there. She wiped her tear-stained face and thought of repairing her makeup, then rejected the idea. What would it matter?

Ellen walked further along towards Ogden Point. She detoured and took the hiking trail to the beach below, which dipped then climbed along the steep banks. She rested on one of the wooden benches spaced along the path. Ellen was so exhausted that her mind began to lose focus. The breeze, slightly cooler than before, made white-capped waves dance in the Strait while sailboats glided by, bobbing gently.

Ellen found herself calming down as her breathing returned to normal.

What now? If you're not going to marry him, what are you going to do? Ellen didn't think she could face her mom and dad with the truth. She had felt bad enough before. Now, they would consider their daughter a fool for getting involved with Barry. She couldn't face any more lectures.

Then what? She searched for an escape hatch.

Could she simply stay here? No, not here. To even think about bumping into Barry would be too much stress to handle. Perhaps Duncan or Nanaimo. She could probably get a job waitressing for a while and maybe live at the YWCA until she started to show-but then what?

An idea struck her. Maybe, she should look into the Planned Parenthood organization. Maybe, they would have somewhere for her to live while she decided whether to keep her baby or give the child up. The thought of that possibility sent her running from the bench as her mind raced for another viable solution.

Ellen lost all sense of time as she alternately rested and walked. As the sun's reflections on the strait turned the ripples into diamonds, she became aware of its ritualistic descent. Usually, this time of evening filled her with a rapturous sense of romance, the colorful adieu offering a feeling of all's well with the world.

But tonight, it just seemed to be saying goodbye.

Goodbye, she answered back. Goodbye. Hmmm. Maybe that's not such a bad idea, Ellen pondered numbly.

She took her sandals off. The heated sand slipped between her toes as she walked further, looking for a shortcut down to the beach. She sat on her bottom and slid down the steep embankment until she landed on the damp, cool sand of the beach.

The tide was beginning to come in as she pattered towards the rocky point. Ellen loved climbing on the rocks as a child, dodging the waves as they tried to catch her. The surf swirled around her ankles as she walked towards the point. Low swells soaked her dress and threatened her balance as she climbed onto the slippery granite rocks.

The wind flapped at her dampened dress, and Ellen began humming a song. It was peaceful here, she mused. No one to disappoint. No one to hurt her. She found her way through another thirty or forty feet of outcroppings and sat down.

Ellen could feel nature's energy, feel the pulsating of the waves against the rock, the brashness of the wind caressing then attacking her. The salt spray soon drenched her, but she didn't notice the chill, only a peaceful acceptance of fate.

CHAPTER 4

"Ellen?" Barry couldn't believe his eyes. "Ellen, stop!" He pushed Bev aside and ran towards Camosun's parking lot. When the beige Topaz pulled out and away, he halted, confused and shaken.

Bev caught up to him. "What's the matter with you? You almost knocked me over."

"Sorry, Bev. I don't know why she's here, but that was Ellen I saw running across the lawn. I didn't know she was coming here today. Why did she take off like that?"

"Really? Don't be so dense. She probably put two and two together and got five. She's never met me, and she comes to surprise you, and here you are with me."

"Oh my God, you're might be right. Ellen probably thinks I'm screwing around. Great. Now, what do I do?" In frustration, he kicked the cement curb, hurt his big toe, and began jumping around on one foot, swearing.

Bev started to giggle, even though he was glaring at her. "Don't think you're going to scare me, big boy. I'll laugh when I damn well feel like laughing, and right now, you're a pretty hilarious sight." He looked so sad, though, that she did try to control herself. After all, it wasn't a funny situation. "C'mon, use your head. If you were her, where would you go?"

Barry looked at his childhood girlfriend and thanked God for her. They had been neighbors for over eleven years, and she had been his first crush. They had both gotten over that and had, over the years, developed a strong sibling love for each other. Which wasn't surprising, as he was an only child, and she was the baby of her family. Bev's closest sister was married and out of the house by the time she was nine.

When Barry moved in next door to her, she was disappointed he was a boy at first, but she forgave him after teaching her how to use a slingshot. The skinny, long-legged tomboy had grown into a luscious, raven-haired young woman, her olive skin setting off her golden-brown eyes, which led to their initial romantic attachment.

Barry had to admit, it must have looked incriminating. Bev had often complained that a lot of fellas figured they were an item. Her long dark hair swung loosely around her shoulders, and her facial features hinted at her Latino background. Barry admired her not entirely for her beauty but also because of who she was inside. She was funny, kind, and intelligent. Truly one of those people you loved to be around. He protected her from guys he didn't think were nice enough, much to her frustration.

Barry blew out a sigh as he ran his fingers through his hair. Dammit to hell. If other people assumed that, it wouldn't be hard to imagine that Ellen got that impression too.

Christ, she must be going bananas. She had always found it hard to believe Barry had fallen in love with her so quickly. After she confirmed the pregnancy, she seemed to need his reassurances constantly. The sight of Beverly and himself together probably made her doubt his love even more than before. But where would she go?

"What would you do, Bev?"

"I dunno. Probably drive to my girlfriend's, or maybe I'd race home and scream and cry for a while. But seeing as she doesn't live here," Beverly shrugged her shoulders. "Maybe she'll find a motel for the night to calm down, then head home tomorrow. Your guess is as good as mine."

"I'll call Paula and ask her what's up, why Ellen came down."

"Good idea. Maybe her friend will know something more," Bev agreed.

They hopped in his Escort and went to his place. He couldn't remember Paula's last name, so he had to call Ellen's mother.

"Hi, Mrs. Dalmy. I was wondering if you could give me Paula's phone number. I want to ask her a favor."

"Sure, but why didn't you ask Ellen. She is there by now, isn't she?"

"Yes, she and my mom have gone to the grocery store," he lied nervously. "So, I thought I'd get the number from you. I want to surprise her with a special gift. Paula might have a clue of something she'd like."

"That's very considerate." After giving him the number, she wished him luck then hung up.

"Whew, I hate lying. I hope Paula knows what's going on." He called her, hoping he'd catch her at home.

Beverly watched the expressions on Barry's face. She was relieved to see him so worried. When he first told her about Ellen, she wondered if he was marrying her only because of the baby. For all his tomfoolery, he was a sensitive guy. Now his present behavior proved to her how deeply he cared. She listened for clues to their current dilemma.

"Thanks a lot, Paula, and by the way, could you think of anything special I could get Ellen? That part I told Mrs. Dalmy wasn't a lie." He paused, and when she promised to think about it, he said goodbye then disconnected.

"She's had a rough week with her mom, so she decided to take a break and come to surprise me. Ellen had planned on meeting my mom and staying with us until Sunday. Then I'd go back with her and make the proposal official with her father."

"Oh, brother. She's not expected home for a couple of days then. She could go anywhere. Did Paula have any other suggestions?"

"Her parents have friends in Duncan that she's close with. She might have gone there. Paula says I should try going to some of Ellen's favorite places like Mount Tolmie, Beacon Hill Park, or the Parliament buildings. Last time Paula came down with her, they spent hours walking around the Inner Harbor and the park." Frustrated, he checked the time. 5:30. Damn, she could be anywhere.

"I'll go with you," Beverly offered.

"No, I better go by myself. Can you let my mom know what's happening? I'll call you if I need you." He knew she was trying to be helpful, but if Ellen saw them together before he had a chance to explain, she'd probably take off again.

Bev wished him luck and waved to him as he squealed out down Shelbourne towards Mount Tolmie. It was closer to his house, so it made sense to search there first.

He cursed the traffic.

Friday, near supper time, couldn't be a worse hour for congested traffic. His nerves jangled, and he lit a cigarette, inhaling deeply while deciding where else she'd go.

He wound his way through to Mayfair Street and started

up the steep curving road to the summit. Locals, as well as tourists, found this spot tranquil as well as spectacular. The whole city was laid out below them, hugging the coastline and bays. It was an excellent place to think things through, to put worries in perspective. Hopefully, he would find Ellen there.

He slammed his vehicle into park and scanned for her beige Topaz. Cars filled every nook and cranny they could use. The foot traffic was heavy as he jogged around the tourists. He might have missed Ellen. He climbed onto a huge rock, searching the crowd. There!

Was that her? Over on the giant cement pad that extended over the eastern side of the summit surrounded by iron railings, a slender brunette in a blue dress strolled across it. He ran down towards the pad, losing sight of her in the swarm of sightseers.

"Ellen?" he called out.

People stared at him strangely as he dodged through them, but he couldn't care less.

He caught up to her and put his hand on her shoulder. "Ellen, wait, listen to me," Barry panted.

The girl turned. She wasn't Ellen.

"Who the hell are you?" Alarm flashed across her face as she shrugged off his hand and jumped away from him, her voice full of fear.

"Oh God, I'm so sorry. I thought you were my fiancé." He backed slowly away, running his fingers through his hair, his face flushed with embarrassment. He did a tour of the area, checking out the picnic areas, then headed back to his car. *Where could she have gone? I need to find her and fast.*

Victoria was a tourist haven in July, and as he made his way downtown, he alternately cursed then thanked the absent-minded, slow-walking sightseers. Their meanderings meant he could scour the sidewalks for her. He had a better chance of locating her than if the traffic was light and moving quickly.

As he passed the Empress Hotel with his eyes peeled for his fiancé, a horse-drawn coach pulled in front of him. Slamming on his brakes with his heart pounding, he began searching for Ellen on foot. He didn't need an accident now. He passed the domed Parliament buildings, then the wax museum before he spied a car vacating a spot.

He glanced at the time, 6:00. He decided to call home on the off-chance that Ellen would have tried to reach him.

"Has she called, Mom?"

"Not yet, dear. Keep looking. I'm sure Ellen will come to her senses and phone here, so check back later. I don't think we should hold up the phone, so you'd better go."

"Right." He said goodbye, thankful he had such a compassionate mother. He paused and wondered where he should go next.

He walked in front of the ornately carved architecture of the British-styled Parliament buildings, dodging tour guides imploring passengers to board double-decker buses or the Victorian horse-drawn carriages. His pace quickened as he hurried past the tall totem poles in Thunderbird Park, his eyes always searching.

Hopeless. This is bloody hopeless. Barry hesitated, debating which way to go. He hoped he wasn't wasting his time searching this area. Barry didn't sense her anywhere nearby, didn't feel her. *I must be going crazy, but I don't think she's here.*

He had to start trusting his gut. It told him to try somewhere else and to hurry. Hot and tired, he jogged back to his car, his mind full of cotton balls.

He could feel the panic building inside of him as he headed towards Beacon Hill Park, another favorite place for

Ellen—and him, although they had never been there together. He drove slowly along the tree-lined boulevards, his concentration divided between dodging cars and looking for the love of his life.

He began to curse himself. Ellen wouldn't be around a crowd. She'd want privacy.

The gazebo!

He parked the car at the next available space, then ran in the direction of the open field beyond the sculptured gardens. It was a grassy field at the park's highest level, which afforded an unparalleled view of the Juan de Fuca Strait. As it was out of the way and plain compared to the rest of the park, it was generally secluded. The octangular wooden structure offered sanctuary in a rain storm, rest for tired hikers, or privacy for lovers. And hopefully, a tranquil refuge for a troubled person.

A few people were in the structure, and a couple reclined on a blanket about fifty feet away, soaking up the last of the day's heat. As the sound of their voices traveled over in the light breeze, Barry envied their happiness. He hoped he'd be able to salvage his and Ellen's.

Panting, he slowed down, not wanting to scare anybody by dashing in. The cedar-shingled observatory was quite large, almost four hundred square feet, with benches lining the three-foot retaining walls, a welcome place to wait out a winter storm.

His spirits drooped. Ellen wasn't here either.

"I'm looking for my fiancé. Did you see a girl with dark brown, shoulder-length hair? She's wearing a blue-patterned dress."

The older couple smiled sympathetically at him.

"No, we haven't, but we've only been here half an hour." The woman pointed to the young couple on the blanket. "They were here when we arrived. Maybe they saw her."

Barry thanked them and approached the pregnant woman and her partner. After apologizing for the intrusion, he asked the same question again.

"No, not here. We've been here since 6:30 or so. Sorry."

"No problem. I'll find her," he said, smiling nervously.

"Hang on a second," said the young woman. "We went for an ice-cream before coming here. I saw a girl who looked similar walking on the grassy area around Clover Point. She appeared pretty upset. I remember feeling sorry for her. It seemed like too beautiful of a day to be sad."

"Thanks, I'll go there now. And don't worry, I promise you, my fiance will be pleased once I give her some good news."

He knew the couple was probably thinking they had a lovers' spat. Many people would probably have refused to give any information. Barry was grateful they had. He wanted them to know he was going to make everything right.

He jogged back to his car, but it was gone. In his hurry to investigate the pavilion, he had ignored the sign indicating it as a drop-off zone only.

"Dammit. Nothing's going right today," Barry grumbled as he jogged down the hill to Dallas Road. He was exhausted, but now there was a new spring to his stride.

Ellen had been seen in the Clover Point less than a few hours ago. Hopefully, she would still be here. He remembered her fascination with the ocean and the playful hours they had spent on the beach in Parksville. *I should have come here first.*

Automatically, he searched for her car as he made his way to the Point. Clover Point was a peninsula jutting out about a quarter-mile. At this time of the evening, romantic couples strolled by hand in hand, appreciating the pallet of evening's blush. Serenity exuded itself here, measurable in its healing power.

A woman wearing a white jacket with a hood drawn up sat quietly on a boulder. He was almost sure it wasn't Ellen, but he approached her anyway.

"Excuse me, could you tell me the time please?" he asked earnestly. He had to see the girl's face.

She turned and smiled. "Sure. It's almost 7:00. Isn't it beautiful tonight?" she asked as if ready to begin a conversation.

"Yea, fantastic. Thanks." He left her, hoping he hadn't been too rude. As he quickly headed along the trail, Barry wondered if Ellen had headed home and whether he was wasting his time searching.

He rang his mother for the third time. "Has she called yet?"

"No, son. Sorry."

"Shit. What a day. My car was towed, so I don't have any wheels. I'm at Clover Point. Could you get Bev to come and get me? I'm running out of daylight, and I need to spread out faster if I'm going to find her."

"Sure. Bev's here right now. She'll be there in less than twenty minutes. I've got dinner set aside for you when you return."

Barry smiled wearily to himself. Trust his mom to think about food. "Thanks, Mom." He scanned the entire parking lot, noting a few beige cars that could've been hers that he'd check out.

The tide was coming in as he examined the pedestrians walking the grassy area along the road. Further down the beach, the splashing waves on a rocky finger caught his eye.

And another movement. He squinted, trying to make out what he saw.

A flutter. And something blue. Somebody was sitting out there. Ellen?

His heart pounded as his adrenaline pumped. How did Ellen manage to climb those slippery stones? The rocky protrusion was off shore from a forty-foot sandstone cliff. He searched for a way to reach her. An incoming tide was already devouring the beach's meager edge. He kicked off his shoes and scrambled down the boulders.

He waded, then swam. Ellen's position looked a lot closer than it was. He fought the incoming tide and the weight of his clothes. Swells pushed him around. Warm salty water, usually his friend, conspired against him by slowing his progress. He wanted to call Ellen but knew she wouldn't hear him.

Whatever gave her the dangerous idea to come way out here? She could hurt herself and their baby. Had she meant to? The question shook him to his core. Swimming, then wading, then swimming again, he eventually reached the rocky point.

"Ellen, Ellen!" he yelled again. He watched her sitting there so quietly with her slender arms wrapped around her knees, her limp hair dripping down her face. He scrambled up the jagged rocks, almost losing his balance as a wave pounded him. She didn't notice him at all. She sat trance-like, gazing out to sea.

"Ellen." He wrapped his arms around her and turned her face to his.

Her hazel eyes stared at him, but he realized she hadn't registered his presence.

He shook her gently, repeating her name. "Ellen, honey.

Sweetheart, what's going on? This is crazy. Why are you out here? Why did you run away from me at the college?"

His words seemed to trigger her consciousness as her eyes narrowed, focusing on his presence. She began to tremble, and as his warmth transferred to her chilled body, he alternately rubbed her arms and legs as he explained what she saw.

"I love you, sweetheart. That girl you saw me with is my neighbor. We're like family, and we grew up together. Bev's been waiting at home with my mom while I've been looking for you."

"Really? I'm sorry, I was sure you had someone else," Ellen whispered. "I couldn't, couldn't... Take me...home," she whispered just before she fainted in his arms.

"Oh no, no, no. Wake up, Ellen. I need you. We need to get back up the rocks together. C'mon honey," he coaxed as he tapped her cheeks gently, then glanced around desperately. As he debated carrying her to shelter at the cliff's edge, he noticed movement on Clover Point.

People waved at him while others unloaded a canoe from the top of a car. They'd noticed his predicament, and help was on the way. He raised his arm in the air, and an answering signal came back.

He fervently hoped it wasn't too late. He cradled the chilled, unconscious body of the woman he loved. For now, there was nothing else he could do.

CHAPTER 5

"Damn, I'll never get this all done in time," Ellen complained as she flicked the duster over the coffee tables. She paused for a moment and picked up her wedding photo. Hard to believe five years with Barry had gone by so fast. Tonight, Paula and Ken were coming over for drinks. Then, they were all going out to dinner to celebrate. Bev and her new boyfriend would be joining them later at the Sticky Wicket to party,

Ellen was thankful that, at last, she and Barry were able to afford a small down payment on this house. As she set crystal wine glasses out on the liquor buffet, she reflected on their first years together.

They had lived with Barry's mother for over a year. Contrary to most mother-in-law stories, they had gotten along well. When Mrs. Peterson passed away, Ellen grieved almost as much as Barry. They had then moved to an inexpensive flat on Gladstone Street, a lovely, Victorian home divided into four apartments. Theirs was on the top floor, and for the next three years, Ellen vacillated between deciding if the cheap rent and the homey gabled rooms were worth the stairs, especially with a child.

Barry had worked day and night in those years, learning by practical experience what he had learned in theory at school. The pay was low at first, but the owners of the Oak Bay Resort treated him well. Barry earned their respect with his innovative ideas and resourcefulness, often receiving a bonus as time went by. The hospitality industry was not known for its high wages, so Barry frequently took weekend fill-in jobs as a bartender.

When Danny began preschool, Ellen worked part-time at the TD bank nearby. They were frugal with their money. After all, Barry had a career plan. She knew they couldn't accomplish their dreams without some penny-pinching.

A few months before Sara was born last June, they took the plunge and bought their first home, a three-bedroom bungalow on Watson Street. It was in dire need of new paint inside and out, along with some plain old elbow grease on the yard, but both Ellen and Barry could see its potential. With a gift down-payment from her parents, their mortgage payment was only slightly higher than the rent they'd been paying. At $91,000.00, it was a good investment and would give them equity in a short time.

Ellen looked around her small home, satisfied that everything was in order. Wine chilling in the fridge, and a platter of appetizers were waiting to be heated and served. Hopefully, Barry would be home early enough to have a private drink with her before Paula and Ken came.

Funny about those two, she mused. They had been their best man and bridesmaid, and they had kept in touch with each other ever since. Ellen suspected that's why Paula chose to go to UBC in Vancouver for her nursing degree, so she was closer to

Ken. They had strong feelings for each other, but their different religions kept them from planning a future. Paula, for all her flippancy, was a devout Catholic. Ken was Jewish. She hoped that Ken and Paula would be strong enough to overcome their differences. In every other way, they complimented each other.

Ellen heard Barry's car turn in the driveway. She ran her hands down the new dress she had made, wondering what he would think of it. Her figure was almost back to her previous size ten. She may be twenty-four this year, but she wasn't going to look like an old married lady for their fifth anniversary. Scouring the pattern books, Ellen had settled on a form-fitting sheath with a scoop neckline. She picked out a black paisley rayon blend and whipped it together in one afternoon. Now, she fretted over the daring length she had hemmed it.

Freshening her soft-pink lip gloss, she studied her reflection in the mirror. The silver eyeshadow above the black eyeliner emphasized her hazel eyes and gave her the sexy, sophisticated look she'd aimed for. Ellen wore her latest dangling silver earrings and matching necklace, then dabbed on her favorite scent, 90210, with the green apple and freesia base.

Hot damn! If this didn't trigger a romantic evening, nothing would. Lately, she'd begun to wonder about Barry's late nights and their diminishing sex lives.

"Ellen?"

Ellen ran down the hall to greet her husband. "Hi hon, Happy Anniversary!" The look in his eyes dispelled her doubts that he had stopped finding her attractive.

"Wow."

She giggled, pleased with his reaction.

"Where did you get that?"

"I wanted something new, something different, so I made it," she explained. "It hardly cost me anything."

"Too bad we're going out," he whispered as he pulled her to him. "We could try something different here too," He nuzzled her ear, then her throat as his busy hands stroked her curves, pressing her closer to him.

"That's what I hoped we might do later. I was beginning to think you forgot about me," Ellen said as she moved her hips suggestively against him.

"Aw c'mon, Ellen, I can't keep up with everything." Barry broke away and started down the hallway. "I'm going to take a shower and shave. Have we got any wine or anything?" He switched the subject quickly, but Ellen knew she had made her point.

Their sex life had always been intensely passionate, but as his work hours grew and the pressures increased, their once precious love life had dwindled.

"Yes, I picked up a few bottles of Napa Valley wines," Ellen replied to his disappearing figure. "The Chardonnay is chilling. The two Cabernets are breathing and ready to go. I'll go check on the appies."

Hearing tiny moans from Sara's room as she passed by, Ellen slipped in quietly, covering her with a light blanket, and popped the soother back into her mouth. She was growing so fast. Where did the time go? She heard Danny kicking at something in the next bedroom and laughing. She smiled to herself. He was a mischievous little devil, full of pep and vinegar.

Her life had changed sp much in the past five years. Danny would start preschool this coming fall. Ellen hoped to return to her part-time bookkeeping job once Sara was in preschool too. She loved her kids dearly, but she also missed the social interactions and the extra money that her job gave her.

Knock, Knock.

The raps sent Ellen skipping down the hallway. She threw open the door and dove in for hugs and kisses. "Hi, guys, it's about time you got here. How about a glass of wine? Barry will join us in a minute. He's in the shower."

"Sounds good to me. We dropped our things off at the Best Western and came straight over. Look at you, getting brave, aren't we?" teased Paula. "That's a good four inches above the knee. I love those flats. We need to go shopping for a pair for me."

"Anytime, Paula. I know where all the deals are."

"I don't mind the length," Ken leered.

Ellen punched his shoulder. "Thanks for the compliment. I wanted to remind Barry how lucky he was five years ago." Ellen poured the wine as her friends wandered about, noticing the decorating changes she'd made this year.

When Barry joined them, he immediately proposed a toast. "To my beautiful, sexy wife. I don't know how she puts up with me sometimes, but I'm glad she does." He tipped his glass to her and winked.

Amid the cheers of approval, Ellen raised her glass and toasted Barry. "To a man who never took no for an answer." Wine glasses clinked again. "And to our best friends who were there then and are still here now. Thank you."

"Ok, if all the toasting is over with, let's get down to some heavy partying. Got any new music?"

"Trust Ken to be unromantic about tonight," Paula complained loudly. "You'd think this was an ordinary evening for you two when I happen to know you hardly ever go out."

"Who cares? As long as we have a ball when we do," Ellen shot back.

Paula wandered about the living room, complimenting her on the design makeover, then snuck down the hallway to peek at Sara. "You're so lucky, Ellen. A perfect family, a boy and a girl. I wonder if I'll ever get there or if I even want to."

"When you finish your nursing degree, you'll have time to decide. I started family life early. You still have lots of time." Ellen poured them more wine while they sat on the sofa catching up with their latest activities.

The men drifted over to the back patio, where Barry lit a cigarette. He was trying to quit smoking, but he hadn't been successful.

Ellen popped the appetizers in the oven. Soon the smell of garlic and shrimp filled the compact home. Ellen had prepared stuffed mushroom caps and an artichoke dip with crisp side vegetables to enjoy with their wine. The men joined them and raved about Ellen's cooking skills.

Soon after they killed the second bottle of wine, they called a cab. Katy arrived to babysit, so they set off to the exclusive French restaurant, Ma Maison, on Hollywood Crescent. Reservation weeks in advance were necessary as their reputation for superb cuisine and excellent service made it a preferred destination for special celebrations.

The refurbished luxurious Mediterranean-styled home discreetly hidden behind a stone four-foot wall was extraordinary by all standards. The white stucco exterior and arched brick walkways interspersed with hanging baskets of vibrant fuchsia, lobelia, and petunias welcomed patrons. Inside, fresh flowers and flickering candlelight enhanced the polished pieces of cherry wood furniture.

They had requested a private table in one of the alcoves

facing the sea, and as the maître d' escorted them, Ellen inhaled in awe. The stunning view of Gonzales Bay framed in the alcove's complementing arched window was beyond her imagination. The thick carpeting beneath her feet silenced their footsteps while background music muffled the surrounding conversations.

After they were seated, Paula breathed a sigh of relief. "Whew, I was so nervous. Look at this place, do you believe it? I could almost see myself tripping and causing a scene."

Barry smiled, obviously more comfortable in this setting than anyone else. "I promised Ellen a classy place for our fifth anniversary, and this is one of the best. The seafood crepes and the peppercorn steak are legendary." He ordered more wine for them, then listened to Ellen and Paula's hushed comments on the decor of the place and its clientele.

"I love the antique brass accents and all the greenery," Paula said.

Ellen nodded. "It does provide privacy. I feel like we stepped into an episode of 'The Rich and Shameless.'"

Barry tapped his spoon to his wine glass to catch their attention. "I have an announcement to make," he said, smiling mysteriously.

"Oh no you don't," Ken said. "All serious stuff is over with."

"Not quite. This is more good news. I'd like to announce that as of tomorrow at 9:00 a.m., I'm the proud owner of a new restaurant in town."

"What? Say that again?" Ellen's face mirrored her confusion. "What are you talking about? We—"

"Alright. Good for you," Ken interrupted. "All that backbreaking work was bound to pay off one of these days."

"Barry? How did you do this?" Ellen questioned again.

"I've been working on this idea for months. I know it's in an old building, and the structure needs a lot of work, but I've developed a great concept. And I've sold it to Pete Zalinsky. He's going to bankroll the project, but I'll be running the show. We're sharing the profits, 55/45 for him. Not a great split, but it's a start."

Ellen blushed as she tried to look as excited as he was. The last thing she needed to do was embarrass him or herself. *Don't make a scene.* "Congratulations, honey." Ellen leaned over and kissed Barry lightly on the lips. She wouldn't bring up any questions tonight. But why hadn't he discussed this project with her?

She could tell by the proud look on his face that he was excited about his new enterprise.

"Where is it?" Ken asked, obviously unable to hold back like her. Barry's eagerness to share his dreams had piqued his curiosity.

"It's on Johnson Street, in one of the old turn-of-the-century brick buildings, half a block before Douglas St. It's within walking distance of the nightclubs like Big Bad John's and Dukes, so if the crowd feels like carrying on after dinner, they're in the right spot."

"Good idea. So, what's the scoop?" Ken asked. "What will you be doing with the place?"

"First of all, we're going to add sky lights to lighten the space and re-do the electrical to code, then re-decorate it in a casual atmosphere. We're going to try and attract the young crowd." Barry's hands were busy gesturing, emphasizing his plans. "We'll have the latest music on the best sound system. Attractive young waiters and waitresses will be serving the customers. Then I'll find top-notch chefs that aren't prima donnas. We'll have a lounge where people will sit and have a drink or two before going to the dining area."

"That sounds perfect," Ken said.

"The food prices will be fair so that guests will want to come back a lot. I want it to be somewhere that people can get together and have a good time, let their hair down, and not have to worry about noise or etiquette."

"That also sounds good to me," Ken added. I'd prefer that to clubbing. An evening of drinks and dinner with friends is more my style now."

"We'll encourage large groups like sports teams, clubs, or any kind of get-together. If they don't feel like dinner, they'll have the option to stay in the lounge and order appetizers as they drink."

Paula liked the idea, too. "Sweet. But you're going to have to do some fancy advertising to put the idea across."

"I've considered that. I'll also check into ads on the internet. Once it gets going, I want to approach the sports groups around Victoria and sponsor them, and do promotions at the colleges and the university. I'll see if I can attract their interest. If it goes well, I might even try some television advertising."

"You need a catchy tune with your advertisement, something that'll grab people's attention too," Ken said. "And a tag-line for marketing. I'm good with stuff like that. Let me work on it."

Ellen saw Barry lean back in his chair, obviously proud and relaxed now that his friends were cheering him on. They were as excited as he was. The waiter arrived and served their meals with a flair. Ken and Paula had decided to share a Chateau Briand, and its arrival brought sighs of appreciation. Ellen and Barry opted for the peppercorn steak, complete with all the trimmings.

Ellen was pleased with the whole evening so far. The food was attractively presented and mouthwatering, the surroundings beyond compare. And three of the most important people in her life were with her.

From that point on, ideas flowed freely between them as they discussed menus, décor, and uniforms. The look of '98 was casual, and most men wore jeans or khakis to go out. Women were more eclectic in their styles, and anything went, from the sexy black or slip dress to maxi skirts and knee boots. The more daring gals sported tube or crop tops with metallic trim and pleather pants or leggings and doc martens.

"Why not have staff wear black jeans and white polo shirts with a logo on them?" Ellen suggested. "Maybe add black or red aprons to spiff it up? That would make the young crowd feel more comfortable, make it *the* place to be."

"Sounds good to me, casual but smart," Barry replied as he pushed the last piece of steak in his mouth. "Man, this was the greatest."

The meal had been excellent and the service superb. Ellen was glad they had been extravagant and come, especially since it was now a double celebration. She couldn't quite finish her dinner. Barry's news had given her nervous butterflies in her stomach. He had done well so far, but continual budgeting had made her anxious about money issues. She realized this was why he had avoided discussing it with her. Although, in her family, both her parents planned major events together. She fervently hoped Barry knew what he was doing.

They left the restaurant and headed downtown to the Sticky Wicket to continue their celebration. Some of Barry's older friends were there, greeting the group warmly and joining in their celebration. Bev and Larry had saved a booth for the six of them.

"Happy Anniversary, you two!" Bev stood up and kissed

them both. She motioned to their waiter, then settled back into the booth beside Larry. "And I hear there are congratulations in order. A new restaurant, Barry! Wow."

"You know? You knew before me?" Ellen's mouth hung open in surprise.

"Who else was he going to talk to if he wanted to keep it a surprise?" Bev giggled. "Don't worry, I was careful. I didn't offer an opinion one way or another. I'm almost a lawyer now, and I know how to avoid things. I just advised him on legal stuff should he decide to go ahead."

"You brat, I'm not sure I could've kept a secret like that without sending a few hints out." Ellen grinned and smacked Bev's hand lightly. "No one better to confide in, though. I'm glad you were there for him."

A bottle of Tattinger Champagne and six flutes appeared on their table. Bev removed the cork and poured them each a glass. "To a great future in the restaurant business. May all your dreams come true." Bev clinked her glass with her childhood friend, then with the rest of the group. "You two deserve it. Congratulations!"

Paula, Bev, and Ellen enjoyed the music, dragging their men to the dance floor or dancing with each other. Ellen and Barry looked around them, grinning with excitement. For the first time in their marriage, their dreams were within arms' reach.

The girls made their way through the crowded and noisy bar to the ladies' room. As soon as they entered, they rolled their eyes. It was so predictable. So many people were smoking pot that Ellen suspected she was an odd ball. And that was considered tame compared to the coke making a big splash around Victoria, creating venues wilder than ever.

"Have you ever smoked a joint?" she asked Paula.

"Yea, a couple of times. Oh, don't look so shocked!" Paula laughed. "Y'know me, curiosity might kill me one day, but now at least, I can say I've tried it. It wasn't as great as I heard it was. It didn't make me feel any cooler either. It made my head spin like crazy, which made me nauseous. That was about it."

"Coke?"

"No way. Too scary for me. I'm good with the booze, and I don't need the other shit."

Bev swiped on a new coat of lip gloss. "Me neither. I need to stay away from that whole scene. It would ruin my career. Besides, we can have fun without being stoned."

"Exactly. You haven't studied this hard just to put yourself in jeopardy. And Paula would only get a strong case of the guilts anyway." Ellen teased. "All that good Catholic breeding paid off. You're an adult, but you still can't enjoy anything illegal, even if you want to."

"No kidding." Paula touched up her pale pink lipstick and dark eyeliner. "You sure look hot tonight, Ellen. You don't look like you have two kids, that's for sure." She checked the zigzag part in her blond-highlighted hair, looping her hair around her ear, probably trying to imitate the Spice Girls shoulder-length bob.

"Good. I'm ready to party. Barry's been so bloody busy lately that he hardly pays any attention to me. But I'm going to make him notice tonight."

"At least now you know why he's been working so much. He loves you, Ellen. He wouldn't ignore you on purpose." Bev ran her fingers through her hair, giving it the messy bedroom look that was all the rage these days, then gave the two girls a finger wave. "See you guys out there."

Paula couldn't believe her eyes when Ellen teetered off balance for a second. She seldom drank enough to be inebriated, yet here she was, well on her way. And it wasn't only that. It was the desperation she heard in her voice.

"Is everything ok with you two?" she asked.

"Just peachy." Ellen hiccupped, then giggled, amused at her friend's concerned expression. "I take care of the kids while he works. And works. And works. If we make *it* every couple of weeks lately, we're lucky." Ellen groaned as she threw her hands up in the air. "Oh, I know I shouldn't bitch, especially now that I know what he's been up to, but sometimes I get so bloody lonely."

"Why don't you pack up the kids and come to Vancouver for a week now and then? I'd love to have you."

"You never know, maybe when Sara's older. C'mon, let's go party. I don't want to waste any time thinking."

The night raced by. Although Barry wasn't usually a big dancer, Ellen was pleased when he couldn't seem to keep his eyes off her. Ellen gyrated and twisted to the music, copying any new dance steps she saw. She felt wild and sexy tonight, and she was going to make sure that no one else would grab his attention. So far, it seemed to be working.

Finally, Barry pulled her out of her chair and into his arms for the last song. There were hardly any waltzes, and as the evening wore on, she ached to hold him close. She knew he had caught the eyes of several guys watching her party tonight and hoped it made him more aware of her. Ellen wouldn't be taken for granted anymore. She wasn't only his life partner or the mother of his children. She was an incredibly sexy young woman.

Ellen saw the molten look in his eyes as he reached for her and her pulse quickened. *It was still there.* He put his arms around her waist, his hands sliding lower to press her closer.

"Mmmm, it's been a while," Ellen whispered as she

pressed her body against his. She hadn't worn a bra tonight, and her nipples hardened through the sleek shift she wore as she brushed them against his chest.

She heard his breath quicken, and he bent to whisper in her ear. "Ell, you're the sexiest woman here, do you know that? I can't wait to get you home and get this off you." Barry blew softly in her ear then teased the shell with his tongue.

"Better wait 'til we get home, honey." Ellen pushed him away from her a tad. She was uncomfortable necking in a public place, but her husky voice belied her casual rebuff.

They glanced around, looking for Ken and Paula, and found them wrapped too, in each other's arms.

"Are you guys coming?" Barry asked. "We're heading out."

"Go for it. We'll close the place with Bev and Larry, then catch a taxi later. We'll see you two in the morning," Ken answered.

Barry went to the bar and asked them to call for a cab. They stepped outside into the cool evening air and chatted about their fun-filled evening while waiting for their ride. Inside the cab, Ellen sat enjoying Barry's hand on her thigh and the fire in his eyes. After the noise of the dance, they didn't talk much. They both knew what they wanted next.

"I had such a good time tonight, honey. A double celebration. You surprised me."

"It's not over yet, sweetheart." He smiled and put his arm around her, caressing her breast lightly. Minutes later, Barry paid for the taxi while Ellen went inside and paid a sleepy babysitter.

"Good thing she lives across the street." Ellen giggled.

While Barry walked the sitter home, Ellen raced to their bedroom and put on her sexiest black nightie. A dab of perfume on her wrists, neck, and belly, then she jumped into bed. She heard him come back down the hallway and giggled in anticipation.

Ellen watched in surprise as Barry began tossing articles of clothing while he hummed the raunchy notes of a strip tease. When he jumped into the room stark naked, Ellen was beside herself with laughter. This playful partner was the Barry who had aroused and married her, then disappeared this past year.

"Whaddya think about that," he growled as he jumped in beside her.

"I think that was worth waiting for. I've never made it with a stripper before."

Passion ignited a frenzy within Ellen as she pressed her tongue against his teeth. As he opened, she darted her tongue inside, slipping in and out. Her fingertips caressed his back. Barry withdrew from her kiss and traced his tongue down her neck to her breasts. He cupped them and circled the already erect nipples with his tongue, teasing them.

As he began tasting her, she purred with desire, writhing beneath him, grinding her pelvis against him. He pinned her hands to the side as he tasted his way past her trembling belly button. Groans, sighs, and expletives filled the room as they expressed their need for each other.

Ellen wasn't ready for this to end. She pushed him over and knelt between his legs. Her fingers began massaging his thighs, slowly moving higher, cupping his manhood gently. Barry pulled her to him, and gladly she paid homage to his throbbing desire before mounting him. Sliding and arching, she found her rhythm.

Ellen lost herself in the increased throbbing deep in her belly as the tension built. Time stopped for them. Nothing mattered except the mounting electrical sensations they were creating for each other. Naughty whispers and whimpers of delight peppered the air as they rode the rhythmic wave of ecstasy. They held each other tight, riding the flow.

They lay beside each other, tousled and damp.

"Dead. I've died and gone to heaven," Ellen panted as she tried to catch her breath.

"Yea, me too." Barry propped himself up on one elbow as he watched her doze off. "You are one sexy lady, you know. You're getting better all the time."

"Mmhmm..." Ellen was already drifting asleep. As long as they could find the time for each other like this, she could take the long hours he put in. She decided that she might as well get used to it because it wouldn't get any better. It may even worsen.

"WHERE THE HELL ARE THE FUCKIN' carpet layers?" Barry screamed into the phone. "I've got a fuckin' grand opening in five days, and my bloody carpets and lino still aren't laid!"

Barry took the last drag on his cigarette and angrily butted it out in the ashtray. "If you think I'm flipping out, watch and see what happens if they don't show up today. I'm fed up with the screwing around you've been giving me," Barry replied, slightly less agitated than a minute ago. "Yea? Well, you'll be hearing from me again if this is another bullshit story. I'll sue your ass off if I can't open on Thursday!" He slammed down the phone and reached for another smoke.

God help him. He felt like he was going around the bend. He already moved his restaurant's grand opening back one month because the electricians' strike delayed him. Now the carpets which were on hold for him were lost in transit somewhere. Everything else was ready and in storage. Mentally he scanned his final checklist.

Barry had hired his staff. The kitchen crew had been practicing the menu at lunchtime for the past week. Barry had called the various service clubs in the area and offered them a free luncheon for up to twenty club members. They had brought in long rectory tables and chairs for seating, and the idea had worked well.

It wasn't only good practice, it was good P.R. They were all patient with the new waiters and anonymously filled out questionnaires at the end of the meal. Barry hoped he would get a more accurate reflection of their reaction, and it did. He scrapped the calamari with curry dip appetizer, then added more specialty salads for the diet conscious. It seemed that between the chefs and Barry, they had designed the perfect menu.

Diversity with a flare. Barry priced everything as an extra, so you could tailor your meal as basic or as extravagant as you like. The trial patrons had loved it.

Pete may have the larger share of the deal, but Barry had all the responsibility. When they agreed that Pete would be a silent partner, that's precisely what he was.

Barry was the one who contacted the draftsman to redesign the two-story hardware store, then arrange for Webber's Construction to do it. He also scouted the best deals for the restaurant, from freezers, coolers, and kitchen appliances to furniture, flooring, and menu design.

Ellen assumed the duty of ordering all the dishes, cutlery, and glassware. She also took over developing the logo and ordering the polo shirts and red aprons. Following precise directions from Barry, Ellen interviewed for staff, narrowing the applicants to fifty. Barry made the final selection of twenty full-time staff and fifteen part-timers.

Their internet and newspaper campaigns advertising *Good Times, Good Food, and Good Friends at the Carvery* were a success that had Victoria jumping to see the place.

Along the walls of The Carvery were the long party booths that could hold eight persons comfortably. The five thousand square foot restaurant had been divided into different levels to give more privacy and dispel the illusion of it being the hardware store it once was.

The lounge, which doubled as a holding area for the dining room, was completely stocked. Ellen suggested decorating the rough-hewn cedar walls with neon signs of the various beers they sold, which brightened the area and made it more welcoming. Four posters five by seven feet showed the hottest rock groups that the staff would be change regularly. Opening posters were of the Spice Girls, Backstreet Boys, and Whitney Houston. A variety to appeal to every kind of pop music. The stereo system was installed with top-of-the-line speakers built-in at strategic points to give the ultimate surround sound.

Barry looked down out of his office loft and imagined his completed dream. Thanks to Pete's money and belief in him, Barry was going to open the funkiest place in town. Come hell or high water, his goal was becoming a reality. Carp Diem, baby! It was time to strut his stuff.

CHAPTER 6

Ellen grabbed the wooden spoon and marched into the living room. "Danny, I've told you and told you to stop it. Now, you're going to get it."

Danny shoved Sara down again as he ran for the back door, half laughing, half crying. She could see his mischievous mind working at top speed.

She lunged forward, snatching him by the arm. "You do not take Sara's toys and wreck them. And stop pushing her down. She's just a little girl, and you're her big brother. You're supposed to help her, not hurt her. Ok?" Ellen asked impatiently.

"Yes, Mom. But I just wanted to fix it," he pouted.

"Don't lie to me, young man. I watched you break her doll's arm off. That's not nice, and you know it."

"I'll be good, Mommy, promise," he whined, beginning to realize she meant business.

As much as she hated to hit him, she lifted the spoon and firmly spanked him three times on the rump before sending him to his room. Dr. Spock had never met her child, she swore. She could reason with him, and he would sit quietly and agree with her, apologizing like a fallen angel. Then ten minutes later, he'd be doing it again.

Now the crying was coming from both ends of the house. She picked up Sara and cuddled her, her mind still on Danny. If only Barry would be home more often, maybe Danny would listen better. These last three years were what she'd expected they'd be: hell.

Ellen's head pounded. The tension of it all was beginning to get to her. She couldn't blame Barry for his long hours. Most days, he never even saw the children arriving home well after their bedtime. She hoped his work with the restaurant would ease after the opening. She took an aspirin and, still carrying Sara, walked to the window.

It was the first week of November, but still relatively mild. The wind blew the twisted barren branches of the apple tree. She and the kids weren't going out as often as they used to, but today would be a perfect day for the park. To hell with the housework.

Quickly, she changed and bundled Sara, making sure to tuck juice boxes and bananas in the stroller.

At Danny's door, she knocked once and tiptoed inside. He lay on his bed and stared at the ceiling, trance-like. His flushed cheeks and tousled hair warmed her heart. She loved him so much it was hard to discipline him. She wiggled his toe.

"I be good, Mommy," he said.

"I know, sweetheart, you'll try. How would you like to go to the park?"

"Awright!" he screamed excitedly. He scampered off the bed, then ran to his toy box. "Can I bring a truck and my ball?"

"Sure, but not a big truck, only small things I can fit in

the stroller." Ellen handed Danny his boots and jacket to put on while she donned her duffel coat.

Within minutes the three of them were on the way to Carnarvon Park. It was a favorite place for them and only about half a mile from their home. She and Danny had gone there regularly before Sara was born.

Carnarvon Park was famous for its Garry Oaks to climb, swings to glide on, and the two plastic jungle gyms with slides. There were also several benches underneath shady trees for tired moms to relax on. In the spring and summer, an irresistible water fountain splashed the braver kids who dared cool off in it. Now it stood forlornly, a receptacle for autumn leaves.

Only one other mother was there with her two children, talking animatedly in Italian. They smiled and nodded to each other as Ellen pushed the stroller towards Danny's favorite jungle gym. She laughed as Danny scampered to the plastic-covered rungs, eager to climb it. She removed Sara from her stroller, taking her hand and leading her to the swing. The fresh breeze gently caressed Ellen's face and made her smile. It was so peaceful here.

Settling Sara into the toddler swing, she pushed her from the front. She had taught Sara to make her legs stiff and to stick them straight out so she could watch her daughter giggle while she pushed on her feet. Making funny faces with her, she kept it up until her daughter grew tired of it.

"Momma. Slide. Momma!" Sara pointed to the slide, so Ellen lifted her from the swing and watched her run towards the small circular funnel that she could use on her own. She liked being a *big girl*.

Ellen sat on a nearby bench and kept an eye on Danny as he ran off with his truck to the sand pile. Ellen guarded their progress as her children explored the park while concentrating on deep breathing for stress control. She gazed up at the popcorn clouds skipping across the blue sky and breathed in the fresh air. The oak and maple trees around her were shedding their golden and red leaves, alternately floating or whirling around them, depending on the wind direction.

Piles of leaves were already raked, and Danny's quick eyes soon found another past-time. The poor gardeners weren't going to thank him for that, Ellen mused as she watched Danny recklessly jump in and scatter them high in the air. Sara and the other two children soon joined him, and their laughter floated across the park.

She reflected on her childhood and suddenly had a strong feeling of loneliness. She hardly ever saw her parents anymore. They would come up for New Year's dinner and an overnighter or two. Then Ellen and Barry would try to spend the Canada Day long weekend with them in July. They urged her to visit more often, but it wasn't easy with two small children unless Barry could join them—and of course, he seldom could.

Well, she decided suddenly, 1999 is going to be different.

Matt and Anna and their two children were arriving from Olympia to visit her parents on their way to spend a week near Long Beach on the West Coast. It had been years since she'd spent any amount of time with them, only keeping in touch now and then with photos through emails. Ellen would bring her children and meet them in Port Alberni for a mini-reunion.

She'd email and ask them to consider spending a few days in Victoria with her before returning home. They could always take the ferry from Victoria to Port Angeles. She realized how much she missed their relationship. It was way past time to rectify that. She wanted her kids to feel the connection of cousins and extended family. Ellen was tired of being lonely, but with Barry's preoccupation and commitment to The Carvery, it was up to her to solve it.

A scream interrupted her daydreams. Ellen jumped up as she recognized Danny's cry. She searched for him and saw him dangling from a metal monkey tree. As Ellen sprinted toward him, a young man leaped from his blanket on the ground. He got there before she did and handed the trembling boy back to her.

"Thank you. Danny, you little rascal, you know you're not supposed to climb so high," Ellen scolded as she held him tightly.

"That scared me, Mommy." Danny stuck his thumb in his mouth. He often reverted to the habit when frightened.

Ellen gently removed it. "You're ok now. Say thank-you to the nice man."

"Thank you, Mister." Danny fled for the sand box and began making roads with his truck again.

"They sure have a lot of energy, don't they?" The stranger commented.

"You're not kidding. Thanks again for helping. It could've been a bad fall. He's so fast." Ellen felt guilty for letting her mind wander and not stopping Danny before he got so high.

"No problem." The stranger glanced over at his sleeping bag and pack sack. "I was watching him race around. Kind of reminded me of my younger brother."

Ellen looked over at his gear. It didn't seem to fit with his looks. His clothes were fairly new and clean, and his hair was slightly over his ears. Not homeless yet, she decided.

"Are you on your way somewhere?" she asked.

"I was. Now I'm here." He smiled.

"Where are you from?" she asked. It was none of her

business, but something about this stranger's kindness touched her. Suddenly she needed to speak to another adult.

He shrugged his shoulders and eyed her carefully. "Nova Scotia."

Ellen noticed the uncertain look in his eyes, and she knew the position he was in. Steady work was sparse on the Canadian east coast. The lure to find his future meant he must have left everyone behind.

"Must be hard," Ellen replied.

"Yup." He smiled at her, then returned to his things. He packed up quickly, then left.

Who was he? Did he have a place to live and work? He seemed lonely. Ellen tossed her head, trying to shrug off a problem that wasn't hers to own.

"Danny let's race to the swings." Ellen chased after him and caught him, twirling him around her. His grubby hands swiped his nose, and she laughed at him. "You are going to have the biggest bubble bath when we get home."

After finishing their snack, Ellen was in a much better mood. She decided to walk to Bev's place for a cup of tea before going home.

Bev was everything Barry said she was, but she was also an extremely busy woman. She was entering her final year of law school, and her schedule was so hectic that it precluded the solid type of friendship that Ellen needed. Ellen was lucky if they got together more than once a month.

Once again, bad timing. Bev's red mustang sat in front of her house. As Ellen was getting Sara out of the stroller, Bev came out of the house, briefcase, and books in hand.

"Hi, Ellen. God, it's nice to see you. Hi Danny." She ruffled his hair in greeting.

"Looks like I picked a bad time," Ellen said as she sat Sara back down.

"Sorry, crazy schedules lately. I'm so glad this is my last year. Not that it will be much better when I get hired, but it will be a change of pace. Look at that sweetheart." Bev bent down to Sara's level and kissed her cheek, then kissed the palm of her outstretched hand. "She's growing up so fast. I've been missing out on so much lately. How are things going?"

"Great. Barry's very pleased with his restaurant. He's busier than he ever imagined he'd be."

"Sweet. He's a genius at that kind of stuff. I'm glad it's all come together so well."

"Yea, so am I. I've started bugging him to get an assistant manager before he burns out. He says he's not ready to share the load yet. He's still excited about the challenge. Barry's turned into a workaholic, which means he's hardly ever home, but it's hard to be upset about it. He loves it."

Bev shifted her books to the other arm, then looked at her watch. "Must be tough on you."

"Not bad. I keep busy, although sometimes I'd kill for an intelligent adult conversation. Look, I'm holding you up, you better get moving, or you'll be late for something."

"True. Hopefully, I can take a break after I finish my fall thesis. How about we make a day of it and go have lunch, then do some shopping?"

"Sounds awesome. I'm in. Let me know when."

"Sorry I couldn't visit, Ellen, but I'll see you soon. Say hi to Barry for me." Bev loaded her things into the car then waved as she drove off.

STORING the playpen in the car's trunk with their suitcases and a duffel bag of essential toys took more time than Ellen had anticipated. She had to repack it twice to get it to close.

She couldn't wait to share Thanksgiving with her parents and cousins.

Ellen went into the house to pick up Sara and her favorite blanket. Strapping her into the car seat, Ellen went back to deal with Sara's brother. Danny sat on the grass, his arms crossed and a frown pasted on his face.

"I want to bring my bike."

"There's no room, Danny. I've told you that. You won't need it anyway—you'll have your cousins to play with. Now get into your car seat so that we can get going."

"No. I want my bike." Danny could be so stubborn sometimes.

"I said now, Danny. In the car. We're going to drive through MacDonald's for a happy meal. You can have your lunch just like we planned. You love Mickey D's, don't you?"

"No."

"Fine. We won't stop, your choice. But we're going now. Do I need to count to three?"

Danny glared at her, then stomped to the car. At six years old, he'd long been able to get into his car seat and buckle the harness himself. Not today.

Ellen sighed. She was hot and edgy. Nothing was going smoothly today. She leaned in and buckled Danny in, kissing him on the head. "Do you want a book to read while we travel or your Pixar friends?"

"I want Woody and Bullseye and Buzz. And I want MacDonald's."

"OK, that we can do. Hang on." Ellen went to the trunk to pull out the duffel bag, then rooted through it to find his toys. She extracted a hand-held, push-button piano for Sara that she loved to play with too. If they didn't fall asleep along the way, she might have to divide the almost three-hour drive with a stop to let their energy out.

It would have been so much easier if Barry had come. He hadn't met Matt and Anna yet. This trip would have been an excellent opportunity for the two guys to get to know each other. But of course, Barry said it was out of the question. Never mind. Once she arrived there, she'd have lots of help with the children while enjoying the camaraderie of family.

After stopping for Danny's lunch and feeding Sara yogurt, she started the journey. She glanced at Sara in the rear-view mirror, who was busy keying in musical notes on her piano and singing along with the tunes. Danny was play-fighting with his characters and imitating their voices. With any luck, their full tummies would make them sleepy, so hopefully, she could get some quiet time for at least part of the trip.

At long last, Danny and Sara would meet their cousins. If Ellen remembered correctly, Jed was almost four years older than Danny, so he'd probably be in grade four now. Lisa was barely a year older than Sara, but she was tall for her age and already involved in swimming and dance. The kids were close enough in age, and they should be easy enough to look after; they'd entertain each other.

Matt's wife Anna had recently finished another course to upgrade her nursing certificate with the help of her sister, who babysat her children. She'd told everyone she was looking forward to returning to work next year when Lisa attended preschool.

Ellen was in awe of Anna's ambition and drive. She lived for the next challenge, so unlike herself.

Ellen's parents had swapped their '40s wartime house

for a spacious ten-year-old home, which included a workshop bordering the back alley. Her mom was especially proud that most of the people who lived in the subdivision were businessmen or upper management in the forest industry. Her dad would have been content to remain in their old residence, but needing more space for a home office and supply storage necessitated an upgrade.

Hard work was paying off. Ellen's parents' dreams were coming true. Ellen was delighted for them.

Driving up to her parents' recent home on Cameron Drive, she noted the improvements they'd done since she was here last. Her parents painted the once-white shutters an emerald green, and then they whitewashed the stucco. In front of the two-story section, the bed of rhododendrons and fresh mulch were ready for fall.

Her dad's face peered out the window, then the front door opened.

"Ellen, I'm so glad you're here. I was beginning to worry."

"Sorry, I'm so late, Dad. Someone had a meltdown on the way. We needed to stop to let him run around and let it all out. Thank God, they're both sleeping right now."

Ellen sighed as her dad wrapped his arms around her and kissed her cheek. Wow. This seldom happened.

She hugged him tightly and returned his kiss. "Where's Mom?"

"She's gone with Anna and Lisa to pick up a few more groceries. Matt's in the backyard with Jed. Let me unpack the trunk for you and get you settled."

The noise of the trunk and luggage shifting woke Sara first. Within a minute, Danny was stirring too. Both were anxious to leave the car.

"Papa! I'm here." Danny disengaged himself from his car

seat and bounced from the car, jumping up and down. He loved his Papa. With the help of a framed photo at home, he remembered the last trip when the two of them had taken the steam engine train to McLean's Mill, a national heritage site. Papa had become a hero in Danny's eyes. "When are we going on the train again, Papa?" Danny tugged at his grandpa's pants. "When, Papa? When?"

"It runs on Saturday morning, so one more sleep, then we'll go with your cousins, Matt and Jed."

"Can't we go now, Papa?"

"Sorry, Danny. It's not working today, so we'll have to wait. Papa's going to help your mom bring in your things. Can you help us?"

"Nope. I'm too small." Danny scampered around his papa and up the stairs.

"I'll bring the playpen in, then take Danny outside to meet Matt and Jed," her father said. "They're playing soccer in the backyard. He can join them while you get settled."

"Exactly what he needs. Tell Matt I'll be out there soon." Ellen gathered Sara in her arms, and by the time she entered the guest bedroom, her dad had assembled the playpen. She freshened Sara with a damp cloth, then changed her into play clothes and tucked her hair into a knit cap with ears.

She grabbed a thick Afghan for them to sit on and headed outdoors to meet Matt and his son.

Pleasure warmed Ellen's heart as she watched her family chase a soccer ball, shouting and encouraging one another. The men tended goal while the boys ran tirelessly between them.

Jed and Danny were vying for attention from Papa, which made her dad very happy. He didn't have a chance to play with his grandson often. Ellen could see he was running out of breath, so she wasn't surprised when he brought it down a notch.

"Ok, boys. Enough of that. We're going to play a new game. Have you ever played T-ball, Danny?"

"No, Papa. I can't."

"Sure, you can. I'm going to show you how." Ellen's dad waved Matt away towards Ellen, giving Matt some time to reconnect with her. He handed a glove to Jed to play fielder while showing Danny how to hold a bat.

"Matt, I'm so glad to see you." Ellen hugged him. "You're still as athletic as ever, keeping up with the two boys."

"Hey, Ellen. Nice to see you, too. I love playing soccer whenever I can." Matt kissed her cheek, then held her at arms' length and looked her over. "You've turned into a beautiful mom. Everything good?"

"Yes, perfect actually," Ellen lied. "These two keep me on my toes, and Barry is busy with his restaurant. The usual."

Matt bent down to play peek-a-boo with the toddler in Ellen's arms. "Who's this sweet angel?"

Sara hid her face in her mother's shoulder, shy of her new cousin. As she peeked to see if the stranger was still there, Matt tickled her foot then pretended to hide behind his hands, earning him a giggle.

"This is Sara. I can't wait to see Lisa?"

"She'll be excited to see you and her cousins too. We've been showing her pictures of your family."

Ellen spread the Afghan on the grass, sat Sara on it with her musical toys, then collapsed on a lawn chair, patting one for Matt. "Sit yourself down and bring me up to date. Tell me, what's new with you guys?"

The back door opened, and Anna called out to Matt to grab Lisa while she helped Aunt Claire with groceries. He ran up the steps, planting a big kiss on his daughter's blond curls, then lifted her into his arms and returned to his lawn chair.

"Not much besides work, kids, and church. That keeps us busy. There's a dental conference at the Wickaninnish Inn next week, so we decided to turn it into a family holiday. We haven't seen your mom and dad in a few years, so Anna suggested visiting here for a few days before heading to the West Coast. I'm glad we did. Jed can afford a week off school, so it's a good time to go. It won't be so easy when the kids get older."

He sat Lisa down beside Sara, introducing his daughter to the younger child. Within minutes, the two girls were chattering, touching each other, then grabbing for the musical toys sitting nearby.

"I know. Time flies, doesn't it? Hard to believe we both have two kids and are doing family holidays. Jed's tall for his age. He must be in grade four now?"

"He's in a split grade four and five." Matt looked over at the scene. "You can't beat this. Uncle Fred is teaching my son to hit a homerun. I remember playing ball with him myself when I was his age. Where does the time go?" Matt shook his head as he looked around him. "Next year, Jed wants to join scouts with his cousin Aaron, so that ought to be interesting."

"Ha...I can picture you volunteering for camp and playing *Chase the Flag*. It seems like yesterday we were the adventurous hikers, off to explore. Now it's our kids."

Matt laughed. "Don't know how much time I'll have for that. My practice is still growing. I'm working five days a week and every second Saturday. But yes, eventually, I'll be doing that kind of thing. I hear that Barry's extremely busy too. Congratulations on your new restaurant. I googled it, and it looks great. I've read many positive reviews on it."

"Thanks. Barry wants to treat you and Anna for dinner there when you come to visit. We'll get a babysitter for the kids and have a relaxing evening. Sound good?"

"Definitely. But only if I'm buying." Matt noticed her frown and explained. "Don't worry, it's a write-off, and you and Barry are only starting the business. Let me do this."

"We'll see. How about we cover the food? You can cover the booze. I doubt Barry would agree to anything more."

"Deal."

Noise from the boys distracted them.

Matt jumped up, jogging to the wrestling match the boys were engaged in. "Boys! Stop." Matt separated them, demanding explanations.

Danny didn't like the idea of taking turns. He had pushed Jed to the ground when Jed tried to take the plastic bat from him. Patiently, Matt talked to both of them. Soon Jed was swinging the bat, with Danny running to retrieve the ball.

"Well, that was fun. The first argument."

"Danny can be headstrong, so I'm sure it won't be the last. I'm surprised he listened so well to you." Ellen tapped her lip with her finger.

How much sharing should she do? She shrugged her shoulders. If she couldn't talk to Matt, she couldn't speak to anyone.

"Our family life is complicated. Barry's only home in the mornings until 11:00 or so, then he's not home until well after they're in bed. My boys' butt heads more than anything else."

"Don't worry. They'll figure it out. Our lifestyle's a lot different. I'm home every night except Wednesdays when I'm committed to my church meeting. Things will change once Anna gets back to work part-time, but we're dedicated to spending as much time as possible with our kids. We bike or go swimming with them every week. We spend a lot of time with Anna's sister and her family. I want to be involved in their lives like my dad was for me."

"Barry's dad died when he was around seven years old, so his vision of family life is different. He doesn't remember much of him, other than what photos tell him. His mother worked full-time once he started school. She was the original super-mom. She did it all, worked, looked after the house as well as the discipline. So, he's comfortable with a routine that has him working while I look after the kids and the house. We talk about that changing once the business is more established. I hope it works that way for us too."

"What else have you been up to, Ellen? Are you planning to go back to work when Sara's older? Weren't you doing some accounting at a bank somewhere?"

"Yes, I was part time at the Canada Trust branch in Oak Bay. They tell me I'm welcome to come back anytime, so we'll see. Right now, my hands are full. I don't think I could do both."

"Who wants a popsicle?" Ellen's mom came outside loaded with goodies for the kids, followed by Anna carrying cold beers for the adults.

"Now, *this* is a reunion." Matt sighed as he guzzled almost half a bottle of chilled beer.

Anna hugged Ellen and gave her a beer too. "So nice to see you. It's been way too long. Look at these kids. They're beautiful."

"So are yours. All kids are, right?" Ellen hadn't realized how parched she'd become. She took a sip, then another to quench her thirst. It was so good to be home, surrounded by her family and cousins. She watched the men with the children and smiled. This was what family life should look like, making memories like these. As photos were taken, Ellen wondered if Barry would regret not being part of these times. She hoped his business was worth it.

SATURDAY MORNING ARRIVED with a blue sky and temperatures in the high sixties. October weather in the Valley was usually mild and comfortable. Surrounded by mountains, the Alberni Valley could experience temperatures in the nineties during the summer, then below freezing temperatures with snow in the winter. Unlike Victoria or Parksville, the mountains trapped the weather, causing definite seasonal differences.

Matt, Ellen, her dad, and two excited boys drove to Athol Street and purchased tickets for the steam engine train ride. Leaving the rejuvenated 1911 Alberni Pacific Roundhouse, they would have an hour's journey to the historic McLean's Sawmill.

Jed and Danny were tearing about, hardly able to contain their excitement. Anna and Ellen's mom decided to stay home with the girls. The noise from the steam engine and the occasional shrieking whistle at road crossings would probably be too frightful for the young ones. The adults carried backpacks with essentials for picnics, water, and potential emergency supplies.

"Danny, get back over here, stay with your papa!" Ellen chased him from the loading platform back into the waiting area.

Ellen's dad caught Danny and threw him in the air, then sat him on his shoulders so he could spot the train's arrival. About thirty people had already shown up to board the train to the restored forestry site.

"Jed, look at this." Matt took his son aside and showed him a site map of the refurbished village with over thirty buildings and structures. Pictures of rebuilt logging trucks, graders, and lumber carriers dotted the camp.

"Wow. Can we go on them? They look really old. Do they still work?"

"I doubt you can go inside, but we can look around them. It says some are still working. See that sawmill? It first started in 1926, and it's fully restored now. That means it still runs too. So does the steam donkey that helped the men move the logs. I don't understand how, but I'm sure we'll find out while we're there. There used to be a bunkhouse for the workers to live in, and they would have meals at a cook shack. It's been repaired too, with stoves and ice boxes."

"Ice boxes?"

"No such things as refrigerators at the camp when they first started, so that's how they kept their food cold. This is going to be fun. We'll see what it was like back then. It was a dangerous life, really tough. Everything is rebuilt to look like it was almost a hundred years ago. Neat, hey?"

"Yup. Umm, Dad?" Jed's voice was barely more than a whisper. He scuffed the toe of his runner into the floor as he avoided looking at him.

"Yes? What's going on, buddy?"

"Umm. I don't think I like Danny much."

"Really?" Matt looked at his son's worried expression.

"He's not very nice. He knocked Lisa over a couple of times, and he stomped on my foot this morning then laughed like crazy. Sometimes he elbows me when no one's looking."

"Hmm. I'll keep an eye out for that. His dad is hardly ever around. I think it's his way of getting attention. He's probably jealous of you."

"Why would he want to make people mad at him?"

"Who knows? But we'll watch out for you. Stick close to me and Uncle Fred, and you'll be ok. Danny will be so excited with everything at the mill that he won't have time to bother you."

Two short whistles sounded.

"All aboard." called the conductor.

An engine with two passenger cars followed by a caboose had just pulled in. Steam shushed from the wheels as it braked.

The family reunited and surrendered their tickets before receiving a stamp on their hand for their return trip home. The boys claimed the window seat on each side of the center aisle, with the men sitting beside them. Ellen sat behind her dad and Danny. The leather seats, perhaps comfortable at one time, were now rock hard.

Soon all the passengers were on board, and the whistle blew to the delight of young and old alike. The wheels groaned and clanged as the train slowly gathered speed. *They were off*. Danny's face was glowing with adventure. Matt glanced over to Ellen and winked at her. This weekend was exactly what they all needed. Family time.

The train passed the Somass Sawmill, then veered off. Before crossing Stamp Ave, it blew a warning whistle. The boys covered their ears and hooted with laughter, causing the adults to grin at their excitement. As they entered a wooded section, a half-mile later, Danny pointed at two horses galloping toward them, with riders in cowboy gear.

"Look, look, Papa! The robbers are here." Danny's voice became shrill with anticipation as he waved at the pair sprinting towards them.

A second later, the conductor announced that bandits

were chasing them, but they could outrun them, not to be worried.

Jed scampered over to Danny's side to have a good look through the open windows at the horses racing alongside. Both cowboys had masks around their eyes and cowboy hats tied under their chins.

"Here they come! Uncle Fred, they're getting closer."

"It's ok, no worries, boys, this train will stay ahead of them for sure. Look, they're backing off now."

"I hoped that they were going to jump on board, just like in the old movies." Jed's hands were gesturing wildly. "That would've been *so* cool."

Uncle Fred moved to the other aisle beside Matt and let the boys sit side by side as they discovered the joys of riding on a steam train.

Ellen snapped photos of the wind blowing through the open windows, mussing the boys' hair. Their eyes were alight with their imagination running wild. As Matt watched the boys enjoying a fantasy play out in front of them, he glanced over at Ellen, pleased to see the rosy glow on her face. He needed to stay in touch with his cousin more often.

~

THANK GOD, Ellen sighed to herself. Almost home from the train station. The boys were dozing in the car, giving the adults some long-needed silence.

"That was a great day, Matt. Feels so good to share it with family. I have several videos to show Barry when we get home. Are we still on for a hike around Sproat Lake Park tomorrow?"

"Anna and I have decided that we'll join you. We'll stop

and have a picnic lunch there, then walk to the First Nations petroglyphs before heading out to Ucluelet. We'll bank another family memory."

"Sounds like fun. I haven't been there since I married. The children and I will be leaving for home Monday morning. It's been a good break. I can't wait for you guys to join us for a few nights."

Matt ruffled Ellen's hair. "We're looking forward to that too, kiddo. Make sure you have a sitter for our night out."

Ellen grinned. "You bet. I'll have Katy over and maybe ask her to bring her friend so that it won't be too crazy for her."

"Good idea. These four are a handful for both of us, let alone teenagers."

THE DAY WAS WARM AGAIN. The sky was bright blue with only an occasional light breeze that rippled through the park's falling maple leaves. Only a few couples were walking about, so choosing a picnic table in the sunshine was easy.

Anna's mom disappeared with a bag of dollar store knickknacks to hide along the path to the First Nations petroglyph. The family trailed a few minutes later. They stepped onto a floating platform to view the worn carvings of mystical lake creatures on a rock face stretching high above them.

"Those are funny-looking fish, Mommy." Danny pointed to one that reminded Ellen of an octopus.

"That one looks like a dog swimming, see the ears?" Jed studied the pictures carefully then glanced towards his dad for answers.

"Probably not a dog, but maybe a wolf. And see this fish?

With the curved back and the fin on top? That could be a whale. First nations people told stories by carving pictures of powerful or scary animals."

"Why?" Both boys responded at the same time.

"We don't know. These were carved a very long time ago before the tribes had tools like we have. They used stone chisels and dyed the paintings with juices of berries, among other things."

Papa lifted Danny onto his shoulders and brought him closer to see the other fish depicted in the scene. "Some folks think they were trying to scare other tribes away from here. It must have taken them a long, long time to carve them deep enough that we can still see them thousands of years later."

As they returned to their picnic area, Aunt Claire told the boys to look around, that sometimes tourists left treasures for people to find near the petroglyphs. A boisterous search between the two boys found small airplane gliders to assemble, whistles, and two little boats with wind-up propellers.

The boys enjoyed flying the airplanes, then went down to the shoreline, taking their shoes and socks off. Wading up to their knees, they wound the boat propellers up, engaging in boat races while the adults prepared lunch. Afterward, Matt and Uncle Fred took the boys to the shore to teach them how to skip rocks, distancing themselves for safety.

A scream pierced the air.

Papa raced over to Danny. "Are you ok, son?"

An errant stone had ricocheted off something, bouncing back sideways. It had caught Danny unaware just as he turned around, hitting him on the upper left cheekbone. Papa picked him up then brought him to the picnic table, checking for damage and trying to calm the sobs and shrieks of anger.

Matt joined his uncle, trying to soothe and quieten Danny while searching for gauze pads in his emergency bag. Jed was beside them, his face white with shock.

"Sorry, Danny, sorry. I didn't mean to hit you. I wasn't aiming at you. Dad, I don't know how that happened." Jed's voice was quavering.

"I know, son. He's going to have a bruise, but he'll be fine. You must have hit some driftwood near the shore, and then it ricocheted back."

"Papa, Jed hurt me. He hurt me on purpose."

"No, he didn't. It was an accident, Danny-boy. You're fine. These things happen. He threw a rock that hit something and made it jump back. You were in the wrong place at the wrong time. It was an accident. He said he was sorry."

"I don't care. I hate my cousin."

"Don't say that. Come on now, Jed feels bad that you were hurt." Papa had made a makeshift gauze icebag from the cooler then placed it against Danny's face. "Hold it there for a few minutes, and it will help." Papa saw Ellen coming over and put his hand up to stop her. "We're fine over here." He noticed that whenever Ellen was near Danny, the boy would become cranky and even more demanding.

Ellen nodded, realizing her dad's intent.

Danny glared at Jed, who was staring at him with a sheepish look on his face. Suddenly, Danny jumped from his papa's care, dropping the ice pack, and ran towards Jed, pushing him over. He sat on him, but before anything else could happen, Matt was there pulling Danny off him.

"Hey buddy, that's not how guys handle accidents. Jed said he was sorry. You don't need to turn this into a fight."

"He hurt me! And I'm going to hurt him."

"That's not how cousins and friends handle things. You both need to shake hands then say you're sorry to each other. After that, you can have fun again."

"I don't want to have fun with him anymore," Danny whined.

"Hmm. Guess you're still a baby then. Babies don't know how to play nice or to say sorry. I thought you were old enough to go to school. I guess I was wrong."

"I am old enough to go to school. I'm in grade one."

"Really? Hmm. Most teachers don't want kids that can't get along with each other or start fights. Accidents happen. Teachers expect kids to shake hands and be friends after." Matt sat on the sand next to Danny, pulling his knees up to his chest as he talked with him. "Kids that can't shake hands get sent home. They don't get to stay at school."

"Really?" Danny sat stock still, thinking about what Jed's dad said to him.

"Yes. So, I think it would be a great idea to show your mom and your papa that you truly are a big boy. Go shake hands with Jed."

Danny looked around at the others who were busy packing the picnic and getting ready to leave. "Ok." Danny scrambled to his feet and walked toward Jed. He offered his hand. "Sorry, Jed. But you hurt me, and it made me mad."

"I'm sorry too, Danny. I didn't hit you on purpose. Are you ok now?"

"Yup. Hardly even hurts now."

Jed came closer and inspected the bruise forming underneath Danny's left eye. "I hope you don't get a black eye."

"Do you think I will? That would make me look tough, wouldn't it?" Danny giggled at the idea and ran back to the water.

Matt watched the boys wade into the water and wind up their boats for a final ride along the shore. He smiled at the two of them, the incident over already. He walked over to his cousin, hitching his thumb behind him at the boys.

"Ellen? Don't worry about things, ok? Accidents happen, and they're just boys. They fight sometimes. Then they make up like they did today. No big deal."

"Oh Matt, sometimes I wonder."

"You're a great mom, Ellen. But never let Danny see he's driving you crazy. He may be young, but he's smart. Once kids that age get your number, they'll push those buttons over and over. Keep it simple. Ignore the small stuff. It's better for both of you that way."

"I can't help it. Sometimes, I worry. Barry's hardly ever home, and those two guys are like oil and water. It's like Danny gets so wound up around Barry that he flies off the handle at anything his dad tells him to do. It's not fun. I'm so embarrassed that he did the same to Jed." Ellen frowned and spread her hands. "Sometimes, I don't know how to handle him."

"Don't lose any sleep over it. A lot is going on in his life right now, so he's acting out. He'll discover how to get along. He'll have to learn more self-control if he wants to get along at school. You'll see."

"I hope so. This single parenting is a lot harder than it looks. Since Sara's born, Danny has a common case of jealousy, add that to the mix, and it's no wonder some days that I'm a nervous wreck."

"Don't let yourself go there, Ellen. It's not a good place. You know that. If you need help, you can afford it–get some. Get a sitter and go shopping if Barry's too busy to take you somewhere. Take some time for yourself, sweetie. It's not good for the kids if you get overstressed, you have to make sure you don't push yourself again."

"I hear you. It's tough sometimes, but I'm ok." Ellen reached up and hugged Matt. "It's so great visiting with you and your family again. I can't wait for you to join us. We'll have fun, I promise."

"We have reservations at the Best Western, but we'll spend most of our time together. I didn't want to overcrowd you." Matt winked at her. "Besides, it's another write-off."

CHAPTER 7

After a whirlwind visit with Matt, Anna, and their children, the return to everyday life was welcome at first. Ellen would catch herself smiling at a memory of the family at McLean's Mill or Sproat Lake.

Barry had welcomed Matt and Anna lavishly. The dinner and service at his restaurant were superb. As expected, a brief argument ensued about the bill, although Barry graciously allowed Matt to pay the liquor tab in the end. The staff was surprised at the generous tip, so everyone was left with a happy memory.

As November progressed, Danny became used to the routine of full school days. Mrs. Scott, a neighbor on the next street over, also had a boy in the same class and would take the two of them to school in the morning. In rainy weather, Ellen picked the kids up in her car after school. But on clear days, she would take Lisa in the stroller and walk the boys back home at 2:30. She often stopped by the park, letting the children expend some energy before returning home.

Sara's afternoon naps gave Ellen time to catch up on

housework, then take time for a cup of tea. She loved looking after her home and children, but the success of Barry's new restaurant also left a void in her heart. Every aspect of The Carvery consumed Barry's life and made her feel isolated.

After the time spent with her family this fall, it was more difficult than ever to return to the mundane and predictable schedule her life had become. She reflected that it was hard to figure out being lonely when she was so busy looking after her family, but it was the closest feeling she could associate with the heaviness inside.

Ellen began looking forward to the clear days when she took the children to the park. She always looked around, hoping to see Stephen, the now-familiar stranger who had helped Danny. She'd never admit how her heart would quicken and how quickly and pleasantly an afternoon could go by if he were present.

Learning that Stephen had been studying social work in Halifax, Ellen was glad when he had resumed studies here. He was supporting himself by bartending weekends. It gave him lots of opportunities to study human behavior, Stephen had commented. He was a sensitive, intuitive person, and Ellen was alternately at ease with him. then uncomfortable. He was three years her junior, so she tried viewing him as the younger brother she never had.

A few weeks before Christmas, she saw him again. He had rented a room over a garage nearby. Ellen often saw him biking home. She watched him approach her as she settled on the bench. As usual, Danny was already on the monkey bars.

"Hello, stranger, I haven't seen you in a few weeks." Ellen smiled warmly, her heart beating slightly faster.

"That long? I was working for Mr. Mike's for a while. But

I quit yesterday. Not enough to live on. People don't tip much there, so I'll look someplace else."

"Why don't you try our restaurant? I'll talk to Barry. He could probably use another bartender. Wages aren't great, but the tips average $70 to 100 per night easily. Then you could afford to continue your studies during the day and live in a decent place."

"How are you going to tell him you know me? I don't think he'd be impressed that you've—adopted me."

She laughed. "I don't think Barry would be impressed that I picked you up in the park alright, but he already knows a few things about you. Danny talks about you sometimes." She suddenly had an idea. "Why don't you volunteer to help with morning Kindergarten for a week or two? I could tell him that's when I met you during your course studies. That would cover us if it slipped that we've met at the park."

"Why even bother, Ellen? Why lie?"

Ellen fidgeted, her gaze flitting anywhere but into his. "Barry's working constantly. Lately, he's showing signs of being jealous. Barry knows I get lonely, and then I guess he worries about that. We've had arguments about how much he works. I don't think Barry could understand a platonic friendship," she explained. She looked down, then stamped her feet, trying to warm them.

"I get it. I'll come tomorrow. Let's see how it goes."

She had watched him debate the idea in his mind. She was pleased when he decided to let her help. She smiled. "Great. We'll have you working as much as you want by Christmas," she promised.

True to her word, Ellen had introduced Stephen's name into the conversation in a timely way, and Stephen was interviewed then hired. Once he completed his certificate in social work, he postponed his plans for a degree. He enjoyed working with the young crowd, and within two years, Barry had promoted him to beverage manager. It took a load off of Barry to hand over the responsibilities of ordering and stocking the liquor supplies, organizing work schedules, and staffing problems.

STEPHEN WAS A WELL-LIKED BOSS. He had a sense of humor combined with a no-nonsense policy that the younger staff appreciated and respected. Barry had grown to depend on him also, often inviting him to the house to discuss business matters and occasionally having dinner with them, much to Stephen's pleasure.

Stephen set the table while he surreptitiously studied the attractive woman cooking before him. It took all his concentration to hide the love he had for her. Stephen dreamt of running his fingers through her thick, wavy hair and tasting those full soft lips. He had grown more attracted to her and had fought to keep his distance when he first began working at The Carvery. After all, she was married with two children. As far as he was concerned, though, it wasn't much of a marriage. She drew him to her like a magnet, yet he was sure she wasn't even aware of it.

Platonic my ass, he thought, as he remembered the countless times he had daydreamed of making love to her. He'd reach a decision, though. He couldn't live without her. Somehow, he'd patiently wait for the time she'd recognize it for more than that.

When she smiled at him, her genuine concern shone through her hazel eyes. He wished there was something more there. But it would come, he was sure of it. She made the move to B.C. less lonesome, gave him something to hope for.

∽

BARRY AND ELLEN moved up accordingly, with the success of their enterprise. They had another appointment to view a home on Lockhaven Place, overlooking Telegraph Cove. Ellen admired the older homes in this upper middle-class area as they drove along, then gasped in disbelief as Barry turned their car into a long, curved driveway. The delicate scent of hyacinths in a bed of daffodils and tulips wafted through her open window.

"Are you sure we can afford this?" Ellen whispered as the real estate agent went ahead to unlock the door.

"No sweat, sweetheart. We've been living on almost the same wage I had when I worked at Oak Bay, right?" She nodded, then he continued, "We've been making great money, and you've been great with the budget. When I sold the shares in Pacific Resources last month, I doubled the money I put in. With the equity of our old house and the fifty thousand I've pulled out of our investments, we'll have this place or one like it, more than half paid when we move in."

He'd been working night and day for the last three years, ensuring the success of The Carvery. This home would be proof of it. As he watched Ellen's face, he was overwhelmed again by her beauty and by his good fortune to have found her. She seldom complained of the long hours he was away from her, but he knew she missed him. The children adored her, and she did an excellent job with them, even if she was a trifle too lenient with Danny. He would put a lot more time in with that one as soon as things calmed down a bit.

The house wasn't right on the water, but at the end of a short rising road on Cadboro Point Peninsula. The view of the cove and the Strait of Juan de Fuca was commanding. The grounds were immaculate, the freshly cropped grass a rich carpet of deep green. Sculptured sections of flowers and shrubs accented the home, and their riotous colors perfectly contrasted the understated blue-gray exterior.

Once inside, they wandered slowly through the home, appreciating the full bay windows featured in the enormous living room. The dining room and study also occupied the front of the house, and their large picture windows promised them spectacular views of the ocean in all her moods. The real estate agent had picked his time well. Early evening in September, Barry and Ellen stood spell-bound, holding hands as the sun began to set.

Thin, wispy clouds stretched across to the distant mountains of Washington State. As the sun sank into the deep blue waters of the Strait, the twilight deepened from their initial pale pink to mauve. The tranquility touched a chord they'd been seeking—peace and relaxation after the hectic schedule their lives had become.

As the mauve faded quickly into twilight, Barry turned to Ellen and pulled her into his arms. "This will be our corner of heaven right here, sweetheart," he said as he kissed her gently.

"Definitely. It's perfect." Ellen replied.

They climbed the winding staircase to the second floor, choosing the rooms that Danny and Sara would have. There were four large bedrooms. The three smaller ones had each their own small ensuite, which had impressed Ellen, but the best was still to come. Their master bedroom was as big as their present living room.

When they checked out the ensuite, they drew their

breaths in awe. A beautifully decorated room complete with a jacuzzi and a king-size marble shower surprised them. A white ledge between the jacuzzi and the tall, narrow windows held a variety of potted plants and ferns. Different shapes and colors of candles surrounded the oval ivory tub, and Ellen couldn't help but feel the sensuality of the room. White wicker shelves held thick fluffy towels just begging to be used.

As Ellen glanced into the several strategically placed mirrors, she saw Barry's gaze on hers, promising her unforgettable nights.

"This is the best part of the whole house," she teased.

"We're going to have fun making up for lost time right here," Barry growled softly.

As they made the final tour through the backyard to meet their agent, they both knew what their decision would be.

THE SPRING after they moved in, Ellen called her parents to come for a weekend. With the spare bedroom now a guest room, they had already made use of it. Paula and Ken, who were engaged and living together in Vancouver, had come over for a weekend. Stephen had spent the night several times also, after lengthy month-end reports. Ellen had put the finishing touches on her dream home and was ready to present the evidence of their hard-earned success to her parents.

Ellen sprinted to the door and flung it open while watching her father's classic '65 Malibu drive up their laneway. She ran outside to greet them, calling the children to join her.

"Dad! Mom!" She hugged her father tightly, smelling the tangy, familiar scent of his Old Spice cologne. "I'm so glad you came." She kissed her mother too and asked how the trip had been.

"Traffic was terrible, dear. Crazy, wasn't it, Fred?" Her mother shook her head, then called Sara and Danny to her, kissed them, and handed them each a box of smarties.

The kids jumped around excitedly, begging Ellen to let them eat their treats right away. Ellen agreed. After all, it wasn't often Papa and Nana came to visit. So what if their clean clothes would soon be a chocolate mess?

"Well, what do you think?" Ellen asked as she spread her arms to encompass the view.

"Fantastic, Ellen. It's gorgeous here," her father replied, gazing around him. He walked the property, alternately praising the landscaping, then the ocean views. "Let me know if you decide to buy a boat and do some fishing. I could show Barry a trick or two."

"I don't know if he's ever fished, Dad. He lost his father when he was very young. I don't think there were many opportunities. Maybe one day, he'll slow down enough to get a boat. I hope so."

"Okay, let's go see inside this mansion," he teased as he helped his wife into the house.

Her mother smiled at her, nodding with admiration at the layout and décor that bespoke Ellen's taste. Hardwood floors shone, area carpets in the living and dining areas welcomed cozy living. The navy-blue countertops atop white cabinets provided an elegant contrast. Combined with window toppers in navy with red and yellow flowers on them, they gave a cheerful ambiance to the heart of the house. Ellen brought them to the spacious family room, which held a large TV, entertainment center, and their toys.

"Let me have your suitcase, Mom. Your bedroom is upstairs. I've painted that room in your favorite soft mauve. I hope you like it."

"Oh sweetie, you've done a beautiful job decorating your home. I'm so proud of you."

Ellen saw her mom's eyes tear up as she looked around her.

"Thanks, Mom. It's been a lot of work for both of us, but we're very excited to be here. We have lots of room to entertain now, so I hope you and Dad come more often and stay."

"I'm sure we'll try. We're getting older now, and your dad tires more easily these days. I know it's easier for us to come here than for you to come to our home, so we'll figure it out. Congratulations, sweetheart. I'm glad you're happy."

Ellen saw the look of pride in her parents' eyes, and suddenly Ellen considered herself honorable again. After nine years of marriage, the guilt of her impromptu wedding finally disappeared. She hadn't made the biggest mistake of her life after all. Look where she was now—Independent, self-sufficient, and on cloud nine.

The weekend passed quickly. Barry had Stephen cover for him while taking his father-in-law golfing Saturday afternoon at the prestigious Uplands Golf Club, overlooking the ocean. Ellen took her mother and the children to the Imax theater to watch a documentary on T-Rex, which was scarier than Ellen had assumed it would be. However, the kids loved it.

They splurged on ice cream afterward at the Gyro Park on Cadboro Bay near her home. Ellen breathed a sigh of contentment. For the first time, mother and daughter met on equal grounds as friends. At last, Barry's success finally earned him the long-sought-after acceptance and appreciation from her mother.

On Sunday, they drove to the Parliament Buildings then toured the picturesque downtown sites, finishing the afternoon in Beacon Hill Park. For the first time, her parents ate dinner with them at Barry's restaurant. They were impressed with the food and the service, although they found it too noisy for their taste.

The raucous din of young people talking and laughing, competing against the music, was a little much for them. However, there was no denying the place was full of people enjoying themselves or the successful life it had provided them.

Ellen waved goodbye later that weekend, with a genuine smile on her lips and in her heart. Finally, she and Barry had earned her parents' approval, as well as their respect.

CHAPTER 8

"What the hell are you talking about?" thundered Barry.

"Cool your jets, man! I'm just letting you know what I heard. What you do is up to you. It might be a pile of bullshit, but it might be true. It's worth checking out, though, isn't it?" Stephen shot back. He walked out of the office, slamming the door. *That's the thanks I get,* Stephen fumed.

Barry stared at the door. Pete wouldn't have betrayed him, would he? Barry knew some people in Victoria raised their eyebrows at Pete Zalinsky.

Old money always had some disdain for people like Pete. Son of an immigrant Ukrainian stevedore, he had the street smarts, the connections, and the guts to take chances. His generosity incurred special favors when called upon. Inside information, illegal as it was, catapulted him into the world of power and wealth. Technically, Pete stayed on this side of the law. That's all that had concerned Barry at the start of their silent partnership. You couldn't fault a guy for being shrewd. Or could you?

Everyone was on tender-hooks with the uncertainty of

the new millennium. The world had survived Y2K, and the boom in Silicon Valley had changed the focus of everyday lives. The cost of living was soaring, which impacted his restaurant.

He'd had to raise his prices twice in the past year when his staff were threatening to leave if they didn't get better benefits. Barry had fumed at that. *Who ever heard of benefits in a restaurant?*

Ever since al Qaeda had bombed the USS Cole in Yemen, there was a tremor of apprehension throughout the world. Markets were trending downwards, which made people look for alternative investments.

Barry recalled Pete advising him to get into real estate development. Pete was hot to develop a section of land on Sawtooth Ridge overlooking Lake Chelan in Washington State. Not only would they make a fortune selling the old stands of Douglas Fir, but the area was also ripe for a resort vacationland. Luxurious condominiums encompassing an 18-hole golf course on the shores of a crystal-clear lake would sell like hot cakes.

Thank God he had been too busy to get even remotely interested. If what Steve told him was true, he'd be lucky to salvage his restaurants. He dialed the phone. "Hi, is Pete in?" Melanie knew his voice, so Barry knew his call would be forwarded, unlike some other callers, he guessed.

"For you, he's always here. Can you hold for a minute?" Melanie asked before completing the connection.

"Barry. How are ya? What can I do for ya?" Pete's familiar booming voice sounded as optimistic as ever.

Barry wavered a moment, then plunged. "Not much right now, although I need some info on some stuff going on around here. Can you meet me for dinner tonight?"

"Sorry, can't. I'm up to my eyeballs in frigging paperwork."

Barry could picture him chewing on his cigar.

"What about drinks later then? Around quitting time, say around midnight?"

"Sure, why not. See ya later." Pete signed off.

Barry sighed. He didn't want Pete getting angry with him, but he had a right to know the scoop too. Barry considered other people he could contact and dialed Wayne Mitchell's number. Wayne was head of the Victoria Real Estate Board and a member of the same Lions club. He lit another cigarette while he waited for Wayne to answer his call.

Shit! Barry pushed his chair back and paced his office, running his fingers through his hair. What the hell was he going to do? Wayne had reluctantly confirmed the story Steve had told him.

It was only a matter of time. Pete was going under. He had invested heavily into land on Sawtooth Ridge. He and others like him hadn't counted on the strong opposition from the environmentalists. They began lobbying state congress, bombarding the press with their issues of saving the vast stands of old-growth Douglas Fir.

Now, it looked like they had won. A bill was presented before congress last week to designate a moratorium on logging on the Ridge until such a time a decision was made whether to designate it a state park. Against such a determined group of nature lovers, money didn't always win.

Barry wondered how much he'd have to raise to buy Pete's share. His restaurants in Victoria, one on Johnson Street and the other on Shelbourne, were highly successful. Last year he opened the third one in Nanaimo, a smaller city, sixty miles north of Victoria. Although promising, it was only turning a slight profit. That potential success was still to come.

Barry was confident it would do even better than the Shelbourne Street Carvery. Nanaimo had a strong industrialized base and an active sports-minded community. That community ensured plenty of outgoing people were ready to party with the money to do it. The three operations' net value was probably worth a little less than a million dollars, with the lion's share being his original Johnson Street Carvery.

He called Steve in. "I have to bat some ideas around. I'm sorry about blowing up at you, but I'm glad you gave me the news. There's a rumor going around about Pete's deal turning sour. I'll meet him tonight and see what position we're in, but I need to calm down first before I blow this thing."

"Shit, man, what can I say?" Steve spread his hands before him.

"I'm going to try and buy him out. I can't raise all of the $350,000, which would be his share, so I'll have to break up the chain. Luckily, he only owns 55% of the first one, although it's worth the most. The rest belongs to me."

"Don't sell that one, Barry. If you have enough equity in the Shelbourne location, sell that one. If you can show a financial plan trimming the operations down on the other two, I'm sure the bank would issue a new mortgage, even if it's slightly higher interest. You've proven yourself. You're the one that made this place work—not Pete. Everyone knows it."

Barry massaged his left temple, then nodded. He had worked his ass off for the first ten years he owned the restaurants, careful to expand only when a good opportunity arose. Last year, he hired managers for each outlet, then cut his sixty-hour work week to an average of forty. His elevated blood pressure and a renewed determination to spend more time at home prompted the decision.

It also gave Barry a chance to branch out and make contacts in the political system. Influential friends made through the Lions' service club had approached him to attend the Liberal party conference. Well-known and respected, Barry was encouraged to run for public office.

He wanted to get involved, but he knew it would have to go on hold for now. His business had to come first. It was time for him to get back to work.

"You can't trust him, Barry. Not anymore. He should've come to you himself and let you know he was in trouble."

"I know. I told Pete to hold back, but he was so sure of himself, he didn't listen. I have to buy him out. Completely."

"Stand your ground, or he'll take you down with him. Make him a low-ball offer. You know he's going to push the numbers up no matter what the first offer is. He's the one that's hurting, and you're his only hope out."

As ashtrays filled to overflowing, the hours dragged on. Neither seemed to notice the stink of smoke that filled the room, the stale air, or the lingering odor of hidden panic. Steve and Barry exhausted every possibility.

No matter what Pete said tonight, Barry decided, it was time to buy him out. He couldn't afford to be associated with the publicity that Pete's predicament would produce.

Tomorrow, The Carvery on Shelbourne would go for sale at a price that investors should snap up quickly. It was a modest place, and although only three years old, it had a good profit margin. Net, he should realize around $200,000 he hoped. Barry knew the bank would be receptive to restructuring the original mortgage on the Johnson Street Carvery. They were always offering him money to expand or upgrade. Steve agreed that a proposal to offer Pete a flat $300,000 would probably be counter-offered at 350,000, which was Barry's hope.

Barry stood up and shook Steve's hand. "Thanks, Steve, you've got me stoked. I'm not taking no for an answer. I'll get out of this mess."

"Be careful. Don't go postal on Pete. He's not someone who will take it. Good luck tonight."

"Thanks, buddy," Barry answered hoarsely, his voice gruff from the constant smoking and talking. He rubbed the back of his neck, trying to loosen the knots of tension. His mouth tasted like shit. He suddenly realized how tired and hungry he was. He reached for his jacket.

"I'm going home. I'll grab a bite to eat, then rest a few hours. I'll be back around 11:00."

"It's all good. I'll look after things here."

BARRY WAS SELDOM home for dinner on weekends, preferring to eat a large lunch before leaving home or eating a late meal at the restaurant. He arrived home unexpectedly, and his exhaustion was evident in his features. Ellen caught a whiff of smelly cigarette smoke clinging to him as he passed by her.

"Hi, hon, what's up? You look beat," Ellen observed as she headed for the fridge, looking for something quick to make him if he was hungry.

"Yea, I'm bone tired. I figured I'd come home for dinner tonight, take a rest. I'll go back later to close up. I'm going to see Pete tonight too."

"There's leftover lasagna, or I could make you a Denver omelet?" She shrugged. "Sorry, I wasn't expecting you."

"How about an omelet and a glass of milk? I'm all coffeed out, and I only need something light. I'm going to grab a quick shower." He climbed the stairs slowly, undoing his tie as he went along.

Ellen quickly chopped some mushrooms, green onions, and tomatoes, then whipped three eggs up. Hearing the shower already running, she'd bet he'd return in his housecoat. Ellen heated the frypan until the butter was sizzling and poured in the ingredients. She pulled out the grated cheddar cheese then set the table, all the while wondering what the problem was.

Barry walked into the kitchen and put his hands on his wife's shoulders. He leaned over to kiss her cheek. "That smells so good. I'm starving."

"Go sit down. It's almost ready." Ellen spread the cheddar onto the middle of the omelet then flipped each side over to form a pocket to melt it. Another minute later, she slid the omelet onto a plate.

Barry poured himself a glass of milk, and another of orange juice, then tipped the container towards Ellen, offering her a drink.

"Sure, juice would be great. You're looking better. Smelling better too."

"Sorry. Tough day."

"Want to talk?" Ellen sat at the table beside him and crossed her legs. "Anything I can do? I haven't seen you this uptight since you started this business."

"I don't know. Maybe. I haven't got it all figured out yet." Barry concentrated on his food. "This is delicious, sweetheart. It's hitting the spot." Barry pushed his empty plate away from him, then leaned back, stifling a yawn. "You're right. It's business again. I've been checking out some rumors today. It looks like Pete's over-extended himself on a real estate deal. He put his share of The Carvery up for collateral". His voice was devoid of emotion, drained.

"What?" she cried out. "How could Pete do that without your consent?"

"Beats me. I hope to get answers tonight."

"So, what do you think is going to happen?"

"I've spent the afternoon talking it over with Stephen, and I've decided to offer to buy him out. I'll sell the Shelbourne Street Carvery then keep the other two. I'll have to trim the operations down and re-organize our finances."

"Why don't you get rid of the Nanaimo branch?" Ellen asked.

"That was my first theory. But it's turning such a good profit even though it's only been open a year. It has almost double the capacity compared to the Shelbourne location. Nanaimo has nothing comparable, so we should do well there with more guidance."

"Which means?" Ellen prodded.

"Which means Steve moves up from liquor management to restaurant manager at Johnson Street. He'll do fine with the promotion. I'll take over the Nanaimo branch. It's too new and too big to send Stephen there. I'll spend Thursday through to Sunday in Nanaimo, then let an assistant manager handle the slower three days. When I'm back here, I'll check the operation here."

"What about the house? Should we sell it? I love it here, but if it has to go, it has to go. We'll get something else when we get back on our feet." Ellen watched Barry pacing back and forth in the kitchen, his anxiety returning as he considered his dilemma. His eyes darted around, looking for the best way out of this mess.

"No way. If absolutely necessary, I may put a second mortgage on it. I hope not. We may have to use our home equity as collateral for a new business restructuring. It depends on how much Pete will want for his portion of Johnson Street and what the net profit is on the Shelbourne sale. I'll have to make up the difference, so I've got to cut corners and push the business even harder for a while."

"What about me? Could I work there doing something? I'm a good bookkeeper," she offered.

"Let's wait and see. What about all the volunteer work you're doing at the school?"

"You know I love it, but it doesn't bring in the paychecks. I could go in to work at 9:00 after the kids go to school. I could arrange for Sara to go to her Tracy's for an hour after school and pick her up on the way home. The girls get along so well. She'd be thrilled with that. Her mom could probably use the extra money each month."

"Thanks, hon." Barry came back then pulled her in his arms, kissing her gently on the lips.

"For what? The omelet or the free labor?" Ellen joked.

"You never doubt me," Barry replied. "Even now, you don't even think twice. You pick up the challenge and march in."

"I've always believed life's a roller coaster with a lot of peaks and valleys before it straightens out. I've never bailed out, and you haven't either, so we're bound to make it." She laughed. "We're too stubborn not to."

Ellen stood behind him as he sat at the table, slowly kneading her fingers into his tense shoulder and neck muscles. Massage was something she enjoyed doing when he came home stressed. It helped him relax and share his problems more often than not. Thankfully, most times, the tension was more from exhaustion than a problem.

Barry crawled into the bed in the wee hours of the morning. He leaned over and kissed Ellen on her forehead. "It's done, sweetheart. We have a deal."

"I tried to wait up for you. I guess I dozed off."

"No worries. We'll talk more tomorrow."

The next few months were hectic. Pete had agreed to the sale, somewhat reluctantly. He wasn't used to being in the passenger seat. With the sale of Shelbourne Street Carvery and the bank's cooperation, Barry was back on track, entirely in charge of his life.

CHAPTER 9

There was no getting around the dilemma. Ellen tried to avoid it, believing that Sara needed more time to settle down in her grade three class.

Her bubbly daughter was showing signs of depression. She picked at her food, barely eating any at dinnertime, then complained of tummy aches. Circles appeared under her eyes, probably from the tossing and turning Ellen heard going on in Sara's bedroom. She would go into her room, smoothing Sara's hair from her sweaty forehead. She'd rearrange her blankets and ask if she were having a nightmare.

Sara's answer was always the same. No nightmare, she just didn't feel good.

Ellen tried to find out what was bothering her, but Sara kept shrugging and refusing to answer. Two days ago, Ellen had enough. If it took an argument, so be it.

She confronted Sara, who burst into tears before she revealed her problem. Now Ellen would meet her teacher on Monday at 3:30, then get to the bottom of it.

"I'M SORRY, Mrs. Andrews, I disagree with you. Sara has always been a happy and cooperative child. There's some sort of problem going on. She's been getting progressively worse about going to school since she entered your class."

"Now look, Mrs. Peterson, I hate to argue, but your child is used to getting her way," the bespectacled, gray-haired teacher declared, her palm slapped the desk as if that was the end of the story. "She's lazy in class and often hasn't completed the board work assigned during the day. I'm simply firm with her."

The hardline response made Ellen's eyebrows rise in surprise. "I don't think a child in grade three should be as tense about going to school as she is. She has trouble sleeping sometimes, and she seems to think you *pick* on her." Ellen crossed her hands on her lap as she tried to keep her composure while calmly discussing the teacher's attitude.

"And, of course, you believe her." Mrs. Andrews's voice was full of contempt for another overprotective parent. "Come to the classroom. See for yourself the work she does compared to other students." She walked briskly past Ellen, her lips pursed, assuming that Ellen would follow.

Ellen could feel her blood begin a slow boil. This narrow-minded woman compromised nothing. It would be her way or no way, she was sure.

Ellen had, over the years, helped out in special school projects when needed, had even volunteer tutored on occasion. It had been evident to her that the new methods of democratic teaching engaged children way more than when she was in school, instilling an enthusiastic desire to learn. This old bat was still practicing an autocratic style where children learned by rote and fear of failure.

"As you can see, Sara is not concentrating. By this time, even though she is left-handed, she should not be reversing her numbers like this. She should be printing fluently, and she's not." Mrs. Andrews flipped to the back of the Key Tab and showed Ellen the lines of practice letters and numbers. "I've been keeping her in for 10 minutes a day to apply herself. There it is. All correctly done. However, in class, she's too busy looking around to concentrate." The frustrated teacher pulled out books from the desks of other children. "Look at her artwork. She's not even trying to color nicely or pay attention to detail. You can't tell me you don't see that."

Ellen could feel her face heat at Mrs. Andrews's condescending tone. She looked at her daughter's scarecrow figures and messy coloring in comparison to the others. "So what? Not everyone is an artist, Mrs. Andrews."

"True. But look in Sara's writing and math books. It's no different. Surely you must recognize that Sara must reach a certain standard?"

Ellen leafed through the books comparing the quality of work. There was a difference. Ellen had noticed that Sara never liked coloring like most children. Her printing was also frequently interspersed with capital and lower-case letters making her work look awkward and messy. Now in comparison to her classmates, Ellen could see how far behind she really was.

"Your daughter is very bright, Mrs. Peterson. A tad immature for her age, but bright. She does well in verbal question-and-answer discussions. She simply chooses not to concentrate when it's time to do the written work. She can do this if she wants to. I fully intend to see her buckle down in my class."

"I know my daughter, Mrs. Andrews. I can't see how

putting pressure on her is going to get her co-operation," Ellen argued again. "She's beginning to hate school."

"Sara hates being told what to do, Mrs. Peterson. It's as simple as that. I'd recommend that you are much firmer in your approach to her school work. We should see a difference by Christmas." Mrs. Andrews put the books away, then walked to the classroom door and held the door open for Ellen as she smiled politely. "Now, if you'll excuse me, I have some tests to mark."

"Of course." Ellen left, feeling frustrated with her attempts to diffuse the growing tension between the teacher and her child. It was hard to believe her bubbly, bright Sara was a lazy daydreamer, incapable of staying at par with her peers. When playing with the neighborhood children, she seemed to be a well-liked, natural leader. What was going on in class that changed her? Concentration problems, distractions, or was something else going on?

"Can't be," Ellen muttered aloud. "That teacher with her high and mighty attitude would throw me off, too." She strode briskly towards her car, trying to harness her exasperation.

"Muttering to yourself again?" Steve asked as he bicycled up beside her.

"Oh, hi, Steve, you startled me. And yes—I'm muttering."

"Danny again?" Steve inquired.

"No. Dan's at junior high now, remember?"

He shook his head in disbelief, then smiled. "You never seem to grow any older, Ell, it's hard to realize your kids are."

"Sure, tell my hairdresser that." She laughed. "Believe me, I'm getting older. I'll have a few more gray hairs by the end of this year if I have to deal with Sara's teacher again. No wonder she hates going to school."

They were standing by her car now, but she didn't want

him to leave. She seldom saw Steve alone now that Barry had hired an accountant to take her place this summer. She needed a friend to confide with her problems. He always seemed to understand where she was coming from.

When Ellen noticed the tips of his ears were red from the wind, his nose redder still, she made her decision. "Have you time for coffee?" Ellen asked. "You look frozen, and I could use some company. Besides, Sara's at her friend's place baking cookies. I don't need to pick her up until 5:00. I'm free as a bird for another hour."

"Why not? But I'm buying." Steve dismounted from his bike and leaned against her car. He noticed the flush of frustration on her cheeks, the sunlight in her hair. Again, it triggered a yearning deep inside him that was getting harder to ignore.

He had gone for a long bike ride this morning, enjoying the crispness of early fall, remembering when he had first met her. He had often tried to give her up in his mind, dating available ladies. Some of them had been great, but after a short while, the thrill of conquest laid aside, he'd realize he'd always compare them with Ellen.

"You're on." Steve winked at her. "Let's go."

STEVE SAW Ellen perk up at the idea of joining him. Whether she knew it or not, she missed him. Her eyes sparkled as she suggested packing his bike into the back of the SUV, offering to take him to Starbucks.

With two hot chocolates and a slice of lemon bread each, they sat down to catch up with their lives. The place was packed, so they took a seat at the bar next to each other. When Steve touched his leg to hers, she didn't pull away. A warm feeling of acceptance spread through her. Very seldom did she have the chance lately to connect with someone who always listened.

"So, what's going on, Ellen? You looked upset. That doesn't usually happen when you're dealing with Sara."

"She has a teacher that should have retired ten years ago. No wonder Sara doesn't like her. I don't either." Ellen's hands flew as she explained the frustrating meeting with Mrs. Andrews.

"So, what are you going to do?" Steve asked.

"I don't know. These stomach aches that Sara's been getting are probably a nervous reaction. She never gets them on the weekend until Sunday night."

Steve put his elbow on the bar and propped his head on an angle to face her. "Talk to the principal then, and if that doesn't improve things, have her switch teachers or schools."

"Can't. The only other grade three class with the available room is a split grade three and four for the brighter students. She'd stick out like a sore thumb there. I think switching schools is out of the question. She'd be even more lost without her friends. Besides, I think there might be something wrong with Sara. Her work was—-scattered. Not bad in some areas, but definitely not on the same level as the others."

"Get her tested then. Have you ever had her eyes checked or her hearing?"

"No. I think Sara's ok that way." Ellen's voice lowered as she fidgeted with her napkin.

Steve heard the anxiety in her voice. "You never know, Ell. You make the appointments to have that done, and I'll check with a few teachers I know that I play soccer with."

Glancing at her watch, Ellen gathered their debris and took it to the recycle bin. "Alright, I have to do something.

Thanks, Steve." Ellen took hold of his arm as they left the coffee shop and leaned her head on his shoulder. "Did I ever tell you what a great listener you are? I've missed you."

"I've missed you too. It's not the same at work without you. I hope I've been able to give you moral support at least."

"You have. You've given me some ideas to check out. I'll drop by the doctor's office and arrange for tests this week if I can." Ellen squeezed his arm. "Thanks again, my friend."

"Don't worry about it. Time to let someone else problem-solve for a change. How about going for lunch two weeks from today? At the Sea Edge? We can go over what we've found out. I'd like to be able to help whenever you need me. That's what friends are for, right?"

"Sure, why not? Text me if you know anything sooner. I hope I can get Sara examined quickly. I'm sure I'll be ready to compare notes by then."

Ellen helped Steve get the bike out of the car and again thanked him for his time and suggestions. She waved goodbye and headed home, feeling much happier. Talking with Steve had relaxed her. She had a course to follow that might give her the answers she needed to help Sara. Ellen breathed in deeply, pleased with the support she sorely needed.

BARRY ARRIVED home on Tuesday afternoon, surprised to learn that Ellen had taken steps to test Sara's sight and hearing. Ellen shared what Sara's work looked like compared to her peers, then her teacher's opinion of Sara's efforts.

"I'm sure with all her experience, Mrs. Andrews should know what's best for Sara," Barry's confidence in his old teacher probably rankled Ellen, but he believed it was true. "She was a substitute teacher for me a few times. She's tough and doesn't put up with any guff, that's for sure. But she gets results."

After they finished a late lunch, they sat on the sofa and enjoyed another coffee. Ellen leaned back, then twirled the last sip of coffee in her cup before polishing it off. "She's behind the times, honey. I don't agree with her method of teaching anymore. Sara feels pressured all the time, and instead of it helping, it's making things worse. She has tummy aches in the morning and doesn't want to go to school." Frustrated, Ellen slapped the cushion beside her. "I know it's early, but I need a glass of wine. Do you want one?"

Barry nodded and waited until she returned with full glasses of cabernet. They clinked glasses and sipped the velvety rich flavor. He noticed Ellen's frown and her troubled eyes as she continued to try to convince him that Sara's problems were coming from Mrs. Andrews. That glass disappeared as quickly as the first. She wiggled her wineglass, suggesting another refill which was very unusual when they discussed their daughter.

"Alright, do what you think is best." Barry returned from the kitchen with another glass of wine for both of them. "If it puts your mind at ease, get the testing done. I think you should spend more time at home with her practicing. Maybe we can encourage her more by offering incentives that might motivate her. Some parents swear by that approach."

"Not Sara. She doesn't have much self-esteem now. What happens if she doesn't measure up to our incentives? She'll feel even worse. Home is the only place she feels comfortable right now. If I add to her stress at home, she might feel even more inferior. I'm glad her vision is good, and today we'll find out about her hearing. The appointment's this afternoon at four o'clock."

"Sara's always been my favorite. Maybe we've babied her too long," Barry murmured. He was staying in Nanaimo much more than he needed to. He had noticed that things around here seemed to be disintegrating but had turned a blind eye.

"At her age, she needs a lot of loving, and there's nothing wrong with that. I know she's a smart kid. She's just having problems. We need to figure out why. If her ears and eyes are good, I want to follow up and get her fine motor skills tested. I think that's arranged through the school."

"It's a waste of time, Ellen. There's nothing wrong with her. She'll outgrow this." As Barry saw the fire in Ellen's eyes, he threw his hands up in defeat. "Go ahead. Do what you want, but you'll see I'm right." Barry put his wineglass down and grabbed the Victoria Colonist newspaper, opening it with a flourish.

THE SUBJECT WAS CLOSED. Ellen glared at him and his indifference to a problem that was so upsetting to her. Her face heated as her frustration mounted.

Why did they have so much trouble parenting? She often wondered if it stemmed from him growing up with a widowed mom. He had never learned how important it was to have a loving and involved father sharing the problems and being part of the solutions.

Ellen was used to Barry's attitude with Danny, but she didn't expect it for Sara. Lately, Barry had more energy and enthusiasm for his business and his politics than for his family. Home was only the place he slept in or ate at.

CHAPTER 10

Still frustrated with their conversation, Ellen rushed through the preparation of a chicken casserole for dinner. She'd pick up a tossed salad and buns from the grocery near the audiologist's office for accompaniment. There was no time for homemade tonight.

She knew it didn't help to slam a cupboard drawer or clash utensils together, but it sure as hell made her feel better. Ellen knew it would grate on Barry's nerves, yet that's what made the noise so satisfying too. She set the oven on a time cook, so it would be ready for when she returned with Sara from her hearing appointment, then left a note for the table to be set. Barry would probably be gone before she returned.

The weekend crawled by. Ellen was despondent. Barry was gone again to Nanaimo, pleased that he had been right about Sara. It would've been such an easy matter to correct if either Sara's eyes or ears were malfunctioning. In one way, she was glad her daughter's senses were fine, yet in another way, she was disappointed.

By 9:00 Saturday night, she couldn't wait any longer to

see Steve. She picked up her cell and speed-dialed the restaurant.

"The Carvery," answered one of their staff cheerfully. The noise of music and people in the background made it difficult for Ellen to hear her.

"May I speak to Steve, please?"

"Sure, I'll transfer the call," the girl replied.

"Steve here."

"Hi, it's Ellen. It sounds busy down there. I guess I should've waited." Ellen gripped her phone tightly, her voice trembling.

"Is everything ok?" his voice at once deepened with concern as she seldom called him.

"I guess so. It's not an emergency or anything... I wanted to talk, that's all. Listen, forget I called. I'll see you Monday."

"No, wait. I'd like to see you. I've got good staff on tonight, so I'm going to leave early. I could be at your place in an hour, ok?"

"I've got a better idea. I'll get the girl next door to babysit, and then I'll meet you at 11:00?"

"Alright. Meet me outside The Carvery. But stay in your car."

"Ok," Ellen whispered.

"Ellen?" Steve said her name loudly. "Did you hear me?"

"Yes. And I said OK. I'll stay in my car."

"Later, then."

Ellen slowly lowered her hand as she turned her phone off. This week had been difficult, organizing appointments for Sara and arguing with Barry. She was so tired of staying at home by herself.

It had been over two months since Barry and she had gone out. And, as usual, the last time had been a Chamber of Commerce function where Barry knew everyone, but she didn't. It was funny how she felt as isolated surrounded by people who meant nothing to her or them as staying at home by herself.

She and Barry were drifting again, their common interests slowly dissolving.

Ellen closed her eyes, running her hand over her face. She didn't know if she was coming or going. Did Barry even see her as a woman anymore? Or only as a homemaker and mother? Somewhere, she had turned into an efficient home manager.

Enough. Tonight, Ellen wanted something different. She wanted to be listened to, talked to, cared for.

She made arrangements for the sitter and waited as time dragged. At 10:30, Ellen went upstairs to change. Not knowing where she and Steve would end up, she chose to wear a beige silk pantsuit, casual but smart. On impulse, she dabbed Red Door on her wrists, then went to check on her children.

She stroked Sara's silky tresses away from her face and kissed her good night.

She knocked twice on Danny's door, then opened it, walked over to his bed, and pulled out one of his earphones so he could hear her. "Bev and I are going to The Carvery for a few drinks. The sitter's here. See you tomorrow."

Danny shrugged.

Feeling guilty about the lie, then wondering why she had bothered, she retreated and closed his door softly.

As she pulled into The Carvery parking lot, Ellen noticed Steve outside, waiting for her.

"Hi. I'm not late, am I?" she asked.

"No, of course not. I didn't want you to wait out here alone." Steve climbed inside her car and smiled at her.

"Thanks. I hope I haven't screwed up your evening."

"Not at all. I'm glad you called. Where would you like to go? We could go have a drink if you like."

"Wherever it's quiet would be nice. Have you had a chance to talk to your friends about Sara?"

"I have. Yesterday I went to the library and checked out the research material they recommended. I've been busy, so I've only read the first few chapters, but I think it's what you're looking for. How did the hearing and sight tests go?"

"All negative," Ellen replied. "Nothing wrong there."

"That fits with what I've learned so far. If you want, we can go to my place, and I could give you the books to read."

"I don't know." Ellen was beginning to feel foolish, wondering why she had been so impulsive. She put her forehead on the steering wheel and sighed.

"I make the best Spanish coffees in town, and we'd have the privacy to talk."

Ellen lifted her head and gazed at Steve, who smiled kindly at her. What was she afraid of? There was nothing wrong with going to a friend's house to gain information that could help Sara.

"Sure, let's go." Ellen started her car and pulled out of the parking lot. "I need some answers."

Ten minutes later, they entered his apartment, a flat in a restored Victorian house on Cook Street. Originally a three-story home, it had been divided into six flats. Ellen had dropped him off there before from work but had never been inside. Steve guided her through the lobby toward a heavy, dark mahogany door with a diamond-shaped transom.

"Wow. That's beautiful." Ellen looked around, taking in the architectural detail surrounding them.

"I've always liked these tall, narrow houses. They remind me of back east." Stephen unlocked the door then ushered her in. "Make yourself at home. I'll put some coffee on."

Ellen took off her coat and draped it on a high-back chair near the door. Then, she slipped off her shoes and wandered into the living room, admiring the colorful Turkish carpet against the hardwood floor. For a bachelor pad, this man had great taste. She sat on his leather sofa and listening to him puttering in the kitchen.

She didn't feel nervous now. Steve was casual and at ease, chatting with her from the kitchen while preparing their drinks. Accepting the steaming mugs of Spanish coffee for them, Ellen placed the drinks on coasters on the long coffee table in front of her. When Steve returned to the kitchen, she idly browsed the jumble of magazines. Several were specialty magazines on photography and scuba diving.

When he returned, she tilted her head towards him. "Do you dive?" Ellen asked as he approached her with a short stack of books in his hand.

"Once in a while. I used to do a lot of it. My parents had a cabin down in Miramichi Bay. Every weekend I could, I used to go and fish or walk the beaches, looking for treasures. I learned to scuba dive when I was fifteen, and even if you don't do it for a long time, you can never get it out of your system. Have you ever dived?"

"No. I love the ocean and boating or sailing, but I'm too much of a chicken to try scuba diving."

"You'd be surprised. Once you see how beautiful and colorful it is, you'd enjoy it."

"Maybe. I guess anything's possible. Are those the books you were talking about?"

Steve threw a few pillows on the carpet and sat down on one in front of the coffee table, spreading the books in front of him. She sat down beside him, reaching for the first book. As he explained what his friends had told him, Ellen leafed through the opening chapters.

Ellen was surprised with '*Teaching Learning Disabled Students*' and the other handbook '*Dyslexia -the Invisible Handicap.*' Excitedly, she read aloud passages that identified the same types of problems Sara was having.

"I can't believe it. These doctors could be using my Sara as an example. Of course, this must be it."

"You can arrange to have her tested for dyslexia at UBC Student Services in Vancouver. You need a referral from your doctor and her school, but if she's diagnosed with a learning disability, you'll have clinical proof. They'll co-ordinate programs with Sara's school, so she'll get the help she needs."

"Steve, this is amazing. Wait until I tell Barry about this. Thank God." Ellen leaned over and kissed him on the cheek as excitement colored her cheeks. "Thank you and your friends. I knew there was something wrong, but I couldn't get any answers."

"Well, now you know how to find them. UBC will give her school a plan to follow and monitor her progress every year or two. There are all sorts of supports if you know where to look for them." Steve leaned over and tapped the end of her nose playfully. "You're a great mom, Ellen. I'm glad I was able to help you with Sara."

Ellen flushed with pleasure at the compliment. "I knew she wasn't stupid or lazy." Ellen eagerly thumbed through the books, looking for more information.

They each took turns reading excerpts from different publications, discussing what it would mean in Sara's particular case.

"The book says that dyslexic children have normal to high IQ. It's a matter of a short circuit in the brain that doesn't allow them to learn in the same way you and I do. If left untreated, by the time the child has reached senior high, they are so frustrated with their attempts that they drop out." Ellen's mouth crumpled as she looked at her friend. "How sad. I could cry for these kids."

"Geeze, listen to this, Ellen. Up to seventy percent of juvenile male inmates are dyslexic. Can you believe that?" Steve continued scanning the article, commenting on the lack of resources that the school system used to solve the issues of failing students.

"Doesn't surprise me. If you can't express what you think in a way the system wants you to, you're labeled. Then these kids feel embarrassed or ashamed. That stupid teacher! Doesn't she ever educate herself to keep up on stuff?" Ellen asked angrily.

"Oh, the younger ones do, but it's hard to change some teachers. Some of the older staff think it's all a cop-out," Steve said. "Would you like another coffee?"

"Sure, one more, then I have to go. I can't believe we've been here so long. Over two hours already."

"But that's good. You have some answers. You sure look and sound a lot better than when you called me earlier."

"I feel great now. I was so confused, and I have to confess, lonely. I had to talk to someone," Ellen said softly. "Thanks for taking time for me."

"No prob." He handed her the coffee, and she put it down on the coffee table. She stretched her arms in front of her to unwind as she lay propped against the sofa.

Ellen sipped her coffee as she relaxed completely. Sharing her problems with Steve and feeling his genuine concern and optimistic attitude helped her unwind. A strong sense of relief that her fears were substantiated coursed through her. Yet now, Ellen felt confident with the knowledge of its solutions. Feeling somewhat overwhelmed, she closed her eyes briefly. Ellen leaned her head against

Steve, so thankful for his help in discovering the answers. She glanced up at Steve, noticing his gentle mouth, then met his eyes.

Uh-oh.

Ellen leaned forward, fussing with the books on the table. Her cheeks flushed, and she dared not look at Steve. The smoldering look he displayed was dangerous. She imagined her eyes could have reflected the same thing. She ran a shaky fingertip over her brow and pushed away from the coffee table.

"Look at the time. I really have to go. Thanks again for your help." Ellen flitted a glance toward him as she gathered her purse. She was surprised to see an amused expression on his face. What was so funny?

"Anytime, Ellen, anytime. I'm glad you were able to see my place. I hope you'll come again. Make sure to let me know how things work out."

"For sure." Ellen stopped at the door, dropping her purse to pull her coat on. Steve picked it up and handed her the books as well. Ellen gave him a peck on the cheek. "And you do make the best Spanish coffee I've ever had. This night has been the best I've had in a long while. You've given me hope."

"Thanks. You've given me hope, too." Steve opened the door and led her to the exterior door.

STEVE WATCHED her get into her car before shutting the door. She hadn't commented on his last remark, but he was sure she'd be thinking about it. Planting the seed, he prayed that one day it would germinate.

CHAPTER 11

Barry was pushing himself to the max, working and promoting the Nanaimo Carvery, then double-checking his Victoria restaurant when he returned home. He was back in the role of the familiar stranger at home. He was sure that Danny was quite relieved with that development.

Last year, Barry had spent more time at home and more effort into bringing Danny into line. He often wondered whether Danny's stubborn withdrawal and lack of enthusiasm were payback for his obsessive commitment to work.

Danny had always been a moody kid, but the last couple of years were worse. Puberty had not been his friend. He never wanted to participate with the family in anything they did. He preferred to be off on his own or in his room. His grades had fallen in school, yet he refused to attempt, although the teachers believed he was bright enough. He often daydreamed and put only the barest effort necessary into his studies to assure a pass.

Barry made him join soccer and baseball. He often

forced him to join them on family evenings out to the movies or bowling.

Nothing seemed to work though, Barry sighed. Danny was as sullen as ever. It was one area he and Ellen disagreed on constantly. Ellen tried to convince him that Danny was a shy person and would come out of it on his own when he felt comfortable enough. Barry believed he was a rude, spoiled brat.

DANNY SENSED the struggle between his parents and smiled inside. He knew what they were thinking. Dan had read a bit on ESP and decided he had it. He knew what they were all thinking, his parents, his teachers, his classmates. They hid it well, but he knew they hated him. When he first realized he was right, he was thrilled. He didn't have to pretend anymore. As long as they left him alone, he couldn't care less.

This last year with Dad at home so much had been awful. It was pitiful watching a grown-up pretend they loved you. He resisted as much as he could without creating a scene. Thank God, it had now returned to normal. Even better than usual because Mom was gone a lot now too. She wouldn't have the time to spend on precious Sara anymore.

The only person he was ever comfortable with was Stephen. If Stephen accompanied them on weekends, Danny would come along peacefully. As the years went by, the rest of the family recognized the special though strange relationship. Stephen never doted on him or pressured him to do anything. He was just there. Steve accepted him as he was and seldom paid attention to Sara's bubbly personality.

Again, now that his dad was gone a lot, Stephen would often stop in and drop off reports and stay for coffee. Like tonight.

"I hear you have your last tournament this weekend. Want a fan?" Stephen asked as Danny passed by the kitchen table.

"I don't care," Danny replied, shrugging his shoulders. "I don't play half the time anyway."

"If I've got time, I'll drop in. Maybe we'll go for a pizza after the game if you feel like it."

"Suit yourself. If you're there, you're there," Danny replied as he grabbed an apple and left to go to bed.

Danny was glad it was almost the end of soccer. Next year, his dad could go to hell. He wasn't ever going to join another sports team.

Once again, he caught the look of dismay on his mother's face as he left. She probably thought I was rude, he mused, but Steve knows I want to see him. He understands the messages I give.

STEVE PATTED ELLEN'S HAND. After finishing the month-end reconciliation, they enjoyed a glass of wine and caught up on their personal lives. "Don't worry about it. He's fourteen, what do you expect? Boys are all the same at that age. Major anti-social."

"Honestly, he drives me crazy sometimes. He can be so sweet to me one day, yet other days he's a rude, selfish brat." She shook her head again, guiltily. "Terrible mother, aren't I for saying such awful things about my son?"

"No, I don't think so. Each kid is different. Some are easier to handle than others. Most parents feel like that now and then, especially during the teen years. You ought to know—you've worked with enough of them."

"That's for sure." Ellen grinned, pulling her hand away from Steve's. Touching him came so naturally, was so comfortable that it was hard not to. She caught the amused look on his face and flushed. She switched back to business, checking the year-end figures. "So, is that everything up to date?"

"Yea. When Barry gets back, he wants to check them before going to the bank. I'm pleased, though. Even with the second mortgage on *my* place, it's showing a good profit. He'll be able to make a lump sum payment soon."

"Thank God. Pete almost ruined us. If it wasn't for your loyalty, I don't know how Barry and I would've made it," she replied.

While she put their coffee cups in the dishwasher, she recalled everything Steve had done. He worked hard and was a great manager. Without him, Barry would've gone crazy trying to cope. Steve had been there to help her with the books, explaining restaurant accounting and inventory practices. When a pipe burst in the hot water tank at home, she'd called him, and he came to look after the problem.

Sometimes, he was simply there when she needed him. Steve had been a life saver.

As she walked him to the door, he casually draped his arm around her. Automatically she put her arm about his waist, then dropped it, blushing self-consciously. She bit her lip, wondering if he shared the same electricity.

"Thanks again for all the extra work, Steve. There'll be a bonus on your next check to show our appreciation."

"Hey, don't worry about it. What are friends for? I seem to remember you helping me out a long time ago." Steve squeezed her shoulder a little tighter.

Ellen broke away. "That was too long ago to remember. I'll see you on Tuesday, maybe. I want to go over some of the accounts with Barry."

"Great. See you later," Steve smiled, his eyes glinting with amusement at her discomfiture.

⁓

SHE LEANED against the closed door, alarmed at these new feelings. Damn, what was she getting herself into?

Suddenly, she remembered when her neighborhood friend had teased her. Susan and her husband had met Steve during a community fundraising barbeque.

"Have you ever wondered why he's never married?" Susan had asked. "He's quite the handsome man. Is he gay?"

"No, he's not gay. He's had quite a few girl friends over the years."

"Nothing serious though, I wonder why. There's something behind it. Maybe Steve's in love with someone who's already married?"

"C'mon, leave the poor guy alone. Marriage isn't for everyone," Ellen defended.

"I bet if a certain woman were free, you'd see a wedding band on his finger," Susan had teased.

"Susan, what are you insinuating? Steve is a very considerate and special person, but he's never been more than a friend to this family. He's *never* made a pass at me either." Ellen had raised her eyebrows in protest as her voice, and her indignation had also risen. "So, get your mind out of the gutter."

"OK, OK. Even if you haven't noticed it, I have. Steve cares about you. He's nice to everyone, but with you, he's even more considerate and–gentler, I guess. Don't you feel that?"

"I hadn't noticed anything different," Ellen lied. She did feel the growing closeness between them, the looks in his eyes sometimes when they were alone. She chose to deliberately ignore them, hoping that her eyes were not mirroring the same desires as his.

Dammit, she had to get a hold of herself. She still loved Barry. Right now, if the emotions between them were a bit stale, it was understandable. She'd stand by him, and the fire would come back. Ellen didn't need to get involved with another man, let alone Steve. She cared too much about both Barry and Steve to hurt or risk losing either one of them.

Stop acting like a teenager, she chastised herself. Ellen latched the door, then leaned against it, trying to re-group her thoughts and chase her unsettling feelings away.

"I like him, Mom." Ellen whirled around.

Danny sat near the top of the stairs, looking down at her.

"I— I—" Ellen stopped stuttering and blurted, "I thought you went to bed."

"I'm going."

"You shouldn't have been so rude earlier. Steve's a good friend to all of us," Ellen replied, trying to change the subject.

Much as she tried, it was hard to get close to and understand her firstborn. The differences between her two children were growing more evident each year. She struggled not to show favoritism, but it was tough when one child was warm and cheerful while the other was withdrawn and sullen.

"You better hit the hay. It's after 11:00."

"Sure, Mom." Danny seldom argued. However, he rarely

did what she wanted him to do either. Danny gave her a secretive smile then headed toward his room, not even saying goodnight.

Ellen was sure the light in his room would be on long after she went to bed. She cleared the table, putting her reports in a legal box that she used to transport them back and forth to the restaurant. Her chin trembled, and tears threatened to spill over. Her emotions were all over the map.

Both her and Barry had been working long hours. The stress of maintaining two businesses and running a family life was taking a toll. Nothing had worked despite Barry's attempts a few years ago to bring motivation and discipline to Danny's routine. Things were back to where they used to be.

Danny had absolutely no fear or desire to please. He did what he wanted when he wanted. Ellen had compromised years ago, letting the minor infractions slide and demanding less of him than was probably wise. She hoped it gave him a chance to accomplish things in his way while leaving her some sanity. Just like Matt advised. She treasured the good times, then locked the tough ones away to forget.

Ellen needed a break, something to look forward to. She pushed her worries aside and concentrated on her summer plans. Matt and Anna had called last week and invited them to their cottage in Safe Haven in August. She hadn't confirmed because of their hectic lifestyle, but tonight she'd decided to accept the offer. She'd bring Danny and Sara with her.

She didn't even have to ask Barry if he'd go. She knew the answer. It had been so relaxing when she'd joined Matt and Anna's family at their cottage a few years ago. Ellen enjoyed keeping in touch with them. It centered her and allowed her children to connect with their cousins.

Susan's teasing nagged her, slipping under her skin and staying there. She didn't want to admit it, yet there was no denying the fact that her attraction to Steve had grown. As Susan had noticed, Steve treated her as a woman, often complimenting her with his eyes or a soft touch. Words weren't always necessary.

It wasn't fair to Barry to compare the two. Now Ellen had another mission to accomplish. For the moment, Barry's wife was the restaurant, and Ellen was his business partner. Until they could get back on their feet, she needed to accept that. She wouldn't or couldn't doubt their love and commitment to each other. The trip to see her cousins was precisely what she needed to break the spell she had fallen into with Steve.

"I'm not joking, Dan. You're coming too. Jed and Aaron will be there to hang out with and do stuff. I know you liked being around your "Uncle" Matt. We'll enjoy the beach together. You'll probably go fishing with the guys. You'll see —it'll be fun."

"No, Mom. Forget it. I'm old enough to stay home on my own. That family makes me sick. They're rich and snobby. They think they're better than everyone else. I feel like shit around them."

"That's not true. Yes, your cousins have a different lifestyle than we do, but I've known them forever. I know they enjoy spending time with us. I've never seen any behavior that tells me any different. It's only your imagination."

"Go ahead, keep your eyes closed, Mom. You always do. Life isn't the rose garden you like to pretend it is. I'm not going, and that's it."

"I need a break, and I want my kids to share it with me. I'm not making excuses for your absence, so get used to it." Ellen narrowed her eyes and lowered her voice to a warning growl. "I'm not making excuses for your absence, so get used to it." She watched her son turn his back and stomp to the door. "I'm not kidding, Dan. We're going, even if I have to bribe you.

Ellen closed her eyes for a second, breathing deeply, wishing she could take back those words.

Danny turned and cocked his head to the side, a slow smile spreading across his face. "What have you got in mind?"

Ellen noticed his eyes narrowing, probably assessing how much he could get out of her. She was used to this kind of arbitration—it had happened before. *Well, whatever it takes.* She squared her shoulders and started the negotiation. "That new sound system for your bedroom? You've been itching for a new one."

"What would be the point, Mom? I could never have it loud enough in the house. You guys would be all over me."

"I'm not playing games, Dan. What do you want?" Ellen felt a flush rising on her face, angry at herself for once again mediating a compromise.

"State-of-the-art laptop. With combination computer speakers and headphones to listen to my music."

"Jesus, do you know how much those things cost?" Ellen's eyes widened. "How desperate do you think I am?"

"How much do you want me to come with you?" Danny smirked, his eyes mocking her. Knowing how important it was for his mom to present a perfect family, he often traded good behavior for special favors. Last time he got tickets for himself and three friends to a Nickelback concert.

"Quality laptop now, speakers at Christmas." Ellen

turned to walk away, then hesitated. "And you better be on your best behavior while we're there. None of your smart-ass behavior, got it?" A lump rose in her throat as she faced the smugness in her son's eyes.

"Chill out, Mom. I'll be the perfect son." Dan grabbed his jacket then left the house, whistling a happy tune.

Tired of feeling guilty for negotiating a deal with Dan, Ellen rubbed the back of her neck, trying to ease the tension. She had planned on having a soak in the jacuzzi, now she pushed the notion away. She didn't want to think anymore tonight. She went to bed, took a melatonin and surrendered to a deep heavy sleep, devoid of dreams of either her son or Steve.

CHAPTER 12

The ferry trip from Victoria to Port Angeles on the MV Coho was as impressive as always. Ellen never failed to be thankful for her Island home or the Strait separating it from Washington State. On a summer's day like this, sailboats with their colorful sheets were plentiful, gliding through the light chop effortlessly. Yachts and small boats alike dotted the seascape while freighters on their way to Seattle or Vancouver commanded the right of way.

Always something to watch, something to appreciate.

"Sara, are you ready, sweetheart?" Ellen gathered their belongings from the luncheon table at the front of the boat.

The outline of the port appeared ahead.

"I am. Want me to take another bag?" Sara extended the handle on her roll-on luggage and attached a duffel bag on top for easier maneuvering.

"No, I've got this one. Danny should be on the top deck. We'll find him, then disembark from the ramp."

"I can't wait to see Lisa. We've been texting back and forth on Instagram. We're going to have a blast."

"I'm sure you will. Please make sure you get Lisa to rest

her leg often. She's only recently stopped using her crutches. She might push herself too hard."

"I know. I can't believe what Lisa's been through lately. And then her mom getting involved in that riot? She still has nightmares about that, you know."

Ellen noted Sara's eyes darkened when she spoke of her cousin's brush with mob anger. "I've no doubt. Scary stuff when your family is involved in something like that. I'm sure they're a lot more careful about where they go now."

Ellen scanned the top deck, then spotted Dan and his backpack nearby, flicking a butt over the railing. Great. Littering and smoking. She sucked in a breath, hoping it was only tobacco. Honestly, that boy pushed every button she had.

"Dan. Over here." Ellen waved to him. She watched him glance around, embarrassed to be called by his mother. Too bad.

"Can you grab this duffel bag too, please? This roller suitcase is heavy enough for me to handle."

Dan hefted the duffel. "How much stuff did you bring for four days?"

"Enough not to do laundry. Besides, you never know how the weather will be."

As they disembarked via the ramp on the deck, Lisa shrieked when she saw her Aunt Anna and Lisa waving enthusiastically. "Over there, Mom. Aunt Kari is here too! I'll meet you there." She ran ahead, eager to see her cousin.

"Great. Good thing I've got earphones. I hate listening to giggling girls."

"They must have two vehicles if Kari's here. I'll send the girls with Kari unless you want to go with her."

Dan lifted his eyebrows in a way that suggested she was crazy. "I don't think so. Send the girls with her."

"Fine." Ellen made her way to the two sisters and hugged them. "Anna, Kari. So nice to see both of you. Look at your tans. You've taken advantage of the good weather I see."

"Yes, it's been awesome. Some light fog in the early morning off the Strait, but it burns off by mid-morning."

"Dan, can you put our luggage in the back of the SUV?" She handed her son her suitcase then hugged her cousin warmly.

"Wow, Danny, you've grown a few inches since I saw you. What grade are you in now?"

"Going into grade nine. And it's Dan now."

"Of course. The guys are out fishing. They'll be home by the time we get back. Why don't we grab some burgers before we head home? Are you hungry?"

"I'm good. We ate on the ferry." Dan closed the back door and hopped into the rear seat, plugging in his earphones to access music.

Ellen glanced backward at her son, and Dan winked at her. So far, so good. She knew he liked keeping his mom on edge. Smart ass.

"Would you like to stop and do some shopping at the quay in Port Angeles? Or go straight to the cottage?"

"Straight to Safe Haven, please. I've been looking forward to beachcombing and lazing about."

"Sounds good. There's an arts festival on Saturday in Port Angeles. We could all go if you're interested." Anna's eyes sparkled in anticipation of Ellen's acceptance, drawing her into the festive spirit.

"Of course, that'll be fun."

The girls chatted away, bringing each other up to date in their lives. Three-quarters of an hour later, after unloading the vehicles, Lisa and Sara immediately changed into bathing suits then skipped towards the beach. Lisa proceeded to show Sara how to mount a paddle board. Giggles and squeals from three excited girls could be heard inside the cottage.

Dan dropped his backpack beside the tent, then set about collecting driftwood along the beach to stockpile beside the firepit.

The stress of the last few months melted away in the lighthearted ambiance the day fostered. Ellen's demeanor was totally relaxed as Anna and Kari shared the fun they'd been having since arriving there. Easy laughter flowed around her, enveloping her in a cocoon of comforting acceptance.

"We're all sorry that Barry couldn't come. He would've enjoyed fishing with the guys, then having a few beers around the campfire."

"True. Unfortunately, Barry's overwhelmed with working and managing both the Victoria and Nanaimo restaurant. He hasn't taken much time off in the last few years. He's so wound up in it, nothing else seems to matter much. I wonder if he'd even know how to relax."

"Never mind, you'll enjoy the break. That's what matters. And the kids will get to know each other again. Aaron and Jed were talking about taking a hike tomorrow with Dan to Marymere Falls. We'll drop them off at Crescent Lodge on the lake around noon and pick them up around 4:00. Unless you'd like to make that a family hike and join them?"

Ellen cocked her head, considering her options, then grinned. "No thanks, let the boys be boys. I'll stay at the beach and relax with a pitcher of Margaritas."

"Alright, that sounds better to me too. We'll get the men to handle the transportation, and then we won't need to worry about driving."

Kari glanced at her watch and gasped. "Good thing we prepped these salads this morning, Anna. The guys should be back soon."

"Let me do something, please." Ellen went to the kitchen sink and washed her hands. "What can I do?"

"I've chopped tomatoes, peppers, and zucchini to add to the pasta. A dressing needs to be made, then mixed with the vegetables. Can you make a Caesar style for it? Kari made a marinated bean salad a few days ago. A couple of warmed loaves of French bread should be enough to go with the BBQ. I also have corn on the cob ready for Matt to grill."

"Heavens, that's way too much food." Ellen's eyes widened at the menu offerings.

"Are you kidding? Three teenage boys, two men, and us four girls? We'll be lucky if there are leftovers."

LOUD CHEERS from the dock brought them all outside as the men proudly showed off their catch of two decent-sized salmon, over twenty pounds, and one around twelve. They'd also decided to jig for cod and were lucky to pick up a greenling.

Jed and Aaron seemed happy to be off the confines of the boat. The banter flowed as they teased each other about who had made the largest catch.

As Dan approached, the boys greeted him and then tried to entice him to fish with them. Dan shook his head and laughed them away, saying he'd rather start the bonfire.

Ray and Matt cleaned and secured the boat, then returned the lunch coolers to the house. A short time later, they brought a replenished cooler of beer and sodas to the

BBQ area near the firepit, where the ladies had claimed the zero-gravity chairs for tanning.

"Ellen, I'm so glad you decided to come. Cheers." Matt clinked his beer to her Margarita glass. "Seems like you ladies are off to a good start." Matt glanced towards the water where Lisa and Sara paddled on boards thirty feet away from the shoreline. "She looks a lot like you at that age and almost as sunny. Those girls are becoming great friends."

"Thanks to Instagram, they've kept up with each other. Sara was extremely excited about coming over." Ellen proposed a toast as she clinked her glass to each of them. "To the family and good times." She peered towards the firepit and lifted her glass to Danny, too, nodding in approval when he gave her the thumbs up. This holiday was going better than she hoped it would.

Ray and Matt had taken a quick dip after their beer to cool off, then decided to enjoy another brew before starting the BBQ. Soon after, Anna called the girls in to shower and help with dinner set up. They took the salads to the picnic table, covering them with umbrella nets. Dan had lit the firepit while Aaron and Jed sat nearby, discussing future plans.

The smell of salmon cooking and corn roasting permeated the air. Soon the talkative group was silent, concentrating on their dinners.

"So, Dan—are you up for a hike tomorrow? I could drop you boys at Crescent Lake with your backpacks and pick you up later. Marymere Falls is only a couple of miles from there, and they're pretty spectacular to see. What do you think?"

"Sweet. Why not? I'm game. I haven't done much hiking, but it can't be that hard if these two are ready to go."

"It's not a tough hike, some interesting terrain around there. We'll drop you guys off on our way to town. Ray and I have to pick up some gear tomorrow morning for Saturday's fishing trip. We'll come back around 4:00 to pick you up. How's that sound?"

Aaron and Jed agreed, then sauntered off down the beach, hollering at Dan to join them. Dan refused the offer and returned to the fire, using the poker to stir the embers again before adding more wood.

DAN LOOKED AROUND HIM, the noisy chatter fading as the evening sky changed colors, welcoming the night. The bonfire crackled and burned brightly against the inky darkness. Looking up, he saw the outer two stars of the Big Dipper pointing to the handle of the Little Dipper. He questioned if those two wonder boys knew their real names, Ursa Major and Ursa Minor. Somehow, he doubted it. They might know how to fish, but Stephen had taught him long ago about the constellations in the sky.

Dan could stare for hours at them, mesmerized by their knowing glow. All the things those stars had seen throughout earth's history boggled his mind. There was a connection between that knowledge and his own awareness of things around him that no one else could fully understand.

"HEY DAN, THIS WAY," Jed called his cousin to join him to cross the single plank bridge across the creek.

"Woosies use a bridge. I'm crossing the creek. I'll meet you on the other side."

"Watch out for the round river rocks. They'll be slippery. I'd be careful of the current there too." Jed warned, shaking his head.

Aaron glanced back towards Jed, whispering. "He won't listen. He's gotta be the tough guy. It'll serve him right to fall on his ass and get swept downstream."

"He won't go that far. There's hardly any current now that it's so shallow, although it's going to be a hard fall if he does. He could twist his ankle or worse."

"He might be your cousin, but he's crazy. Did you see how close he came to going over the edge of the falls?"

"Yea. I think he scared himself too, not that he'd admit it. What the hell would we have done if that'd happened?" Jed frowned at the thought of the trouble they would've had.

"Are we gonna tell our dads?"

"No way. Maybe once we get home, then again, maybe not. I don't need a lecture about looking after my younger cousin. You know the old saying, *you can't fix stupid*. That's him. Not only that, he can be pretty scary sometimes. I don't need him mad at us."

"Gotchya. Lucky bugger, look at him. He's going to make it."

A sudden splash and a yelp caused Aaron and Jed to squelch a smile as they looked down to see Dan scrambling from the stream to the far bank. "Not a word, Aaron. Pretend you didn't see anything."

"Hey guys, come on in. Water's great. Time to cool off."

"Ah, thanks, but I'll wait until we get to the lake." Jed hollered down.

"Suit yourself. I think I'll stop and have a coke while you

catch up." Dan stared up at them, still carefully going foot over foot on the rough, cedar-planked bridge.

A half-hour later, they were back at Crescent Lake, near the Lodge. They stripped down to their bathing trunks and dove into the clear, cold lake.

∽

As Matt pulled up to pick up the boys, they saw them laughing and splashing with each other. "Hmm. Guess that was a success. They look like they've been having fun."

Ray put his hand over his brow to shield the bright sun from his eyes and smiled. "I wondered how it'd go. It seems like Dan's a loner, so I honestly didn't know how our boys would do with him."

"Let's join them for a swim and head back. We'll see how things go tomorrow when we take them fishing."

"Are you sure Dan's going to come? When you asked him this morning, he said he'd pass."

"Oh, he'll be coming. The girls are going to an arts festival tomorrow, and I'm not leaving him alone. He'll be ok once we get out on the water."

"If he doesn't want to fish, maybe we can teach him to steer the boat. It's a big ocean. As long as he doesn't go in circles, he can't go wrong. I haven't met a kid yet that doesn't enjoy doing that."

Matt and Ray shucked their shirts and sandals, then joined the boys in the water, enjoying a game of water tag. When hunger finally reminded them of the time, they came out, drying themselves in the hot sun before loading into the SUV to go home.

∽

ELLEN LEANED back on the wooden bench, letting the sea breeze cool her. She closed her eyes and smiled, both inside and out.

What a great weekend. Everyone connected so well, and even Dan had been on good behavior. The only exception was around dinner time last night. He had slipped away to wander the shoreline then had lost track of the time he later explained. Nobody seemed to be upset about his absence, but Ellen had noticed Matt look at him thoughtfully for a minute before telling him to help himself to the leftovers.

The art festival was a huge success. Ellen couldn't remember ever having so much innocent fun. The artist's posters of Lisa and Sara and one of the three ladies were hilarious. It had captured the essence of their outing. Thankfully they found a Michael's outlet that could scan and reprint them so each family would have a memory of that summer's day.

Ellen's heart was replenished with joyous optimism. So what if she had to bribe Dan to come? It was well worth it.

She had great memories to take out and cherish whenever she felt lonely. Ellen was going home ready to handle anything life threw at her.

CHAPTER 13

"Well, I can see the holiday was a success. Look at the tans you picked up." Barry smiled as he drew Ellen into his arms and kissed her. He reached over and tussled Sara's hair. "Hey, kiddo, I missed you. You look great." Barry looked towards his son, who was already heading into the house. "Hey, Dan! Grab a suitcase, will you?"

Dan stopped in his tracks and glanced over his shoulder. "Yea. I'll be right back." He continued into the house, slamming the door behind him.

"Leave him be. He's tired. There's not that much to bring in anyway."

"Ellen. Really? Didn't you promised not to make excuses for him anymore?"

"I'm not. It's a fact. We're exhausted, that's all."

"Then you go in, and I'll bring the luggage indoors. Go on. I'll put the bags in the laundry room. Why not freshen up and get some wine out for us to celebrate? I've missed you and Sara."

"That's nice to hear. Matt mentioned he hopes you come next year if you have things under control." Ellen watched his reaction and was relieved to see that the invite was well received. "How about ordering in dinner tonight?"

"I'm already ahead of you with that. I've ordered a couple of pizzas and a lasagna for a six o'clock delivery. I hope that's ok."

"That's perfect. Nice and easy." Ellen hugged him and kissed his cheek. "I've missed you too, honey. I've so much to tell you. All of it's good." Her husband's eager-to-please expression spoke volumes. It wasn't often that she left him on his own, so she was surprised that he had even missed them.

Noticing the wrinkles at the corner of her husband's eyes as he returned her smile, she realized her man was getting older and more attractive every year. The way his eyes lit up when they arrived home told her that he appreciated her too. This break had done them both a world of good. She trailed a finger down the side of his face to his mouth, astonished and delighted when he licked it.

"Get a room, you two," Sara quipped as she passed them with her duffel bag.

A flurry of activity kept the household busy for the next few hours, showers and laundry being top priorities. Barry wandered about listening to Sara's accounts of paddle boarding and the arts festival. He asked about Dan's behavior and was surprised when he found that he had participated in both a hike and a fishing trip. Very unusual.

After dinner, Sara and Danny disappeared, appearing anxious to get back to their regular routine. Barry shooed his wife to the living room to relax while he cleaned up the dining room table.

He came and sat beside her on the sofa, offering her a glass of chardonnay while he sipped a shot of Drambuie. "How about you and I go for dinner tomorrow night?"

"Sure, sounds good. It's so nice to have you home in the evening. And having you two nights in a row? It makes me feel special."

"You are, sweetheart." Barry's eyebrows lifted suggestively. "Why don't you go up and pour yourself a bath, then I'll come up and give you a neck massage while you're soaking?"

Ellen giggled. He knew her so well. There was nothing like a massage while relaxing in the tub. She'd put in scented bath oil to make his fingers glide easier. His hands were magic when it came to kneading her tense muscles, then even more expert when it came to arousing her. "You don't have to tell me twice. This week keeps getting better and better."

THE NEXT EVENING, Barry bit into his last succulent bite of rosemary and garlic-infused lamb rack. His tongue savored the blend as he rolled his eyes heavenward. "I've heard the chef here is the best in Victoria. Now I know it's true."

"I'll be back for the grilled halibut with peach salsa and asparagus. Wow." Ellen discreetly wiped the corners of her mouth with the navy linen napkin. "Such a different menu. It was hard to choose."

"These five-star restaurants usually carry only three or four main course meals, but they're creative and served to perfection. It's worth the price when you have something to celebrate."

The waiter appeared discreetly, pouring them another glass of Chianti Classico. The candlelight, soft music, and wine softened the mood.

Barry captured her hands in his and grinned. "You look so relaxed. I think this break was good for you, Ell."

"I am. I enjoyed myself, so did the kids."

They chatted more about the trip as they slowly finished their wine. Ellen's eyes opened wide as she saw the waiter approach with a bottle of Mumm's champagne. She looked at Barry, her eyebrow raised in question.

She waited impatiently until the waiter left, then asked, "What's up? Have I missed something?"

"To your freedom again, Ellen." Barry toasted happily.

Ellen's eyes widened even more. "Pardon?"

"The bank's gone over our fiscal year for both restaurants, and they are impressed with our business operations. I made a lump sum payment on the mortgage of twenty thousand dollars. They were so proud of our success that they've dropped their lending rate and gave us prime financing. It's saving us a bundle."

"Great news, Barry. Congratulations! We should throw a staff party. I know everyone has been working hard and going the extra mile for us."

"You're right. I'll get Steve to organize something for September." Barry leaned towards her and clinked their flutes for a toast. "I'll also be cutting my hours back. The stress isn't worth working seven days a week anymore. I've missed you."

Barry's voice softened as his eyes sparkled with impending news. "More importantly, you're free. You were a great help during the past few years. Now that the crunch is over, you can stay home again and do whatever you used to do."

Ellen returned the smile and sipped her champagne, torn between being happy to have the 'free' time and sad for leaving an interesting and demanding job. This experience had made her feel valuable aside from the mothering aspect.

"I'm not sure I want to give it up, sweetheart," she replied. "I like being involved in our business and meeting the people you deal with." Ellen saw the disbelief in his face, so she patted his hand. "I'm thrilled with your news. Don't worry, if you don't need me, that's okay. I'll find some other work to do. Maybe go back to the bank."

"But you don't need to. I've appreciated everything you've done, Ell." Barry sat straighter, looking puzzled by her reaction. "Things at home are running smoothly now during the summer, but don't forget what it was like during the last school year. I'm worried about September."

"Let's not go there, Barry. We'll figure it out later. I don't want this evening to lose its magic."

"Alright, darling. You're right. Ready to dance?"

"Oh yes, it's been a long time," Ellen murmured as she wrapped her arms around his neck for a slow waltz.

He held her lightly, and she sensed he was miles away in thought.

"Now what?" Ellen pulled herself away from him, searching for an answer as she studied his eyes. "Weren't we leaving all discussions of the children at home tonight?"

"We are. Why?"

"It feels like you're miles away from here, with your attention on something else," she murmured.

"Sorry, babe." Barry kissed her cheek in apology. "I guess I did drift. I've been approached to join the Liberal party to run for a spot on the committee for fundraising. I'm not sure what to do."

Ellen couldn't believe he was serious. "You're only starting to cut down the hours you work in Nanaimo. Now, you're going to add another job? Or is that why you're cutting back?"

"I had planned on reducing my work week ever since I promoted Steve to assistant manager. He's damn good. He's taken a lot of stress off my shoulders."

Ellen tilted her head to the side, studying him. "I understood we were working toward more quality time at home."

"We are. The party is centered here, so it's not like I'd be away all the time. There are conventions in Vancouver and Kamloops sometimes, but I can bring you with me."

The song had ended, and so had the romantic evening.

"Why do you want to join? You've got the Lions Club and your businesses, isn't your life demanding enough?" Instead of lingering for another dance, Ellen turned abruptly and returned to her seat.

Barry sat and reached for her hand. "Ell, that's exactly it. I'm too busy to commit to politics unless I free up some time. You know I've always hoped to run for office one day. I'd have to give up the Lions. It'd be worth it, though, the contacts I could make." His eyes shone, anticipating the challenge.

Ellen looked at him and smiled despite herself. He was as eager as a little kid to jump in and get it when he wanted something. She knew Barry wanted more than what they had now. He wanted prestige. Well, so be it.

Ellen closed her eyes for a few seconds, then licked her lips. When her eyes flew open, she fixed her gaze on him, making sure he knew what her opinion was. "Fine. Go for it —on one condition: Don't shut me out. We don't have enough time for each other now as it is. I get lonely."

"We'll go out more, you'll see," Barry promised. "Let's go home and celebrate some more. It's my turn for a massage tonight. I'm thinking warm coconut oil?" His eyebrows moved up and down suggestively while his hand discreetly slid up her thigh, squeezing gently.

Ellen shook her head and giggled. "What are we waiting for?"

He was in high spirits, thinking about new possibilities, so she might as well be too.

But then another niggling idea flitted through her mind. All the way around, this change might be the best thing for Dan as well as Barry. The conflict between her son and her husband couldn't worsen if Barry was busy and seldom home.

Barry woke the next morning and stretched. He growled softly like a contented lion. That's how he felt. Robust, successful, and replete. It had been a long time since he'd let loose this way.

Last night had been fantastic. He was thankful that Ellen had persuaded him not to talk about family issues. He didn't look forward to dealing with Dan, but it had to be addressed.

After a hot shower, he went downstairs and put a pot of coffee on. Looking outside, he saw Ellen kneeling in the flower beds, weeding a colorful bed of begonias. He knocked on the window then motioned a sipping action, and she nodded. Ellen removed her gloves and came into the house.

"Ready for coffee?" Barry asked as he tilted the pot towards her.

"You bet. You slept in today. Tired, were you?"

Barry looked over at his wife, pretending to be coy, then smiled. "Maybe. Your point?"

"No point. Just wondering how busy you would be today."

"I have to go in soon and cover the lunch crowd." Barry's tone deepened, and he motioned for Ellen to sit down. "Before I go, there are a few things we need to talk about."

He waited until Ellen was comfortable.

"We have a problem that we need to discuss. It's less than a month away from school. One of the reasons I was so pleased that we could afford for you to stay at home was for the kids." Barry sat down beside her, taking one of her hands in his, squeezing lightly.

"Sara's seems okay now, but I'm worried about what's coming up. Last year she had a tough time. She was moody and didn't want to go to school. That's not like her. I'd feel a lot better if you stayed at home—we can afford it, so why not?" Barry could see her ambivalence and held his breath.

"Let's see how it goes. If it makes a difference to Sara if I'm home or not, we'll decide then." Ellen shrugged her shoulders.

Barry cleared his throat. He needed to tread softly into the next subject. "It's not only Sara. Dan's going into grade nine in September, and you might be busier than you think. It'll be easier if you're on top of it all from the start."

Barry stood up again, pacing. He drew in a deep breath, slowly releasing it before he continued. "It's no secret that Dan and I don't get along. I know you've been trying to keep the peace between us for years. But it needs to stop. No more pussyfooting around with him. I'll keep my nose out of it, but if he gets into any serious trouble, I want to know." Barry ran his fingers through his hair, trying to settle his nerves, knowing the dangerous waters he was treading with her.

"He'll be OK. I think he'll fit in better in high school. He was always too serious to horse around like the other kids his age."

Barry noted his wife was twirling her wedding ring around her finger, a common sign that she was nervous. He sat beside her again, tilting her chin up so he could hold her gaze. "I'm not kidding, Ell. Don't hide anything from me. I know you have before. I let it go because how serious can the trouble be when he's eight or ten or twelve years old? Although I may not be around often, I've picked up the tension escalating in our home. Now he's a teenager, and he'll be exposed to a lot of stuff in high school. He could—"

"You're acting like you expect the worse," Ellen interrupted. "Give him a break and judge him after he's been in it awhile, for God's sake." Ellen tore her hand away, stood up, and began pacing the kitchen.

"Fine, fine. Have it your way. But don't be blind, Ell. I've left you to handle him because I didn't want to argue with you or with him in the few hours I had to share with the family. But now I need to know what's going on, whether I'm at home more or not."

"I get that, but you need to understand him too. He has his good points, but you never see them."

"Maybe that's true, but you have to admit that Dan's always testing us, pushing our buttons. It's made me suspicious of everything he does. I'm always on guard, and I don't know what to expect." Barry rubbed the back of his neck as his gaze jumped around the room, debating the best way to approach her.

"I'm worried for you, Ell. And for Sara. Maybe he'll outgrow this attitude. I hope so. But he has to show us some respect. He may not love me, and I can handle that." Barry paused, his voice softening as he gazed at his wife. "I'm trying to protect you, Ell. I won't tolerate hostility at home or school. No more defending him or hiding things from me."

"I don't hide things from you. I—"

"You do!"

Ellen pursed her lips, clearly not liking him interrupting her or disagreeing with her.

"You make excuses. And I'm damn sure I don't know everything that goes on around here." He threw the last of his coffee out into the sink, then ran his fingers through his hair. "Dan has to have consequences for his behavior. I'm sorry, Ell, but we're not doing him any favors by letting him get away with things. Got it?" A low growl of frustration escaped from his narrowed lips as he stomped out of the house, quickly returning to plant a kiss on the top of Ellen's head. "Sorry, sweetheart, but I had to set this straight."

ELLEN WATCHED him leave the house without replying. "Wonderful. Flippin' wonderful." Ellen's chest constricted, and a prickling sensation began in her scalp.

Well, it had been a great interlude. Now reality and stress were back. It was hard enough when Barry worked six to seven days a week between the two restaurants. But his absence also allowed her to find a way to have peace in her home.

With Barry reducing his days away to three, then only two or three here in Victoria, it would result in a different dynamic. Even adding in the extra responsibilities of joining the Liberal Party, Barry might still spend more time at home than he had been.

Having her, two guys adjust to each other was going to be tough on all of them. Fireworks? You bet.

Maybe she should stay home. Being a peacemaker took a lot of time anticipating and diverting a crisis. Maybe Barry's involvement in politics would take more time than he believed it would. Maybe her home wouldn't become a battleground.

Ellen dropped her head onto her folded hands and closed her eyes. Please, God, help me find a way.

CHAPTER 14

Barry had hired Jolene Thompson as assistant manager for the Nanaimo Carvery. At both interviews, she had worn a conservative pant suit, heavy framed glasses, and had styled her auburn hair swept back into a chignon. He had been impressed with her practical ideas and her work experience. Divorced once, she had no children and no distractions to keep her from committing herself totally to a new challenge with his restaurant.

Slowly, over the following months, their friendship grew. After hectic late-night closing routines, they began taking breathers. Neither one was able to leave work and go directly home to sleep. They were often too hyped about a problem at work or a particularly good evening. It became a habit to close up shop, finish their paperwork, and sit in the quiet darkened lounge to drink or two. Barry remembered their first time together.

He had poured her a Caesar and watched her quickly down it. "Wow, you were thirsty. The next one will have to be a virgin Caesar if you're going to drive. I hope this doesn't mean you have a problem," Barry joked.

"Nope. I'm parched, plain and simple, and you know two drinks are my limit after work. We've done very well again this month. I told you if we started sponsoring some of the baseball tournaments around town, this place would explode."

"I know, I know. You were right again." He poured her another Caesar, virgin this time, then tilted his drink towards her, toasting her. "You've been a good investment for this place, Jolene. I think you deserve a raise."

"I agree." She raised her eyebrow and laughed. "How about 20%?"

"Whoa. I said a raise, not a piece of the action." Barry teased, enjoying the mischievous light in her eyes.

It was easy to be with her. She was up front about everything. Barry knew exactly where he stood with her, and so did the rest of the staff. She enjoyed life and didn't have time for petty problems.

"Look, you know I'm worth it. Keep me motivated, then I'll follow you anywhere. Make me mad, and I'll go make someone else rich."

"Make it 15% net, and you've got a deal. We both win." He watched her as she walked towards the bar, her hips swinging ever so discreetly as she went to make them both their second drink.

There was something about her, he reflected. She stopped wearing her dark, wavy hair in a tight bun. Instead, the waves settled onto her shoulders, causing more than one lustful glance. Last week, she had started wearing contact lenses. Barry had never really noticed her deep violet eyes before, her long dark lashes. It was as if she'd shed an outer wrap and let him see the butterfly underneath.

She turned and walked towards him with the drinks.

Her high heels tapped the floor lightly, commanding him to watch the long legs approach him.

"Cheers."

"Cheers. To more records being made." Barry patted the bench beside him then gestured to her hair. "Have I told you how much I like your hair this way?"

"No, you haven't. At least not in words." Her purred reply made a thrill shoot through him. She held his gaze as she crossed her legs, letting her skirt ride higher up her thighs.

Barry couldn't keep his eyes off them. He forced himself to look upwards and saw the amusement in her eyes. He could see that she knew precisely what she was doing. "You had me fooled, Jolene. When I hired you, I couldn't imagine you being so casual and sexy. You looked so serious. Totally professional."

Jolene's eyes narrowed. "I had to be. If I'd have walked in looking like this, you wouldn't even have considered me. I feel comfortable now, showing you my other side. I can be a successful, ambitious career woman as well as a sexy one." She tipped her glass towards him, inviting a comment.

"I'm beginning to see that," Barry replied softly, unsure of where the conversation was going, yet he was powerless to stop it.

"Are you still staying at the Tides Lodge?" she asked.

"Yes. The Lodge does all my laundry and cleans up the place. It's easy for me."

"Whatever you're comfortable with, I guess," she murmured. She ran her tongue around the salty edge of her drink, then lifted her eyes to capture Barry's attention.

"Why haven't you moved out of that dump? You work hard. You deserve a place where you can have people over occasionally and have a life while you're here." Jolene paused and wrapped her lips around her straw, then sucked a long draw of her Caesar. "If you're interested, there's a one-bedroom suite available in my apartment block."

"Probably wouldn't be any more expensive than what I'm paying now." He wasn't sure if she offered him anything more than a homey atmosphere, but he decided to find out. "Care to show me your apartment? If I like it, I'll apply for the other one".

"Sure." Jolene finished her drink then grabbed her purse. "Follow me—if you can keep up."

He laughed with sheer delight. Jolene's speeding tickets in her restored XR7 were legendary.

Together they locked up the restaurant, then went out to the parking lot, and hopped into their respective cars. Barry had a tough time keeping her tail lights visible as he pushed his aging Volvo after her sports car. She weaved her way through Nanaimo's clubbing district to Departure Bay Road, then took a left on Vista Place. There were a series of well-kept apartment blocks facing each other. He followed her into the parking lot, where she waited.

"Slowpoke."

"You're quite the speed demon," Barry countered. "One of these days, they're going to lift your license."

"Not likely," she retorted. "My uncle works in the traffic court files. It's amazing how much stuff he loses."

Her laughter was contagious. Barry joined in, shaking his head.

"I have to admit. You're quite the gal."

"What? Does it matter that my uncle does me a few favors? I do some for him too, so we're even. Oh, don't look so shocked," she chastised as she led him through the security doors to her building.

Jolene was a woman used to getting her way.

She led him to the elevator and pressed the 6th-floor button.

"Your apartment would be on the 4th floor. It used to belong to a friend. It'd be about the same size as mine."

Barry nodded, unable to keep his eyes off of her. Being in her apartment was tempting fate, but he knew he couldn't resist. He didn't want to.

He was tired of listening to Ellen's complaints about the kids and how he was never home. He was tired of being such a damn responsible person. He was tired of the long hours, the strain of keeping both businesses operating at peak efficiency.

He stared at Jolene's full lips, his gaze flickering back to hers, trying to decide if he was reading her right.

JOLENE RAN the tip of her tongue around her top lip and lowered her eyes. She was treading a fine line. She wanted him with every inch of her being, yet she dared not risk her position. He was the type who would retreat from her more usual direct approach. She didn't want to lose this fish. She wanted him to bite the hook, knowing it, wanting it, and loving it.

Jolene had caught and married one man already, so she knew that marriage would never be in the cards for her again. Then again, neither would a string of affairs satisfy her. She wanted a long-term relationship with someone who didn't demand all of her time, space, or life. Barry would be perfect. She knew how important his family was to him.

"Coming?" she murmured as the elevator opened. She

unlocked her door then entered, shedding her shoes as Barry entered behind her.

"Mmhmm. Nice place." Barry said as he closed the door and tossed his jacket on the coat rack beside hers. Jolene led the way inside, but when the heat from Barry's hand on her hip drew her attention, she turned. She raised her eyebrow when she saw the molten look in his eyes.

Not giving either of them time to reconsider, Jolene pulled him to her, kissing him hungrily. She pressed herself against him, her warm body inviting him to explore, her tongue invading his mouth, demanding a response. His hands traveled over her body, discovering her voluptuous curves, causing his breath to hitch as he groaned in anticipation. She broke away from him, her face flushed, her eyes sparkling.

"Are you sure?" she asked.

"Yes. God, yes," he replied, removing his clothes as fast as she was.

They barely found their way to the sofa before the rise of passion claimed them. The release was quick and explosive, then Jolene led him to her bedroom afterward, overruling his apology.

"Don't. Not necessary. There's a long night ahead, full of surprises." She slipped between the satin sheets beside him, whispering her need for him. She ran her fingers down his abs, swishing her long hair on his chest as she nipped and kissed her way down to his manhood. Listening to Barry swearing softly, his hands gripping her head, she twirled her tongue around him, her lips teasing another erection within minutes. Jolene released him, then wiping her mouth, she straddled him as she proceeded to drive him insane.

The erotica Jolene enjoyed was met with enthusiasm.

She'd make sure Barry would never regret his decision to bed her.

In the hours that followed, they reveled in each other's arms. Jolene guided him skillfully, fulfilling fantasies he had previously only imagined.

THE EARLY MONTHS with Jolene caught Barry by surprise. Whenever he returned to Nanaimo, there was a spring in his step, an excitement that coursed through him every time he saw her, knowing that she wanted him. Him! She was like a drug that he couldn't get enough of.

Her knowing smile, the tip of her tongue licking her lips as she gave him a wink. The anticipation of a quickie text. He never knew if it was a blow job in the wine cellar or a coffee break in his office. Sometimes she was tender, sometimes she was demanding. Jolene enjoyed keeping him on his toes, never knowing what to expect. He could get an instant hard-on, just picturing her bent over his desk with her skirt up around her waist as he took her into nirvana with him. He'd never met a woman capable of multi orgasms, always ready for more.

Jolene expected and wanted nothing more than an interlude of hot, no-barred sex. She had nothing to lose. Lately, Barry recognized the truth that he was only a convenience for her. He was the one who was risking his whole way of life.

Jolene had been an aberration. They both knew it was currently dying a slow death. With Jolene, work was work, and sex was sex. She had no desire to share his life or his interests.

Less than a year later, Barry realized he was tired of

keeping track of his lies. Fear crept into the titillating chances he'd been taking, undermining the enjoyment. Their trysts were not as frequent or as sensual as they once were, merely a satisfying blow off of steam. The fantasy they were involved in was dissolving.

Barry closed the door to his office and speed-dialed his long-time friend and confidant. As usual, her answering machine picked up.

"Bev? How busy are you? I'll be back in Victoria tonight. I was wondering if you'd like to have a few drinks with me tomorrow night? Say 9:30? Call or text me and let me know if that works for you. Thanks, buddy."

BARRY STOOD up and greeted Bev as she walked into the lounge. For a Thursday night, it was fairly quiet, and only a few tables were occupied, which suited him fine. He leaned over and bussed her on the cheek, then let her sit before he settled himself.

"That was a surprising call. It's been a while since I've seen you. Is everything OK?" Bev dumped her briefcase and jacket on the chair next to her.

"Better than it was last year at this time. What will you have to drink?"

"White wine, please."

Barry went to the bar and opened a chilled bottle of Far Niente Chardonnay, a favorite of hers. He poured a glass then brought the rest to the table. He placed a coaster on the table, set her drink down, then took his seat across from her.

"Ooh. The good stuff. Something to celebrate or something to work out? Which is it?"

"Both. Our Nanaimo branch is doing extremely well.

The new manager I brought in is sharp. She chased the sports teams, and our business has boomed."

"That's great news. She?"

"Yes, that's the tough part." Barry sipped his single malt and lowered his eyes to the table, slowly turning his glass around and around between both hands. "I've been stupid, Bev. A real fool."

"Oh my God, Barry. You didn't." Bev's mouth hung open for a moment before she picked up her wine and took a healthy slug of it before continuing. "Is it serious?"

"No, not for either of us. We were very discreet. My manager's extremely independent and self-confident. She made that clear almost from the start—it was a sexual relationship only."

"Whoa, you don't hear of that often. I never pegged you for a casual sex kind of guy. What happened?"

"Stress. Working my Victoria and Nanaimo branches seven days a week, twelve to fourteen hours a day. Trouble at home with the kids. The usual stuff a guy uses to justify a mid-life crisis." Barry rubbed the back of his neck, still avoiding Bev's gaze. "I felt trapped, always working, always settling some crisis at home. Jolene was a temptation I couldn't resist." Frowning, he slowly raised his eyes, wondering what he'd see.

"How long has the affair gone on?"

Barry blew a sigh from his lips. "About eight or nine months."

"So now what? Is it over?" Bev's eyes searched his face, probably looking for a hint of why he'd told her.

"It's been dying for the past month or so. We both knew it would happen. I need some advice. What do I do? I was such a horny fool, excited that a hot woman like her wanted me."

"Have you told Ellen? Do you *want* to tell Ellen?"

"No, and no, not unless I have to. What do you advise? What should I do now? I don't want to worry about her popping up down the road, telling Ellen and the world about how stupid we were." Barry finished the last sip of his drink, then hung his head in shame.

"That's your decision. You know that Ellen probably won't forgive you, and it would be the end of your marriage." Bev leaned forward, her voice a loud whisper filled with exasperation. "You think you had stress before? Imagine the gossip and your reputation going down the drain. Imagine alimony and child custody. What the *hell* were you thinking?"

"I know, I know. Ellen knows something's not right, but I've told her it's the stress that's bothering me." Barry felt his lip trembling and struggled to keep the tears out of his eyes, blinking furiously.

"Ah, Barry." Bev put her hand over his, patting it gently. "I can't say I'm shocked. You two were married so young. It wouldn't have been hard for your manager to tempt you. I gather this is your first affair?"

"First and last. I swear to God, if I can set this straight, I'll earn Ellen's respect and trust again. I've never stopped loving her."

"Again, your decision, but think about this. What does telling Ellen about the affair solve? Does it ease your conscience? Will it make her feel better that you've told her something that could destroy both of you? If you're absolutely sure this will never happen again, then I might have a suggestion."

"There's no doubt in my mind that I will remain faithful to my wife. I'm candid with you, Bev. I'm ashamed of myself. I don't want to lose her." Barry pushed his chair back and went to the bar, and poured himself another shot. When he returned, he saw Bev refilling her wine glass.

"You've never been a player, Barry. I believe you, and I believe in second chances. So, here's an idea to think about. Write this woman a beautiful letter of recommendation and offer her a generous severance package on the condition that she signs a non-disclosure agreement."

"Do you think that will work?"

"Yes, I know it does. I've done several in the past five years. And if this woman wants to retain her reputation for future employment, she'll be quite happy to accept your offer."

"I knew I could count on you to help me out. That's a great idea. What do you suggest for severance?"

"For ordinary termination, it's two weeks for every year of service, but you say it's been less than a year? I'd suggest two or three months. It will tide her over until her next job with no hard feelings."

"Will you do the paperwork for me?" Barry reached over and grasped Bev's hand. When she nodded yes, he lifted her hand and kissed her fingers. "Thank you. I promise you won't be sorry."

As Barry relived his relationship with Jolene, he realized his colossal mistake and was thankful Bev had helped him bail out of it. Now, Barry needed to accept his part in the breakdown of his marriage. He hoped he could pull it together and start over. Barry missed the intimacy he and Ellen shared, how they used to dream and plan for the future. And when they finished making love, he missed that special unity they shared as if they had built a fortress no one could destroy.

He despised himself. Barry wanted and needed honesty and truth back in his life, to live with a clear conscience again.

Was it too late? Could Ellen become the fire in his blood again, the reason his life had meaning? Could he still put a sparkle in her eye?

He had to try.

First things first.

He went back to Nanaimo to settle his past indiscretion. He let go of his apartment and changed his management team. Jolene had accepted his generous severance package and a glowing letter of recommendation with a shrug and a smile. It wouldn't take her long to find another challenge and another lover.

CHAPTER 15

Gradually, Barry renewed his commitment to spend more of his time in Victoria again. He hoped Ellen would never know of his betrayal. Barry wanted Ellen back as his wife and his friend. He yearned for their earlier years.

Perhaps this phony crisis with Sara was a way for Ellen to feel important or to get his attention. Who knew? He had to try to be more understanding. It was time for him to man up. He had to admit if only to himself, his guilt was making him just as hard to live with as Ellen's pre-occupation with her children. It was easier to justify his affair if he blamed his discontent on Ellen.

It was time to find out if their marriage was salvageable. It was time to put as much effort into their relationship as he had in his business. He needed to get his act together if he wanted to save his marriage and pursue a political career.

BY LATE FALL, Ellen was pleased with the results coming from the school system. It took a few months of forcing the issue, but ultimately she prevailed. The fastest way to get an assessment done at UBC was for her and Sara to travel there. The appointments were scheduled into two sessions, which necessitated an overnight stay.

Ellen took the opportunity to take Sara to a production of Stars on Ice. She wanted this trip to have more than the stress of specialist appointments, there needed to be good memories for them. This trip was the first step towards getting Sara the help she needed to feel good about herself and enjoy her life at school.

Ellen's decision to switch Sara's schools was one she was confident about. Sara's new grade three teacher was a man. Mr. Erickson had a kind face and encouraged the best in each of his students. He was open to the suggestions coming from UBC and applied for a teacher's aide to come in for a few hours every day. The aide wouldn't only be for Sara but for any child Mr. Erickson recommended. Ellen knew that made Sara feel better that she wasn't the only one who received special attention. Tracy also received tutoring for math, which cemented a new friendship between the two.

Ellen hadn't seen Steve privately since their time at his apartment. Guilt or embarrassment? She wasn't exactly sure what her reasoning was. After all, Steve had started the ball rolling for Sara, and now the new techniques were beginning to show results. She really ought to make an effort to bring Steve up to date, especially now that she wasn't working at the restaurant anymore. Enough silly procrastination.

"Steve? Hmm. I'm surprised. You don't usually answer the phone." She thought she'd be leaving a message for him at work. What he did with it would be in his court, but at least she'd kept her word.

"Hey there, stranger. How's it going?"

"Good, thanks, extremely good in fact. I wanted to let you know how things are going with Sara. It's taken a while to straighten things out, but I'm pleased with what's happening so far."

"Great. Listen, I have to rush a drink order out. How about we meet for coffee again?"

"I don't know, Steve." Ellen heard her voice soften, aware that her cheeks were flushing. She was glad she was doing this over the phone, so he couldn't see how flustered she was. "I'm not sure I can."

"Barry's coming here after his dinner meeting to close out and run the stats for the month, so I'll be home just after 9:00. I'm anxious to hear about your progress. Barry doesn't talk about family life at work, so I haven't asked any questions. I hope you come. It's been a while." Ice and glasses clinked along with the clattering of utensils in the background.

She wasn't sure what to say. "I'm not sure I can make it. I'll try."

"I have to get these drinks out, sorry. See you later, I hope." Steve disconnected his cell, not bothering to wait for her answer.

Was it just her own emotions that were making her feel guilty? Had she misunderstood their last meeting at his place? If so, then she was acting like an idiot.

Sara arrived home first, excited with her mark on her language test. A happy face and a remark *well done!* was written on top. Sitting on her favorite armchair, Ellen called her over and reached to wrap her in a hug.

"Excellent work, Sara." Ellen looked at her letter formation and flipped the page over to check that one as well. "And not one reversal on either page. Congratulations!" Ellen snuggled her again, kissing the top of her head.

"I went to write the letter b, and I tasted grape, so I did it the right way. This is fun, Mom. I don't feel dumb anymore."

"You were *never* dumb, Sara. Never. You just learn differently than some kids. Got it?"

"Yup. I get it. I can still go where I want to go, but I might have to go the scenic route."

"Exactly. Are you hungry? Want a snack before dinner?"

"Nope, I'm good. I'm going to play Minecraft on my tablet. Call me when dinner's ready." Sara bounced away, tearing up the stairs to where her favorite pastime waited.

Barry left at 5:00 for his Liberal party dinner meeting, reminding Ellen that he'd be going to the restaurant afterward to review the month's statistics and close up.

Ellen smiled, then went to the fridge and poured herself a glass of wine. She sipped her chardonnay while chopping vegetables for a stir fry. This meal was something Ellen often cooked when Barry wasn't home for dinner. Quick, easy, and nutritious, and done so often that she could continue her thoughts as if on automation.

She took the thinly sliced marinated pork out to coat with a cornstarch toss. After sautéing the ingredients, she seasoned with teriyaki or Thai sauce. Poured over noodles or rice, it was something Ellen prepped at least once a week, occasionally substituting pork with chicken or prawns.

As she cooked, she pondered Steve's request to meet him again at his place. Why not? At her last visit, she had felt rebuffed with Barry's lack of support when it came to Sara, so of course, she yearned for attention. He was a close family friend, that was all. Surely, she was mistaken about the evening's end.

Ellen had reassured herself there was nothing untoward in her and Steve's behavior by the time dinner was over. Good friends, that's all they were to each other.

Since he'd joined them, Barry always kept a bottle or two of Steve's favorite Russian Ridge Pinot Noir in their wine cellar to give as gifts for celebrating restaurant milestones. She'd bring one tonight. Getting to the bottom of Sara's difficulties in school deserved an above-average celebration.

Dan announced he was heading out for a while and would be back later. He didn't volunteer information of where he was going or with whom. Ellen didn't bother trying to drag it out of him. She spent time with Sara, checking over her homework, then sent her to get ready for bed.

Ellen had called the sitter in for 9:00, promising an outing of no more than two hours. She freshened up with new makeup, then scanned her closet. Ellen picked some warm black leggings and a peacock blue knitted pullover that went down past her hips. She retrieved the bottle of Russian Pinot Noir, picked up several of Sara's test results, and was ready to leave by the time Missy arrived.

Ellen texted Steve as she parked her car. A minute later, the outside door opened, and Steve waved her in.

"Good, you're here. I wasn't sure that you'd come."

Ellen handed him the expensive bottle of wine and smiled. "Of course, I came. We have something to celebrate."

"I'll open it and let it breathe a bit. Make yourself at home."

Ellen removed her jacket and perused his home, struck again with his taste in décor. Soft music played in the background, old tunes from Elton John's heyday. Ellen sorted Sara's papers to display them on the coffee table better, then sat on the leather sofa.

"I wondered if you'd bring some of Sara's work. I gather you've seen an improvement?"

"Not only in her work but in her personality. Since she received her assessment, I've joined the local chapter of ACLD, and I've been helping her at home. It's amazing what's changed by using different senses to learn."

"What's ACLD?"

"Adults and Children with Learning Disabilities. You were right. Once I knew what the problem was, I was able to access all sorts of information."

"Her printing and math papers look normal, no reversals or anything." Steve looked over the paperwork, then at Ellen. "You must be ecstatic for her."

"I am. I tried a technique using Sara's sense of taste. Believe it or not, it works. I outlined her common reversals with a wet stylus on paper, then shook drink crystals over them. Each letter or numeral had its own flavor. Within two weeks, her reversals were gone. She said when she went to print them, she'd taste the flavor and write it the correct way."

"Beats the hell out of practicing line after line as you told me she used to."

"Which reminds me, I also switched her schools. No more Mrs. Andrews. She's doing well with the male teacher she has now. You wouldn't believe the difference this has made for her. No more tummy aches. No more whining about going to school. She's cheerful now."

"I'm glad you didn't give up on her, and I was able to help. Are you ready for that glass of wine?" Steve tilted his head towards the kitchen.

"Love one."

"I'll be right back."

Ellen heard the fridge open and some kind of preparation going on in there. No surprise when he returned with a small plate of cheeses and grapes. He returned to get the goblets.

"To success. Congratulations, Ellen. We made a good team on that one." Steve clinked his glass to hers.

"Yes, we did. Thank you again for everything." She twirled the wine, watching the legs before sipping the ambrosia. "Wow. This wine may become my favorite, too."

Steve smiled. "It can be addictive, alright. So, what else is new? How's Dan doing?"

"Same old, same old. He's a teenager, what can I say? My cousin Matt told me years ago not to sweat the small stuff. I've got that down pat now. It's easier."

"Good. Dan will grow out of the attitude sooner or later. Now that you've helped Sara, have you decided what you're going to do next? Are you going back to work?"

"I haven't decided. I might. Or I've been thinking about taking a course. I've loved helping Sara, so I'm considering a teacher's aide certificate." Ellen went on to tell him about her recent idea, sipping her wine and enjoying his astute observations.

He knew her so well.

"Another glass? We might as well finish it off. They're not big bottles."

"Sure, why not."

Steve took her glass and went into the kitchen.

Ellen leaned back against the sofa, now listening to more music from Bonnie Tyler.

Content. Relaxed. The constant tension Ellen lived with every day had melted away. Time spent with Steve was always comfortable and stress-free.

When he returned, she accepted her glass and held onto it for a split second more than necessary. She placed her glass on the coffee table beside his.

Steve's adrenaline pumped, and his heart filled with happiness. All of her actions showed she loved and trusted him. The way she looked at him when she leaned back encouraged him.

He put his arm around her, and with his other hand, he tilted her chin up. "Ellen." His eyes locked in hers, swimming in their hazel depths.

She lifted her lips to him, and he heard himself groan as he bent to kiss her full lips. Heaven. Everything he had ever wanted. Her lips were soft and warm as he showered them with short, sweet kisses, murmuring her name.

Ellen quivered as she wrapped her arms around him, murmuring his name as she ran her fingers through his hair. Through half-closed lids, he watched her close her eyes and felt her lips tremble as much as her hands. When she pushed her breasts against his muscled chest, a thrill soared through him.

Steve moaned as her lips feathered kisses down his neck, her warm breath sending shivers down his spine. His body leaned into hers, slowly pushing her down onto the cushion, his arm cradling her head. Sensations swirled around him, driving him into a vortex of need.

Steve slid his hand underneath her sweater, covering her breast and squeezing lightly, fingering the tight bud. Then Ellen slipped her hands under his sweatshirt, running her hands over his torso. Steve could feel her heartbeat quickening in time with his own as he lifted her sweater to press his lips against her breast.

"Oh my God, Steve." Ellen's passionate response suddenly froze, causing her to push away from him.

Steve tried to hang onto her hand as she sat up and

scooted farther away on the sofa. He could see the guilt flitting across her face when a moment ago, there was only the flush of passion.

"Ellen, don't run away from me. I love you. I've loved you for years. You must have known that. Now I know you love me too," Steve whispered urgently. Gently, he reached for her arms and made her face him again as he kissed her closed eyes. "I've waited so long for this, don't pull away from me, honey. This is right for us."

"I can't. I can't do this. We're just friends, and it can't be anything else. It can't be."

"It's sure taken you a long time to notice your feelings about me. I was beginning to think you'd never see it, never feel it." Steve's finger caressed her cheek, moving down to her lips, outlining the fullness.

Ellen raised her eyes to him, drinking in his every feature. His expressive light blue eyes, alight with a fire of desire she'd never seen before. Ellen traced the tiny scar on his left cheekbone on her way to threading her fingers through his wavy blonde hair. She pulled his head down again for a searing kiss that electrified them both.

"What am I doing?"

Ellen pulled away from him and lowered her eyes. Steve watched as she struggled to control her emotions. Her face was beyond flushed, only emphasizing how deeply she had responded. Steve watched her fingertips rub her forehead as her gaze flitted about the room.

"Where did that come from?" Ellen stood up to put some space between them. "I don't know what got into me. I didn't mean for that to happen." Her voice was barely a whisper now.

"Ellen, stop it. Trust me. This was meant to be. Does anyone else know you as I do? Care about you like I do?"

"It doesn't matter, Steve. I'm married. I have a family. This can't happen." She wasn't very coherent anymore. Ellen stumbled as she moved towards the door, reaching for her coat.

Steve followed her, spreading his hands out for an explanation. "What about love? What is a marriage without love? What you and Barry had is gone. You know it. You were lonely tonight—-you're lonely often, whether he's at home or not. How can you keep up marriage as two separate people?"

Steve was by her side, imploring her to listen. "Ellen!"

"I have to go." Ellen frantically pulled the door open.

Following her down the hallway, Steve tugged at her coat to try and stop her, but she wrenched herself free.

"Sweetheart, stop. This was meant to be. You must know that. Wait, please wait. We have to talk." Steve's voice deepened with panic as he continued begging her to listen.

Ellen saw the distress on his face. It broke her heart probably as much as his was breaking right now. "No. Please. Give me some time to think." Ellen pushed the outdoor latch, then hurried outside, resisting his attempts to accompany her. "I'll call you in a few days," she promised, barely able to make eye contact with him.

As the door hissed closed behind her, Steve banged his fist against the wall. Now, what the hell would happen? She had to come back to him, he swore. *Had to.* He rubbed the back of his neck, then briskly ruffled his hair, trying to regain his composure. He shouldn't have kissed her, but he had waited so long, and the mood had seemed so perfect.

He returned to his apartment and sunk into the sofa, grabbing his wine glass and downing the remnants. Now that he had pushed his feelings into the open, he realized the enormity of the risk. Their relationship couldn't continue as it was. Either it would blossom and develop, or it would die. From the look on Ellen's face when she left, Steve didn't like his odds.

Perhaps what had happened was for the best. Steve had postponed his own life for much too long, never having the courage before to force the issue. Still feeling her warm, soft lips on his while their bodies found each other, he'd never forget her first intuitive responses before reasoning had set in.

He'd never forget that connection. At least he knew that Ellen loved him too. There was no doubt in his mind, but it was probably too late. She'd never be able to break the bond she had with Barry and their children. Tomorrow, he'd tender his resignation and remind Barry how lucky he was. He couldn't bear bumping into her at work or in meetings with Barry. It was time to let her go.

ELLEN DROVE HOME QUICKLY, barely aware of where she was, her subconscious taking control of the directions to go home. *How could this happen?*

One part of her was horrified at her behavior. A pregnant bride was a stain on her past that she had made up for, but it was nothing compared to being an adulteress. She tried to be a good Christian wife and mother. The notion of having an affair with Steve had never crossed her mind before.

Or had it? All the way home, she belittled herself, ashamed of her behavior. After paying the babysitter, she slowly climbed the stairs, profound exhaustion seeming to sap every ounce of energy she had left. In her bedroom, she stopped and looked at the confused woman in her mirror. *Who are you?*

A heavy heart settled on her as she crawled into her lonely bed. Finally, in the privacy and darkness of her room, she thought honestly about that brief five-minute interlude. If only she could shut out her responsibilities. Butterflies in her stomach slowly circled lower, reminding her of how passionately she had responded to Steve, how complete she had felt with him. If there was such a thing as soulmates, she was sure that's what she'd felt.

But the nuns had taught her well. She shuddered at the idea of being a divorcee, the shame she'd feel if she broke up her family. She couldn't even imagine what it would do to the kids. Although she now realized her attraction to Steve had been growing for a long time, it was also something that needed to stop. Having an affair out of boredom was stupid. If she wanted excitement in her life, she needed to find her passion in something that gave her joy and pride.

Tears spilled down her cheeks as she acknowledged her marriage was definitely in trouble. Their relationship wasn't working anymore. Something had to give. She couldn't remember the last time she was carefree and excited. It was time for Ellen to explore new horizons other than motherhood if she wanted her marriage to work. Past time.

Ellen sluggishly went about her usual routine in the morning, looking for a way out of her dilemma. It was as if her troubled thoughts could travel when at 11:00 a.m., she received a telephone call from her old school friend.

"Hi, stranger! How are you?" Paula's expressive voice bubbled.

"Paula, it's great to hear from you. What's up?"

"Ken's going away for a few days on a business seminar

to Seattle. It's been such a long time since I saw you. I hoped you'd be able to play hooky and come over for a while."

"I'd love to, but Barry's leaving tomorrow to head back to Nanaimo for four days."

"So? Your kids aren't babies. Isn't there anyone there who could take them for a few days? They wouldn't be a lot of trouble, I'm sure. C'mon, Ell, run away with me," Paula coaxed.

Ellen's mind raced, checking out the possibilities. Sara could go to Tracy's home. If allowed to, she'd live there half the time, anyway. Dan was another problem. But maybe it was time to give him a chance to prove himself. Certainly, there was no friend close enough to him for her to call on.

"Ok, Paula, I'll see what I can do," Ellen chirped excitedly. This getaway was exactly what she needed. Breathing room and another perspective.

"Sweet! Can you call me back tonight?"

"Sure." At this point, Ellen wasn't at all worried about what Barry would think.

If the kids could be handled, he'd have to accept her impetuous getaway. If Barry didn't like it, he could rearrange his schedule and stay home. She needed this.

"Paula, wait. I don't have to call you back. Come hell or high water. I'll be on the 10:00 ferry. Pick me up, and I'll buy you lunch."

"Double sweet. See you tomorrow." Paula disconnected, obviously delighted with the unexpected outcome.

Ellen rolled her shoulders and rocked her head from side to side. She needed a break, a fresh perspective, and Paula was just the person to share her problems with. Ellen was tired of putting herself last, always accommodating the children or Barry. After phoning Tracy's mother and arranging for Sara's stay, she called Barry.

"Hi, hon, what's up?" He sounded worried.

She knew he wasn't used to her contacting him at work.

"Paula just phoned me. She needs me to come over for a few days. I've decided to go. I'll leave in the morning. I've made arrangements for Sara. Tonight, I'll set down rules for Dan. It'd help if you could leave for Nanaimo on Thursday morning instead of the evening. Then he'd only be alone one night before I'm home on Friday."

"Couldn't you wait until I come home on Sunday? You'd have three full days then."

"No, I can't *wait*. Not this time. This is girl stuff. I've got to go right away," Ellen said.

"What's the panic? I really don't think you should go. Dan's not trustworthy, so who knows what he'll do. Stay home, Ell."

"Don't order me like that, Barry. I'm going. This is important. If you don't trust Dan, then *you* stay home until I return." Ellen's face flushed, and her heart pounded as she pushed back. She was done taking orders.

"What the hell's gotten into you? You're not yourself these days."

"How do you know? You're hardly ever here. You're only mad because I'm not agreeing with every bloody thing you tell me. I'm not your goddamned employee." Ellen gripped the phone tighter, trying to control the shrillness in her voice.

"Ok, ok. Look, I know we haven't spent much time together lately. I promise I'll take some time off soon." Barry lowered his voice and his tone. "Go ahead if it's that important. I'll call Nanaimo and let them know I won't be there until Saturday morning. I'm not leaving Dan alone. I'll get Lucas to cover for me."

"Good. I'm getting to a point where I feel like screaming.

It seems you forget that I have needs and opinions too. Life's not *all* about you and your business." Ellen took a deep breath to calm herself, then noticed the dead silence. "Look, I'm sorry I blew up."

"Don't sweat it. I think I needed that. I don't mean to ignore you. It's just that I look after business, and you look after the family, and..."

Ellen gritted her teeth and lowered her voice to a growl. "What decade are you in? No wonder I'm feeling lonely. If that's all I am to you is a nanny, then you need to wake up. And wake up fast."

"Alright, alright. Go and have a ball, ok? Maybe you'll come back in a better mood."

"Maybe I will." Ellen lowered her tone. "We need to spend some time discussing this, Barry. Think about it. I'll probably see you Friday evening."

"Fine. I love you, Ell."

"Hmm." Ellen disconnected. A niggling of guilt for being so headstrong teased at her conscience, but she pushed it aside. If he figured saying he loved her would smooth things over, as usual, he was sadly mistaken.

ELLEN'S WALK quickened as her mood and step became measurably lighter as she collected her luggage at the ferry terminal and then jumped into Paula's car. They grinned foolishly at each other, then chattered and laughed incessantly on the forty-five-minute ride to Paula's home in White Rock.

"Do you realize how long it's been?" Paula asked.

"You betchya. Almost fifteen years. I've never left Barry

with the kids before unless you count the week I spent in Port Alberni when my dad had his heart attack."

Ellen followed her friend into the condo and set her overnight bag down. "You've changed the décor since we were here last. I love the warm colors you've painted on the walls. Very brave of you."

"Ken talked me into it, and I'm happy with the results. Your bedroom is the first door on the left."

Ellen brought her suitcase into her room and lifted it on the bed. "It feels weird being here by myself, but I'm glad you called. Perfect timing, actually."

"Why? What's going on? You never did tell me what made you accept my invitation this time."

"Who knows? Nothing and everything." Ellen shrugged her shoulders. "I needed to get away, do something fun for a change." She turned aside, busy putting her toiletries away on the dresser top. "By the way, what have you got planned for tonight?"

Knowing Paula, Ellen was sure they wouldn't be sitting at home. Having company meant going out.

Paula and Ken had finally married three years ago but had decided not to have children. They were used to traveling and entertaining. Children didn't fit in the lifestyle they enjoyed.

"Why don't we take the sky-train into Vancouver, have some dinner, and go to Brandi's on Hornby? The music and sound system are fantastic, and it's always packed, so we can dance and people watch."

"Sweet. I guess that means we better get the lead out and hit some shops. I think we deserve a new outfit for that, don't you?"

Paula agreed, albeit surprised at Ellen's effervescent, daring mood. Ellen had been her friend for most of her life, and although she was a loyal friend, Paula had occasionally been frustrated with her prim and proper ways. Her constant consideration of everyone else except herself could get annoying. At times, Paula would think of her sarcastically as Saint Ellen. This little jaunt was totally out of character. Something was out of whack, no doubt about it.

The feeling of apprehension came and went as the afternoon flew by while they explored the trendy boutiques in White Rock.

Ellen flitted about in a state of nervous energy, experimenting with bold colors and fashions she usually avoided. They finally splurged on new outfits for the evening, and on impulse, Paula lured Ellen into a lingerie boutique. Paula bought some scented massage oil and a black negligee trimmed in faux fur, guaranteed to thrill.

"C'mon, Ellen -haven't you ever used this stuff? After all the years of marriage, don't you find your sex life boring sometimes?"

"Paula," Ellen's hushed voice was full of shock. This store had quietened her down considerably.

"Oh, don't be such a prude. What's wrong with putting a little spice in the bedroom? Ken loves it when I come home with something new. And I don't have to worry about him wandering around either." Paula laughed at Ellen's discomfiture. She nodded across the mall to *Black Friday*.

"Have you ever been in there? I love to surprise Ken now and then with something sexy too. They have the hottest G-strings for guys. He likes turning me on too but don't, for God's sake, tell Barry he wears them. Ken would kill me."

They left the boutique, but not until after Paula had coaxed Ellen into buying some lotions and a revealing satin and lace teddy. "Now, wasn't that a blast? That ought to send a few sparks flying when you get home. Shall we go and get him something too?"

"No way. He'll wonder what I've been up to if I come home with that. These purchases will be enough to raise his eyebrows."

"It better raise more than his eyebrows," quipped Paula, and they both giggled. "Be honest, Ellen, have you ever thought of anyone else? I'm damn sure you haven't fooled around, but you two got married very young."

Ellen looked at her, surprised at her intuition. "Me? Why would I?"

"Hmm. Now there's a non-answer. What's up? Never mind, save it until we get home. We, my dear, are going to have several drinks and talk."

"Isn't that what we've been doing all day?"

Ellen breathed a sigh of relief when Paula abandoned the conversation and concentrated on driving home through the heavy Lower Mainland traffic. After unpacking their purchases, Paula poured each a glass of wine and sat down.

There was no getting away from her now, and as Ellen sipped her wine, The load she carried began to lighten just in anticipation.

After she swore Paula to secrecy, she told her of the trouble in her marriage and how they had slowly drifted apart until they were now barely more than companions in the same house. On their second bottle of wine came the secret of her growing attraction to Steve and how close she had come to being sexually involved with him.

"Why didn't you?"

"Honestly, I don't know. I hadn't realized how often I turned to Steve and how often he was there for me, listening to me or helping me. Suddenly the electricity was there, and I knew I wanted him as much as he wanted me."

"He never let on before. How he felt?"

"Maybe he did, and I didn't see it. We'd been discussing the problems Sara had at school and trying to find a solution. I agreed to meet him at his apartment to pick up information from his teaching friends. Everything was going so well. He'd made us a few Spanish coffees, and I was so relaxed and excited about the possibilities of getting Sara assessed for learning disabilities. I went back three months later to tell him what I'd discovered and bring him up to date with Sara's progress. I brought his favorite wine as a thank you, and one thing led to another. Then, bang. All of a sudden, he kissed me."

"Wow. I take it you were surprised? Please don't tell me you ran away."

"Oh my God, Paula, I'd forgotten how that fire felt. The heat, the tenderness, that feeling in the pit of your belly. My whole body was trembling. The passion in his eyes, the gentle way he held me, it was amazing."

"Did you kiss him back?"

"You bet I did. It almost took my breath away. Then as we were getting more comfortable, I came to my senses and chickened out. I panicked and ran. And the bitch of it was, I think he understood."

"Ah, sweetie, you got yourself a problem there. He loves you, doesn't he? It wasn't entirely about sex, was it?" Paula went to the fridge and grabbed another bottle of Chardonnay, and refilled their glasses.

"I keep going over and over it. It was the connection I longed for all evening. It was heaven, and I won't deny that. He says he loves me and has for a long time." Ellen shrugged, then her voice dropped in wonder. "And I might love him too. I deeply care about him and think about him a lot. But I still love Barry too. I don't want to lose my kids or disgrace my parents again."

"Damn Barry!" Ellen's shocked expression must have surprised Paula. "You heard me. I could kill him for ignoring you so much. I thought he was such a good father and husband."

"He is. It's me. He works hard for us, and I know he loves us. It just hasn't been enough for me lately. I've been lonely, and I guess Steve saw it. I should have seen the signs and not let myself be alone with him."

"Come off it. Barry's slowly been abandoning you, letting you take on all the responsibility for the family and giving you nothing in the way of emotional support. If you had his attention and loving, you wouldn't have been in that position."

"Maybe." Ellen tapped her finger to her lips, thinking. "I guess that's why I'm so attracted to Steve. He's genuinely interested in my life. He gives me the confidence I haven't had with Barry for a long time. He's supportive, and he treats me with the respect that I deserve. Like I'm important as a person, not only a wife or mother."

"So, what's the problem? You have a right to be happy too. If you can't have an affair, why don't you get a divorce?"

"Are you crazy?" Ellen almost shouted at her. "I couldn't put the kids through the pain of shared custody or of taking sides. That wouldn't be good for them at all, for any of us for that matter." Ellen's lip trembled as she looked at Paula glaring at her. "I know it's confusing, but I love Barry too. He's been part of my life for so long. He's part of who I am."

"Ellen, grow up!"

"Pardon me?"

"You heard me!" Paula slammed her wine glass on the coffee table. "Grow. Up. How can you be satisfied if you live your life for everyone else? It's time you make your own decisions based on what *you* want." Paula's voice was strident, almost harsh. "I love you with all my heart, but sometimes you drive me crazy. Do you know what my nickname for you has been over the years? *Saint Ellen.* You're always trying to be perfect. News flash – *no one's perfect*."

Ellen, surprised at her friend's brusqueness, slowly nodded. "I guess I've always been obsessed with doing the right thing for my family. I've never been assertive. I don't know if I can do that. First, I was a daughter. Then I was a wife and mother. I don't know who I am without those titles."

Paula reached over and squeezed her best friend's hand. "I know. Your life has been wrapped around your family for so long that you've lost sight of yourself. You need to value yourself and make other people pay attention to your happiness too."

Ellen rubbed her temple where a headache now throbbed. Too many things had been going on that she didn't want to analyze. It was so much easier to ignore the problems in her life.

"Why can't things go back like they were, Paula?" she cried. "I don't want to lose anybody or anything." Ellen's eyes watered. She clenched her hands against her mouth, trying to hold back her tears. She'd cried enough lately, yet it had solved nothing.

Paula patted her shoulder gently. "You, my dear, have got to get real. Nobody can turn back the clock, and even if you could, you might not come out ahead."

"Maybe we'd better cut back on the wine for a while," Ellen mumbled.

Paula went to the cupboard and pulled out a charcuterie board she had prepped in the morning. When she offered the tray to Ellen, Ellen shook her head. Paula popped a few olives in her mouth then made herself comfortable again, wondering how far she should go.

"People change. Situations change." Paula pointed at Ellen. "You-*you* have to decide what you want or need, then have the guts to go for it. Be brave. Talk it out, fight for what you want."

"I don't know, Paula, it's hard for me to be honest and say what's bugging me or to complain. I feel like I'm selfish."

"It's tough, but it's the only way you're going to find happiness. It's *not* selfish. It's called *self-care*. If you're feeling ignored and unappreciated, I'll bloody guarantee that Barry does too. You can't ignore the shit that's been going on for the past several years and keep pretending it's alright." Paula munched on a few crackers with cheese, giving Ellen time to think. She washed it down with the rest of her wine before continuing. "If you can't do it alone, get some counseling. And get Barry to go too."

"That might be the answer for me. But Barry won't go, that's for sure." Ellen took another sip of her wine then took a deep breath, trying to calm herself. "Oh brother, what a mess. Ok, when I get back, I'll see what this lingerie can do to break the ice in the bedroom. Maybe Barry and I can work this out. I hope so. I'll go from there."

"And while you're at it, start thinking about what you find interesting, what you'd do if you had a career. You need to find another outlet for your energy, other than your family."

"You must be a mind reader. Lately, I've been wondering what my passion would've been if I hadn't married."

"There you go. You're smart and a great problem solver, so figure it out. Challenge yourself. Reaching for your dreams is liberating, believe me."

"I guess. Can we stop now? My brain is starting to go fuzzy with all this talk and wine." Ellen leaned her head back against the sofa and closed her eyes.

"Of course." Paula went into the kitchen to tidy up, then hollered for Ellen to get ready for the evening.

Ellen massaged her temples slowly, opened her eyes then went to the bathroom to freshen up. Although she had drunk more than usual, she had a clear plan of action for the problems she'd long ignored. The talking had lifted the mysterious burden from her as she recognized what she'd been afraid to face. No more putting it off. It was time for her to make some choices.

"Thanks," Ellen said to her friend as she re-entered the living room.

"No prob. Let's drop it now and go have some fun."

"Sweet. I'm more than ready."

THREE DAYS LATER, as Ellen waved goodbye to her friend at the ferry, she silently thanked God for her no-nonsense, supportive ally.

They had a wonderful evening the first night, joining some of Paula's fascinating friends at Brandi's. They partied until the music ended before heading home. The second night they spent at Paula's place and ordered a Chinese buffet. They spent the rest of the evening talking endlessly about anything and everything. A renewed closeness developed again between them that had been missing for a long time. Paula seemed to give her the strength to take risks, to strive for her own goals.

If only this feeling she had now would last.

ELLEN CLIMBED the stairs to go topside on the Queen of Alberni, where scattered benches welcomed the heartier traveler. Stiff sea breezes buffeted her, so she took refuge behind a plexiglass divider where she sat to think.

Paula had been right. If she wasn't satisfied with her situation, it was up to her to change it. Not up to Steve or Barry. Up to her. All along, it had been so easy for her to blame someone else for her growing frustration and resentment. Or to ignore it altogether.

Resentment?? Ellen wondered why that word had popped into her head. Resent who, Resent what?

In a conscious effort not to set aside this unsettling feeling, she delved down, looking for answers she had kept from herself for far too long. She let her mind wander through a kaleidoscope of memories, both good and bad, remembering the joys she had experienced earlier in their marriage.

Although it had been an early start, she and Barry had approached it with all the vigor and optimism of youth. Barry had remained the confident workaholic he'd been from the beginning. Yet, somewhere along the way, things had changed. She had changed, and she wondered if Barry had even noticed.

These days, all her energies went into the children. She recognized the grudge she held against Barry. He had allowed her to grow apart from him, yet had she confronted him? Would it have made a difference?

She tossed the questions about, debating her role in the situation.

Because Steve was more perceptive, did it mean that he was a better man? Was he worth losing her family? Wasn't that part of her commitment to her husband? To be able to communicate and work out problems in their marriage? Had she given Barry a chance?

"He's not a mind reader," She blurted aloud just as the ferry's whistle blew, startling her.

For the first time, she had allowed herself to be introspective, a behavior that she had always worried was only one step away from selfishness.

Introspection was a trait highly condemned by her parents and her religious schooling. But how could she analyze her feelings if she ignored them or buried them? Paula's admonition to grow up had snapped something inside her. She had fooled herself into believing that if she looked after others well, made their days brighter, she'd be satisfied too. How naïve.

Ellen took a deep breath of salt air, watching the pier approach. She lifted her head high and threw her shoulders back. Time to grow up. Stop looking for others to guide her. Stop being afraid.

As she disembarked, she embraced the challenge ahead of her for a better future. What that would hold was still a mystery, but she wanted something better. She deserved to have a life of her own, to be appreciated and valued. Unless she became more assertive and stood up for herself, it wouldn't happen.

Shock therapy, like what Paula gave her, was what Barry needed. She was more than the young, impressionable, eager to please girl that he married. She couldn't ignore the widening gap between them or stay stuck in the role she'd tried to perfect as the perfect wife. It was time to explore her options. To make herself happy.

She retrieved her luggage and returned to the overnight parking area to collect her car. Even though butterflies circled inside, she was confident she was on the right track to get control of her life. All she had to do was stand tall and not cave in.

~

As soon as Ellen stepped inside her home's foyer, she noticed a vase of yellow rosebuds on the entrance table. Wow. She checked the date, wondering if she'd forgotten something, but nothing jumped out at her. Hmmm. She bent to smell the delicate scent. Nice. But if he thought they could erase the way he talked to her, he was sadly mistaken. Things were going to change, and it might as well start now.

"Ellen?" Barry's nervous voice preceded him. He stepped forward and drew her into a hug. Ellen's body tensed, her shoulders arching back as she remembered her vow to stay strong and voice her opinion. She gave his back a soft pat, then pulled away, using the excuse of setting her purse on the table to get out of his arms. She couldn't let her guard down.

"You're home in the middle of the day?" Ellen noticed Barry's flushed face. Was there a problem? "Is everything ok?"

"No problem, I missed you, that's all," he said. He reached for her jacket, but Ellen shrugged out of it and hung it up herself.

"Hmm. Maybe I should go away more often," she said.

"You...you shocked the hell out of me on Tuesday," he replied.

"Kind of surprised me too," Ellen conceded, quietly accepting a drink from him.

"I have another surprise for you then, one that's long

overdue." His eyes locked onto hers, a mischievous look crossed his face. Barry beckoned her to sit beside him.

Tentatively, she sat. She wondered if Barry had been having the same problems but been braver than her. All of a sudden, she hoped not. A fierce determination gripped her as she realized that she wanted to give their marriage another shot. Ellen nervously sipped her drink, then cleared her throat.

"Barry, this past year has been challenging."

"I know, Ell. I'm so sorry. I've let you shoulder too much of the responsibility around here. I promise we're going to work this out. I want to see the sparkle in your eyes again." He handed her an envelope. "I picked these up today." He stood close to her as she opened it. "I hope this will be something you want as much as I do."

Ellen glanced from the envelope to her husband's eyes and recognized the uncertainty. She held his gaze as she tore it open. As Ellen looked at the contents, tears came to her eyes. Two airline tickets to Hawaii in February gave her the answer.

"Excellent idea. I've been edgy lately, unsure of what I could do to be happy inside again. There are so many things we need to discuss." Ellen sighed, then wrapped her arms around his neck and kissed him soundly. "Honey, I think this will be perfect. The honeymoon we never had."

Relief flooded over them as they toasted each other with another glass of wine, the tension disintegrating into an exciting, newfound hope.

CHAPTER 16

Celebrating their sixteenth anniversary the following July found Ellen reviewing the year. There was a lot to be thankful for and few regrets.

The Hawaiian holiday they took together after Christmas had been an antidote to a dying relationship. Her mom had made their life easier by agreeing to stay and care for the children while they were gone. Even the loss of Steve from the restaurant had not been enough to cancel the plans. If Barry suspected the depth of their friendship, he never alluded to it, yet somehow Ellen sensed he knew.

Barry reverted to the romantic man she had married, thoughtful and sensitive to her needs. They played tourist, renting a convertible, and drove around Oahu, finding secluded beaches to picnic and enjoy the swimming. They talked about everything and nothing, so by the time the three weeks were up, they had a handle on a solution. Not everything was better, but now she felt cared for, listened to, and an essential part of his life.

After their February holiday, Ellen looked into classes at Camosun College. She enjoyed helping Sara and decided to pursue a career as a teacher's aide. Sara and Ellen often sat at the kitchen island, doing homework together, cheering each other on, and commenting on Barry's attempts at cooking.

Barry, Ellen, and Sara spent almost every second weekend re-discovering favorite haunts on Vancouver Island. In May, they found a *For Sale* ad for a two-bedroom chalet with a loft on Comox Lake near Courtenay. On a whim, they viewed it and bought it the same day.

Barry, aware of his near loss, strove to make Ellen excited about new possibilities. He hired a local contractor to add a third bedroom to the loft in their Comox Lake getaway. Then an updated well and septic field was added before the landscape was redesigned. Barry enjoyed helping to construct a new cedar dock and float house. When completed in August, they spent as much time there as they could.

Dan usually preferred to stay at their home in Victoria, even if it meant surprise checks by the new manager at The Carvery, along with impromptu parental phone calls.

Without the stress of their son's presence, tranquility reigned in their new sanctuary, and it fostered a renewal of optimism. Ellen knew carefree happiness she had seldom experienced since early in her marriage.

All summer, Ellen and Sara worked together, using new techniques to overcome her worst problems with schoolwork. Ellen tirelessly researched the subject of children with learning disabilities and was amazed at some of her discoveries. Once she realized that all people learn in more ways than listening and reading, her imagination caught fire. Together, she and her daughter searched the internet for learning strategies that would help Sara excel.

Ellen was optimistic that Sara would feel more confident

when school started again in September. She hoped that this would be the start of a more fulfilling school life.

"Mom, guess what?" Sara shrieked as she returned from school one day near the end of November.

"What, sweetie?" Ellen was busy spooning the last tray of cookie dough.

"I received an award today for the most improved student this month." Sara was jumping up and down, punching her left arm in the air. "Woo-hoo!"

"Alright. I'm so proud of you." Ellen hugged her vibrating, young daughter tightly. "See, you've got this down pat now. The sky's the limit, and you can do whatever you want."

Sara giggled, as if still in disbelief, then said, "Yup, I can. I'm going upstairs and chat with Lisa on Instagram. Tell her my news."

"Go for it, sweetie. Want to have a family outing to Dairy Queen for dessert tonight? Or if you'd rather, I could run and get a frozen DQ cake for all of us to share at home?"

"Why not just you and me? You're the one who's been helping me."

"You're right. You and I will celebrate on our own. Now go tell Lisa." She smiled at her daughter's exuberance, letting a sigh of relief escape her lips. *What a difference two years had made for the both of them.* Ellen worked two to three days a week in a special education class at the Monterey Middle School and had never been happier.

Ellen's heart filled with pride with Sara's educational success and hoped this would end Sara's problems. Sara's IQ was 110. If she could remain positive and work hard with the tools available to her, anything was possible. Ellen experienced a wave of relief course through her, knowing they had found a way around the maze of dyslexia.

Relief was not a word she could use about Dan. It seemed that most of her family's troubles now centered around Dan and his father. Before, there were issues with the restaurants, or Sara or Steve. Each time Ellen solved one challenge, another situation would crop up and threaten to overcome her.

However, the self-confidence she developed while taking the teacher's aide course changed her outlook. Ellen had created an identity of her own now. Nothing seemed impossible. Of course, it was easier now that she spent more time sharing her problems with Barry. She didn't have to handle situations entirely on her own. When Ellen considered their family's future, a new optimism flowed through her, even though Dan continued to try their patience.

He still excluded himself from almost all family outings. To tell the truth, Ellen mused as she slipped the tray of cookies in the oven, it was a reprieve for the rest of them. His sullen manner aggravated Barry, which made Sara nervous, which in turn made Ellen apprehensive.

In the past year, Dan had come out of his self-imposed isolation. When he'd started going to a local band's rehearsals, both Barry and Ellen were against it. His renewed interest in heavy metal was putting the household on edge. *Stryper's* CD *Reborn* or *Nine Inch Nails'* new release *With Teeth* would blaze whenever they weren't home, causing the neighbors to complain.

It was almost better than rap, but only because of the language. Ellen swore Dan liked them precisely because it aggravated everyone else.

Coming home unexpectedly one afternoon, Ellen

opened the door to the family room and put her hands to her ears, then growled in frustration. Dan was leaning back in his computer chair, his eyes closed, and his hand was pounding the desk in time to the drum. As if mesmerized by the heavy bass and screeching metal guitars, he appeared to be in a world of his own. Not again!

"Danny! Shut that damn racket off!"

Of course, there was no response, so she flicked the lights on and off to catch his attention.

When that didn't work, she strode over to him and yanked his chair around to face her. "Didn't we agreed you'd keep it down? We don't need the cops here again on a noise complaint."

"Fine. I was leaving anyway. The band is practicing after dinner in their garage. I'm helping with the acoustics."

"I'm not sure they're a good influence on you. We've never even met these guys. You never tell us anything about your friends. How old are they?" Ellen had her arms crossed, waiting for an answer.

Dan returned her glare. "You guys are always on my back to go out. Now I am, and you still aren't happy. At least I'll be outta here, so you won't have to put up with me." He shoved his chair away from his computer, almost tipping it over. "I'm gone. See you whenever."

"What about homework?" Ellen tried to prevent him from leaving by blocking the doorway. "And what's with those jeans? Since when do you wear them hanging off your butt like that?"

"Look around, Mom. Lotsa guys do. Get off my back." Dan pushed her aside forcefully and marched to the back door, grabbing his jacket from the hook.

"Dan!" Barry entered the family room, catching the tail end of the conversation.

Dan continued out the door and slammed it. Outside, he turned as he passed the window and sneered at Barry in a mocking gesture as if daring him to follow.

"God, that kid. One day I'm going to send him flying."

"You and who else?" Ellen remarked. "He's taller than you and must weigh twenty pounds more."

"So what? I'll teach that little sonofabitch a few manners."

"OK, OK, calm down," Ellen soothed while her stomach churned.

Those brief seconds Dan had glared at her had frightened her. Her son was now an unpredictable boy in a man's body, able to intimidate her at will. She tried to pretend the possibility for violence didn't exist. What do you do, she wondered, give up? Confront his anger??

She, for one, was too afraid. How could Dan have turned out so different from his sister?

"That little jerk better watch himself, or so help me God, he'll see the back of my hand before I kick his ass out on the street." Barry's eyes flashed as his fists clenched and unclenched.

"He's still our son, and there's no way that's going to happen," Ellen stated decisively, her hands on her hips. "Got it?"

"You're too soft on him. That's why he gives you the crap he does. He knows better than to talk to me like that. You better open your eyes with him and be careful. I don't trust him."

"What do you think he's going to do? He's different—there's no doubt about it. But there's still a chance he'll change once he matures. I'm not giving up." Ellen's eyes welled up, her insides shaking when Barry had verbally echoed her deepest fears. She turned from him and walked to her favorite viewpoint of the Strait with her back to him.

"I don't know. I stopped wearing blinders a long time ago. Face it. There's something haywire with our son. Maybe he's not all there upstairs-who knows? I'm simply asking you to be careful. If he starts pushing his weight around here, he's gone. I won't endanger our family's health and well-being." Barry spread his arms around, emphasizing his point. He went to the fridge and took out a cold beer, twisting the cap off then guzzling almost half of it.

Ellen put her hands on her hips and shook her head, her lips pursed at yet another family argument. Not surprisingly, Barry went outside to cool off and finish his brew. She knew he was probably trying to figure out a solution to Dan's belligerent behavior. *Good Luck.* Ellen retreated to the study and dropped into her overstuffed chair. She drew comfort in the ocean view ahead while she zoned out her anxiety.

When Barry calmed down, he came inside and approached Ellen, who still sat beside the bay window with her feet on the wide window ledge, looking outside at the choppy waves slamming onto the rocky outcroppings in the bay. He knew she was identifying with the turbulent moods of the Strait. Left undisturbed, it would calm her. He put his arm around her and kissed the nape of her neck lightly, thankful once more that despite their earlier problems, they were still together.

"Don't take it so hard. It's not your fault. You're an excellent mom. Besides, you're probably right. I get too uptight around him." He patted her shoulder gently and retreated.

Ellen didn't trust herself to speak, yet she appreciated his effort to mollify her and ease her tension. The trouble was, she had the same fear of their future with Dan. She was beginning to see their child through the eyes of someone else instead of the eyes of a mother, and she didn't like what she saw.

~

TONIGHT, barely a month after that incident, Ellen anxiously stood by the front window, looking for Dan. He was supposed to be at home early to babysit Sara while they went to dinner to celebrate their anniversary. It was already 6:30, and he still wasn't home. Ellen had prepared a simple dinner of chili and buns for them to devour, but Sara gave up waiting for Dan and had wolfed down her favorite dish an hour ago.

Barry was due home by 7:00 from Nanaimo, then after a quick shower and shave, they'd leave for dinner reservations at 8:00. Ellen walked back inside, debating whether to call for a backup babysitter or not. She didn't want the evening to start on the wrong foot, so finally, she did call a sitter to come for 7:30. If Danny came home later, Missy could go home and still get a whole evening's pay.

It was worth it to her for the peace of mind. Pleased with her preventative measure, she poured herself a glass of wine to help her unwind. Dan was not going to spoil her anniversary.

Much later, after a sumptuous candlelit dinner, Barry brought up the subject. "Wasn't Dan supposed to be babysitting tonight?"

"He wasn't sure what time he'd be home. He was helping the band move to another garage for practicing. So, I made a backup plan in case he lost track of time. I didn't want anything to spoil our evening." Ellen covered for him even now, a peace-making gesture she had developed a long time ago. She didn't consider it was lying exactly, merely a way to keep the family running smoothly.

"Goes to show how important he finds our anniversary."

"Come on, don't start. We promised the evening belonged only to us. Kids aren't included."

"You're right. Amazing how conversations drift toward them sooner or later, but no more tonight, I promise. Do you realize in another eight or ten years, they'll both be gone? Then it'll be only the two of us."

Ellen enjoyed seeing her husband's eyes dance with mischief. "Whatever will we do?" Ellen's eyebrows danced up and down. "No more fights to referee, no more homework hassles... a cleaner house." She clinked her glass to his.

"We'll close all the curtains, then run around naked. No more eyes to catch us."

"Trust you to think of that."

"Why not? Sometimes, I regret not having any time to ourselves when we were first married, to horse around and do foolish things."

"I've thought about that too. When we were first married, I used to feel so old. When I turned twenty, I honestly felt like I was thirty—I used to envy Paula's freedom, then I'd feel guilty about thinking that way. Now I'm glad we started so young. We'll be in our early forties and be free to do our own thing."

"And I can hardly wait," he reached for his wife's hand and stroked it. "What would you like to do next? Dancing? Maybe hit the casino?"

"How about a walk first? It's so beautiful tonight, then we could go dancing if you're up for it."

"Sure." Barry paid the bill, then helped Ellen from the chair. Together, hand in hand, they left and walked down Oswego Street towards the downtown core. Walking past the Wax Museum and Undersea Gardens, they watched the yachts and sailboats moored nearby.

Victoria in the summer was a romantic place to be. The city took great pride in its Victorian background, with the Empress Hotel and Parliament Buildings taking center stage on the Inner Harbor. Tubs of colorful baskets complemented the finely corniced and sculpted architecture, always kept so spotlessly clean. Starry-eyed lovers meandered about, dreaming of a simpler time. The warm evening air was slowly cooling thanks to the light ocean breeze.

"We're so lucky." Ellen stopped and leaned over the cement railing to the buskers below on the lower level of the walkway. "To enjoy this every day is a real gift."

"I told you if you followed me, we'd find heaven together. And you know what I love about you?"

"Besides the obvious?" Ellen's lighthearted response drew a smile. "No. Please tell me."

"You always notice things, appreciate things. Whether it's the architecture, the landscaping, or the natural beauty of living here, you always admire it. You never take it for granted." Barry lifted her hand and kissed the top of it. "You make me see it with new eyes."

"Thank you. I can't help expressing how I feel about living here." Ellen tugged his hand, and they wandered down the steps to the Lower Causeway.

Holding hands, Barry and Ellen wandered about, passing other couples, young and old, caught up in the magic of nature's evening tribute. The still waters of the Inner Harbor mirrored the sun's setting rays, awash in colors flamboyantly salmon and purple. Discreet street musicians and buskers displayed their arts, being careful not to disturb the peaceful ambiance. No cares existed outside this time.

"Perfect." Barry switched from holding hands to wrapping an arm around his wife, pulling him close to her.

"Mmhmm, it's magical here."

"Just like you. Happy Anniversary, Ell."

"Thank you. I can't think of a place I'd rather be on our anniversary than here with you." Ellen reached over his chest and hugged him tightly, resting her head on his shoulder.

"I hope you'll feel the same way for our twenty-fifth," Barry whispered as he tipped her head upwards and kissed her passionately.

"Things will only get better for us, Barry. I can feel it."

"That's right, and they will." He twirled his wife away, then back towards him, his eyes sparkling. "Do you still want to go dancing, or would you rather go home and make love?" Barry's tone was suggestively purring as his eyebrows danced.

Ellen laughed. "We can do that anytime. Shall we try the dance lounge at the Chateau Victoria?"

"Good choice." They ambled through the city center towards Government Street, talking aimlessly about trivial things they saw, enjoying the last vestiges of late twilight. The lounge was almost packed, and a four-piece band was playing. Uptown country music attracted many couples in their mid-30s. They saw several people they knew, so it turned out to be a festive evening full of laughter.

They took a taxi and arrived home not long after 2:00 a.m. As previously agreed upon, Barry went upstairs for a quick shower while Ellen dealt with the babysitter.

"Hi, Missy. I see Dan didn't get home. I guess you've earned a lot of money tonight," Ellen effused, full of humor.

"Ah..." Missy fidgeted with her hands.

"What's the matter? Did you have a problem with Sara?"

"Not with Sara, Mrs. Peterson." All of a sudden, Missy burst into tears. "I didn't know where you were! I called the Inn, but you had already left."

"What's the matter? What happened?" Ellen's voice deepened with concern as she placed a hand on Missy's shoulder.

"It was Dan. He came home around 9:30. He was really pissed off about something. Sara brushed by him on the way to the kitchen, and he—" Missy began to tremble as she struggled to control her tears.

"Go on, tell me. What did he do?" Ellen spoke softly and stroked Missy's shoulders to calm her down.

"He shoved Sara hard and sent her flying across the room. He started screaming at her, and when I tried to stop him, he told me to F-off! I was so scared. You should've seen him." By now, Missy was hyperventilating as she relived the terror.

"Oh my God, where's Sara? Is she OK?"

"I think so. She's sleeping upstairs now."

"Aw sweetie, I'm so sorry." Ellen hugged her and rocked her back and forth as she patted her back. "Do you know where Dan went?"

"No. After he swore at me, he started ranting on about something. I sent Sara to your bedroom and told her to lock the door. I was sure he would hit me too, so I ran home, but my parents were out too. I was going to call the cops, but I didn't know what you'd say." Missy's trembling had quietened as Ellen continued to stroke Missy's arms gently.

Now that she was semi-composed, she was able to talk more coherently. "While I was at home trying to figure out what to do, the phone rang, and it was Sara, telling me Dan had left. She begged me to come back, so I did. Together, we locked the house up good and tight. If he'd have come back,

I would've called the cops," she vowed. "I had the cell beside me, ready just in case. I've never seen anyone so angry before."

"You did the right thing. Thank you for coming back. I'm very sorry. We were enjoying ourselves so much that we forgot to call in and let you know where we'd be. I'm sorry, Missy." Ellen couldn't apologize enough for the fear their babysitter had felt.

Missy turned away, and Ellen heard her trembling voice mutter something.

"Sorry, Missy. I didn't hear you. What did you say?"

"Mrs. Peterson, I can't babysit for you anymore," Missy sounded almost apologetic as she declared her feelings.

"I understand completely. I'd never ask you to put yourself at risk again. We'll be punishing Dan for this, so I doubt he'll ever perform like that again, but I don't blame you one bit. I'm very sorry."

Ellen hugged her again, then paid her double the usual rate. From the front steps, she watched Missy walk home across the street. As soon as she saw Missy safely enter her own home, she shut the door and sprinted upstairs, her heart pounding wildly.

Sara's room was across the hall from hers. Ellen quietly opened her door. The night light was on, shedding an eerie glow across the room.

My God, my God. Please let Sara be unhurt.

Ellen perched on the side of her daughter's bed, searching for signs of abuse. Sara's puffy eyes were proof of the traumatic evening. As Ellen gently pulled the covers down, she saw an already ugly bruise forming on her left bicep. Her trembling fingers pulled the covers back up as she struggled to understand.

Sara moaned briefly, then her eyes opened instantly, full

of alarm. As she saw her mother sitting there, she sat up and wrapped her arms around her mom.

"Mom!" Her sobbing broke Ellen's heart.

Breathing deeply, Ellen tried to control herself so that she wouldn't add to her daughter's terror.

"You're safe now, sweetheart. Your father and I are home."

"Good. I hate Danny, Mom, he's crazy! He hurt me tonight. I'm scared of him."

"Sshh...I know all about it. Missy told me. It's over now, and it won't ever happen again." Ellen made Sara look at her directly and forced confidence into her voice. "Trust me. It won't *ever* happen again. I'll talk to Dan, and he'll be punished. He'll have to apologize and behave, or he'll have to leave. Understand?"

Sara nodded through her tears. Ellen hoped they were tears of relief rather than from fear. She rocked her daughter for a few minutes before tucking her back into bed and kissing her forehead.

Ellen continued, "Let's keep this our secret for now. You know how your dad would blow up if he knew. He's still your brother, and I think if he promises to behave, we should give him one more chance."

"I don't think he'll listen, Mom. I'm scared to be alone with him now."

Ellen saw the doubt still lingering in Sara's eyes. Once again, she reassured her. "You won't be. Please believe me. Danny will never hurt you again. I promise. Tomorrow, we'll go for a walk somewhere. We'll talk more. You name the place."

Sara nodded. "Mount Tolmie?"

"Ellen, are you coming?" Barry called from their bedroom.

"In a minute!" Ellen called back with false cheerfulness. "Yes, we can go there, then we'll splurge and have lunch." Seeing the relief in her daughter's eyes, she kissed her precious sweetheart one more time before heading to her bedroom.

Barry's eagerness to continue their romantic evening in bed was evident, so Ellen compelled herself to push aside her troubles. She had become adept at compartmentalizing. As she had vowed earlier, Dan would not spoil her evening. Watching herself in a mirror, Ellen took several slow, deep breaths. She practiced smiling with her eyes, making them twinkle before slipping into a new blue satin teddy and joining her husband.

Barry had lit several candles around the bedroom. As his wife sauntered towards him, he poured them each some wine, toasting her. "Happy Anniversary, honey." He clinked glasses with her, watching her drink deeply. Barry took the wine from her, then angled her face towards him, kissing her passionately.

Ellen wrapped her arms around his neck, holding him tightly while her hips teased against his. Thank God they had made a new start in their relationship. She didn't think she'd be able to handle their family life alone.

Their lovemaking had become more sensual since their trip to Hawaii. Thanks to Paula's suggestions and renewed commitment, their sex life had more vigor and interest than ever. They spent time leisurely building their passion to a flashpoint, using scented oils and delicate fingertip massages.

Unbeknownst to Ellen, Barry's new experience added some spice to their routine. Now, if they didn't have the time to make love properly, they abstained, preferring good sex to the quick release they had grown accustomed.

Long after her exhausted, slightly inebriated, and satiated husband fell asleep, Ellen pondered on the violence of the evening. *What had ever possessed Dan to explode like that?* Thoughtfully, she looked for clues to her son's newest belligerence.

To her innermost self and only under duress could she admit how damaging his presence was in their home. Even when Dan was helpful and considerate, which God knew wasn't often, everyone tiptoed around him. Thankful that he condescended to be a family member for a while, they each appreciated a reprieve while mentally wondering when the biting remarks or his sullen moods would resume.

Ellen knew that Barry had isolated himself from his only son to preserve their fragile family unit, much as Ellen had insulated herself. An agreement had long existed to recognize that as hard as Dan was to live with, as frustrating as he was to love, he was still their son. Ellen could tolerate almost anything to preserve their family relationship, dysfunctional as it was.

Dan's threatening behavior now put their relationship on edge. Their home was a sanctuary, a safe haven inviolate to aggression. Over the years, she attempted to develop an understanding and closeness, but Dan shunned each effort with thinly veiled disinterest or outright ridicule. She had spent many afternoons crying about her inabilities to reach him and love him, as she did Sara.

Eventually, she accepted the reality and learned how to live passively with her son, enjoying the good times without expecting them. She dreaded confronting him, however, she had come to the end of her patience. Her eyelids, heavy with exhaustion, drooped, and a deep, dreamless sleep released her from any more recriminations.

Much later, through a thick fog of sleep, she became

aware of footsteps climbing the stairs. Her first instinct was to roll over and ignore the sound. Then she became dimly aware that it wasn't Barry coming home late. He was lying next to her. She awoke startled, realizing that it must be Dan.

Contemplating whether she should speak to him, she heard him again heading back down the stairs. With her heart palpitating wildly, Ellen arose and wrapped her thick terry housecoat around her. She wanted to see his condition. Stealthily, she shut the bedroom door behind her, wanting to resolve the conflict herself.

As she came down the circular staircase, she noticed the kitchen light on. Ellen should've guessed he'd be hungry. Quietly entering the kitchen, she stood watching her son rummaging in the fridge. He seemed to have grown a foot in the past six months, and his tall frame needed more padding. She noticed he needed a haircut again. His dark brown hair hung way over his jacket collar.

How she wished she could hug him and have him hug her. She wanted his love much more than she suspected he wanted hers. Now and then, she still allowed herself to hope he'd change as he grew older.

He jumped as he turned and saw her. "Jesus, Mom, you scared the shit out of me."

"Watch your language, Dan," she said automatically. "Hungry? There's leftover chili. Or do you want me to make you something else?"

He eyed her carefully, then apparently decided it might be a good idea to accept her offering. "Sure. Is there any roast beef left?"

"Yes. Would you like a sandwich?"

"Sure." Danny poured himself a glass of milk, then sat at the table with his back to her.

Civil. I can live with civil. I can't live with violence. Ellen glanced at her son as she sliced the two sandwiches in half, then added some pickles on the side. *At least he looks sober, and he doesn't look like he's on anything. Maybe this was going to be an excellent time to talk after all.*

"Here you go." Ellen put the plate down in front of him and sat beside him.

He didn't say anything as he concentrated on filling his empty stomach. Ellen fetched the quart of milk again.

"Mom. Have you ever thought I was crazy?"

Ellen almost dropped the quart. *Danny instigating a conversation—and about himself? Wow.*

She poured him a refill and sat down, thinking carefully of how to answer that. "No, although occasionally you do things that make me wonder where your head is. Do you think you're crazy?"

"Sometimes. Like tonight, man. I forgot about your anniversary, and I got mad. When I got home, that bitch was here babysitting Sara."

"Dan."

"Sorry." Dan rolled his eyes, then continued. "Miss Goody-Goody had a card right there at the entry for you. Those flowers and chocolates were probably from Sara, too." Dan pushed the plate away and glanced around the kitchen, avoiding direct visual contact with her.

"The flowers came from Ken and Paula, and Sara bought us some Roger's Chocolate."

"Figures. She looks at me like I'm scum, and I lost it. When she walked by me, I couldn't help myself, and I shoved her. Then she started to whine, so I smacked her—just to give her something to really cry about."

Dan shook his head, his fists clenching and unclenching. "I shouldn't have. I should've gone straight upstairs like I usually do."

A wave of nausea rolled in Ellen's stomach as she pictured the violence her son had committed on his sister. What in God's name had come over him? Now, he looked remorseful, but Ellen couldn't be sure that it wasn't an act. She had lost trust in him a long time ago. Maybe he did care. She had always hoped so. "Do you get mad a lot?"

"Yea, I guess I do." His voice grew louder, his words running into each other. "I'm not stupid, y'know. I can see right through you guys. I know what you're thinking. So yea, I get mad." His eyes narrowed as he glared at his mother, flashing daggers of anger towards her. He stood and began pacing the kitchen floor, his hands gesturing wildly.

"Dan, calm down. You're a hard kid to live with, but we love you."

"Yea, right. Just like you love Sara, hey?" He stopped and scowled at her, daring her to contradict him.

"Don't be jealous. We do love you. Granted, not in the same way we love Sara—you won't let us do that, but we do love you."

Ellen watched her son step closer to her, trying to intimidate her. She pulled her shoulders back and stared right back at him, refusing to take the bait and argue further with him. She could tell he was surprised that she was not alarmed, or worse yet, crying.

"You guys don't get it, do you? Sometimes I don't even know that I do. I know what people think, and I get a kick out of screwing things up for them. Like I know Dad hates me, and so does Sara. And you—you feel sorry for me. Like I'm a total reject. Always making excuses for who I am. Well, maybe I like who I am."

"No one here hates you. You're so moody. It's hard for us

to ignore that and pretend everything is smooth sailing." Ellen paused briefly. "Dan, be honest with me. Have you been doing drugs?"

"No!" Dan smacked his hand on the counter. "I don't believe it. You're looking for an excuse again, but can't you see? It's just who I am, and I'm *not* taking any drugs."

"I had to ask. Things seem to be getting worse for you and us. If there's a reason, we could work it out."

"Face it, Mom, I've always been like this. You've never been able to control me or figure me out. I can't even do it." His angry tone dropped, and his voice deepened as he looked away from her. "Most of the time, I feel like I don't belong here, that this is all a big stage. Or a big lie. Sometimes I hear things in my head that you wouldn't believe. *I* don't even believe it. That's why the music's so loud sometimes. To drown it out."

"Dan," her voice softened as Ellen looked at the back of her son, his shoulders slumped with what might be despair. "Would you like to see a therapist? Y'know, maybe I should've done this before."

The urge to comfort him rose in her chest. Where had her little ruffian so full of curiosity and energy gone? Those idyllic days of treasure hunting at the park or the beach seemed to belong to another lifetime. Ellen's forefinger tapped her top lip, wondering how far to go.

"Maybe it would do you good. Do all of us good. Being a teenager is tough and maybe—"

"Forget it, Mom. I am what I am. I'll straighten myself out -I'll be the angel you've always wanted. Watch me. I can do anything I put my mind to." Dan turned to face his mom, searching for what? Understanding?

"That's not the point. We don't expect you to be an angel, but we want you to be happy, not just faking it. We want the whole family to get along." Ellen approached him, putting her hand on his shoulder. "Family life's to be enjoyed, not just tolerated. If you need help, let's get some."

Dan flicked her hand from his shoulder. "Don't worry, Mom. I won't hurt your precious Sara again."

She had to pull herself together. Emotional responses had never worked. Dan needed to suffer the consequences, spend time deciding his place in their family, and make decisions for his future. It was long overdue. Her heart jumped in her chest, but Ellen had to stay strong and disciplined.

"I'm disappointed and troubled. You're aware of the rules around here. I saw Sara's arm, and it makes me sick that you've done that. She's never going to forget that, you know. I understand that you also scared the heck out of Missy. You're lucky she didn't phone the police."

Ellen looked directly into Dan's eyes and held his gaze. Before she had seen remorse, now all she saw was a hardness in his eyes before he shrugged and half turned his back to her.

She toughened, too, as her voice became harsh. "I don't care what the problem is or how big it is. You need to find a way to deal with it *without anger.*" Ellen crossed her arms to show she meant business. "I don't ever want to see violence in this house again. Do you understand? I won't tolerate it under this roof. Never again! Got it?"

Dan turned to glare at her. "Yes, ma'am."

"It's over with now, but consider yourself grounded for a month. I expect you to give your sister an apology, as well as Missy and her parents. Think about what I said, Dan. Counseling could—"

"Back off, I got it! I'm going to bed." Dan got up, touched his two fingers to his forehead, and gave her a sarcastic salute, then quickly walked to the stairs. As he started to climb them, he turned. "It's not your fault, y'know. And I do love you." Dan bolted up the stairs, two at a time.

"Love you too," she replied softly to the empty room. Dan had caught her unaware and had scooted off before he could hear her reply. Her mind reeled from the brief, confusing tete a tete. *What was going on?*

It had been many years since she heard him say he loved her. It triggered a scent of baby powder as she remembered the snuggles they used to share. Where had that little tike gone?

Ellen collapsed on a kitchen chair, her head in her hands. She went over their recent conversation and his confusing remarks. His attitude had swung from remorse to disinterest, then to anger before returning to some sort of caring again. He knew in his own way that he was contradicting himself, yet he didn't want help.

She'd stated her views clearly. As much as she loved her son, she was done. The little rascal who held her heart was long gone. If he abused anyone in this house again and refused therapy, she'd pack his suitcase and let him go.

Over the years, Dan had intimidated and resisted all her attempts to find a solution to his moods. Ellen had learned the hard way that she couldn't make Dan do anything he didn't want to.

The troubled times with Dan had taken their toll. Again tonight, he'd refused her suggestions to get help. Unless he committed to professional counseling, they couldn't maintain the family relationship anymore.

One day, with any luck, he would mature enough to seek it on his own and create a good life for himself. That's all she wanted.

Exhausted, she shut the lights out and climbed the stairs

to her bedroom. To Ellen's dismay, she found herself willing to give him up to have peace in her and Sara and Barry's lives. Ashamed and yet strengthened by her awareness and decision, she crept back into her warm bed, falling asleep almost instantly, almost satisfied.

CHAPTER 17

February in Victoria. A time of contrasts. Blue skies and icy, gale-force winds. Crocuses pushing their way through frost layered ground. Leaves and flowers were sending their first buds out gingerly, testing the reception. Discreet bursts of energy in the lethargic world of winter.

Ellen sat with a quilt on her lap in her study, watching the dancing whitecaps skipping across the Strait, following the thin ethereal clouds as they whipped by.

February 22, Dan's nineteenth birthday. It would've been a good day to celebrate. The teen years were almost gone. Technically, he was an adult now.

At least she knew Dan was on the mainland. Two years after he disappeared, he attempted a weekend visit to let them know he made a life for himself. He worked for a garage station somewhere in Surrey and hoped to start a working apprenticeship with them.

Their son only made it through one night with them, leaving early the following morning. He left a note saying he was going back to work. With no cell number, or address, or even the name of the garage he worked for, they had no way to reach him. Not surprising that Dan chose to have their relationship on his terms only.

Ellen hoped he was happy and that he had friends. He'd gone to live his own life by his own rules. In her heart, she knew that was probably the best thing for all of them. They never heard from him on birthdays or at Christmas. It was as if he was no longer a part of their family.

That hurt.

She'd half expected she'd cry today, but she hadn't. There were no tears left. Ellen's tears of regret and recriminations were all shed a long time ago.

The terror and pain of that fateful night when she and Dan had argued finally dulled. When he exploded with foul language after being reprimanded for once again breaking curfew, Ellen had warned him to stop, that he was throwing away the second chance she'd given him. But that only amped his anger. She stood her ground which caused him to lash out verbally, then shove her aside before storming from the house. His parting shot had left bruises that had long since faded, but she feared the ache in her heart would never recede.

The calendar registered four years, yet it seemed like a lifetime ago when Ellen packed Dan's suitcase along with a duffel bag, then left them out beside the garage. She had the locks also changed, fearing repercussions. Two days later, they were gone. She guessed enough horrible things had been said that he had nothing left to add.

Barry knew part of what happened, but Dan had chosen a night that his dad was working in Nanaimo to explode. What Barry learned was enough. Ellen didn't need her husband to cross the line and hate their son.

Now, Ellen mourned her steely ultimatum. Thinking that he'd return when he was good and hungry, they waited.

After two weeks, they reported him missing with the police. The RCMP had done a cursory search, but teenage runaways were common. They soon forgot about Dan over more urgent matters. About a month after he disappeared, Dan left a message on voice mail to say he was staying with friends and was fine. He didn't say where he was or who he was with, nor was there any apology. But at least they knew he was alive.

It was what I wanted, wasn't it? Ellen passed her hand over her face, stopping to press her fingers against her trembling lips. *I wanted him to behave or be gone. Now he's gone.*

Time had a way of healing deep wounds, she supposed. Much to Ellen's chagrin, she'd find that weeks had gone by without her thinking of her son. His birthday triggered this bout of depression. Other times her despair would be caused by a poster in a store window of an *Opeth* or *Nine Inch Nails* newest release.

Barry had cleaned out Dan's room not long after his phone call. The door remained closed. Ellen still ran across reminders of her son. Cleaning out the attic for charity donations, she found a cardboard box full of his favorite Pixar toys. They generated another series of memories and sleepless nights with all the inevitable questions.

Barry could reassure her a thousand times that she wasn't to blame. Dan brought on the confrontation by his behavior. That was true, although now she wondered if she could've handled it differently. Would it have helped if she'd demanded family counseling or psychiatric therapy for Dan?

Maybe, maybe not. A deep sigh escaped Ellen as she

pondered her past decisions. Had she done the worst thing a mother could do? She'd sent her son packing. Ellen thought it'd be a wake-up call. She thought he'd come back, ready to start some therapy with them to heal their family.

It never happened.

Ellen denied herself credit for the many attempts she had made over the years. She viewed them as feeble now, without substance. She should have recognized he needed professional help.

Ellen pinched the bridge of her nose as she tried to toss the regrets from her mind. She bit her lip and forced herself from her overstuffed Queen Anne. A walk would help improve her mood and get her thinking about other things. Otherwise, she'd go down the path of never-ending regrets.

"God, forgive me." She started saying the daily novena she began after he stormed out of the house. Part penance and part bargaining. If she prayed long and hard enough, perhaps God would look after Dan and forgive her. Ellen wrapped a scarf around her neck, then slipped her gloves on to brace the icy wind.

BARRY SAW her leave the house, not surprised to see Ellen heading outdoors, her hands folded in prayer, a repetitious litany pouring from her lips. He gritted his teeth in anger. *How dare his son hurt his mother like this.* He stared at the back of his beloved wife, noting her slumped shoulders, her gait slow and slightly askew. He knew it would be like this today. It was the reason he had taken the day off.

He understood so much more now. He'd resisted counseling when Ellen suggested it after Dan left, but watching her recuperate and build a new identity for herself made him realize the benefits. Learning to parent and assume household chores hadn't come naturally to him, although when Ellen returned to school, he learned to cook, do laundry, and help with homework. When she arrived home with the table set and a messy kitchen, the look on her face restored his self-esteem as a husband and father. Now, he was more than the provider. He was an essential part of the family.

Over time, without the constant tension of living with Dan's moods, the relationship between him and Ellen had blossomed. Barry learned to distract her when Ellen's misguided conscience seized her emotions. Sometimes, it was simple, putting on one of her favorite CDs and pulling her up to dance with him or taking her out for a walk along the shoreline, dodging the surf as they searched for treasures.

Times like those took more patience than he thought he had, as he wrestled with his anger towards his son. But it helped when after the second year, both he and Ellen agreed to stop discussing Dan. They had talked everything to death, they'd decided, and their son had made a decision that satisfied him.

Barry soon realized that getting away from Victoria to the cabin at Comox Lake seemed to bring out the best in his wife. He hoped that today's suggestion to escape there might be enough to help her through this difficult stretch. Dan's birthdays were always worse than any other time.

Ellen's laughter as they enjoyed boating, hiking, or sitting around a campfire made his heart sing. He'd often catch Sara looking at them, her eyes filled with happiness. With time, Ellen's carefree attitude proved that Dan's departure had been best for all involved.

Quickly, Barry grabbed a jacket and ran to catch up with

her. He took her hand in his, making her pause for a moment. "Do you mind if I join you? I could use a walk."

"If you want. I won't be long, though. I'll be fine."

Barry saw her trembling smile. She was trying to be so brave.

"No, I'd like to come. I've been thinking about taking a break. Why don't we head to the lake for a few days? What do you think? Let's go up to the chalet, see how it's fared so far during the winter."

Barry welcomed the grateful look Ellen gave him. He'd concentrated on building their marriage after the brief, shameful affair he had. He promised himself if given a second chance, he would spend his life showing her how much he loved and appreciated her. Trimming his hours to cover the pre-dinner prep time and then close-ups, Barry handed over the bulk of the operations to his managers.

After twenty-plus years, his business now took second place to his family. His priority was his wife. A gentler, more loyal soul couldn't be found, he was sure.

"What about Sara?" she asked.

"We'll surprise her and pick her up at lunchtime. There's a good supply of tinned and dry goods at the cabin, so we could stop and pick up fresh groceries in Courtenay and rough it. What do you say?"

"Why not?" Ellen masked her sorrow, then smiled. "When we get back, I'll pack us a few things. We'll be spontaneous and make do with what we have, alright?"

"Sure. Grab some jeans and sweatshirts for all of us. Nothing fancy. If it's nice tomorrow, we'll build a bonfire and tidy up the place. We might as well get some work done."

A blazing bonfire and the tranquil lake setting would be a perfect antidote for today. Barry watched Ellen perk up as she anticipated the getaway. A new bounce in her step showed her enthusiasm as they continued their walk while making plans to close up the house.

Nestled in the Beaufort Range around Comox Lake, their chalet offered them a sanctuary to enjoy. Although much smaller than their home in Victoria, it had all the amenities for either short or long stays. The chalet itself was constructed from cedar logs with an enormous fireplace dominating the north wall. The smooth rounded stones captured a feeling of an era gone by. Picture windows gave them a view of the lake just beyond the treed front yard.

When they bought the two-acre site the year before Dan left, they decided to leave it as natural as possible. Except for a few trees removed to give more light to the house, the rest of the property remained wild. Beneath the evergreen trees, salal and moss grew thick on the ground. Other than picking up fallen branches and burning them periodically, there was no lawn to cut, no flowers to tend. They spent their time swimming, boating, fishing, and hiking.

Barry's mind flitted through the contented times they had there. He wondered if Dan would ever become a part of their lives again, then pushed the thought aside. Only time would tell.

CHAPTER 18

Ellen was thrilled when Barry sold the controlling interest in both restaurants a year ago, then relocated to Comox. A new start. Their Victoria home filled with persistent reminders of their failures with Dan wasn't conducive to Ellen's mental health. She constantly fought a sense of guilt and bouts of depression.

With the sale of their water view home, they began looking for another view property for their home base. They found an older and smaller home overlooking Goose Spit, the Naval Cadet Base, and Forbidden Plateau in the distance. With the difference between Victoria and Comox real estate prices, there was enough left over to do a makeover to Ellen's satisfaction.

When Lisa surprised them with a visit from Bella Coola, Ellen emailed Matt immediately to let him know she was staying with them. Many girl-talks over bonfires on the beach helped to put Lisa back together. Perspective from outsiders seemed to have gotten through to her, but she was adamant that she was not returning to a community lifestyle.

Only two months after living with them, Lisa and her family reached a compromise. Lisa would be going to the same university that Sara would be attending. Meanwhile, she was upgrading her qualifications and living in a furnished studio apartment in Saanich. Her parents would cover her expenses for the first year then assess the situation afterward. Lisa was confident that surrounding herself with a younger generation with a broader viewpoint would be exactly what she needed.

Sara was as excited as Lisa with the plans. Next August, they'd look for an apartment to share with Sara's childhood friend, Tracy. It was going to be a blast.

ELLEN SAT BESIDE HER DAUGHTER, watching her copy her favorite recipes into a file she named Mom's home cooking on her computer. University life would be quite the change for her daughter, but she knew Sara was ready.

Sara had learned how important organization and routine were with her dyslexia, and Ellen was proud of her. Sara had tacked a long checklist to the wallboard in her bedroom, which she often added to.

"I can't wait to start looking for an apartment for Tracy, Lisa, and me. Don't worry. I'll find one we can afford close to the University."

"That's important, but so is the location. We want you in a safe neighborhood, even if it's a little more expensive. Stay away from the apartments that cater to students. The temptation to party will distract you."

"I know, Mom. We've gone over this before. I'll email you a few different places that might work, and then you can come down and check them out."

"Ok. We'll come down, and Dad will sign the lease while I help you girls get some second-hand furniture and set you up. The rent that Lisa and Tracy give you should be enough to keep you going. It will be a good experience learning how to budget while going to school." At Sara's frown, Ellen patted her hand. "You'll be fine. I've given you a ledger and shown you how to keep track of things. Like Dad told you, we're here to help in emergencies, but you girls need to learn some life lessons, too."

"We will." Sara put her tablet down and leaned back, tapping her finger on the table while looking at her mom. "Are you going to be OK without me? Sometimes, I worry about you, especially since Dad got elected as an MLA."

"Of course, Sara. I'll miss you, that's for sure, but you're only a few hours away. We'll get together often. As far as your dad goes, you know him. Sometimes I wonder if he'll ever slow down enough to enjoy total retirement. But you've seen how happy he is. I'm proud that he followed his dreams."

"Me too, but what are you going to do with yourself?"

"Heavens, Sara. There are so many things for me to choose from, it might be difficult. I'm looking forward to spreading my wings and trying different ideas. I can volunteer, play more golf, take some cooking or art classes. Please, don't worry about me. This is *your* time in the sun. Enjoy it."

"I guess so. It's hard to believe you were married at my age. Didn't you ever regret being tied down so young?"

"There was a time that I missed the freedom to be crazy and spontaneous. It's a big responsibility to be a parent and handle marriage and household." Ellen leaned over and grasped her daughter's hand. "Never doubt that I was happy with my choice. Besides, look at me now. Still young," Ellen rocked her head back and forth and winked at Sara. "Healthy, a lot wiser, and in charge of my life. I can do whatever I want. Don't you worry about your mom. You need to focus on your future now."

Sara stood from the table and stepped over to her mom, and hugged her tightly. "You're the best mom ever. You're probably going to get a lot of calls from me on how to do things. You'll probably start screening my calls."

"Never, sweetheart. There's always time for you."

Sara went to the fridge and routed around for a snack, then announced her plan for a walk to clear her mind. Ellen smiled. Sara was in heaven these days, excited about her future. Both her parents enjoyed seeing her so carefree and happy. She deserved this period of flamboyance. Soon enough, it'd be back to the demanding study necessary to become a physiotherapist.

ELLEN WAS SO nervous and excited. Butterflies flitted about her stomach, making her queasy. After almost seven years, they were finally going to have a chance to spend time with Dan again. She looked around their chalet for the third time, satisfied that everything was ready. Ellen went outside and made her way down to the landing. Their nineteen-foot motorboat and a canoe gently bobbed against the pier, waiting for action.

Yesterday, Barry had gone and purchased two more casting rods and freshwater tackle, along with a slalom board for water skiing. He was as nervous as she was, although not as optimistic.

They had spent a weekend with Dan over four years

prior while still living in Victoria. It had been a tense and exhausting ordeal. Everyone was on their best behavior, but it was easy to see the tight rope Dan treaded to stay that way. He was stretched as taut as a violin. It was a relief when he shortened the visit as supposedly, *work* needed him back.

In the past year, they began to get a phone call from their son now and then. Often at the end, there'd be a hint for support. However, Barry seldom acted upon it. He overruled Ellen's suggestions to subsidize Dan regularly. As Barry suspected, the calls grew fewer and farther apart.

It didn't matter now. This time would be different. Dan was bringing two friends with him on Saturday to spend a week to ten days with them. At twenty-two, Dan should be mature enough with his friends at his side to enjoy a relaxing time on the lake. Hopefully, the family would get to know each other again and enjoy the reunion.

She had enough groceries for an army. Tonight, she planned on a barbecue of marinated sirloin steaks. Later there'd be the inevitable campfire in the pit. If they weren't full from supper, she had lots of wieners and marshmallows for roasting.

The weather was cooperating, and it was warm and clear. It never sweltered here, seldom more than eighty-three or eighty-four degrees, a comfortable summer heat. It cooled down quickly at night. The high mountains and the Forbidden Plateau glacier on the western corner of the lake ensured it. Looking at the morning light reflecting from the rippling waters of the lake, Ellen again appreciated the treasure she had grown to cherish.

Sara was due to arrive tomorrow to spend a week with them before the university started. Ellen crossed her fingers, hoping this holiday would run smoothly. She knew Sara had misgivings about its success.

The truth was, so did Ellen. However, a burning desire to see her family reunited and sharing good times washed through her. Surely, the time had come.

Honk, Honk! Ellen heard Barry's Jeep Cherokee pull into the property. Excited, she ran up the slope to meet them. Following behind was a sharp-looking four-door, red Tacoma pickup with two strangers that appeared to be Dan's age in it. Dan was riding with Barry and now came out to greet his mom.

"Hi, Mom." He came over and kissed her cheek.

Ellen noted the smell of beer on his breath but threw an arm around his neck and kissed his cheek. She pulled back and scanned his face, noting how much he'd matured. He was broad-shouldered and almost as tall as his dad now. "You're looking good, Dan. I'm so glad you came. It's been a long time."

Dan nodded, then turned to his companions. "These are my friends, Neil and Mike."

"Hi, Mrs. Peterson, thanks for having us," Neil sang out, obviously in a holiday mood.

Mike echoed him and turned to unload the car.

"C'mon, let's show you guys around," Ellen said happily. "Anyone hungry?"

"We're always hungry," shot back Neil.

"Great. Barry, why don't you show them around, and I'll get the barbecue going. We'll have hamburgers for lunch, and then they can go swimming or whatever suits them."

"That's my mom, always taking care of the belly."

Ellen scanned him from head to toe, smiling at his humorous sarcasm. "You look like you could use some good cooking. I can see your ribs."

"Yea, well, the guys and me don't cook much. We go on a lot of liquid diets, if y'know what I mean." Dan went to the passenger seat in the Tacoma pickup and hauled out two cases of beer.

Mike snickered, and Neil, unobtrusively tactful, closed the cab door. If there was any more, Ellen couldn't see it. Neil opened the other side door and dragged a couple of sports bags and a duffel bag out.

"Shall I put this in the house?" Neil asked politely.

"Sure. Take the stairs up to the loft. There are bunk beds and a cot in there." Ellen smiled back. Already she had decided she liked that one.

As Ellen gathered the condiments for lunch, she watched the boys tromp up to the loft, dump their gear, then loudly tease each other about sleeping arrangements. She heard Barry yell for them.

"C'mon, guys, I'll show you the boats."

The troop trampled down to the dock, surveying everything around them.

"Sweet. That's a nice looking machine you have there, Mr. Peterson. What size motor is it?" asked Mike.

"There's an 85 Merc on it, and I've got a 9.9 kicker to add on when we take it from here to the ocean. We don't go often, but it's nice to have the option to go fishing for salmon."

"You never used to fish at all. Are you any good at it?" Dan asked.

"Not great. I love being out there, though. So does Sara. But I can't pry her out of bed at daybreak, so we often miss the bite. We catch the odd one, and then we explore the coastline. We're happy with that."

"We never used to do any of that kind of stuff when I was a kid. Guess you were too busy then, hey?"

"Different times, Dan. I *guess* I've mellowed some. I was

too much of a go-getter in those days." Barry chose to ignore the bitter sarcasm in his son's voice.

"You're not kidding. I remember thinking that Steve was more my father than you were."

Barry eyed him sharply. Although the words were cutting, his tone wasn't. Barry wasn't sure if Danny was simply making an observation or if he was trying to torment him.

"I guess nobody's perfect." He shrugged his shoulders and switched the subject, walking towards the ski equipment. "Anyone water ski? There are two sets of skis plus a slalom board."

"I haven't done that in years. Can we go after lunch?" Mike was already there, kneeling to examine the slalom board, running his hands over the smooth surface.

"Sure. I'll drive, but someone will have to spot for you. Neil, Dan, has either of you skied?"

Neither one of them had, but both wanted to try.

Dan stepped out of the conversation to look over the nearby canoe. "Mind if I go for a paddle?"

"Go ahead -but not far. Lunch will be ready soon. By the way, we might as well go over the rules now. You guys can use the boats anytime you want. But no booze, no night cruising, no crazy boating, and *never* ski without a spotter. Got it?"

"Yea," they each replied, excited to have such a free rein on it all.

"And don't forget life jackets," Barry warned. "I'll give you boat operation lessons after lunch, so you'll know what you're doing. It's not hard, and it just takes a little practice."

Dan had already left the dock, hesitantly rowing, trying to get the canoe going where he wanted.

"Hey man, don't you know how to row that thing? Haven't you ever been camping?" Mike teased.

"Nope. Dad was always too busy." Dan paddled harder but only succeeded in going into another circle. "This isn't as easy as it looks," Dan yelled back.

Mike laughed even harder. He quickly shucked his jeans and shirt, then dove into the water. Mike swam to the canoe, shaking the sides, taunting his friend. Of course, the inevitable happened, and the canoe turned over, dumping Dan into the lake.

A free for all ensued when Neil jumped in and joined them, each boy dunking the other until spent. Tiredly, they recovered the paddle then steered the canoe home, emerging refreshed and relaxed.

Ellen and Barry watched the good-natured antics with pleasure.

"That was the best idea you've had, honey," Ellen remarked. "Look how happy they are. Bringing those friends will be good for him. It's probably taken the stress off. I can't ever remember seeing him have so much fun."

"True. I hope it's not all because of the beer. I don't want them drinking a lot—it's too dangerous if they're swimming or boating."

"They were probably nervous about coming here and had a few to loosen up. I'm sure it won't be a problem."

"I hope not. It's starting off well."

The guys were returning to the sundeck, laughing and joking. They were in such high spirits that Ellen's spirits soared. She couldn't help smiling as she watched them interacting with each other. Above all, she wanted her son to be happy. Although his family life had been troubled, it looked like he had finally found a place where he belonged.

Dan came back for his second burger and stood close beside his mother. "I forgot how pretty you are," he said quietly.

"Oh Dan, I'm so glad you're here," she replied softly. Ellen suppressed the urge to hug him. "You must be going blind, though. Haven't you noticed the silver in my hair?"

"And a few more lines around your eyes," he added.

"Aah. Those are laugh lines, so they're allowed."

"Laugh lines? Or worry lines?"

"Look, Dan, there's no use hanging on to the past, looking for blame or for the reason why. I'm sure we've all done enough of that since you left. You look good, you look happy, so we're happy. We'll go from here, OK?"

"Sure, Mom."

The others had drifted, giving them privacy. Barry showed Neil and Mike the storage shed where he stored the fishing gear and skis. When Dan joined them, Barry brought the guys to the lake's shore. He showed them the various hazards and landmarks so they could find their way around.

Their property occupied about 120' of waterfront in a large bay. So far, the Petersons were the only ones who had developed the land, and they enjoyed having their private paradise. Now and then, a boat would moor in the bay, using the natural breakwater on their right to protect them from the brisk south-westerly winds.

The house was situated high on the land, enabling them to see around the point. Often, they'd watch mother nature whip the lake into a frenzy, with waves exploding on the rocky protrusion safeguarding their bay. A buoy, barely visible from the house, marked the shallow reef preceding the peninsula for the novice boaters.

Barry was especially cautious in explaining the dangers of the point. The lake level could drop ten feet or more in a dry summer, as Comox Lake supplied the surrounding district with water. Then the hidden craggy rocks, usually low enough below the surface to cause no harm, posed a serious threat to unadvised boaters.

Then, Barry showed them the silhouette of Forbidden Plateau, the local ski mountain, and told them of the many hiking trails.

"My favorite is the glacier trail on the north-western corner of the lake. Anyway, Sara will be here tomorrow. She knows most of the trails well. If any of you want to go, I'm sure she'd be glad to show you."

"Not my style, Mr. Peterson, but thanks anyway," said Mike. "I'm a real fish - I love the water. I only come up for air, food, or booze."

"I wouldn't mind hiking up to the glacier," Neil said. "I don't know about Dan. It'd probably be too slow for him. He kinda likes the fast stuff."

"Whatever you guys decide, just enjoy yourself within the rules here, OK?"

"Yea, sure, no worries."

Dan had wandered away but soon caught up with them. Not long after, Barry decided to take them skiing. It took several attempts for Mike to get up on the skis, but as Ellen watched through her binoculars, it didn't take long for him to start jumping the backwash and splashing sheets of water.

Dan tried skiing next, and due to his size and strength, he was also up skiing after only four attempts. However, he followed straight after the boat, happy enough to be touring the lake without trying any stunts. He fell a few times, most often on the long corners.

After his third attempt at picking up Dan from a spill, Barry clenched his teeth and threw the line out to him again.

"Keep your legs straight and your skis parallel. When the rope is tight, then yell *hit it,* then we'll take off again."

"I did yell *hit it!* You were too damn slow. You were dragging me. Next time, punch it," Dan yelled back.

"Just make sure the line is tight when you holler," Barry said, then returned to the controls.

"Neil, watch the rope. When it starts to straighten out, let me know and tap my shoulder when Dan yells. Maybe we'll get him up this time."

"Don't sweat it, Mr. Peterson. When Dan gets fed up, he's mad at everyone. The best thing to do is ignore him and let him be on his own for a while. Might be almost time to head home."

"Do you guys have a lot of trouble with him?"

"Off and on, I guess. Dan's cool for months, and then bang, he's the grouchiest son of a bitch you ever saw. Whoops, sorry about the language."

"It's alright." Barry grinned back.

"That's it—go!" Neil tapped his shoulder, and Barry chomped on the motor.

Thankfully Dan came up, and they headed back towards their bay. Neil declined his turn, preferring to wait another day.

Ellen noted that the boys were all more subdued when they returned, but she attributed it all to the healthy exhaustion a day of sunshine and skiing can produce. They ate ravenously, then snoozed on lawn chairs, their tousled hair and tanned, youthful bodies stretched out in various positions of sleep.

Boys. Ellen smiled.

Barry caught her smile and was happy for her. Laughter and sunshine eased the lines in his treasured wife's face. There was a new vitality surrounding her, energizing her.

He had no desire to let her know of Dan's mood swing or his conversation with Neil. Ellen deserved to believe Dan was a typical son, though Barry knew she needed to see more evidence of it. Unless something significant came up, Barry would hide his son's present imperfections.

He didn't want to see one crease of worry on her face, not one iota of apprehension in her manner.

That evening, Barry took his wife for a walk down the gravel road that led to a small, gently cascading waterfall about a mile down their road. They held hands as they usually did, recollecting the day's events.

The sun began its descent behind the mountains, and shadows sprung alongside the road. Through the trees, they saw the lake shimmering in last light. Here and there, campfires were lit, the bright yellow fires casting sparks swirling high into the sky.

The aroma of cedar and evergreen scented the air around them. Barry glanced at his wife while she joyfully discussed the successful reunion of their son in their lives. Full of love, of satisfaction, and optimism. Barry hoped the stars in her eyes would remain there forever. She deserved it.

At first, she and Barry whispered, then settled into a silent reflection and appreciation of the world around them. As they re-entered their driveway, they heard music playing, then saw the boys gathered around the fire, drinking.

"Wanna beer, Mr. Peterson? Mrs. Peterson?" Mike offered.

"Sure, why not?" Barry answered while Ellen nodded her thanks.

Mike handed them each a bottle of chilled Kokanee. After the long walk, the crisp, cool brew quenched their thirst. They sat beside the boys, joining in the conversation at times. Although generally, they sat back and enjoyed the camaraderie that flowed between them.

Mike and Neil were spontaneous, easy-going fellows that kept the conversations active and amusing. Dan joined in at times, but seemed to isolate himself from their chatter. He gazed into the fire, lost in his thoughts.

The friends kept the fire stoked, sending sparks flying into the night sky. Before long, Barry and Ellen retired for the evening. Barry returned with an aluminum five-gallon pail of water with warnings to douse the fire before hitting the sack, then left the guys alone under the starlit sky. Barry and Ellen fell asleep contentedly, listening to the hum of their youthful voices.

Sara arrived Sunday and, true to her nature, immediately welcomed Dan and his friends. Each day, she and Neil would load a backpack and head somewhere to discover the hidden beauties of the area. They got along famously, joking together and helping each other over rough terrain.

Ellen wondered if what she saw had any sparks of romance in it, then decided to let the kids handle it themselves. She'd keep her nose out of it unless Sara brought the subject up herself. Que sera, sera.

Whenever Mike and Danny could get Ellen to spot for them, they did a lot of water skiing. When she or Barry was unavailable, the boys would take the canoe and rods out to try their luck with trout fishing.

Dan took off by himself on Monday, paddled over to one of the creeks that emptied into the lake, and fished it, bringing home four rainbow trout for appetizers before dinner. The delicate taste of the tender pale pink flesh made the troublesome preparations worthwhile. Dan shook off the praise he received, but Ellen could see he was proud.

He left again after dinner for a solitary walk, still not back at 11:00.

"I wonder if we should go look for him? He might've lost his way."

"No, Mrs. Peterson, I think you should just leave him alone. He's been good so far, but it must be starting to get to him, being around so many people for this long. He does this a lot. He's quite a loner." Neil shrugged off her concern.

"He can't get lost, Ell. The main road is obvious. His friends are right. Dan will be ok."

"I know. My middle name must be *worry.*" Ellen laughed off her motherly unease.

"I'm surprised you haven't already started with the lectures about me living with my friends in Victoria," Sara teased.

"It's coming. I'm giving you a break for now, but it's coming," Ellen shot back.

Sure enough, Dan soon arrived, strolling back to another evening beside a hypnotic campfire. Ellen stayed another half-hour longer, then nodded to Barry to let the youth have their privacy.

THE FOLLOWING MORNING, as Ellen threw another load of towels into the wash, she reflected over the past four days. It was everything she had hoped it would be. Dan's friends created enough diversion that no one really noticed or paid attention even when he grew sullen or moody.

There was too much beer drinking for Ellen's liking,

although the boys hadn't created a scene or made themselves obnoxious. Even though it was a summer holiday for the guys, they were conscientious in doing their share around the chalet, the dock, and the grounds, helping with barbecues and cleaning up afterward. Ellen was impressed.

Sara had tried to include her brother on hiking trips and went out of her way to be near him. Dan didn't always accept her overtures, but he was civil with her. He had approached Ellen and Barry separately, striking up conversations about his job and life in Surrey. At other times, he'd abruptly leave the group and march off alone for hours at a time.

His friends thought nothing of it, obviously used to his idiosyncrasies.

On Tuesday, Barry left to attend an emergency meeting at his constituency office to consider averting a mill closure. A report from both sides was waiting for his study. The local forestry economy had been slipping for a while. Western Cedar Coalition professed to be in danger of going bankrupt, which would throw over three hundred men out of work and create a terrible effect on the regional economy.

"I don't know how long this is going to take, Ell. I have several people I want to get an opinion from after reading the report. There will be a meeting in Vancouver to negotiate a settlement that the company and the union can live with. I've heard both sides will be looking for a government handout, but that's not going to happen."

"With your business background, I'm sure you'll be able to mediate some kind of deal." Ellen put her hands on either side of his face, then stepped on her tiptoes and looked straight into his eyes. "I have faith in you."

"Thanks. If I'm pushed into a corner, I might be able to

arrange some kind of tax break for two or three years until the economy turns around. That would probably be enough to keep the men working." Barry finished packing his duffel bag with two changes of clothes, then grabbed his briefcase. "I'm worried about leaving you alone with the guys, Ell."

"Don't be silly. Sara's here with me, and we haven't had any problems so far. I doubt there will be any while you're gone either."

"Don't take any shit from them and make sure they abide by the rules. I've already given them a warning, so they know what I expect from them while I'm gone. And be careful with that ankle of yours—make the guys do the grunt work around here."

"For heaven's sake, they're not kids anymore. They'll be fine. I'll be fine." Ellen gave her husband a little push towards the door. "Now go. The sooner you get this settled, the sooner you'll be back."

"I'll call you when I know what's going on. I shouldn't be more than three or four days." Barry leaned forward and absent-mindedly kissed his wife before heading out the door towards his vehicle. Already his mind was sprinting ahead to the job at hand.

Ellen waved as she watched him leave the property. *When had he turned into such a worrywart?*

Since she twisted her ankle two days ago, Ellen didn't accompany the young men as much as she used to. Instead, she lay on a lounge chair with her binoculars and kept track of their pranks. One of them would usually come and spend some time with her. She was more than happy being the observer as the participant.

Thursday morning, found Ellen emptying the dishwasher. Barry was still gone on business, although on his call last night, he thought he'd be back Saturday afternoon.

She grabbed a fresh coffee and limped towards her favorite chair that faced the shoreline. Ellen watched the overcast sky and shivered. A windstorm was brewing. The tips of the evergreens were swaying in the breeze, and the waves on the lake were choppy.

Deciding that it would be as good a day as any to catch up on chores in town, Ellen made a list of groceries she needed. Then she poked her head inside the boys' bedroom door. "I'm going for groceries. Anything special you'd like?"

"Yea! I'm dying for junk food," Mike exclaimed. "How about some pizza?" Mike pulled his wallet out and gave her a couple of twenties despite her protest.

"OK. That's enough. One extra-large meat lovers and another with the works. You got it." Ellen shoved the money into the side compartment of her purse, ready to leave. "Sara and Neil have already left on a hike to the glacier. It's kind of a lousy day out there, so I doubt you'll go boating. How about chopping more wood and stacking it by the pit?"

"Sure, Mrs. Peterson, no sweat," Mike replied as Dan groaned in protest.

"I'll probably be back in a few hours."

Today, Sara and Neil had left bright and early to take the summer trail to Forbidden Plateau. It would be a full day's hike, and Ellen had agreed to pick them up at 8:00 pm at the old post office in Cumberland. That way, they'd have more time to explore without becoming too exhausted.

Ellen was pleased with the new relationships growing during this trip. She thought of the good times they'd shared already as she negotiated the trail to their parking lot. Her ankle was still tender as Ellen hobbled towards the car, and she contemplated whether to leave the trip to the next day. Then she could get Sara to help.

The heck with it, she might as well use the inclement

weather to her advantage. She'd take her time and get the job done with today. It was surprising how much food the group had been eaten in less than a week.

CHAPTER 19

Ellen returned four hours later, her car laden with groceries, her hair cut and styled. She decided on the spur of the moment to take time out, relax and get pampered.

Her foot was throbbing now, and she scanned the area, looking for Dan and Mike to help her unload the car. She honked the horn several times and called them, but no one answered. The pickup truck was still there, so she knew they were still around.

Frowning, Ellen looped her shoulder strap from her purse around her neck, grabbed the dairy bag, and balanced the pizzas against her side with the other arm. Thankfully, the door wasn't fully closed, so she edged it open with her foot. She set the food on the kitchen counter as her temperature rose. The boys would have to damn well bring in the rest.

"What a bunch of pigs." Ellen's disgust grew as she looked around her. She wrinkled her nose at the revolting smell of stale cigarette smoke. She blew a strand of hair from her forehead as she leaned against the counter, relieving the weight on her ankle. "Look at this mess," she growled. "Well, they can damn well clean it up, I'm not."

She couldn't leave the perishables sit. Muttering to herself, she quickly cleared the counters from their messy lunch and put the milk in the fridge. Job accomplished, she poured herself a glass of orange juice, then popped a few Tylenol from her purse.

She limped into the living room to rest her swollen ankle. She had strained it too much, and it needed ice, but that would have to wait a few minutes until the pain eased.

"Dammit." Ellen seldom swore, but her nerves were frazzled. As she looked around her, she realized what else Dan and Mike had been doing.

This morning the living room had been neat, and now it was littered with probably a dozen beer cans as well as an overflowing ashtray. *How dare they?*

She hobbled to the window, hoping to see the motorboat still moored. It wasn't. Swearing, she grabbed the binoculars then stumbled down to the beach, noting that the boys hadn't chopped the wood either.

"Dammit, they didn't even get that done. If Dan and Mike have taken the skis, I'm going to kill them."

Frustrated and edgy with ankle pain, she made her way to the beach, falling exhausted into the lawn chair nearest the dogwood tree. She hissed as her foot pounded. Rubbing her swollen ankle carefully, Ellen leaned back to relax before reaching for her binoculars.

She scanned the lake, looking for their boat. There were only a couple out there on this windy day, yet it was difficult to tell which one was theirs.

"Damn you guys. Can't trust them for a minute." Her fingers were trembling so hard she had trouble focusing the binoculars. She sat them on her lap then took several long, deep breaths to calm herself.

"Oh, no," she moaned. Her glance fell upon the skis at the end of the pier.

The slalom was missing. Mike was the only one good enough to slalom, so that meant Dan had to be driving. Barry warned them against boating, let alone skiing when drinking. On top of it all, there'd be no spotter with them today. Great.

Calm down. You're over-reacting. These aren't children—they're grown adults. They'll be fine. Over and over, Ellen repeated this until she almost believed it.

Ellen caught the flash of a boat coming towards her. As she waited for it to appear larger, she saw it was hauling a skier. Within seconds she recognized the familiar blue and white hull and sighed with relief.

Boy, were they going to get an earful.

She watched as Dan steered the boat in a figure eight. Was he deliberately trying to dump Mike? Ellen wondered at what kids called fun nowadays. It was plain dangerous and stupid in these choppy waters. *Don't they ever think?*

As she watched Danny get out of the figurine, she marveled at Mike's expertise. Skiing must be a talent you never lose entirely because Mike had recaptured his skills within the week, which, of course, didn't always sit well with his jealous friend.

"Oh no, Dan. You're too close!" Ellen yelled. She dropped the binoculars, waving her arms in the air, trying to warn him. "Dan! Danny!"

He was heading across the bay and, at the last minute, swerved to enter it. He was much too close to the peninsula. The swing of the tow rope would send Mike into the rocky point. Mike would have to let go, or he'd smash against the boulders.

"Danny! Mike, let go, let go-o!" Ellen screamed again as she continued waving. Too late. Poor judgment or callous daring claimed Mike as he struck something underneath the waves and leaped into the air.

Ellen screamed, but like before, to no avail. With the distance and the westerly wind, her voice couldn't carry. Frantically, she picked up her binoculars again and increased the focus, searching for Mike to emerge from the water. Danny turned the boat around and came back slowly, the loose tow rope skipping across the choppy water.

Ellen breathed a deep sigh of relief as she saw Mike raise his arm. Thank God! He's ok. Mike's ok. Mike's head bobbed through the boat's wake and the return wave action from the rocks.

Apprehensively, she prayed that he wasn't critically hurt as she waited for Danny to retrieve him. She saw Danny looking in the boat for something.

"A paddle, stupid—hand him the paddle. Or throw him a life jacket."

From the way Mike floated in the water, Ellen could see he hadn't been smart enough to put one on. She frowned.

Danny grabbed an oar then held it out to Mike. Ellen watched Mike grope for it. Zeroing in closer, she could see blood flowing down from his scalp. Why didn't Danny jump in there? Mike looked groggy, barely able to hang onto it.

Mike managed to grab hold of the oar, then suddenly Danny stopped pulling him in. Instead, he tugged the oar away from Mike then glanced around him.

"What the hell? Danny? What the hell?" Ellen watched in horror. Her heart split into a thousand pieces.

She couldn't believe what she saw.

Deliberately, Dan swung the oar overhand with both arms, slamming it on top of Mike's head.

Mike's arms flailed as he went underneath the choppy water. Danny's grip on the oar must have loosened because Mike came up gasping.

Again, Danny brought the oar down on his friend's head and pressed him downwards. This time there was no sign of struggle. Mike disappeared, and a minute later, Danny lifted his oar and put it back into the gunnel on the boat.

Ellen dropped the binoculars in her lap. An icy feeling of dread overcame her. *Did I just see what I think I saw?* A tingle of fear ran through her. Uh Uh. *No way. It couldn't be.*

She refocused her binoculars with shaky fingers, searching the waves for Mike. Nothing. Mike probably dove and swam over to the other side of the boat to escape Dan's horsing around.

A slow burn consumed her. If these guys were pulling a prank, there'd be shit flying when they came in. *Where was Mike?* Maybe the blood she saw was not as bad as she thought. Mix a little blood and water, and it probably looked worse than it was.

Had Mike decided to hide among the boulders? After the paddle incident, he might be trying to scare Dan or protect himself. *Smartasses!*

Ellen continued to watch the rocks and the shoreline for any sign of Mike. Nothing. She focused on Danny, sitting in the boat as relaxed as can be, slowly circling the point.

Ellen shook so hard that her binoculars fell from her grasp onto the ground. *What if something terrible had happened to Mike?* She closed her eyes and rubbed her forehead, trying to get that vision out of her head.

Her heartbeat pounded in her ears as she dropped her head into her hands. She gulped for breath and tried to control the panic that overcame her. Slowly, she regained control of her breathing.

Was what she'd thought she'd seen possible? No. This was a prank. Or an accident. But if it was a severe injury, what was Dan waiting for? Why didn't he jump in the water and help Mike or come back to shore for help?

She'd better get her first aid kit ready. Ellen grabbed the binoculars and made her way back up the path, staying in the shadows to be safe.

Safe from what?

Her son wouldn't hurt his friend on purpose. Why should she be afraid? Ellen pushed her worry away but followed her instincts to continue in the cover of the trees.

What would Barry say about this? He'd be furious, and rightly so. How could she explain this, or would the guys hide the incident? They still had a few more days to enjoy.

Ellen hoped the subject wouldn't come up. If they didn't say anything, she wouldn't either. Boys will be boys.

She glanced back to the bay. The boat was still there. It would give her time to think, to decide her next move. Carefully planting one foot in front of the other, she made her way back to the house and straight to the bathroom. Running cold water into the sink, Ellen splashed water over her face several times. Blotting her face dry, she looked into the mirror.

Why the hell had Danny done something so stupid? He could've drowned his friend, then what would've happened? Questions tumbled one after another as she stared at her reflection. Her eyes were wild with panic. Her chin and lips were trembling. Ellen placed her hand over her mouth as she struggled to control her breathing.

The color returned to her face slowly, and the waves of nausea had receded. Now that the initial terror had subsided, her panting gradually diminished into more calming breaths, and she could think clearly. Was Mike as badly hurt as it appeared? Ellen went to the linen closet to look for the first aid kit.

Please, God, let it be nothing serious.

"Mom! Mo-o-m!"

Ellen's heart palpitated wildly as she tried to get a grip on her emotions. *God, help me.*

The door crashed open.

"Mom! Mom, I was calling you! We had an accident. Oh my God, Mom, I'm so sorry." Dan seemed overwhelmed with panic. His eyes were opened wide in a flushed face. His breath was coming heavy and fast as if he couldn't believe what had happened. Tears filled Dan's eyes as he begged her to listen. "Mom."

"What happened?"

"Mom, Mike wiped out. I can't find him. I've looked and looked." His eyes darted in apparent confusion.

Ellen belatedly realized Dan was dripping wet. *Why was he wet?*

"What are you talking about?" Ellen stalled.

"Dad warned us against booze and boating, and we didn't listen. I mean, we only had a few beers each. We didn't think it would be a big deal. God, I should've listened." He threw his hands up.

"Danny, explain yourself!"

"We took the boat out to do some skiing. It was too rough for me, but Mike wanted to try slalom. We were on our way back. I guess I drove too close to the rocks around the point. Mike should've let go, but he kept following. The next thing I know, he's sailing through the air. I went back to get him, but he was gone. His board was broken. Parts of it were floating on the water, but he disappeared." Dan was pacing now, back and forth from the kitchen to the living room.

"What the hell were you guys doing out there? From the looks of the living room, you'd been drinking, and then you go skiing without life jackets or a spotter? What's the matter with you?"

"Give it a break, Mom. Don't you think I feel bad enough? Besides, we were careful. When he fell in, I thought he was joking around, trying to scare me, so I started yelling at him - telling him to smarten up." Dan stopped in front of her. His arms hung at his side, his fingers nervously pulling at his shorts. His lips were trembling now, and his eyes widened in panic.

"Slow down, Dan. You have to tell me exactly what happened. Was he bleeding?"

"I don't know. I told you I didn't see Mike. I yelled, but he didn't answer, Mom. Nothing. Then I got scared and jumped in. I started looking for him. But Mike was gone." Dan began sniffling then grabbed his head with both hands. "He's gone, Mom."

"Oh my God." Her quiet statement was more a reflection of disbelief in her son's ability to tell such a bare-faced lie.

Dan nodded, taking her oath to mean one of sorrow, of acceptance of his details of the accident.

"Call 911. You need to call the police, Mom. Or the search and rescue, or somebody. Mom, you gotta help me," he cried as he crumpled into the kitchen chair, his head hung in apparent disbelief.

Ellen gravitated towards him, and unable to stop herself, she lay her hand on his shoulder, massaging it. *He's right. I should've helped him a long time ago.* She had failed to see what an amoral and manipulative person he was. With the proper help, he might not have turned out this way.

"It's ok, son, I'll help," she heard herself say. Maybe this was the answer.

He certainly did appear remorseful.

If she hadn't seen it with her own eyes, she would've believed his story. Without a doubt, he gave the impression of a panicked friend. His face twisted in apparent remorse for being so reckless. He appeared devastated that Mike was missing.

But there was no denying that there was no mention of Mike surfacing or the initial attempt to save him with the oar. Let alone the callous decision to send his friend to a watery grave.

The hope that she had misinterpreted what she witnessed was torn to shreds. If one thing in his story was a lie, then it all was.

Ellen turned away and pressed her knuckles against her lips, stifling a cry of anguish. What should she do? She knew what the right thing to do would be. Call the police and reveal the truth. But how would that help?

The truth was that this could destroy Barry's career. A politician's life was only as good as his reputation. Smear that, and he'd be out. He'd never regain the admiration of his colleagues and constituents again.

If she told the truth, it'd also mean that Dan would go to jail, probably for life. Already, Dan was to blame for one life extinguished today, one family devastated, as well as the friends like Neil who would grieve him. If she could get Dan counseling, wouldn't it be better to save this family than destroy it?

The arrogance of youth. Now, two families and friends were paying the price. Damn! Too many thoughts tumbled through her brain in quick succession. What was she going to do?

"Mom!" Dan cried again. "Do something."

"Yes, yes. I'll call the police." Ellen briskly rubbed her arms, trying to ground herself from the trance she had slipped into. This was not the time for indecision. She found her phone, and with trembling fingers, she dialed 911 on her cell.

"RCMP Courtenay. What's the nature of your call?"

"I need your help. My son was involved in a boating accident, and his friend's missing. At least Dan can't find him."

"Your name, please."

"Mrs. Ellen Peterson. We have a summer home on Comox Lake about four miles past the old logging bridge. There's a sign on the driveway."

"When did this happen?" The officer's voice was calm but curt.

"Ummm. I don't know exactly. Danny, how long ago did Mike go down?"

"I'm not sure. Maybe twenty minutes ago? Maybe less?"

Ellen relayed the information, then listened intently.

"An officer will be dispatched ASAP. We'll notify search and rescue to meet us at your home."

"Thank you, sir," Ellen replied and hung up. It usually took her about twenty-five minutes to go to town, so she estimated they'd arrive by 2:00 or so.

"They're on the way, Dan. Now tell me again. What happened? You'll have to be prepared to tell the police when they arrive."

"I gotta clean this place. There are beer cans everywhere. I'll be in so much shit." He headed towards the living room.

"No. Leave it. Maybe it will prove to the police that you were both impaired. Besides, when Search and Rescue find Mike, they'll do an autopsy and know the situation. They'll probably want to do a breathalyzer and blood test on you too."

"Fine. Let them. I don't care! My best friend dies. Because of me." Dan sat at the kitchen table, collapsing his head on his forearms.

"Tell me again what happened," Ellen encouraged softly. She observed her son as he began recounting the events. Ellen forced herself to see it through his eyes. Everything fit with what she saw—all except the final scene.

"He never even came up, Mom. I thought he was trying to scare me and went hiding along the boulders. I called him and looked around. I was starting to get pissed off. It didn't look like a bad fall. I wasn't *that* close to the rocks." Dan rubbed the back of his neck, then spread his hands out. "Then I got scared that maybe it wasn't a joke, so I threw the anchor out and jumped in." Dan stood and started pacing again, running his fingers through his damp hair.

Ellen went to the laundry room and picked up a thick beach towel. "Here, Dan. Use this before you go into shock."

She watched him towel dry his hair, then wrap the towel around his shoulders. His jaw clenched, and his lips drew into a thin line as he tried to calm himself and continue with his story. "The wind was picking up, and the waves were hitting the rocks hard. I went under, but it was hard to control where I wanted to go. It was a lot deeper there than I thought, and there's a pretty strong current too. I kept diving, but I couldn't even see the bottom or him. Fuck, I was so scared." Dan stopped in front of the picture window and gazed at the lake.

"Language, Dan." The automatic rebuke slipped from Ellen's mouth. She wasn't surprised when he ignored her.

"How stupid could we be? It's my fault, Mom, my mistake. We were drinking, and I shouldn't have taken the boat out. But I didn't kill him, Mom. It was an accident." Dan turned slowly, his shoulders slumped, watching for his mom's response. "Am I going to jail?"

"I have no idea what will happen. I have to make a few phone calls. I'll call your dad first. Then I better call Mike's parents, I guess. Do you know their number?"

"No. The Blackwells live on 142nd Street near the Guildford Mall. Maybe we should wait, though. Maybe they'll find him, and he'll be ok."

Ellen nodded and decided she'd better let the police handle it once they knew the outcome. She closed her eyes and said a prayer. No way could Ellen handle delivering that news. She called Barry's office and told his receptionist she had an emergency. Her shaky voice emphasized the trauma she was feeling.

"He's at the Fairmont Hotel where the forestry negotiations are taking place. I'll put a crisis call through to his business cell for you. That's the best I can do, Mrs. Peterson."

Ellen thanked her and disconnected. While waiting for Barry's response, Ellen made coffee for both of them. Shock and the wet clothes teamed to give Danny the shivers. Ellen advised him against changing. She wanted his appearance a matter of public record.

The phone rang, and Ellen repeated the tragic situation to her stunned husband.

"Goddamn idiots! They were drinking, weren't they?"

"Yes. It looks like it," Ellen replied coolly. She was holding on stiffly to her emotions, winding them tighter and tighter around herself.

She'd persevere. They all would. And Dan would be alright too.

"I'll call in a few favors and get a Heli from Vancouver

Harbor. I'll be there within a few hours. Be cooperative, but don't let the authorities badger you. This was an accident. A stupid and tragic accident. Tell them the basic information they'll need to find Mike. I'll call Bev. She's a good lawyer, and I know she'll drop everything and fly up. If the cops try to pin this on Dan, tell him to clam up until we get there." He told Ellen he'd call Mike's parents after speaking with the police and the SAR crew.

Ellen could tell that Barry was furious. She knew he'd be angry with himself for leaving her alone with the boys. Barry always thought she let Dan walk over her and said that we could never trust him. It looks like he was right.

"I'll see you soon. I'll do my best." Ellen disconnected slowly, then stood up, rubbing her arms again, trying to dispel the chill that had come over her body. She grabbed the coffee pot and refilled his mug. She couldn't sit down beside her son again, so she began putting the rest of the groceries away. The silence between the two of them grew.

"Now what, Mom? What else should we do?"

"Let's go back down to the beach," Ellen needed to do something, anything other than wait in the house. "Get the binoculars from the counter. Maybe he's surfaced somewhere. We might be able to find him before the Search and Rescue arrive."

"There's no use, Mom."

"Get them! We can try at least."

CHAPTER 20

It seemed like hours before Ellen heard the crunch of tires coming down her driveway. Two police cars followed by a yellow van sped in. The search and rescue vehicle hauled a small boat with a zodiac atop, which immediately wound its way down to the water's edge.

An RCMP officer approached Ellen and her son near the shoreline and opened his notebook. "My name's Corporal Wilson. Are you the party that called in the emergency?"

"Yes, sir, we are. This is my son, Dan Peterson. He was driving the boat."

"Who is the person we're looking for?" Wilson asked Danny.

"Mike Blackwell, a friend of mine. We were out skiing."

"We'll get into that later. Show me where you saw your friend go down. The volunteer search and rescue crew are ready to start and need instructions." He gestured to one of the men heading toward them.

"Over to your right about half a mile, near the end of that point? Right around there. Mike was on a slalom board, and I cut it too close, I guess. He should've let go of the rope."

"Got that, Gerald?" asked the officer.

"Right. We'll mark it and start a grid, then work from there. What's your name?

"Dan Peterson."

"Ok, Dan. Did you see him come up at all?"

"Nope, we didn't have a spotter. When I realized he had gone down, I turned around and coasted back, looking for him. I saw the broken ski, but I never saw him."

As the corporal moved over to speak to Ellen, Gerald approached Dan.

"Any alcohol or drugs involved here?" he asked quietly.

"Uh..." Dan appeared trapped, worried.

"Look, I'm just here to help you find your friend. I can smell the booze on you, and I don't give a shit if you were both drinking or not. That's none of my business. But it makes a difference on how we search."

"Between both of us, we probably drank a case of beer in the house." Dan shrugged his shoulders defensively. "I grabbed a half-sack when we went in the boat. We weren't drunk or anything. He might've had six or seven beers over three or four hours. Shit." Danny's shoulder drooped, and his voice cracked with emotion. "Shit."

"Alright, Dan. We'll find him. You look pale, you'd better sit down a while. Corporal Wilson will be back to talk with you."

"Thanks."

When Wilson returned, he went over the story again with Dan. As Ellen hovered nearby, she was amazed by the accuracy with which Dan retold the tragedy. It never wavered from the deceit he told her. As he related the story again, his reactions rang true. When Sergeant Browning arrived following the SARS unit and approached Dan, Wilson peeled away and approached Ellen.

"Mrs. Peterson, I'd like to ask you a few questions, please. You look exhausted. Do you need to sit down?"

"Yes, please. Can we go inside?"

"Sure," Wilson noted her limp and reached over to offer his arm. "Hold on, if you'd like help. What happened to your foot?"

"I sprained it a few days ago. On this uneven ground, it's awkward to walk without it hurting." Ellen wrapped her hand around the crook of his arm as they made their way into the house.

"Would you like coffee, Officer?"

Wilson shook his head. "No, thanks. Have a seat, and let's get this started. You're probably exhausted from this tragedy, but I do need to know more." When Ellen nodded and slipped into the kitchen chair beside him, he continued. "It looks like the guys were drinking. Didn't you try and stop them from boating?"

Ellen cocked her head to the side and lifted her eyebrows, her voice rising. "I wasn't here. Of course, I would've stopped them from leaving if I was home." She blew a breath out and closed her eyes briefly, her shoulders slumping. "Sorry, that wasn't necessary." Ellen's voice quietened as she continued. "I left this morning to get groceries and do a few things in town. When I returned about four hours later, this is what greeted me." Ellen waved her hand towards the living room. "We set down strict rules about boating. No drinking and no skiing if there wasn't anyone to spot for them. And of course, always wear a life jacket."

"Doesn't look like they listened to any of those rules today."

"They certainly didn't. I can't believe what's happened. Wait 'til my husband returns. He's going to be livid."

"When did you realize the boat was gone?"

"I put a few groceries away, and I was furious with the way Dan and Mike had left the house. I was determined not to clean up after them, but my ankle was aching, so I sat down in the living room. That's when I noticed the boat was gone."

"Did you see the accident? It seems like you have a panoramic view from your living room."

"No, I didn't." Ellen lowered her gaze, and pinched the bridge of her nose, then despairingly shook her head as she tried to gain control of herself and her story. "I took two Tylenol, then decided to put the rest of the groceries away. I was angry and thinking about what I'd do when the guys got home. The next thing I heard was Dan yelling for me as he came onto the porch. The rest you know about."

Corporal Wilson continued asking the same questions she'd heard before. A strange feeling of numbness overtook her, and Ellen recited the same answers Dan had relayed to the officer an hour earlier.

The officer finally closed his book when he realized that nothing new would be obtained from Mrs. Peterson. She appeared to be sliding into a state of shock, which was understandable.

Wilson needed to call the office and set up procedures to take a breathalyzer on Dan today, as well as start a police file on the incident. He'd advise the Surrey RCMP to be prepared to contact Mike's parents. Wilson would go over his notes, then interview both Dan and his mom again, perhaps tomorrow. The corporal placed a hand on Ellen's shoulder. "I'm sorry about this, Mrs. Peterson. It's a real tragedy. I'll be outside with the SARS crew. We'll talk again soon."

Ellen nodded and returned outside to watch the rescue activity and keep an eye on Dan. She lowered herself into one of the Adirondack chairs on the sundeck, rubbing her temples to clear her mind from the fog that had overtaken it.

Sergeant Browning now introduced himself after overseeing and starting the rescue search, bringing Dan with him. Again, Dan repeated his story as Ellen listened while the Sergeant took his own notes. She wondered how often she'd hear the tale. Looking at Mrs. Peterson, the sergeant compassionately closed his notebook and told her he'd coordinate with Wilson for her account. He jerked his head at Dan, then told him to follow him down to the shore.

Alone, at last, Ellen breathed a sigh of relief. She closed her eyes and concentrated on letting the tension seep from her body. How long could she listen to this? The sound of arrival made Ellen glance up the gravel laneway. Barry was home, thank God.

Barry sprinted up the porch to the sundeck and pulled Ellen into his arms. She seemed as limp as a rag. He supposed she was in shock. Who wouldn't be?

A frisson of anger ran up his spine. "Ell, are you ok?" He ran his hands up and down her arms, trying to get her circulation going or get some kind of response.

"No, I'm not. I'm sick about this." Ellen leaned her head against Barry's shoulder. "I can't believe this is happening. Mike's parents will be devastated." Ellen moved aside to the railing to watch the activity below.

"Dad!" Dan called and excused himself from Sergeant Browning.

Barry grabbed his arm and pulled him aside, growling

softly. "What the hell were you guys thinking? Jesus Christ, don't you ever listen?"

"Cut it out, Dad. I feel bad enough as it is. Don't you think I know?"

"Maybe, but it doesn't do any good now, does it? I'm sorry about your friend. His poor parents." Barry shook his head.

By this time, Sergeant Browning joined them as Dan repeated to his father the sorry details of the accident once again.

Ellen moved to the railing, watching the activity below, trying not to listen. She was barely aware of the words now. Everything seemed to have dulled, and sounds were muffled, lost in the haze of her confusion. She couldn't stand there any longer. Ellen limped slowly towards the back door. Questions ran through her brain to which she had no good answers.

Eventually, Barry followed her back into the house and made more coffee for them, then called one of the women Ellen befriended from St. Joseph's Church. Hannah offered to help for the next few days. Thank God because Ellen seemed incapable of accomplishing anything. She simply sat on the sofa, watching the rescue activity.

Four divers working in pairs were covering the area near the accident, methodically coming up then relaying information to the coordinator on the zodiac. Buoys closed off the location to the curious, with only one other rescue boat assisting them.

Their watercraft was left dockside and examined several times. A police photographer snapped pictures of everything—the boat, the shoreline, inside and outside their home.

Ellen closed her eyes, then leaned back in her armchair.

A nightmare, Ellen thought. A flipping nightmare. She wished she could wake up, yet every time she opened her eyes, the same scene was in front of her.

Minutes passed as hours in the interminable wait. Suddenly, there was a surge of activity. Sergeant Browning came up to the house to advise them that they found Mike's body. He told them he expected Dan and Ellen to follow him to the station. An ambulance was already there, so the body was being sent to the coroner's office. Dan came in soon after the sergeant left and then showered, changing into jeans and a sweatshirt.

Ellen began to cry softly. Too much. This tragedy was too much to bear. Barry gathered her in his arms and carried her to their bedroom, covering her with a quilt.

"I can't go to the station or the morgue. I honestly can't." Ellen turned her face away from him, curling up into a fetal position.

"Don't worry about anything. I'll go down with Dan. Try and rest, honey. I'll be back soon."

"Say goodbye to Mike for me," Ellen mumbled before squeezing her eyes closed. She needed to shut this whole day out of her heart and mind.

Barry promised he would, then kissed her forehead and left, closing the door behind him. He went to the living room and poured himself a finger of scotch. What a disaster. How was Ellen going to manage this? One thing at a time. He downed his drink, welcoming the burn in his throat.

Dan was sitting on a lawn chair on the patio, looking at the water. This identification wasn't going to be easy. Barry closed his eyes briefly as he swiped a hand over his face, then rubbed his chin fiercely. Time to man up. He wondered how his son was handling this now, whether it had finally hit home. *Stupid kids.*

Barry watched the zodiac pull up onshore, and the volunteers congregate. Barry walked down to meet them. The search that took almost three hours was concluded. The strain of it showed on the divers' faces. He spoke with each of them, thanking them for their service.

Gerald came over and talked with Barry again before leaving. "He drifted with the current about a mile and a half. He was down very deep, over 30 feet. He must have had a lot of alcohol in his system to have sunk so far." Gerald's voice had a slight tremor in it.

Barry could see the exhaustion on his face.

"Were you the one that found him?"

"Yea. Me and my partner. It looked like he was sitting there waiting for us, his arms outstretched. Goddamn stupid waste," he muttered and turned away. Not fast enough to hide the tears in his eyes.

This man had courage, Barry acknowledged. Hell, they all did. Otherwise, they'd never be able to perform these services over and over again.

They were a quiet bunch now, stripping off their suits and re-loading their equipment into their van. The small pilot boat was loaded onto a trailer and pulled out of the water. Barry helped them load the zodiac atop it, then strap it down. He offered them coffee, but the team refused. Their job was done, and they wanted to leave before their emotions caught up with them.

"I'm sorry we had to call you. We won't forget this," Barry promised as he reached to shake his hand. "Thank you."

"No problem," Gerald replied. "Most of us have kids. Take it easy on yours. He's suffered a lot already, but there's more to come. He's going to need your support," Gerald advised as he stepped into his van.

Barry nodded and waved as he watched them solemnly depart.

When this situation cleared, he would look into the local search and rescue organization, then see what it needed. Most of these operations suffered from tight budget constraints resulting in a lack of equipment. After today, Barry vowed to see it given priority funding.

Barry climbed the path to the chalet slowly. His heart pounded as he thought of what was next. He clenched and unclenched his fists beside him, trying to strengthen his resolve. No use postponing the inevitable.

"Dan? We have to go to the station."

"No, Dad, I can't." Dan looked warmer and calmer now, yet he hadn't moved since the sergeant told them Dan needed to go the station.

"You have to. The body has to be identified for the police, and the RCMP may still have questions. Technically, they could charge you with criminal negligence. And who knows what else? You told me they took a breathalyzer on you, right?"

"Yea."

"Then they're going to know how reckless you both were. Act like a man, son, and face it. This part is one of the last things you can do for Mike. If you show the police how troubled you feel, your remorse, it could help your case. You're not finished with this yet."

The investigation would likely rest on the discretion of the RCMP. Dan would probably get off with a fine and a suspended sentence unless it were evident that the accident was planned or deliberate. It'd also depend on how Mike's parents handled their loss and if they were likely to press charges.

Dan closed his eyes for a moment, then nodded. "I'll get my jacket."

It was the hardest thing Barry had ever done, helping Dan identify the young man that laid in the body bag. His once vibrant features were waxen and still. But for the vagaries of fate, it could've been his son there. Barry mourned the recklessness of youth, their infallible beliefs in themselves.

Sergeant Browning wasn't immune to their distress. After the identification was complete, he told them to go home and return to the station the following afternoon.

A handshake later, Barry crooked his finger to his son. "Time to go, Dan. We'll come back tomorrow."

As the son of the local MLA, the sergeant was not worried that Dan would disappear. The sergeant's first instincts were that it had been a foolhardy adventure that turned tragic.

The fact that Dan Peterson came from a good family weighed heavily in his favor. Dan had also seemed regretful and cooperative, although now he had retreated into silence. Quite understandable. The sergeant sighed deeply. One or two people would drown in Comox Lake every summer, usually children or a drunk adolescent. What a waste.

Dan slid into the passenger seat, secured himself then pulled the bill on his ball cap down. Barry guessed his son was probably tapped out. Hell, they were all exhausted.

It had been a horrible, nerve-wracking day for everyone. Barry started the vehicle and drove back to the chalet. No one could do anything else today that would change the outcome.

~

Once inside the chalet, Hannah greeted the men with a nod. "Nice pot of creamy clam chowder here, Barry. I've made a platter of sandwiches too. Have a seat, you two. I'll get the bowls."

Dan shrugged out of his jacket. "Sorry, I can't right now. I'm wiped. I'm going to bed." On second thought, as he passed the table, he grabbed a few sandwiches on a plate then sent them a silent salute of thanks as he headed for his room.

Hannah handed Barry a large steaming bowl of soup. "By the way, I haven't seen Sara about. Is she here?"

"Oh, God. She's spending the week here. I hadn't even thought of her or Neil." Barry jumped from his chair and sprinted up the stairs to the loft. "Dan, where's Neil and Sara?"

Dan lifted his eyes in surprise. "Shit, I forgot about them. They went hiking real early this morning. Mom's supposed to pick them up at the post office in Cumberland tonight at 8:00."

"It's already 6:30. You and I better get Sara and Neil. Maybe we could tell them there rather than have your mom go through this again."

"What about me? How many times have I told the story already? I've had enough too."

"I know, I know. Look, stay home. I'll get them. I'll tell the kids."

"Thanks, Dad. I'm going to crash out." Danny waited until his dad's footsteps clomped down the stairs. Once alone, however, his shoulders straightened, and a smile broke across his face. He punched his right arm up in the air as a sign of triumph. *I did it. I didn't plan to, but I did it. And I got away with it.* Pleased with himself, he laid across his bed, ate his sandwiches, then fell deep asleep.

CHAPTER 21

Barry moved about organizing the household over the following week. He and Dan met with the Blackwells, who arranged to have their son's body flown back to Surrey. Even deep in shock, they exercised considerable compassion towards Dan and refused to allow him to shoulder all the blame. After all, Mike had been drinking too and should've shown more common sense. He was almost two years older than Dan and should have been more responsible.

The Peterson family chartered a small plane to fly them back and forth to Vancouver for the funeral. Dan remained on the mainland, returning to his job as a mechanic.

Four months later, in early January, Dan was back in Courtenay attending the court case for dangerous boating causing death. Barry was there also, in support of his son, but Ellen couldn't make herself appear.

Bev was able to negotiate a plea deal. Dan received a suspension for operating a boat for two years, along with an order to abstain from alcohol for the same period. He'd also be required to perform one hundred hours of community service in Surrey.

When the case adjourned, Bev hugged Barry, then shook Dan's hand. "I'm happy to see the leniency in your sentence, Dan. It helped that Mike's parents sent a letter stating they didn't hold you totally responsible. This tragedy has been a tough lesson."

"It has been tough. Thanks for your help, Mrs. Williams." Dan shook her hand firmly, hoping his attempt at sincerity looked genuine. "Thanks, Dad. Tell Mom I said hello." Dan shook his father's hand then turned away, anxious to get back to the mainland and away from this suffocating nightmare.

"Dan—aren't you coming to the house? Your mom wasn't well enough to take the stress here, but she wanted to see you."

"Sorry. I need to catch the ferry. I took the day off work for this, but I'm scheduled for a shift tomorrow. I'll catch her next time." Dan gave them his two-finger salute then left the courtroom, totally oblivious to the impression he'd left them.

"That's it?" Bev asked. "You'd think he'd have gone home with you, even if only for an hour or two."

"I'm afraid that's Dan. I hate to say it, but he looks after himself first. This is no surprise. And honestly? Ellen's not herself these days. Dan knows how to press her buttons and mine, so I'm glad he's leaving." Barry shook his hand. "Don't forget to send the bill to me. You'll never get a penny out of Dan. Paying bills is apparently the only thing he likes me for."

Bev shook her head slightly, then tapped him on the shoulder. "Then don't waste any more energy on him. Let him go his own way. Concentrate on Ellen and Sara. When you're up for it, Larry and I will come for a visit. It's been a while since we spent a weekend with you and Ellen. Give her a hug for me, and tell her to call anytime she needs to talk."

"Sounds good. We need to make some new memories, or we'll have to sell the place. I know that Ellen hasn't been able to go there since the accident. If I had my way, I'd never have our son in our home again. He's brought nothing but trouble for us. Who knows, I may change my mind if he ever grows up, but—" Barry spread his hands out and wiggled them.

"I hear you. Dan's always been difficult. And I can't say that I blame Ellen for not wanting to go back there. Maybe in a few years, when the memories dull a little, she'll be able to start over." Bev shrugged. "Who knows? But she's got you to lean on. You'll figure it out." Bev gave a finger wave and gathered her briefcase and shoulder bag. They parted ways, each wondering if their success, in this case, was really for the best.

THE TRAGEDY of Mike's death forged a bond between Neil and Sara that made them nearly inseparable. When Neil advised the Petersons that he intended to move and find work in Victoria, it was no surprise. Barry closed the chalet for the rest of the summer, then hired Hannah to put everything in order.

After Mike's funeral, Dan returned to work. Sara left to get on with the business of settling in Victoria for school. By mid-September, everyone was back on track with their lives, still somewhat battered but back in the routine of the living.

BARRY WATCHED HIS WIFE AGE. When her plan to have Dan relocate to Comox failed, her anxiety became worse. The disaster had triggered a depression in her, the likes he had never seen before. Either she was talking a blue streak in a high-pitched voice, running around their home, cleaning everything in sight, or she sat.

Some days he'd arise in the morning to see her sitting in her rocker, gazing outside, focusing on nothing. She wouldn't comb her hair, and she wouldn't talk. It was driving him crazy. Always slender, she was now gaunt, her face and figure slowly disintegrating as surely as her spirit.

Barry talked to Sara often on the phone. She pressed him to see their family doctor and get an opinion on her mother's mental health. She was sure her mother was on the verge of a breakdown. Ellen refused to go to the clinic, so Dr. Wiseman made a house call. He agreed with Sara and Barry, then offered to make arrangements to see Dr. Hallden, one of the best psychiatrists on the Island.

Barry and Sara composed a document for Dr. Hallden explaining the summer boating tragedy. They also included separate opinions on the different times in their lives that Ellen had troubles with Dan and how his behavior had affected the family. After an afternoon visit with Ellen, Dr. Hallden made an appointment for Barry to see him.

Dr. Hallden believed that forced treatment should be the last option. Whenever Barry and Ellen were ready, all they had to do was call him for an intake appointment or book a series of meetings in his private office. The chances that Ellen would return to her usual self were small without therapy, but it could happen over time. Barry felt comfortable with the idea. He'd help her any way he could.

He just couldn't stand the thought of putting her in a clinic.

~

ELLEN MADE it clear she wanted no one's help. She didn't have the strength. At times, Ellen had a hard time even breathing. It seemed to take so much energy. She vaguely knew she was slipping her hold on life, but she honestly didn't care.

When she did try to focus on the people in the family pictures, she hurt. Pain welled up inside her like a rubber balloon, expanding then growing until she thought she'd puke. It was infinitely safer where she was, peaceful even. She moved about like an automaton, only doing the basics when she was alone. But when Barry or anyone else arrived, she'd become as inconspicuous as possible, hiding within her shell.

She was aware of their conversations, aware of their concern but utterly numb to it all. Ellen wanted to be left alone. By herself in their Comox home overlooking Goose Spit, she'd take her bath and tidy up a bit. On impulse one morning, she went into Sara's room to borrow a clean housecoat.

There, sitting on the dresser, was an envelope of pictures. Curious, Ellen reached inside and pulled them out. Happy pictures of Sara's graduation made Ellen smile and feeling braver. She continued flipping through them.

Pictures of the three of them at the lake. Ellen's heart began to thump.

Pictures of Dan napping on the lawn chair. Thump, thump, thump! Her heart beat faster, yet she was unable to stop herself from continuing.

A snapshot of the pier, Barry loading fishing gear in the canoe, smiling. Thump, thump, thump!

Oh my God. There it was—the three young men horsing around on the pier, the skis and tow rope sitting on the deck.

"No-o-o!" Ellen dropped the pictures and ran out of the room then into her bedroom, slamming the door. Wails poured torrentially from her body as she slumped against the door. Ellen was powerless as fear tore deep inside of her. Her trembling hands covered her ears as she tried to stifle the screams vibrating through her body and mind.

BARRY SHUT the ignition then grabbed his golf clubs from the back of his SUV. He was aware that Ellen performed minor personal and household tasks when she was by herself. Now Barry left her for a few hours each day, hoping she'd garner more interest in life when she busied herself. As he approached the side door, he heard her high-pitched screams.

He dropped the clubs and ran inside, calling her name. "Ellen? Ellen?" He raced through the kitchen and living room. Spotting Sara's open door, he rushed inside, noting the scattered photographs. Scanning them briefly, he knew what had happened.

"Ell, honey, I'm coming," he cried out as he ran down the hall towards their bedroom. He pushed against the door and felt the weight behind it.

On the other side, Ellen's moans deepened, their pitch rising, the wailing about to start again.

"Ell, my sweetheart, let me in. Move over, honey. I'll help you." Barry jiggled the doorknob, trying to pry the door open. "Ellen?"

Too late, a resounding cry of anguish spilled from her lungs, piercing the air with its palpable pain. Barry tried again to dislodge the door without hurting her. Giving up, he ran to the living room and phoned Dr. Hallden's number.

"This is an emergency. I've spoken to Dr. Hallden about my wife. She's locked in her room, screaming."

"Is she in immediate danger?" asked the receptionist.

"No, I don't think so. Ellen won't let me in. I don't even know if she knows I'm there. What shall I do?"

"Hold the line a moment. Your name again, sir?"

He waited impatiently. He shouldn't have procrastinated so long, he realized belatedly.

"Mr. Peterson?"

"Yes, Doctor. My wife-"

"Yes, sir, my receptionist told me. I'll call an ambulance and have her transported to St. Joseph's Hospital in Comox, and then I'll meet you there. Meanwhile, sit beside the door, and keep talking to her. It may register."

"Thanks, Dr. Hallden."

Dr. Hallden hung up, and Barry ran to their bedroom. He could hear her sobbing hysterically, could feel the vibration through the door.

"Hold on, sweetheart. I'll help you. You're going to be ok. Nobody's going to hurt you, Ell." He continued consoling her until the wailing began again. He leaned his exhausted body against the wall, then let his head drop in his hands.

If only I knew what we were fighting, he thought helplessly. God help her - help us, he prayed.

CHAPTER 22

"Did you have a good weekend, Ellen?" Dr. Hallden asked.

"Yes."

"Have you thought any more about your plans? Or what you're going to do?"

"Not really."

Dr. Hallden sighed. She wasn't cooperative today. From his notes, he remembered her agitation whenever Dan's name was brought up.

"So, do you think spring will ever get here?" Dr. Hallden asked, switching the subject for a while.

"Definitely. Did you see the purple crocuses beside the pathway? They're beautiful." Her voice had a lilt to it as she remembered the flowers.

"Would you like to go for a walk?"

"I'd like that. I'll go get my sweater."

Dr. Hallden waited for her return. When she first came here, she spoke to no one and had no interest in her surroundings. Ellen progressed a long way in that respect, partially because she was removed from the source of her anxiety, her family.

She couldn't stay here forever. Now that she had regained most of her strength, she managed her day-to-day life reasonably well. Now, it was time to go digging and forge ahead.

Dr. Hallden greeted her with a smile as together they walked outdoors. Surreptitiously, he watched her reactions and waited for her to relax.

"It's almost time to plant bedding flowers," Dr. Hallden remarked. "Or don't you plan on having any this year?"

Ellen ignored him as she concentrated on the new growth sprouting outdoors. They continued walking until they reached a bench which gave them a beautiful view of the Salish Sea. Although it was slightly overcast today, sailboats were out, dotting the bay.

"Do you remember what we were talking about on Friday? We talked about Sara and how bright she was. We talked about Dan. You wondered if there was something wrong with him. You told me that he always seemed so unhappy."

"Yes."

Dr. Hallden was relieved that Ellen was finally more comfortable with him. She probably felt safe with him, able to be totally honest about all her feelings, without the worry of having to justify herself.

"Did you ever confront him and ask him what was bothering him or how he felt about the family?"

"Yes. One night when Barry and I had gone out, he became frustrated and angry. He hit Sara, scaring her and the babysitter to death. Then he left. It was almost dawn when I heard him come home." Ellen paused for a long minute. "I got up then went to the kitchen," Ellen fidgeted with the button on her sweater.

"Go on, what happened?" Dr. Hallden encouraged.

"I can't. I feel sick."

"Exactly how are you feeling?"

"Like I'm going to be nauseous. It feels like there's an air bubble right here." She pointed to her sternum. "I think I must have overeaten at lunch."

"I don't think so, Ellen. You're trying to fight your memories. You don't want to face them." Dr. Hallden sat silently as they watched the seagulls dip and dive to the ocean below them. He reached over and laid his hand on her arm. "You know I'm your friend, as well as your doctor," he began.

She nodded.

"This next part may be painful, but stay with me. Trust me. Let these memories surface. If you feel like swearing or crying or getting sick - go ahead. A little vomit outside here isn't going to harm anything, and it certainly won't bother me. Do whatever you need to do, but don't give up. Once you get this pain out of you, you'll feel much better. I guarantee it. I want to help you, but you have to trust me. OK?"

"OK."

"Alright. Close your eyes for a bit. Take several deep cleansing breaths. Breathe in slowly. Hold. Exhale fully." He joined in the exercise for a couple of minutes. "Alright, Ellen. You're in the kitchen, with Dan, and—you're angry?"

"Not really. I was frustrated." Ellen looked away then returned to meet Dr. Hallden's gaze. She took a deep breath. "That's not true. I was incredibly angry. But I don't let him see it. I wasn't sure what to say, so I make him something to eat. He looks everywhere but at me, then he starts talking."

Dr. Hallden watched her eyes flutter and close as her breathing quickened. "About what?"

"He wanted to know if I thought he was crazy. He started to tell me how nobody has ever understood him. Sometimes, he didn't even understand himself. He also said he could see through everyone, that he knew what they were thinking." Her voice was still calm, but tears trickled slowly down her cheeks. She opened her eyes and searched his for what? Compassion? "He said he could never measure up to what we wanted him to be."

"What did you say?"

"I asked him if he had been taking any drugs or anything. He became angry, then said I was only looking for an excuse for his behavior, but there was none."

"Did you believe him?"

Ellen wiggled her hand in the air. "I wasn't sure. He denied it, but I think he may have used drugs, or at least tried them. I don't know. He probably didn't tell me the truth. He didn't share much, he only told me what he thought I wanted to hear."

"What did you do then?"

"I put my hand on his shoulder for a minute." Ellen closed her eyes tightly, remembering the moment of connection. "He'd never let me hug him. I wasn't sure how to approach him about his worries. Then, we talked about the fight he had with Sara." Her eyes popped open and she stared at Dr. Hallden, her fists clenched.

"God help me." She coughed, almost choking on her tears and her words. "I should've done more. I should've done something -but I didn't know what to do. Dan would never listen to us. What was I supposed to do?" Ellen's eyes begged him for an answer before she lost control and began sobbing.

Dr. Hallden let her cry then handed her his handkerchief. That's better, he noted. It's the first time she had ever let any strong emotions show. This woman had so much pain in her. It was time to let it go.

Background information from Barry, suggested there was a history of mental health problems with Dan. It could well be that he suffered with mild schizophrenia or a form of bi-polar tendencies. At the very least, he was good at manipulating his mother, and stirring up trouble with his dad. Ellen was feeling a lot of guilt he realized, but he was sure there was more he hadn't heard.

"I understand that shortly after, Dan ran away from home. Did he keep in touch?"

"I asked him to leave, after his second violent outburst. I'd warned him. I packed his bags and left them outside. He disappeared then for a long time." Ellen reached for a tissue and blew her nose, regaining control of her composure.

"Sara and your husband mentioned those episodes to me. How did you feel when he left?"

"Awful. Part of me hoped he'd come back, but part of me craved peace in our home. He eventually let us know he was staying with friends, but wouldn't give us any way to reach him. He ended up in Surrey, working his way up to a mechanic's apprentice. He was always good with tinkering. You don't have to deal directly with people, so it seemed to be right up his alley."

"So, once he got established, did he call regularly, or come and visit?"

"Only once, for one day. The visit didn't go well, it was very stressful. Like most apprentices, he was always broke, of course. We sent him a few money transfers here and there. In the end, Barry refused to do anymore because he didn't think Dan was making good use of the money. The last time Dan called us, it sounded like he was at a wild party, so it pissed Barry off."

"When was the last time you saw Dan?"

"He joined us at our summer home last year. We told him he was welcome to bring friends with him, so he did. One was a roommate, and the other worked in a tech repair shop across the street. We hoped it would make a difference having his friends with him. And it did. Things were going well."

Ellen shivered then stood up. "It's getting colder." She wrapped her arms around herself, hugging her sweater tight to her body. "That glacier wind goes right through me."

She looked exhausted, but when a patient switched subjects that quickly, Dr. Hallden was always suspicious. In his experience, he'd found that abrupt changes usually meant the patient wanted to avoid or hide something. She really did look exhausted. Almost four months after her intake, the prodding and encouragement was beginning to pay off. He had gained her trust alright, but had only received apathetic and general observations about her life, no problems or strong feelings.

He was getting close to the heart of this. To hell with his schedule, he was going to stay with her. He had a feeling they were awfully close to a breakthrough.

"How about a cup of tea, Ellen? I've some free time now." He slapped his hands together then blew on them as if to warm them.

Ellen shrugged her shoulders, then nodded her agreement as she walked briskly back inside to get warm.

Dr. Hallden watched the expressions flit across her face. Exhaustion, suspicion then lastly, acceptance. He had noticed she'd often relate something minor, then 'forget' the point of her story. Or how she selectively structured her memories.

She remembered good times, but not any bad things.

Her family, according to her, had been close and supportive of each other. Dr. Hallden was sure that was a lie she told herself. Now the years of lies and compartmentalizing had taken their toll. The sooner she allowed every member of that family to have their weaknesses as well as their good points, the sooner she'd unload her unwarranted guilt and failures from her mind. She had shared this much, but there was more. He was sure of it.

They went inside, walked to the cafeteria, and loaded a tray with teapots, cups, and a brownie each.

"Looks good for a change. I haven't had much of an appetite, but things are starting to appeal to me lately. And this looks delicious."

Dr. Hallden smiled then nodded towards the lounge area, which was off-limits at this time. "Being a doctor has privileges," he quipped. "We'll have our tea in there."

They drank their tea in comfortable silence.

The break in therapy was good for Ellen, and her color was returning to her face. Her wind-blown, chestnut hair was lightly laced with silver at her temples. She must have been beautiful when she was younger because Ellen was still striking even with the stress she'd experienced lately. Her hazel eyes dominated her face, and although the morning had been tough on her, she held her chin high and looked quite dignified sitting there, sipping her tea and nibbling on her brownie.

"So, did you enjoy Dan's visit this summer?" Dr. Hallden began.

"Yes, although I had forgotten how rambunctious he can be. Sometimes, he and his friends helped around the house. Mostly though, they went water skiing." She slapped her teacup down, and her fingers flew to her temples and rubbed them. Suddenly, she felt a prickly sensation underneath her scalp, and a tendril of fear quickened her breathing. *Why?*

"What are you remembering, Ellen?"

"Nothing much." Ellen tapped her temples, a habit she used when she felt a headache coming on. When her breath returned to normal, she sipped her tea, then leaned back in her chair and resumed talking.

"The guys like to sit on the beach, suntan, and have a few beers. They'd water ski off and on all day. One of them, named Neil, had become attached to Sara. The two of them used to do a lot of hiking up towards the glacier near Forbidden Plateau."

"Did Dan talk to you again about his problems - or any issues he was having?"

"No, he seemed happier than ever before. Oh, he went off on his own occasionally - but that's how he's always been. The three friends used to wrestle and bug the devil out of each other. Most times, Dan looked like he was on top of the world swimming, skiing..." Her voice faltered. "Oh my God," she whispered.

She closed her eyes and saw flashes of Danny driving the ski boat. She rocked in her seat, her fingertips rubbing her temples in a circular motion. She saw Dan steer the boat in a figure eight, then Mike clowning around on the slalom. They knew they weren't allowed to go skiing without a spotter, but that morning liquor had clouded their judgment, and they went anyway.

"Be careful," she whispered, unaware of where she presently was. Although her eyes were open now, she wasn't here with Dr. Hallden. An incident had triggered her memory, and she was back in time at the lake.

Dr. Hallden sat quietly, watching Ellen relive something. This was it, he hoped. If only she could let it keep coming.

"Watch out, Dan. You're getting too close." She watched her son approach the rocky islet on the point outside their bay.

Mike wiped out, and the tow line skipped along the top of the water. Dan glanced back and watched his friend go down, then circled back to him. She saw herself using the binoculars, searching to locate Mike. Minutes later, she glimpsed his head and arm grope up from the water.

"Thank God, he's ok," she breathed a sigh of relief. She noticed Dan reach for a paddle and hand it to Mike.

"No, oh no, God no!"

Dr. Hallden watched her tremble as her anguished voice ground out its plea.

"No, Dan, No!" She snapped her eyes shut and started crying hysterically.

Dr. Hallden set his hand on her arm. "Ellen." Dr. Hallden's voice grew more forceful. "Ellen, tell me. What do you remember?"

"I—I can't believe it. Dan hit him. He hit him! He didn't get the paddle to help him. He used it to strike him and hold him underwater." She sobbed convulsively now. "Mike, Mike, you poor kid. How could Dan do that to you?"

Dr. Hallden held both her hands now, rubbing the tops of them with his thumbs for a long while, encouraging her to breathe deeply. So, this was what had triggered her breakdown. He knew from Barry that a boating accident had taken the life of one of Dan's friends. Dan couldn't locate him after Mike wiped out on his slalom board near a dangerous point. He had dived in several times looking for him, then finally returned home to tell his mom.

And as there was no lookout with them or any known witnesses, the official cause of death was ruled accidental. Mike's autopsy showed a large contusion resulting in a probable concussion on his head. With a blood alcohol level content of .18, his ability to swim and recover from the injury had been severely compromised. In all the confusion, alcohol, and trauma, instead of rising out of the water, he had gone the other way.

Ellen had been the only one to witness the tragedy. Dr. Hallden wondered how she saw it. "I thought no one was at home when the accident happened?"

"Dan didn't know I was home. I had just arrived from picking up groceries. When I came inside, there were beer cans everywhere, and I was furious. I couldn't see the boat usually moored at the pier, so I grabbed the binoculars, trying to find them." Ellen raised her gaze slowly to Dr. Hallden's compassionate face and shivered.

"I saw the whole thing, but I wasn't sure what it was that I actually saw. I couldn't believe my eyes. I refused to accept what I witnessed," Ellen whispered.

"Did you tell Dan that you saw the accident?"

"Are you kidding? After listening to him explain what happened, I was so shocked, so frightened. I wondered what he'd do to me if I confronted him. Then before I knew it, it was too late. He'd told the same story to too many people. He never wavered one bit. I began to doubt what I saw. I wanted to believe him so badly."

Ellen lowered her gaze to the crumpled tissues in her hands. "I tried to justify my silence. I couldn't send my son to jail or let Mike's death cause a scandal for Barry, could I? I believed if I could lock it away, I could live with it."

"So, you decided to forget what you saw and go with Dan's story."

Ellen nodded. She reached for more tissues as her eyes filled again with tears. "I tried to forget it completely, but I couldn't stop feeling awful. I should have forced Dan to have therapy when he was young, get the right help for him."

"You were not to blame, Ellen. Unless a psychiatrist diagnoses Dan as criminally insane, it was his choice to drown his friend. He grew up in a loving family and refused any suggestions to get help. You told me that."

"I know. But if I'd have pushed my son..."

"You should know by now that you can't force anyone to get help. Dan was old enough when you had the conversation with him. It was his choice to back off and leave." Dr. Hallden stood up then pulled Ellen to her feet. He smiled gently. "I think you've had enough for today. I'm very proud of your progress. You should be too. My nurse will contact you for a short session tomorrow so I can check to see how you're doing, Ok?"

"But what happens now? Will you have to tell the police? Will Dan be arrested?"

"Nothing's going to happen anytime soon. We'll talk about the next step when you're able to cope better. Right now, I want you to feel especially proud of yourself. You've done the right thing. You've let the truth come out. That's the first step."

Dr. Hallden guided her to her room. He motioned a nurse to come with him. He helped her to bed, and then the nurse covered her with a blanket. Ellen was still holding on to his hand.

"Now you know why you're here. You can't hide the truth any longer. If Dan accepts help, he'll get it, but either way, he's got to face his actions and deal with the consequences. You can't do it for him. Sara and Barry want you back, Ellen. Don't you want to be back home?"

"No, it hurts too much every time I see them. I love my

family, but I can't handle the way I feel when I'm around them."

"I'll help you. Together we'll get you better, then we'll see about the family. Ok? No more forgetting, no more making excuses."

"Mmmhmm." She agreed. She was so tired that she felt woozy. But for the first time in a long while, hope stirred inside her alongside the fear. Now someone else knew the truth, and she wasn't the only one. Thank God. As exhaustion crept over her, the heavy burden she'd carried for so long lightened.

Being numb and existing like she was now wasn't the answer either. *Who knows, maybe Dr. Hallden can help me. Maybe I can handle living again.*

Dr. Hallden watched her shut out the world, this time with sleep. Now he had something definite to work with. Ellen had let the terror escape and shared it with him. It would be his job to make her realize the crime was not hers. He'd teach her to reject her feelings of guilt and responsibility, so she could come back to living life fully.

"Please sit down, Mr. Peterson. I'm glad you could come on such short notice," Dr. Hallden said as he shook Barry's hand.

"No problem, Doctor. I hope this is good news." Barry cleared his throat nervously, his fingers fidgeting in his lap.

"Some good, some bad." Dr. Hallden eyed Barry carefully. "Have you heard from your children lately?"

"Sara and I keep in touch regularly. I call Dan's place usually every month to try to talk to him about his mom. He never answers, so I leave a message on his cell to call me back, but he seldom does. And when he does, it's a brief conversation. Although, that's not exactly surprising."

"How has he handled his mother's breakdown?"

"He refuses to talk about his mom or her health. I've asked him a few times to visit, but he's always too busy. I haven't seen him since the summer."

"Do you get the feeling he's avoiding you?"

"No more than usual."

"There may be a much stronger reason he doesn't want to associate with you or the family at this time." Dr. Hallden held Barry's eyes, trying to ascertain what his reaction might be.

"Oh?"

"Ellen has had a traumatic experience last week, remembering the boating accident. I've talked to her again today. She's agreed to see you when she feels stronger. It could be a few weeks or a month. Whenever she's ready, I'll arrange it. I think it would be beneficial if you and I had a few sessions also before you see her. I want you prepared."

"Really? Fine, whatever it takes. That means she'll come home soon, right?"

"One day at a time, Mr. Peterson. Ellen's moved forward, but she's got a lot of mixed-up feelings to sort through."

"About what? What happened?"

Dr. Hallden cleared his throat, uncomfortable with the story he had to tell. He leaned forwards, his arms on his knees. It was never easy to be the bearer of bad news.

"For God's sake, tell me."

"Ellen believes she saw Dan murder Mike."

Total silence permeated the room.

A moan escaped from Barry. "Oh, God. Oh my God." Barry stared into Dr. Hallden's eyes, searching for comprehension.

"But how? Why?"

"I'll let Ellen tell you the whole story, but basically, it starts when she arrived home and realized the boys had been drinking. She noticed the boat and the slalom ski were gone. She took the binoculars down to the beach."

"And she saw the whole thing. Oh my God," Barry whispered. Tears welled in his eyes as he imagined her shock, her pain. "And she stayed there all day, listening to his lies—over and over again."

"She tried to protect him, as well as you and Sara," Dr. Hallden explained.

Barry's shock turned into anger. "I'm going to kill him. That little sonofabitch!"

"No, you're not even going to touch him. Ellen needs you to keep your senses. She can't run interference anymore. No matter what he's done, she loves him."

"Now, what do we do? Call the RCMP or what?"

"Not yet. Dan's not going anywhere. He feels quite safe with his secret. What I have to do is work with your wife. Help her understand she's not to blame and that you believe in her."

"I do. I always have. Ellen should know that."

"I've seen the love you have for her. But I'm not sure she believes she's worthy of that. I have to help her let go of her obsessive feelings of guilt, of responsibility."

"Why does she do that?"

"It's a circle, Mr. Peterson. She feels pressured to be a perfect wife, a perfect mother. By the time we sort things out, the Ellen you know will have changed. Maybe a lot. You know she can't go back to being the person she was, don't you?"

"I have no idea, but I guess that'd be true. What can I do? I love her."

"Stay in the background. Let your wife find the courage to discover all parts of herself. Ellen needs to realize she isn't responsible for anyone's behavior but her own. No more needless guilt. She has to want to come back, not simply because her family wants her to. Understand?"

"Are you trying to tell me she might not want to come back to me?"

"At this point, I honestly don't know. I'm only saying we have to give Ellen space. Don't push her. Take it one day at a time."

BARRY STABBED his cigarette out on the patio, popped a mint in his mouth, then walked briskly back inside to the third door on the left. He took a deep breath then knocked lightly. He couldn't believe how nervous he was.

For the past month, he had participated in weekly sessions with Dr. Hallden, going over their family life. He realized by abdicating his parenting role and concentrating on his business life, Ellen had become the peacemaker in her make-believe perfect home. What she couldn't make better, she would *'forget'* and ignore until she couldn't face it anymore.

Would she ever forgive him? Would their love survive this? He should've been a better husband and father. He wasn't sure how he should act with Ellen or how he should greet her. He could see himself at one end of a path of broken glass, with Ellen at the other end. Would they ever be able to cross it and be happy together again?

"Come in," Dr. Hallden urged as he opened the door.

Barry entered the room, and his gaze found Ellen's. She stared at him, her hazel eyes bright with unshed tears.

"Ell," Barry whispered her name, then went to her immediately, kneeling in front of her as he grasped her outstretched hands. He lifted her hand and kissed it. "It's so good to see you. You don't know how much I've missed you, sweetheart."

"Ah, Barry. I'm sorry I've hurt you." Her attempt at smiling was contorted by pain, yet she held herself together.

"Don't be sorry, sweetheart. Nothing is your fault. I'm here now, and I'm right beside you. Everything will work out. You'll see. I love you." He pushed aside a lock of wavy hair that had fallen across her face and kissed her forehead.

As Ellen gazed lovingly at him, Barry's heart palpitated wildly. He was encouraged even more when she nodded and gripped his hand tighter.

"I love you too, always have. I think I always will. Sit beside me, honey." Ellen motioned to the chair beside her. "I need you."

Barry's throat closed with emotion as he leaned towards her and kissed her cheek. He would never let her down again. She'd count on him as her friend, her lover, and her protector. Together they would get through whatever life had in store for them. "I need you too, sweetheart. I'll be beside you forever, whenever and wherever you need me." Barry looked towards Dr. Hallden and let out a sigh of relief.

Ellen raised her chin ever so slightly. With her hand clasped firmly in Barry's, she asked, "Where do we start?"

Thanks for reading *All for Peace*. If you haven't already read book 1 in my Safe Haven series, keep reading for an excerpt from *All for Love*.

DEAR READER

I hope you enjoyed reading Ellen and Barry's story as much as I enjoyed writing it. If you did, please post a review online. Reviews are incredibly helpful to an author's success. They help readers find the books they love and motivate authors to keep writing those books.

You can review wherever you purchased *All for Peace* and also on Goodreads and BookBub.

I love hearing from readers and plan to release more books soon. So visit my website www.LynnBoire.com, sign up for my newsletter, or email me at Lynn@LynnBoire.com to stay in touch and learn about my new releases.

An excerpt from *All for Love* is on the next page.

Cheers,
Lynn Boire

ALL FOR LOVE - EXCERPT

CHAPTER 1

Anna Taylor rolled her eyes at the final blessing and glanced at her husband Matt's flushed face. She elbowed Jed to stop his fidgeting, sending him a warning glare to pay attention. At fifteen, he was starting to complain about going to church and missing his weekend practice. Standing beside his father, his youthful attitude seemed incongruous with his height nearing his father's 6'2". On Matt's other side, Lisa leaned towards her father, singing along with him for the closing hymn. Anna knew they'd be expected to stay for coffee and fellowship afterwards, which could lead to half the day being lost.

"Matt, we can't stay this morning," she whispered as they began to file out. "Kari and Ray are coming to celebrate their anniversary. I need to get everything ready."

"Really, Anna? Really?" Matt's eyebrows lifted as his hazel eyes challenged her. "You couldn't have hosted your sister's event yesterday, and let me have my Sunday? You know what these days mean to me. You *know* how important these sessions are. There's not much time left."

The exasperation in Matt's voice made her eyes widen. She was sure she'd mentioned the dinner a few days ago. She looked away, uncomfortable meeting his eyes.

Purchase *All for Love* and find out what happens next.

DEDICATION

I find inspiration from many sources—newspaper or magazine articles, conversations with friends or family, and sometimes from my dreams. Some things are more bizarre than you'd imagine could happen. My favorite creative thought is "What if" that would happen to one of my loved ones or me? How would I react? And I go from there and let my imagination run wild. I love to create a place where a reader can either escape to or identify with, and of course, ending on a positive note.

So, to all my friends and family who scout out new possibilities for me, thanks for your belief in me. And a world of appreciation to my husband, who encourages me daily and expresses his pride in my work. As an author, I'm finally following my life-long dream—and I've never been happier.

In this day and age, we all have an opportunity to interact with the world, digitally, at least. So, if you enjoyed this book, I'd be honored if you'd leave a short but honest review on any of the online bookstores you patronize, so that others might take a chance on my stories written on the beautiful west coast of Canada.

ACKNOWLEDGMENTS

I've started this creative journey late in life, and I admit that technology can sometimes intimidate me, and make me doubt the wisdom of following my dreams. Writing a book is only part of the journey, there's so much more that needs to be done to bring my ideas to print. Joining the Vancouver Island Romance Authors group introduced me to a world of information and support. My mentor, Jacqui Nelson, continues to impress me with her knowledge, patience and ability to teach this old dog new tricks in every aspect. Thanks to all of you.

ALSO BY LYNN BOIRE

∽

THE SAFE HAVEN SERIES

All for Love

A Safe Haven Cli-Fi Suspense Novel

Obsession. Betrayal. Chaos.

Matt Taylor secretly builds a Safe Haven far from the chaos in Washington State. Will his dream for a secure and sustainable lifestyle be everything he hoped for?

All for Family

A Safe Haven Rediscovery Novel

Reunite. Respect. Restore.

After Anna Taylor honors her professional commitments to her community in Olympia, she finally joins her family in Bella Coola. Together they and five other families tackle the challenges of thriving and surviving in an intentional community.

All for Peace

A Safe Haven Self-Discovery Novel

Secrets. Murder. Insanity.

Matt's cousin, Ellen Peterson, avoids conflict at all costs to maintain her illusion of a peaceful and successful family.

But secrets can kill. Can Ellen live with that?

ABOUT THE AUTHOR

Lynn Boire enjoyed a successful career in dental office management, but it was never her passion. Always a voracious reader, she began a process of self-discovery in the '80s and realized creative writing was her passion and future.

Lynn writes contemporary suspense that reveals how women who avoid conflicts whenever possible in their relationships, find the confidence in themselves to voice their opinions. As they become more independent, they gain the inner strength to take control and enrich their lives.

Lynn lives in a seaside town on Vancouver Island in British Columbia, Canada. She uses her deep appreciation of every part of her island home for the background in her stories. She feels a spiritual connection whenever she's near a body of water. Nature puts everything in perspective, and all her doubts and worries float away. Even if a storm's strength frightens her, it also reminds her that—no matter what—all things pass. Lynn is blessed with many friends and family, including her husband, two grown children, a grandson and his daughter, and a stepdaughter and her family.

LynnBoire.com

amazon.com/author/lynnboire
goodreads.com/author/show/20765007.Lynn_Boire
bookbub.com/authors/lynn-boire
facebook.com/lynnboire

Made in the USA
Monee, IL
03 December 2021